What do you do
When The *Love* You Lost Forever
Comes Back Into Your Life?

GOOD TO
Have You
BACK

a Novel

Toriana Jones

This is a work of fiction. All of the characters, organizations and events portrayed in this novel are either products of the author's imagination or are used fictitiously.

Book design by Dashawn Taylor @ HotBookCovers.com

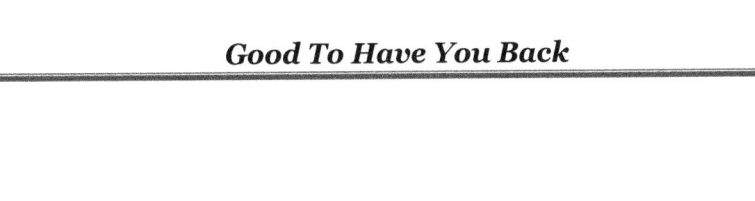

I give God all the glory for blessing me with such an amazing gift.

Good To Have You Back
by
Toriana Jones

Good To Have You Back

Prologue

What do you want to talk about Annabelle Billingsley asked her patient Gabriella?

Antonio, he asked me to marry him.

Wow, congratulations. That's great news Annabelle said with a smile before noticing the deep set frown on Gabriella's beautiful face. No smile, no laughter, no enthusiasm; talk about lack of emotion.

What's the problem?

I don't want to get married.

Why not? It's clear that Antonio loves you. What are you so afraid of?

Being hurt again, being let down, lied to, cheated on. Need I say more?

Gabi, you've got to let go. You can't make Antonio pay for what Ramero did to you. Antonio's a different man and he has not made you think otherwise in the 2 ½ years the two of you have been dating. Before you convict him on Ramero's charges give him a chance.

Gabriella sighed; I just don't want to be hurt.

So what did you say in response to his question?

Nothing, I cried like a baby.

Whoa, that poor man. You still haven't told him what happened yet?

I don't know how to tell him. I don't want him to think differently of me.

Gabi you've got to let all that out. Ever wonder why you can't love? Why you can't move on? You're afraid to let go of your past. Antonio hasn't stuck around this long for nothing. You and I both know you've done everything in your power to push him away. He's still here, that should tell you something.

Okay, what if I tell him and he does not want to see me again?

What if you tell him and he loves you even more, understands you better and still wants to marry you? You'll never know until you try.

But what if I don't want to get married?

Tell him that. Tell him everything. I'm sure he will understand or at least try to. I don't think you have anything to worry about with Antonio. That man loves you and he's been in your corner since the day you met him. Nothing scares him. You better hold on to him. He's a good man. Even Anne Keller can see that.

Good To Have You Back

Gabriella sat at her desk inside the insurance agency she had worked for a number of years. In the beginning she loved her job. Now it wasn't fulfilling. She hated coming in every morning and was bored with the work it took her no time, no energy, no real thought to do. An alert popped up on her screen notifying her that she had a new email message. Her colleague Megan Morgan sent out an invite to her boyfriend's listening party for the band he played in. The alert on her cell phone notified her of a text message. Antonio wanted to confirm their lunch date. She replied with I will see you at 1 @ Chadwick's.

Right at 12 her boss Elena Roberts called her into her office.

Have a seat. I've been meaning to go over your annual review with you for quite some time now. Elena picked up a folder and skimmed through it. You're doing exceptionally well. I have some new job duties I would like for you to take on. More learning opportunities and the possibility of promotion she winked. While Elena babbled on and on all Gabriella understood at the end of the meeting was that once again there was no raise although she was due one, as well as a promotion. They continued to pile more and more work on her but didn't want to compensate for her duties.

With a bright smile as if she had just told Gabriella good news that benefited them both Elena asked So what do you think? Think you can handle your new job responsibilities?

I know I could but I won't. Without much thought about where she would be employed tomorrow Gabriella told her I quit. Thank you for the opportunity but no thanks. I'm just not feeling this anymore she said with a wave of her hand. What, Elena said as she removed her glasses from her face. You can't quit. We're in the middle of closing and it's the end of the year. Nobody can crunch numbers the way that you can.

I know it and you know it Gabriella told her as she stood. Perhaps in the future Staten will value it's hard working employees and not treat them like slaves. I have taken all I can take she said as she removed her badge and sat it atop Elena's desk. I'll be leaving for lunch at 12:30 and I won't be back. Good day she said as she left Elena's office with a smile that she felt from the inside out. She saved all the personal items she had on her PC to a flash drive, deleted all her folders, made sure nothing of hers was left on their hard drive. She grabbed a few boxes from the mail room and packed away her things. Other employees sat by watching without comment.

Gabi, what's going on Christina Bradford, the owner's wife asked as she was walking by. She didn't understand why their most valued employee was packing her things.

Gabriella, can I talk to you for a minute, please?

Glancing at her watch Gabriella responded I can give you 20 at the most but I'm out of here at 12:45. Gabriella felt like she had wasted enough of her life at Staten.

Inside Christina's office she closed the door behind them and asked Can I get you something to drink? Anything to snack on?

No, I'm fine. Thank you.

What is going on she asked as Elena called an emergency meeting in the conference room.

Christina dialed her husband Oscar's cell number and asked Can you come to my office please? We have an urgent matter to discuss. More urgent than this emergency meeting, I'm sure.

Oscar came into the office saw the two boxes packed with Gabriella's things and asked What's going on?

Christina asked Gabi, is this about your annual review?

Among other things.

Let's talk about this please.

At this point there really is nothing to talk about. I quit.

You quit? You've got to be kidding me. I pay you $35 dollars an hour. What do you mean you quit? Nobody else is going to pay you nearly as much and include all the benefits Christina pointed out. Oscar slumped in his seat never uttering a word.

Christina, Gabriella sighed I'm not sure we are speaking of my pay. You see, I've been on a $20 an hour budget for the last 4 years. Aside from that the only benefits I have are the norm, medical, dental, vision and life.

What she asked as she looked at Oscar then back at Gabriella before looking at Oscar again. I personally authorized your raise and modified your benefits 4 years ago to compensate for the hard work you've put in over the years. You have a company car, an apartment in Valley Ranch and...she named off a number of other things while looking through a folder she'd pulled out of her drawer. Oscar was coughing as if he was about to cough up a lung and excused himself from the room.

Christina continued, *Your company credit card even allows you to cover personal expenses with no limit. You haven't had a problem using that* she said as she placed the credit card bills in front of Gabriella to review.

Christina she said without glancing at the bills *I promise you that none of those charges belong to me. I wasn't even aware that there was a company credit card, let alone anything else you've named. If that were the case I would not be packed. You might want to discuss this with Elena.* She pulled check stubs from her purse, passed them to Christina and gave her printed emails and letters in which she had addressed to Elena and Oscar since Christina was rarely in the office.

Christina sat back in her seat and asked *What in the hell is going on around here?* She picked up her phone and dialed a few numbers.

Margaret can you pull the books dating back 4 years ago for Gabriella Pennington, be sure to include any paperwork relating to signatures, passwords and pin numbers. Get started on this ASAP. She hung up and dialed another number.

Lalita, you have keys and records for all employee property right? Okay, pull Gabriella Pennington's file and have the things at that address delivered to the security office at Fellowes Tower. Pull the lease on the vehicle and make sure that no one outside of you, Homer and Alice handle this. Thank you.

Gabriella if you will please allow me time to work this out. I assure you it is all a big misunderstanding. I personally do not want you to leave the company.

Christina nothing you say or offer me will make me come back. I have already left. Mentally I have been gone for months. I'm late for lunch. It has been a pleasure working with you. Of all the people in this office I enjoyed working with you most. I wish you continued success.

Oh Gabi she said as she hugged her. *I will call you in a few days. Please don't change your number or move away, okay? And I wish you the best. You have made Staten what it is, most times by yourself and I truly thank you for that. I honestly should have paid more attention to the business, to you and now I regret not doing so because I'm losing so much right now.*

In less than 3 hours Christina learned that Elena and her husband were having an affair. The condo they charged to the company account was supposed to be all expense paid for Gabriella but in reality the two of them made it their home away from home. The condo had pictures of the two of them traveling around the world on the company's dime. There were even sex tapes they'd made while in various positions using different objects and a number of sexual partners, let alone sexual preferences. The car that was listed as Gabriella's company car was an E class Mercedes in which Oscar had purchased for Elena. All this had been going on for a number of years.

Chapter 1

Gabriella took a nice hot shower and sat down with a bowl of Blue Bell's Banana Pudding ice cream. She felt good about her decision to quit Staten despite not knowing where her new income would come from. She had way too much on her plate to be constantly taking on more and more work without being compensated for it. After Christina found out what was going on she filed for a divorce using her findings as evidence and filed fraud charges against Oscar and Elena. After selling the company to a long time interested party she mailed Gabriella a check that would more than cover the expenses she would have used over the last 4 years, including a vehicle. Christina felt that Gabriella deserved at least half of what she made selling Staten since she was the one to get the company where it was with little or no pay while others reaped the benefits and bogged her down with work.

Gabriella had no clue what to do with all the money, at least not right off. She took a few days to make some serious plans about what to do with her life. She invested a lot of money in stocks and bonds. She purchased a small SUV because she liked the design and didn't have to spend a whole lot of money. She stumbled across a 3 bedroom townhome in foreclosure for less than thirty five thousand. That purchase was made once the inspector determined there was nothing wrong with the property. She made some minor changes, added a few extras before going out to buy furniture to fix the place up. Another thing she decided on was to self-publish her book which would cost a little over eight hundred for the cover, ISBN, bar code and printing for paper and hardback copies to be distributed to local bookstores.

She had been so busy over the last few weeks that Antonio wondered if maybe she was seeing someone else or just tired of him. She hadn't brought the proposal back up or explained what made her cry the way she had the night he proposed. He tried to forget about her. A part of him was saying be patient, she will come around. He had been going back and forth with her for over a year and things just didn't seem to be going anywhere relationship wise.

Gabriella dialed Antonio's number one Friday evening. Hey, how was your day? Long and tiring he responded. How was yours?

Productive, I was able to accomplish more in one day than I have in years she said with a cheerful voice.

Oh well, that's great. Care to share?

Yes, that's why I called. Was wondering if you would like to go grab a bite to eat tonight. If you don't already have plans maybe come spend the weekend with me she said hopeful. She knew she hadn't been the easiest person to get along with. She had shut him out too many times to count even when he didn't deserve it. Over the past few weeks she had practically put him on the back burner while she thought things over. Thinking is good, clarity even better but it would be nice to let the people closest to you know what's going on.

Cool. I don't have any plans. What time should I pick you up?

I'll pick you up if you don't mind. Unless you just have to drive.

No I'm good. If you want to you can pick me up within 45 minutes to an hour. Gives me time to shower and change.

When she picked Antonio up he was dressed in a brown Christian Audiger shirt that showed off his muscular build along with a pair of blue jeans. He looked good enough to eat. She stepped from her SUV with a smile wearing a khaki slip dress with Coach sandals. Her hair was pulled back into an elegant ponytail. She wrapped her arms around him, inhaled his scent before briefly kissing his cheek. I missed you.

Missed you too woman. What's been up with you lately? You found a boyfriend? He asked these things while still holding on to her and starring into her eyes the way a man looks at a woman he adores.

We have a lot to talk about but no, a boyfriend is not one of them.

You sure? Cause a brother was starting to feel neglected. You been alright though?

Yes, better than ever.

What's this? A rental he asked as he opened the driver's side door she'd gotten out of minutes before.

We have a lot to talk about she repeated.

They decided to have dinner at Ruth Chris. The atmosphere was nice and cozy. Despite the crowd of patrons the service was nice and fast. Before they had the opportunity to dive into conversation their dinner was on the table. Neither of them had bothered with lunch so they both were starved and wasted no time chowing down. Before long their plates were nearly empty.

Sorry Gabriella apologized as she wiped her mouth.

No need, I know how your work load gets pretty busy and you tend to skip lunch. I take it you did the same thing today?

Haven't had much of an appetite lately.

Why is that?

Because you were on my mind and you have been avoiding me. Why?

She sighed, I haven't been completely honest about my past and I don't know how to tell you all that I've been through.

How about starting with the truth from beginning to end?

Before she could utter another word Ramero stood in front of their table with his cousin Shamar.

Gabi he said with a smile before leaning over to kiss her cheek. It's good to see you.

What's up Shamar asked?

How have you been Ramero asked ignoring the fact that Antonio was sitting there. When Gabriella didn't answer he looked into her eyes with a menacing look. Fine, have it your way. We will talk later. He walked off leaving Gabriella holding her breath as tears threatened to spill from her eyes.

Who was that Antonio asked as he watched Ramero walk away. It wasn't until he was out the door that he focused his attention on Gabriella. His look went to one of concern as he got up and took the seat beside her. Gabi, what's wrong Ma? You gotta talk to me he told her as he wrapped his arms around her.

Ramero's my ex she said as he wiped away her tears.

Okay but that doesn't explain why your reaction is what it is.

Antonio can we just go, please? I don't want to be here anymore. She dropped money to cover their bill plus the tip before getting up from the table and almost hitting the floor. Antonio lifted her up into his arms or at least planned to when she argued that she was okay. He put an arm around her shoulder and told her At least let me drive. She passed him the keys. Instead of driving to her place he drove to his. He picked a sleeping Gabriella up in his arms and carried her inside. He lit candles inside his bathroom, turned on the music, started a hot bubble bath using Eucalyptus Peppermint Body Wash from Bath & Body Works. He undressed her, lifted her up into his arms again and placed her in the awaiting bath. He bathed her as if you would a newborn baby without starring or making her uncomfortable. Afterwards he dried her off, placed her in bed, removed everything except his boxers and got into bed pulling her onto his chest where she slept peacefully in his arms for the first time in years.

Antonio's house phone is what awakened them the next morning. His brother Adam was at his front door to borrow money. Aside from the ringing phone his constant beating on the door caused Gabriella to jump.
What's going on she asked in alarm?
Antonio kissed her forehead, Calm down Gabi. It's just Adam he said as he searched her face. He came to borrow money. You okay?
She threw herself back on the bed pulling another pillow over her head as she screamed into it.
Antonio left the room to answer the front door after closing the bedroom door behind him. He hoped to make Adam's visit quick so he could get back to Gabriella. Adam made his way inside and asked You got any breakfast food man? I'm starved.
Some cereal, there's some turkey bacon and sausage in there too. If you cook make enough for me and...
Gabi's here?
Yeah. Make yourself at home he said as he turned to leave the room.
Gabriella was awake and dressed in yesterday's clothes. What are you doing Antonio asked?
I'm about to go home and...
And what? Yeah right, you're not going anywhere.
I need to change clothes.
He opened a drawer, pulled out a t-shirt and a pair of sweats that he passed to her. Here, put these on.
She starred at him. He starred back. Adam's making breakfast. We're supposed to be spending the weekend together, remember? You're not going anywhere without me until Sunday night, if I let you out of my sight then.
She smiled for the first time since Ramero showed up at the restaurant. Antonio after breakfast I need to go to my place to...
I'm going with you. He walked into the bathroom, passed her a toothbrush and a face towel. He stood beside her at the sink where they both brushed their teeth and washed their faces.

We're going to have our conversation about last night before this day is over with.

Yes sir.

Gabi, I'm serious.

Okay. Ramero's my ex and he's also the reason I don't trust anyone.

You don't trust me? Well I guess that's obvious because if you did you would have told me all this long ago.

She turned to look into his eyes but he started out of the bathroom. She grabbed his hand, he snatched it away and kept walking.

Antonio, I do trust you she said barely above a whisper. If I didn't I wouldn't be here right now.

Why do you keep me at arm's length? You tell me just enough to shut me up. Gabi that's not enough for me.

What do you want to know?

I want to know everything, the good, the bad and the ugly.

Antonio I have a horrible past.

He saw the pain, the tears, the worry. He pulled her into his arms. Gabi, nothing can be that bad.

Adam stuck around a couple of hours after breakfast enjoying his brother and Gabi's company.

You ready Antonio asked her?

Yeah, I have some confessions to make.

You're cheating on me?

No she laughed.

You're pregnant?

God no, I would have to have sex to get pregnant and…

You used to be a man?

Shut up she laughed as she playfully pushed him.

So what is it man?

I quit my job.

Cool he said calmly knowing how her job stressed and depressed her at the same time. You find something else?

No. I've decided to self publish my book she said waiting to hear the negativity she was sure to come.

Congratulations he told her as he picked her up in his arms twirling her around on the sidewalk while kissing her cheeks. You need help with anything?

Smiling she said No, I'm good. Thanks

When did you do all this?

A few weeks ago.

Oh yeah, we keeping secrets now he asked never letting her feet touch the ground.

Not intentionally, I just didn't know how you would take it that's all.

Do me a favor.

What's that?

Stop worrying about how I'm going to respond to things and just tell me what's on your mind.

I moved.

Where to?

Madison Gardens

Whoa, did you get a contract already?

She laughed again, No. The day I quit my job was the last time you and I went out for lunch. I had another annual review with no raise, no mention of a promotion, only more work added to my job description. I couldn't take it anymore.

That's understandable, the job was stressing you out and it wasn't paying enough. I would have done the same thing…

But what?

I don't understand why you would move into such an expensive community without having a job. Now that I don't understand.

The day I quit I had a talk with Mrs. Bradford. She was not pleased with my leaving the company. She was convinced that she had compensated me enough to where I would never leave the company. Had I been given the many benefits she had outlined in her proposal for me 4 years ago I probably never would have.

I don't understand.

4 years ago Christina promoted me to VP over accounting, gave me $35 an hour, a company paid vehicle of my choice, all paid living expenses, a company credit card in which I could use for whatever and an ass load of other amenities.

What?

Elena, my boss, she never presented the proposal to me. Instead she kept feeding me bullshit about how they couldn't give me a raise or a promotion. Meanwhile her and Christina's husband had made a new life living off what was supposed to be my salary. The company car, Elena drove. The condo, she and Oscar lived in when Christina was away on business which was often enough. They even used the company credit card to shop, take trips and do a number of other things while passing everything off as my expenses. If Christina had not shown up the day I quit I would have never known. I could have been sued for all that money.

Damn.

I know right?

So did they pay you back for the 4 years you weren't being paid?

Yes, all that and then some.

That's what's up.

Chapter 2

So, Ramero, was he your first love?
Yes she sighed, I once thought he was my everything.
And then what happened?
He used me and dropped me like a pile of garbage. Basically he left me to die.
How so?
He got caught up in a federal drug case. To shorten his sentence he started snitching on people. He made them think it was me. Not only was he trying to put all his charges on me and set me up as the ring leader he also wanted everyone on the outside to think I was the one snitching so he could get off scott-free. He even went so far as to allow two men to rape me to prove that I deserved what was coming to me and that he had nothing to do with it.
Were you really raped?
Yes she sighed but that's not the end of it. He owed one guy a half million dollars, he told the guy I ran off with his money. He made me his sex slave for over a year. He at first held me against my will, threatened me with guns, beatings, death. He had infant children that he would leave with me and his bodyguards from time to time. His kids fell in love with me, as did he. But because of what he'd done to me in the past I could never love him. He finally gave me the opportunity to tell him what really happened. He hated himself for it.
Antonio stood there stunned. Damn Gabi, no wonder you won't let me touch you.
She sighed, I've been going to counseling. I'm getting help talking out my problems, my past mistakes and I'm desperately trying to move on with my life. I was once told I would never amount to anything and that I would be dead before I turned 21. Well I'm about to be 25 and I'm still alive so I figured its' time to start living. I go to counseling three times a week. I hope you understand why I'm not so easily trusting of everyone. I've been through far more than what I've shared with you today. If I could, I would tell you more but its' too painful and too much for me to talk about in one setting. For someone that cares about me I'm sure it's even harder for them to hear it.

Ramero showed up at Images the salon Gabriella had been going to since she was in the 9th grade. He waited for her to walk out of the salon. She wore her hair in loose curls, face free of makeup rocking an electric blue sundress by Bebe with a pair of sandals on her pretty pedicured feet. She was still just as beautiful as the day he met her at a track meet when she was in the 7th grade. Juicy he called out to her, stopping her in her tracks as she walked ahead of him. Slow up, I just want to talk to you for a minute.

You and I have nothing to talk about.

But we do, look he pleaded. I want to apologize for all the things I did and said to you. I know right now that don't mean shit, probably never will but I needed to say it to you.

Thank you Ramero she said as she started walking again without turning around.

Satin told me something when I came home and I need to know if it's true. Again she stopped. Gabi, please.

Yes it's true. I was pregnant with your baby but he died while I was giving birth and I almost died too after being beaten for 72 hours by men that thought I was trying to put them away for life with stories I couldn't have possibly told because I never knew. She gave that time to sink in before saying Ramero, that's not the first child we lost. Your daughter managed to breathe for 2 whole hours before she died from a gunshot wound to her chest when you shot me in the stomach. She wiped away tears and sighed, is there anything else you want to know before I walk away one last time?

Whatever happened with you and Tech?

He fucked me for over a year before he fell in love with me and gave me back my freedom.

Were you ever pregnant by him?

Yes but you made sure I lost that one too when you set me up to be kidnapped, beaten because you heard I was no longer being tortured but cared for by the man you despised.

You know Tech is dead right?

Got a phone call this morning. He died of heart failure they say.

A broken heart is what I heard because he never stopped loving you. You going to his funeral?

Yeah I will be there.

She had to convince Antonio that she would be okay traveling to New York alone to attend Tago "Tech" Diaz's funeral.

When she arrived in New York Tech's brother Drago picked her up from the airport and greeted her with a welcoming hug and cheek kisses.

Good to see you Bella, only I wish it were under better circumstances.

You and me both. How have you been? How are Isabella and Fernando holding up?

The whole family is distraught, it's chaotic. I honestly don't know what to do.

With what?

With everything he said sadly. Tech was the one that held this all together.

Yeah, he was damn good at it too Gabriella said with a sad smile.

Can I ask you a question?

Sure, go ahead.

Did you ever love my brother?

Gabriella turned the radio down, lost her smile as her eyes glazed over with tears. I loved him but I hated him at the same time.

Why?

Did he ever tell you how we hooked up?

He said he won a bet but over the years talking about you made him sad and I always thought there was more to the story.

There is or at least there was but Drago I'm not quite sure this conversation is fit for the day. I don't think you could handle it on top of everything else that's going on.

Speak for yourself Bella, I'm a man. Trust me, I can handle it. Now if it's too much for you I can understand.

Do you really want to know?

Yes I want to know how you could walk away from the man that worshiped the ground you walked on and gave you the world.

Drago do you remember the way it was when you first came to live with Tago?

Yes he taught me everything.

Between me and Tago I mean, do you remember?

Yes, it was as if you hated him. The two of you would always argue and fight.

Your brother never put his hands on me, at least not in that way. I was brought to Tago's against my will. I was there to pay off a debt and for a whole year I was your brother's whore so to speak.

What? Yeah right. I don't believe this shit. How dare you use my brother's name in vain? That man loved you.

In the end he did but in the beginning I was just his pussy.

But why? What did you owe him?

I didn't owe him anything. My ex- boyfriend and him were in business together. My ex got locked up and did away with half a million of your brother's money. The Feds took over the case so my ex started singing like a canary. When word got out that someone was snitching he wanted to take the blame off himself so he somehow convinced everyone involved that I was doing the talking. He also convinced Tago that I ran off with his money. Tago never believed I was guilty of snitching but he did believe I took his money. So for one year he made me work off his money by having sex with him. She laughed sadly, I never could understand it all. Had I met Tago before all this and been single I'd have fucked him without a thought. I tried to explain this to him on many occasions but he never believed me. He trusted Ramero just that much.

Ramero?

Yes, he was my ex.

Get the fuck out of here. When my brother said he was in love with Ramero's girl he was talking about you? I thought that was what the two of you fought about all the time, him messing around with other women.

When Tago got serious about me it scared him. There were no other women at that point.

So how did he ever find out the truth?

By the time he did I was already pregnant with his child and he wanted to keep it. I wanted to keep her too. I had even planned to settle down with Tago despite all that happened but then I went out shopping one day. Ramero and his boys kidnapped me. They beat me and tortured me until I lost the baby. Ramero was okay with me working off his debt as Tago's whore but he couldn't stomach Tago and I being together in that sense. While Tago searched for me they went through my things back at the house. I kept a notebook, I wrote down everything that had happened from the time all this mess with Ramero started. Tago read it and he finally realized I had been telling the truth all along.

Man, I don't believe this shit. My brother could have had any woman he wanted. Why would he need you to have sex with him to pay off a debt?

That's the part I never understood.

And Ramero where is he now?

He's supposed to be at the funeral. He made it a point to let me know that.

Does my brother know he did this to you?

No, I never told him because I didn't want him to do something stupid and end up in prison. The Feds were all over him but couldn't make the charges stick. I knew if he even made a threat he would be gone. I didn't want that to happen.

So how did you leave?

After a while what Tago did to me started to bother him and he let me go.

You know my brother never got over you leaving right?

So I've heard. I really wish things could have been different. In another life I'd have married your brother and gave him everything but I had so much taken away from me during all that. I just couldn't take anymore so I walked away. I had to.

Whatever happened with Ramero? How did he get out? He was just as big in this as my brother. And if he was snitching, why ain't nobody after him now?

Last I heard there was a confidential informant working the case and they granted him immunity because he was also involved with more than one undercover agent on an intimate level.

Chapter 3

Drago pulled up in front of Tago's mansion, the door was opened for Gabriella. Bella the doorman greeted her with a long hug. So nice to see you, still beautiful as ever he said as he kissed her cheeks.

Thanks Gordon, and you're still just as handsome I see.

Bella, Bella, Bella Fernando said as he jumped into her arms hands wrapped around her neck as he planted kisses all over her face. I missed you he cried, so much.

I missed you too Fernando, more than you will ever know she said while kissing at his tears as she held him in her arms as if he were still an infant. He was now 8 years old and a big boy.

Drago told him Fernando, get down. Bella can't carry you. You should be carrying her.

They all laughed.

Isabella rounded the stairs and screamed at the top of her lungs when she saw Gabriella. She hugged her long and hard while whispering in her ear I really, really need you.

I'm here baby she assured her. I'm here, tell me what's going on.

Drago said come on, let's go to the family room. The family room was only used for big discussions. Upon entering Gabriella noticed the oil painted portrait of first her, Tago and the kids while she was 9 months pregnant and then another of just her and Tago. Isabella smiled at the picture, at 12 she remembered a whole lot more than Fernando did and clearly understood why Gabriella left. She had overheard many arguments between her parents. She still considered Gabriella to be her Mommy, the only mother she had ever known.

So, how have you been? How is school?

I miss you Bella. I really miss you. I know things between you and my father weren't right and that's why you left but I wished and prayed things would get better. I wanted you to come home. Daddy was horrible after you left. He missed you but didn't have the guts to beg you for forgiveness and beg you to come home Isabella cried. Now who is going to take care of us?

Gabriella closed her eyes as her own tears fell. Isabella, don't you worry, okay? Uncle Drago and I will figure this out. She looked to Drago for confirmation. Drago mouthed, thank you.

When Gabriella got time alone she dialed Antonio.

About damn time you called. You okay woman?

Yes I'm fine. Sorry it took me so long.

How are you holding up? How are the kids?

I'm good. Oh my God Tony, they have gotten so big she said through tears.

Have they decided who's going to get the kids yet?

Isabella mentioned it but no, aside from that there has been too much heartache to cover that topic.

Still thinking about bringing them back with you?

Yes she answered truthfully, but if there are other options I will look into them first. Antonio please...

No need to explain Gabi. I'd want you to do the same for my children.

Thank you for being so understanding.

You've had a hard enough life as it is. I'm here to make it easier for you. I told you that and I meant it.

So if Isabella and Fernando come live with me you won't have a problem with that?

As long as they don't come with more drama and you're happy, I'm good Gabi. I promise.

Okay well let me get down here and put something in my stomach. I'm starved.

You better quit doing that.

Doing what?

Going all day without eating.

My appetite just came back.

Why was it gone in the first place he asked thinking it was because of Tago.

I don't want to lose you she answered truthfully.

Why would you lose me?

I have a horrible past and with all this just makes my life that much more complicated and nobody wants to take on too much. Especially not all the baggage I have.

Gabriella I want you to hear me and hear me loud and clear. I'm going to be around until you run me off and I don't scare easily. All I ask is that you not keep anything from me, be up front and honest with me about everything and we're good. No secrets.

No secrets.

Alright love, go do your thang.

Antonio

Yeah baby

Thank you

You're welcome anytime, remember that always and forever.

Drago escorted his niece and nephew along with Gabriella down the aisle to sit on the first row at the church. There were over a thousand guest in attendance. Some people had to be turned away. They stood in the parking lot, on the street, all over the place.

You okay Drago asked Gabriella as he put an arm around her. She nodded her head slowly, desperately trying to be strong for the kids. She made it through the sermon, through the Benediction, through the prayer. It was the viewing of the body that took the fight out of her, the part that made her fall apart.

Drago and two of his uncles escorted her and the kids back to an awaiting limousine that took them back to the house. Gabriella and the kids slept in Tago's bedroom for the rest of the day. When night fell Drago woke them with food and sat down to talk with them. He and Gabriella had agreed that they should allow the children to decide where they wanted to reside, although he had specific instructions from Tago that the kids should go with Gabriella. With all that he'd learned he felt like that was too much to ask of her and had no problem taking his niece and nephew in along with the 6 kids he already had at home. It would be an adjustment for sure but they would manage if they had to.

How are you feeling Isabella asked Gabriella?

Sad she answered honestly.

Yeah me too she said as she lay her head on Gabriella's shoulder. I miss my Daddy so much.

Me too Fernando cried as he crawled into Gabriella's lap. She wrapped her arms around them both as they all cried silent tears. Drago watched the three of them together and smiled. He now understood why his brother wanted his kids to go to Gabi, why he never stopped loving her as the years continued to pass by. He understood why his brother died from loneliness. Gabriella was irreplaceable and Tago knew that.

Mommy, Fernando said aloud.

Yes baby Gabriella said without reservation.

I wanna stay with you.

Okay she answered. Okay.

Are you going to stay here Isabella asked?

No baby, I live in Georgia now.

So we're going to move to Georgia?

I'm going wherever Mommy goes Fernando said as he snuggled into her.

Me too, Mommy where do you live in Georgia? Do they have good schools? Are there cute boys?

Boys, you better quit thinking about boys right now Gabriella responded before Drago could. Your primary focus is school. Getting an education is important. Boys are a distraction you don't need. Are we clear?

Yes maam she said as she kissed her cheek.

Drago smiled at Gabriella are you sure about this? Tago said that you were involved with someone down there. What is he going to think about all this? Does he know about my brother?

Antonio knows everything from beginning to end.

What does he think about the kids coming to live with you or have you discussed that part yet?

Second thing that came to mind after I received the phone call.

What was the first?

Pain and the loss of possibilities between us.

You and Tago you mean?

Yes

And how did Antonio feel about all that?

He's very understanding she said as she kissed the top of the kids' heads.

Bella

Drago, little brother can we please not think past this moment?

Okay, okay. I am going to go home to check on my fam but I will be back before it gets too late.

Drago

Yes

Stay home with your wife and kids. I have everything under control here and I could use the time alone with them just as I'm sure your wife could use the time alone with you. If you're anything like Tago was death is the only thing that will bring you home she said sadly.

Good To Have You Back

You sure Bella? I could come back.

Go, be safe and call us when you get there.

Yes maam.

Very funny.

That night Gabriella had a long talk with the kids about their father, about their move to Georgia.

She told them about writing a book, about her townhouse and how it would be a big step down from what they were used to.

Mommy, will we have to go to private school Isabella asked?

What do you want to do baby?

Public school. The private school people are so uppity and they're no fun at all.

School is not just about fun Isabella. You're there to learn. I'll let you try out public school but I promise you, if you get out of line I'm going to give you hell.

Yes maam.

The doorbell rang, now it was after midnight. Gabriella had put the kids to bed and was laying in Tago's bed reading over a proposal from a publishing company.

Gordon said Bella, there is a Mr. Sanchez here to see you.

At this hour Mr. Gordon? Send him on his way and tell him to come back at a decent hour.

Yes maam

Gordon

He smiled, okay Bella I got you.

Gordon came back a few minutes later, presented her with a business card and said Mr. Sanchez will be back tomorrow at 2.

Thank you.

How you holding up Gordon asked as he fixed her a bowl of fruit and a glass of Ginger Ale.

I can't believe Tago's not here and I miss him she cried softly.

Oh Bella, I wish you and Tago could have met under better circumstances. I know the two of you would still be together right now, married and happily in love. How are things for you in Georgia?

Great, I finally did something with my writing. I self- published it a month ago and I'm already receiving proposals from publishing companies.

Well that's great news. I'm so proud of you he said as he kissed her cheek. Are you still working at that insurance company?

No sir, I quit.

Well good for you, you know Tago hated that you refused his help.

Tago was so used to everyone needing him, taking from him and I didn't want to be one of those people. I loved him but I couldn't get past all that I'd been through. All that I'd lost.

Three babies and all that abuse Bella, it's no wonder you're still around. And I hear there's a man in your life?

Yes, Antonio.

How long have you known him?

3 years today

The two of you in a relationship?

We are now.

Great, that's good to hear Bella. I always prayed you would find happiness. Are you in counseling?

Yes sir, for the past 4 years now.

You have always been such an incredible woman Bella and you deserve happiness.

The house phone rang, Gordon answered. Yes, we're having a talk right now. Sure, come on over. Bella, Drago wants to know if he can bring you anything?

Yes indeed Gabriella smiled. I want a #4 from Whataburger, extra toast and a chocolate shake.

I see some things never change Gordon says with a smile.

Drago arrived while Gabriella had an enlightening conversation with Antonio. Yes I've thought about that. To Drago she said thanks bro, I'm starved.

Gabriella spent two weeks in New York getting the kids packed and ready for their move to Georgia. Drago, Gordon, Uncles Juan and Diego would make the trip along with them.

Antonio picked them up from the airport and pulled Gabriella into his arms planting soft kisses on her cheeks. I missed you he told her.

I missed you too she said as she wrapped her arms around him. Antonio this is Fernando and this is Isabella.

Antonio hugged them both, asked questions in an attempt to get to know them. Gabriella later introduced him to the Uncles.

Drago asked Bella, you sure you're okay with this?

Will you stop asking me that? Of course I'm okay. Are you okay, with everything?

Damn Drago said as he took a seat on Gabriella's sofa in her den. Gabriella fixed him a shot of Hennessy and took a seat beside him.

Damn what, talk to me.

I miss my brother he said sadly.

We all do Drago.

Even you?

Especially me she said as she stood to fix her own drink.

Chapter 4

Six months later Gabriella was sitting in a coffee shop reading Victoria Christopher –Murray's *Too Little Too Late* when someone slid into the booth she sat in comfortably.

Excuse me she said when they bumped her leg. She removed the book from her face and asked what is the damn problem?

Ramero sat there smiling. Lose the attitude Juicy, it's just me.

What the hell do you want?

He bit his lip and said why can't you just smile for me one time?

Maybe because everything about you makes me frown she said as she stood up and gathered her things.

Excuse me she said politely as she tried to remove herself from the one sided booth they sat in.

Have a seat.

Get out of my way.

Sit the fuck down and let me talk to you. I'm not getting up until I say what I gotta say.

I don't give a damn what you have to say Ramero.

Oh you don't he asked as he showed her the gun he held at his waist. She smiled as she eased her back onto her seat and opened her purse. She pointed her 380 at him and asked What the fuck you gone do to me now that you haven't already done?

Put the gun away. Damn woman, I just want to talk to you.

Get the fuck out of my way and stop following me around you dumb fuck she said as he moved out of her way. She tucked her gun safely inside her purse and stood up. She walked away with her head held high.

Juicy he called out to her as she walked out the door. This ain't over. You and me gone have this conversation one way or another. You know how I get down. I suggest you make this easy on yourself. I'd hate for you to lose any more kids.

Gabriella whipped around and got in his face. Look here you piece of shit. I'm not afraid of you anymore. Your threats don't mean shit to me and I fucking dare you to lay a hand on my kids.

Them ain't your fucking kids. You were just Tago's whore. Don't play yourself.

You know better than that. If you really believed I was Tago's whore you wouldn't be here right now. He might have fucked me in the beginning but he fell in love with me.

You ain't nothing but a slut. How you gone fuck my homeboy after I get locked up?

Ramero, you trifiling bastard. You used me to pay off your debt. You never counted on Tago falling in love with me and me ending up pregnant.

Nah, never counted on that. Never thought you would stoop so fucking low. You of all people.

Gabriella started to walk away. Ramero threatened, your little life is about to fall apart.

Not before you lose yours she warned.

Antonio walked into Gabriella's house with Fernando dribbling a basketball. Fernando Diaz if you don't stop bouncing that ball in this house she yelled.

Sorry Ma.

And stop calling me Ma.

Sorry Mommy.

Isabella came in talking on her cell phone as if no one else was in the room. Isabella, Gabriella said with an edge to her voice. Isabella continued chatting away. Isabella, get off the phone. Isabella she yelled, get off the phone NOW! Get upstairs and clean up your room.

Yes maam

You have a rough day Antonio asked?

Mommy Isabella called out, Can I go to Jackie's when I get done?

No and don't talk to me until your rooms are cleaned she fussed.

Antonio wrapped his arms around Gabriella. She quickly shrugged him off. Gabi, what's going on baby?

Nothing, are you staying for dinner?

Fernando brought dirty clothes from upstairs. Gabriella fussed about that because she had asked for the laundry to be brought downstairs the night before. Isabella made the mistake of asking another question about Jackie's. Gabriella was on the verge of screaming on them again.

Man, what happened to you today Isabella asked as she headed for the stairs. Isabella, get back here right now.

Yes maam.

If you want your lips to remain on your face you better watch who you're talking to. Understand?

Yes maam, I'm sorry Mommy but you really are in a bad mood.

Yeah Fernando responded as he wrapped his arms around her waist. What's wrong with my Mommy?

Antonio watched her. Gabi, why don't you go take a shower. Get comfortable while I make dinner.

She was about to protest when Isabella said Mommy, I will help with dinner. Me too, Fernando said proudly as he kissed her cheek.

Later that night as Antonio lay in bed beside Gabriella he asked You wanna tell me what's going on?

It's nothing.

Bullshit he said as her cell phone rang. It was after midnight. She ignored the Unknown call until the house phone started to ring.

Hello she answered calmly. Yes this is the Pennington-Diaz residence.

Ramero was calling to let her know he knew what school the kids attended, what their schedules are on a daily basis and who their friends were. With everything he said she frowned even more. She said You have the wrong number. Don't ever call my house again.

Who was that Antonio asked?

A telemarketer.

After midnight? Yeah right. Gabriella, who was that?

A telemarketer.

What the fuck ever he said as he got out of bed, put on his clothes and walked out of the bedroom.

Before she could protest her house phone rang again, she ignored it. Her cell phone started up.

You gone get that Antonio asked? I'm sure it's just another telemarketer, wouldn't want it to wake the kids.

As the weeks passed by Gabriella's actions and attitude only got worse. She was pushing Antonio away again. He wasn't too happy about that.

Gabi, you busy he asked when he called?

Leaving the grocery store. What's up? How's your day?

I want to see you, need to talk to you today.

Okay, what is this about?

About you and your attitude lately. You're shutting me out again. You promised me no secrets. I want to know what's bothering you and I want to know now.

Excuse me Juicy can I holla at you for a minute Ramero asked behind her. She turned around noticed the same two men that raped her and frowned.

Antonio…

Ramero snatched her phone and tossed it across the parking lot.

I heard your boo left you everything he owned. I need a loan. I'm good for it right?

Go to hell.

Look, I don't want to hurt you again or anyone close to you so I suggest you get that half a mil I need.

Why don't you get your mom to pay for it in pussy? Ramero slapped her hard. She dropped her bags. He never expected her to swing back. She slapped him so fast he didn't have time to move. The two men grabbed her and roughed her up a little bit.

Half a mil by Saturday or I kill the kids during basketball practice. You should be tired of attending funerals.

I won't be tired until yours is over with she said as she spat in his face.

You dumb bitch he said as he slapped her while the two men held her. He pulled out his gun and warned everyone else to mind their business. Get my money. I'm done talking to you.

When Gabriella got home Antonio was there. She shielded her face with the bags of groceries she carried. Gabi he said calmly, I called you back like 20 times. What happened to your phone? You okay he asked as he grabbed the bags from her hands.

What the fuck happened to your face?

It's nothing…I

Don't lie to me.

Some young kids tried to rob me and…

Bullshit. As much as he tried to find out what happened she would never reveal it. He told her he was going home once the kids were in bed. He got half way home before turning back around because he didn't want to give up on her. He rang the doorbell, she answered holding a shot gun.

Gabriella he said as he took the gun from her, what are you afraid of?

It's Ramero, he's back.

What do you mean he's back?

He's been popping up, making threats, asking for money.

Is he the one that did this to your face?

Yes she cried. Antonio I don't want you to get involved.

You think I'm just going to stand by and let this happen? You and the kids need to go to New York for a while.

But what about school?

Get with the teachers, get their school work and go.

What are you going to do?

Whatever's necessary Gabi, whatever I have to do.

Gabriella decided she was no longer running from Ramero. She didn't want Antonio to get involved and she wasn't about to call Drago. Instead she called Satin, Ramero's cousin and asked his whereabouts. Satin gladly gave her the information she needed. Ramero was staying with some chick in Bankhead. She had been out of town visiting her family for a week. Ramero sent his two henchmen along to keep an eye on her so he would be all alone. Gabriella formulated a plan. She told Antonio that their flight was scheduled to leave Friday, it was just Monday. Antonio tried his best to stick around or at least know where she would be at all times. On this particular day he had taken Fernando to basketball practice. Isabella was at her friend Jackie's, whose parents would protect her as if she were one of their own. She called Ramero from a prepaid cell phone. He answered in a groggy voice.

Yeah, what up?

Ramero, its' me.

Juicy, what up baby? I was just thinking about you.

Please spare me the details.

I remember when we used to tell each other everything.

Yeah well you fucked that up a long time ago.

Come on now Juicy, I said I'm sorry. How many times you gone make a brother beg for forgiveness?

You couldn't possibly want forgiveness threatening me the way you do. What a crazy way to ask for it.

My bad, look I just need that money I asked for.

What do you need with all that money anyway?

Matters that, you just get it to me and you won't have no problems. Understood?

Ramero you're so full of shit. Who do you owe and why? Don't lie to me either.

Your threats don't scare me. If you were going to do something you would have done it by now.

He sighed, I don't want to hurt you anymore. I just need this money. If I don't come up with the money…

What happened with your little CI girlfriend? She can't help you?

She's dead.

Dead? How did that happen?

She got killed in a car accident about a year ago.

Damn, as long as y'all were fucking around she didn't leave you anything she laughed?

Nah, turns out I wasn't the only cat she was fucking around with. She had a federal agent on her team. She left everything to him.

Gabriella tried to think of a way to get him to reveal more information. She realized that all she had to do was be the Juicy he wanted her to be. So she just listened as he rambled on and on.

Juicy you still there?

Yes, I'm here, just trippen off all that's going on with you.

Yeah karma's a muthafucka. I wish I could take it all back.

Too late for that, you've done far too much.

The one thing I regret the most is losing you.

You didn't lose me. You used the things you did and pinned it all on me to get yourself a get out of jail free card. Well you're out of jail, you should be thrilled. Everybody else is either locked up for 10 or more years or dead. Gabriella thought about Tago and fought hard not to get emotional over the phone. You should worship the ground I walk on but instead you're threatening to harm my children.

They're not your children. They're Tago's children.

Yeah and you would put your life at risk by making that threat.
I'm desperate, besides I know you don't want to see no more bloodshed. So you'll just do what you gotta do. Yo Juicy why you ain't never tell Tech what really went down?
What makes you think I didn't?
Because if you did and the nigga was as in love as you claim then I'd be dead right now he said with a laugh. Guess you were just his whore after all. And a good piece of pussy you were. Damn, I sho nuff miss that. Even after all them other niggas done ran through you I still want a taste.
Gabriella started with the tears. Ramero, why? I don't understand. I thought you loved me.
I love money baby, more than anything. I never meant for you to get caught up in this shit but I had to have my freedom to make more money by any means necessary. Coming where I'm from I was on a real come up. I was tired of being broke. He listened to her cry and got all soft. Yo Gabi, stop crying. You know that's my weakness. I'm sorry alright? I know you probably won't ever forgive me but if you give me this money I'll leave you alone. Straight up. I wouldn't ask if I didn't need it.
I'll give you the money but don't keep threatening me about it. Who the hell you know just has half a mil laying around the house?
Okay, alright thanks.

Gabriella called Ramero again on Thursday and asked where are you?
At the crib he responded, why, what's up?
Meet me at Radisson Hotel in an hour.
Alright
When he arrived at the hotel he called her cell phone she answered Room 2111
When he walked into the room he smiled at the suitcase laying open on the bed with the money in it. I knew you would come through for me Juicy.
She smiled as she watched him walk over and count some of the money. He glanced at her saw her curves in the fitted Versace dress she wore. There was some kind of banquet going on at the hotel that night. She had entered undetected and picked up a room key from the front desk with ease. He licked his lips and asked who you fucking with now?
Nobody

You mean to tell me ain't nobody hitting this he asked as he walked up behind her.

No

When's the last time?

Almost 5 years ago, with Tago.

Damn, goddamn

She backed away and said here is all your money.

Can we just, you know, one for the road?

If I say no, then what?

Why would you say no? You haven't had dick in 5 years and I was the best you ever had. You were the best I ever had too he admitted. Nobody can top my Juicy. So what's up? You gone let a nigga in or what?

I don't have time. You know my kids schedules just as well as I do. It's time for me to pick them up from school.

Well how about we hook up later? Nobody has practice tonight.

You're not coming to my place.

Come to mines he said as he called out the address.

I'll call you and let you know.

Yeah you do that. Think about me between them thighs and all the things I used to do to drive you wild he said with a smirk.

Antonio was supposed to meet with Ahmad and some of his boys to attend their cousin Lewis' bachelor party in Miami that night. He kept telling her he would be back the following morning to take them to the airport. She assured him that she would be fine. The kids would be staying over at Jackie's for the night so Gabriella could handle her business.

Ramero was downing shots of Grey Goose anticipating Gabriella's arrival. He couldn't wait to put it to her. He was so drunk by the time she arrived out in the wilderness that she didn't even have to make the steps she thought she would. He was ready to get right to it but she convinced him to have a drink with her. He was so drunk and so relaxed around Gabriella that he started rambling on and on about the things he had done, the people he owed. She got it all on tape. She spiked his drink and had him unconscious in a matter of minutes. She found the money she had given him, took it back and Fed Ex'd the recorded tape after making copies to every major connect she had found out about while doing her research. She made it home right on time for Antonio's phone call.

Y'all alright? I should have just came and stayed the night with you.
Well it's not too late you know.
Oh yeah, will you wait up for me?
Yes indeed.
Be there shortly.

Chapter 5

When Antonio showed up he rang the doorbell. Gabriella wasn't expecting him so soon and had just stepped out of the shower. She wrapped a towel around her body, another around her head and walked out to the front door.
Hey, come on in she tells him.
He picks her up in his arms and kisses her lips slowly while locking the door behind them.
What's got you all hot and bothered she asks with a grin?
Them goddamn strippers he laughed. I knew I shouldn't have went.
Why not?
Cause I'm horny and I can't get none.
Why can't you get any?
Because the kids are here and you ain't trying to give me none no way.
How would you know? You never even asked.
I wanted to he said as he licked his lips slow and seductively.
The kids aren't here.
Where are they?
At Jackie's she said as she kissed him again.
He kissed her back but stopped when his cell rang. Give me a minute to take this call he said as he placed her feet on the ground. He walked into the den and held a conversation with the caller for a good 20 minutes before coming back into the room that Gabriella was in.
I need to go make a run. You will be alright till I get back?
Yes, be careful she pouted.
I will, lock all these doors. Set the alarm.
Yes sir.
Around 4AM he called to say he wouldn't make it back. They stayed on the phone until 7AM. When 11AM came he was back and loading their luggage into the trunk of his car. He hadn't really touched Gabriella since he'd come back. She wondered what last night was all about. It didn't help that he didn't have much to say to her either. The kids were like chatter boxes that morning asking question after question. Gabriella and Antonio never got a chance to discuss things. At the airport Antonio hugged the kids and barely held on to Gabriella. She sat on the plane fuming.

Drago picked them up from the airport. He was happy to see both her and the kids. By the time the weekend ended Drago received a phone call that Ramero was found dead. He tried his best to keep the excitement out of his voice. Gabriella overheard part of the conversation and breathed a sigh of relief. She called the airlines to book flights back home. By 8PM on Sunday they were heading back. Instead of calling Antonio she called a car service to take them home from the airport.

Antonio checked on the house every day. When Monday rolled around he made his way over there. Gabriella was getting out of her car with bags of groceries. Antonio pulled in behind her.

When did you get back he asked?

Yesterday

Well damn, I ain't good for a phone call?

It was late when we arrived.

He grabbed bags from the car and followed her inside. I guess you heard about Ramero?

That would be why we're back.

You find out what happened?

He's dead, everything else is irrelevant to me.

You okay?

Yes, I'm fine she said as she moved about the kitchen putting away groceries when a loud knock stopped her.

You expecting company Antonio asked?

No she said as she heads towards the front door. With everything that has been going on Antonio insists on answering it.

I'm here to see a Gabriella Pennington.

And you are?

Howard Ross with Franklin, Turner and Hughes

What is this about?

Ramero Hernandez

She's moved on with her life and has no contact with him.

I'm aware of that. Actually this is in regards to his life insurance policies. Is Miss Pennington available?

Gabriella stepped from behind Antonio and said I'm Gabriella Pennington.

He shook her hand as she welcomed him inside. Turns out that Ramero had 4 insurance policies. Aside from Satin he didn't have any other living relatives. Gabriella put up a damn good front when Mr. Ross spoke of his death. She could have won an academy award for best actress based on that performance. Even Antonio was moved by it and he knew everything she had gone through in behind him.

Miss Pennington, it is my duty to sign these checks over to you.

I don't want the money.

Both Antonio and Mr. Ross looked at her like she was crazy. Okay I'll take half but give the other half to Satin Hernandez, his cousin.

Whatever you wish Miss Pennington. His funeral arrangements have already been made, If you want to attend...

I don't she answered quickly. If it wasn't for the 2 kids we almost had together and all the drama he put me through I wouldn't even take half the money but I deserve at least that much.

A couple of days later Satin called Gabriella up and through tears said Thank you.

They held a heartfelt conversation for a good 2 hours.

Mommy Fernando said when he came in from school is Antonio going to take me to practice today?

Antonio hasn't called. Did he tell you he would?

Yes maam.

Okay well he'll be here. Antonio had been keeping his distance ever since the night before they went to New York. When Gabriella asked what was going on he'd tell her nothing. Eventually she got tired of asking and just left it alone.

He showed up 20 minutes before 5. Gabriella was dressed in a fitted pant suit. She was having dinner with a few friends and the kids would stay over to Jackie's for the night.

What's up he asked when he walked in?

Hey Fernando has been waiting on you. He didn't know if you were going to make it or not.

I told him I would.

Fernando, Tony's here. She left the living room to go into her bedroom to finish dressing.

Mommy can I have five dollars please?

I just gave you twenty dollars this morning. I know you didn't spend all of it.

I want to save it for the game on Friday.

Fernando spend the five dollars you have.

But what about Friday?

We will discuss Friday when it gets here.

Okay

Remember you are to go to Jackie's. Mr. Hightower will be here to pick you up, so call him when practice is over.

You look pretty Mommy.

Thanks baby she said as she hugged and kissed him. You be good and enjoy practice.

I will, have fun Mommy and be careful.

Will do. To Antonio she said thanks.

No problem, Where you on your way to?

Dinner with some friends.

Cool.

Later on that night Gabriella stepped up in Morrison's, a night club with Satin and mingled with the crowd. Antonio was in VIP smoking a blunt and holding a conversation with Brian out of Chicago about doing business down that way. Some chick walked up and caught their attention long enough for him to miss Gabriella's model stroll up the winding staircase into VIP. She ordered a Mimosa and took a seat at the bar.

I see a lot of new faces Satin says as she smiles at a dude across the way.

One guy in particular held Gabriella's eye. He was watching her just as much she was watching him. Damn he's fine Satin pointed out.

Yes indeed Gabriella smiled. She turned back around in her seat and conversed with Satin. The gentleman came over, introduced himself as Alejandro. He offered to buy them drinks.

No thank you Gabriella spoke, we're good.

I've seen you somewhere before.

New York, 2001 at the Player's Ball.

You were with Tago.

Gabriella smiled, surprised that he referred to him by his government name. Most people referred to him as Tech, only relatives and close friends referred to him as Tago. Yes.

Gabi he asked surprised.

Yes, it's me.

But I thought…

You thought I was dead?

Yeah I mean, what happened? Why did you leave New York?

It was too much going on.

With the Fed case?

With everything.

How are you doing now? I mean, you look beautiful.

Thanks, I'm great. How are you?

I'm alive.

That's a blessing. How's your Mom and Adrianna?

He smiled surprised she remembered their names. My mom is good. She just got news that her cancer is gone.

Amen.

Yes indeed, she's growing her hair back and trying to move on with her life.

And Adrianna, how is she?

He frowned, ugh she's in a mental institution.

What?

Yeah she went through some things that fucked her up and she ain't been right ever since.

Wow, I'm sorry to hear that.

I guess it was fate that I ran into you here.

Why do you say that?

When my Mom first got diagnosed she asked about you and I didn't have the heart to tell her what I'd been told because I wasn't sure if I believed it myself. She kept asking for you until Adrianna told her you were dead. Moms never believed it and would still ask for you to this day. I visited Adrianna yesterday. She had the picture the two of you took that night at the ball and for the first time in 4 years she smiled when I said your name.

Where is she?

Maxwell Behavioral.

Gabriella ordered another drink, asked Satin and Alejandro if they wanted anything. After more conversation she needed to get away to clear her head. She excused herself to the bathroom and then wandered off. She ran into Ahmad and a few of his college buddies.

Wassup sis he asked as he hugged her. What you doing up here? I didn't even know you go out.

I don't, at least I haven't been in a while. Just thought I would get out tonight.

My brother know you here?

No and could probably care less.

Yeah right, you trippen. Want me to get you a drink?

No, I'm good. Thanks

Where you running off to?

Back up to VIP

Who you with?

Me and my homegirl Satin

She cute?

Yeah she smiled.

I'm rolling with you.

This time when they stepped up in VIP Antonio noticed her.

What's up Antonio asked when he walked over to her.

Ain't nothing, what's up with you?

Satin came over and said Gabi, Six is going to Donovan's. You wanna roll?

Yeah that's cool.

Fuck you mean, yeah that's cool Antonio asked as he grabbed her. Who the fuck is Six and what you need with a Bed & Breakfast when you got em both at home?

Gabriella smirked, you really give a fuck huh? Well that's good to know but I'm grown and I don't answer to nobody but God.

Well you answering to me tonight or your ass ain't going nowhere but home.

Boy stop, you're trippen. You ain't had shit to say to me since you left my house before I went to New York. Keep up with that shit. I don't need you paying attention to me now she said as she tried to walk off.

Gabriella he said as he grabbed her arm just as Alejandro walked up. You straight G he asked as he looked at Gabriella.

Yeah I'm good. Antonio this is Alejandro. Alejandro, Antonio.

Good To Have You Back

Alejandro dapped him up and asked you going for omelettes or you still into cooking breakfast?
I'm going for omelettes. To Antonio she asked you going or staying?
Yo Ahmad, take my truck. I'm out he said as he grabbed her hand and walked out the front door.
Satin this is Antonio. Antonio, my good friend Satin.
Nice to finally meet you Satin said as she extended her hand to him.
Same here.
Six asked, Satin you riding with me Ma?
Yeah, see you there she said to Gabriella.

Alejandro watched Antonio and Gabriella together without making it obvious. He always had a thing for Gabriella since they met at the Player's Ball. It wasn't just the fact that she was beautiful or fine. Gabriella was very intelligent, very loyal and she knew the game just as well as any major connect.
Alejandro ran into Gabriella a few weeks later in Palisades Center Mall back in New York. She was coming out of the BCBG store with a young girl that reminded him of Tago. Once he got closer he realized it was Tago's daughter Isabella.
Gabi he called out to her.
Alejandro, hey what's up she asked as she accepted the hug he offered.
Damn woman, you got enough bags he joked? What's up Muffin he asked Isabella.
Hi Alex she smiled.
How long you here for he asked Gabriella?
Until Sunday.
Where's Fernando?
Around here somewhere with Drago and Jesus.
What you getting into later?
I'm not sure, why what's up?
Was wondering if you would like to go see my sister with me and my Mom.
Yeah that's cool. Let me get the kids situated and I'll come by.
Cool.
Drago walked up and asked who dat?
That's Alex, he and Daddy used to play cards together Isabella responded.

What he want he asked looking right at Gabriella?
Are you trying to check me she asked with a laugh?
Nah I'm just trying to see what's up.
Just an old friend.
Better be, don't make me get Antonio up here.
Please, what he gone do?
Alright Drago warned.

Chapter 6

Gabriella got the kids situated at the house. After going back and forth with Drago about where she was going he finally allowed her to leave. He gave her specific instructions on when to call as if she was his child. He wanted text messages of license plate numbers, vehicle descriptions and exact locations. Carmen, Mrs. Lucia Dominguez's housekeeper greeted Gabriella at the door. Good afternoon, you must be Gabriella.

Yes

Mrs. Lucia will be so happy to see you. Please come in.

Gabi, Mrs. Lucia said as she wrapped her arms around her and held her tightly. How have you been?

Gabriella and Lucia sat talking for hours before Alejandro arrived. His little brother Mateo came in behind him.

Mom whose car is in...Gabi he squealed as he hugged her.

Oh my, look at you. You've gotten so big Gabriella told him.

Two chicks stood at the door with blank looks on their faces.

Alejandro said Gabi, I didn't think you would show.

Why?

He shrugged his shoulders and shook his head with a smile.

Don't ever doubt me. I always mean what I say. Are you ready? I have strict instructions to be home before 10 o'clock.

By who, your boyfriend?

I don't have one she laughed. By Drago and the kids, if I'm not back they will put out a search party on me.

How are Isabella and Fernando Lucia asked?

Two of the most amazing kids I know she smiled like a proud parent. They're doing great.

I commend you for taking them in. You're such an Angel.

Alejandro looked puzzled for a minute but shook it off.

They spent 4 hours visiting Adrianna and everybody commented that she was not her usual self today but in a good way. She was just as happy to see Gabriella as the rest of them had been. Adrianna used to date Tago's friend Pedro before he was killed in a bad drug deal. She and Gabriella had become

close over the years. When Adrianna hooked up with Ricardo he and Tago
didn't get along so he wouldn't allow her to see Gabriella.
When they left the institution Gabriella was in tears. Alejandro pulled her into his
arms and held her.
Come on now G. I've never known you to be a big cry baby.
His Mom elbowed him. You leave my baby alone. Gabi, you okay hun?
Yes maam she said as she wiped away her tears.
Alejandro asked You okay once they got back to his Mom's house.
Oh now you wanna be sympathetic she laughed as she punched him.
I'm sorry.
Why?
For saying that to you, it's just that I've never seen you cry before.
Is that a bad thing?
Yeah considering that I know a little about what you went through. You never
told me the rest but Adrianna always said it wasn't pretty.
What happened to her?
She won't say but I think it has something to do with Ricardo.
What makes you think that?
Instincts.
Okay, what?
We have a lot to talk about.
I guess we do.
You sure o'l dude ain't your man?
Am I sure? Of course I'm sure. What's it to you anyway?
He smiled, I want you. That has never been a secret. I want you more now than
I did back then but I ain't trying to step on nobody's toes or nothing. Since you
say that ain't your man, what's up with you and me?
You didn't have time for me then and judging off how you're living she said as
she pointed to the Maserati they had stepped out of, you won't have time for me
now. And the women she said as a chick pulled up in a Corvette and honked the
horn. You know I don't do drama.
Smiling he said I got plenty of time for you G. Don't sleep on me. As for the
women he said as the chick sat in the car rolling her eyes, You know you gone
always come first. He winked at her before telling her Gone on inside. Make that
phone call to let the fam know you made it back safely. I'll be inside in a minute.

Hurry up.

I will Ma, calm your nerves.

As soon as Gabriella walked into the house later Drago said Antonio called. Why you ain't been answering your phone. Don't you know people be worried about you?

Drago, not now.

What you mean not now? What's wrong?

She continued to the kids' bedrooms to check on them. They were watching Scooby Doo when she peeked inside Fernando's room. Mommy you're home.

Yes, I'm home. Where else would I be? Hi Leandra. Hi Corrine.

Hi Auntie Gabi surrounded by small children she hugged them all. Where is everybody?

Manuel, Hector and Jesus are asleep. Raven is with Natasha, Drago responded. Can I talk to you for a minute?

Drago can't it wait she asked as she settled down with kids.

It was after midnight when she came out of the room and headed to Tago's bedroom. Bella

Drago can I take a shower first please? You're really starting to bug me.

Yeah but hurry up. Don't try to fall asleep either.

Once out a long hot shower Gabriella dressed in leggings and a long t-shirt before making her way to the bar. She fixed herself a glass of wine then found Drago in the kitchen.

Alright Lil Bro, let me have it.

What's up with you and Antonio?

What do you mean?

When I told him you were with Alejandro he seemed frustrated.

Serves his ass right.

What do you mean?

What did he tell you?

That he's on his way here.

For what?

He was just that upset with you.

How does he even know where to come?

I told him, besides Uncle Juan is picking him up from the airport as we speak.

And he's coming here?
Yes
Are you out of your mind? Where will he sleep?
With you I suppose, isn't that where he sleeps in Georgia?
Drago, you're not funny. I will not disrespect Tago like that.
Drago smiled, Okay. I will put him in a guestroom. Didn't realize you had that big of a problem with it.
Next time you should ask me before you make decisions on my behalf.
I'm sorry.

Antonio arrived around 2 in the morning. Where's Gabriella?
She's asleep. I'll set you up in the guestroom. She insists.
Cool he tells Mr. Gordon. How are the kids?
Happy, whenever Bella's around they're always happy.
The next morning Gabriella was up making breakfast and singing Selena's Dreaming Of You. The kids were watching cartoons on the big screen in the family room.
Drago came in and tried to sneak a piece of bacon. Get out of this kitchen she fussed at him.
I'm starved.
I have 7 kids to feed, wait your turn.
I'll help you with their plates.
No thank you, I have everything under control. Why don't you go make sure the whole house is awake and ready for breakfast?
Yes maam.
Drago
He laughed as he stole his bacon and ran off.
Later on that day Gabriella was at the butchers buying steaks for Sunday dinner when she ran into Ricardo coming out of the barbershop a few doors down.
Well, well, well I see some things never change he said as he circled her with a smile.
Hello Ricardo
Please call me Ricky. All my friends do. How have you been?
Alive and well.
I can see that you are blessed in many areas.

Gabriella shook her head as more guys came out the shop. Ricardo one of them asked Ay yo, who is this Mamacita?

This is Tago's baby mama Gabriella.

Word? Goddamn one of them responded.

Gabriella smirked I'm not just his baby mama. I'm also his wife.

Was, Ricardo announced. I'm terribly sorry for your loss. If you ever need anything, anything, look me up. I'm in the book.

Cute she told him as she walked into the butcher shop. He followed her inside and asked Really I'd like to sit and talk with you.

Imagine that, finally something we can agree on.

You name the time and place.

Lombardi's at 1 on Monday.

Why not tomorrow?

Some of us have priorities, mines happens to be family.

Yes, right. Lombardi's. Monday at 1

Monday Drago and Antonio left to go to New Jersey. The kids were all with Natasha so Gabriella was free to move about the city. As she sat in Lombardi's waiting on Ricardo to arrive she thought about Alejandro. He picked that time to call.

Yes she answered.

What's up, you busy?

Not at all, what's up with you?

I want to see you today if at all possible.

I'm sure it's possible. Where will you be in the next hour or so?

How about we give it 2-3 hours tops? That too late?

No that's good. I'll call you.

Make sure you do that G.

Ricardo said Sorry I'm late, had a business meeting that ran over. Gabriella was already eating. She chewed the food she had in her mouth and took a sip of her raspberry lemonade. You would never make it with me.

What do you mean?

You just lost cool points for being late and what the fuck were you thinking when you sprayed that funky ass cologne she asked while scrunching up her nose.

Next time I will wear something else he smiled. I won't be late again he said as if he knew there would be a next time. He was so used to having his way with the ladies. Only reason Gabriella gave him the time of day is to find out what happened with Adrianna. She had him all relaxed until Alejandro stood in front of their table wearing a pissed of expression with the Corvette chick standing right beside him.

Fuck you doing with this nigga he asked.

She looked at him biting her lip and said we are having lunch Alejandro. She extended her hand to the chick that stood beside him but he grabbed it before they could shake.

Let me holla at you for a minute he told her through clinched teeth.

You're embarrassing the hell out of me Gabriella mumbled.

What you doing with that nigga?

I told you…

Gabriella, don't fuck with me. Get in your car and go the fuck home.

You get in your car and go home without Mary Poppins.

He smiled at her jealousy. She smiled too. Alejandro it's not what you think.

What is it then?

I want to know what happened to Adrianna.

Leave it alone G. When Adrianna starts talking we will know what happened. And what if she doesn't?

He starred into her eyes, felt her pain and said Let me handle this. I promise you I got it under control. Alright? He kissed her cheek and moved hair from her face before saying Go home. I'll call you in an hour.

She hit the lock, opened the door of her Mercedes and got inside.

An hour later he calls and asks Where are you?

At the house.

I'm about to come through and scoop you up.

Please don't, how about we just meet somewhere.

What we hiding for?

We're not hiding. We will meet at your Mom's.

When?

Now

Just before she walked out the door Antonio called. What's up? What you doing?

About to go to the mall.
We probably won't be back until mid-morning, about to go to Bottoms Up.
Alright.
You cool at the house by yourself?
Yes Antonio, I'm fine.
I know that. I asked if you were okay there by yourself.
Yes, I'm okay. What's been up with you lately? Are we ever going to talk about that?
What's there to talk about? Ain't nothing going on.
That's the point.
What you mean?
We were about to get hot and heavy then you leave and don't come back until it's time to take us to the airport. Since then you haven't come close to me. Why?
No reason. I just think we need to chill.
Oh yeah, and when did you plan on telling me?
I'm telling you now.
Gabriella smirked, Yeah, okay. Whatever.
We will be through there in a couple of hours.
Yeah she said before hanging up.

Why you all frowned up Alejandro asked as he opened his Mom's front door.
No reason.
You ain't still trippen about me back at the restaurant right he asked as he locked the front door back, hit the alarm for his Bentley and walked out to the car.
No, where are we going?
Out to lunch. Do you mind?
No, I don't.
Well get that damn frown off your face he said as he opened the passenger side door.
They enjoyed a late lunch and conversation at Carmine's.
So what's up with you and o'l dude?
Who?
Don't try to play me. The one from the club.

Antonio? Nothing.

What you mean nothing? The way that nigga was trippen I thought y'all were together.

Gabriella didn't comment. Alejandro didn't let it slide. You gone answer my question?

I told you nothing.

Why?

What you mean why?

Why ain't there nothing going on?

Because he ain't feeling me like that.

Good, cause I am.

Gabriella looked at him and smiled, he smiled back.

What you getting into tonight?

Taking my kids to the movies, maybe bowling afterwards.

That's what's up. Any chance you and me can spend the whole day together here in New York?

I doubt it. Drago already wants to know my every move. Now that Antonio's here…

Oh he here? Where he at?

Out with Drago somewhere.

They cool like that?

Yeah I guess.

What he doing here?

I don't know, he came the night we went to visit Adrianna.

He know you was with me?

Yes

How?

Drago told him.

Is that why he came to New York?

Does it matter?

I'm just trying to figure all this out. Alejandro said as he leaned back in his seat starring at her.

The nigga staying at Tago's too?

Yes. Drago invited him.

You say that like you got a problem with it.

I do.
Why?
Because it's disrespectful.
To who?
Tago

Gabriella and the kids went to the movies and then decided to go skating afterwards. The rink didn't close until 1AM. By the time they made it home both Drago and Antonio were worked up.
Man where the fuck you been Drago asked as soon as they came through the door.
Watch your mouth in front of the kids. I told you we were going skating.
It's damn near 2 o'clock in the morning. What skating rink you know open this late Antonio asked.
To Isabella and Fernando Gabriella tells them Go take your showers. Brush your teeth, wash your face, put your pajamas on and I'll be in in a minute.
Yes maam they both mumbled as they hugged her and kissed her cheeks before hugging Drago and Antonio.
As soon as they were out of hearing range Gabriella said Let's get something straight. First of all I'm grown and I don't have to answer to nobody. If I tell you we're going skating that's where the hell we were at. It closed at 1 and we stopped for wings and shakes at Donovan's. Secondly I ain't gotta tell neither one of you shit. I do it out of respect, so don't get it twisted. I'm not all the time hounding y'all about where you're going, where you been.
We just looking out for you Drago told her.
I understand that D but watch how you come at me from now on. Why you all the time worried about me you need to go home to your wife. She has called me at least 20 times looking for your ass. And you she said to Antonio Chill the fuck out.

Chapter 7

The next morning Uncle Juan picked the kids up before 9. They had already eaten breakfast and were ready to leave. Gabriella called Alejandro and told him today is the day.

Oh yeah, where you at?

About to leave the house.

Well I'm at home G. I didn't get in until 7 this morning but you're more than welcome to come chill with me.

Where do you live?

William Beaver. 15 William Street.

Okay I will be there in a minute.

Sure you will he laughed thinking she was joking.

Where you on your way to Antonio asked when she came from the back fully dressed in a pair of slacks and a blouse with soft curls in her hair.

Out. If you need to leave my car is in the front. Here are the keys.

An hour later she pulls up to the door of Alejandro's condos, steps from the car before passing the valet parking attendant the keys to Tago's Bentley GT coupe. She was escorted to the 15th floor and made her way to suite 1511. Alejandro stood with the door open wearing a wife beater and boxers with a morning hard on and a smile.

Unh huh, you didn't think I was coming huh she asked as she stood in front of him. He picked her up in his arms and kissed her lips soft and sensuously.

Nah I didn't believe you, can't even front. She kissed him back and asked are you always this alert in the morning?

He smirked before shifting himself. You got me like this.

Me huh? Well I guess I'll just have to solve your problem.

Yeah maybe you should he laughed thinking she was joking.

What she did next was remove all her clothes and get into his bed naked. He smiled Alright, I'm gone have yo ass hemmed up in here he said as he removed his own clothes and got in the bed beside her.

G, you know I ain't trippen if you don't give me none right? I'm just happy you're here.

Good to know but I'm seriously going to trip if you don't give me none.

Good To Have You Back

Oh yeah he asked as he kissed her lips offering some tongue. Before long his lips and tongue were dancing all over her body. All that coupled with his hands had her shaking. He strapped on a condom after getting her just where he needed her to be and slowly eased himself inside of her. He fell in love with her all over again. The way he molded into her, the snug fit, the expressions on her face, the sounds she made, the way she bit his shoulder, the way she called out his name. All that had him in a trance. She felt so good that for a long time after he was inside her he held it there and just starred deeply into her eyes.

Bonita he moaned. Ooh Gabriella, goddamn woman. She smiled before laughing at the expression on his face.

What's so funny he asks still moaning as he moves in and out of her causing her to moan and make those sexy facial expressions. They spent the next 3 hours making love before taking a break and cuddling up in his bed.

Why were you laughing at me he asked as he played in her hair.

You act like you ain't had pussy in a long time.

Man, you know how long I've been dreaming about getting up in this he asked as his dick got hard just thinking about it. And I ain't never and I do mean never had anything that can compare he said as he kissed her forehead. What about you? Been a long time huh?

Yes

How long? A few months?

Much longer than you think.

How long?

Since Tago she answered as she snatched up her ringing cell phone and answered it without viewing the caller ID. Yes little brother she asked Drago.

How did you know it was me?

Who else would be calling me?

Antonio. Where you at? I'm just asking because what?

Because what, you answer that question.

I wanna know.

Drago I'm okay. Stop worrying about me.

Alejandro got up to use the bathroom swinging long john every which way, Gabriella smiled. D, did you need something?

What time will you be back?

I might not come home tonight.

You're bullshitten right?
What if I wasn't?
You better be. Bella come on now, I don't know what you trying to prove but damn don't do the shit while he here.
What are you talking about?
I know who you're with.
Oh really she asked not the least bit surprised.
Yeah and I suggest you wrap your shit up and head back to the crib cause yo boy is a tad bit antsy.
Drago
Bella come on, do it for me. Please
Okay, okay. I'll be there in a couple of hours.
Thank you

What's up Alejandro asked as he came out of the bathroom and lifted her into his arms. He carried her into his spacious bathroom, placed her inside the bathtub on his lap. It ain't too hot for you is it he asked?
No, just right.
Okay, so what's up?
I gotta go home in a couple of hours.
Why, what's up with the kids?
It's Drago
What about him he asked as he lifts her up and puts on a condom before easing her down on him.
She moans loudly, ooh shit Alejandro. Shit, shit, shit. Aaah, ooh Alejandro. The whole time he's making love to her he's starring into her eyes.
Gabi he says between his own moans.
Mmm, yes she asked as she closed her eyes.
Te Amo Gabriella! Yo no desea que esto sea la ultima vez bien? No deje que esto sea la ultima vez. (I love you Gabriella! I don't want this to be the last time. Alright? Don't let this be the last time.)
Te Amo demasiado Alejandro! Esta no sera la ultima vez prometo, prometo damn. Ooh aahh (I love you too Alejandro! This won't be the last time. I promise, damn. I promise, ooh aahh)

After making love in the shower Alejandro prepared lunch of grilled fish, shrimp and mixed vegetables with rice. She enjoyed it before making her way home to a pissed off Antonio.

Where you been?
I told you I was going out.
Out where? Just saying out ain't good enough for me.
Well I'm back now so it really doesn't matter she said as she walked past him into the kitchen. She grabbed a bottled water from the refrigerator and posted up with her back against the counter. Her text message alert went off. When she read the text message from Alejandro she almost spit out her drink laughing.
Man, tienes un nigga por aqui todos y shit lento. I no es nunca tienen este problema. No puedo ni levantarme. Que tienes ahi? (Man you got a nigga over here all sluggish and shit. I ain't never had this problem. I can't even get up. What you got in there)
What's so funny Antonio asked?
Nothing she said as she replied back with Kryptonite
Alejandro replied back with a smiley face and I can't wait to see you again. Her reply was ditto as she walked into Tago's bedroom closing the door behind her and falling back on his California king sized mattress with a satisfied smile.
Her cell phone rang and she answered Yes Drago. I'm home.
Good, where's Antonio?
On the other side of the door.
Antonio knocked on the door and asked can I talk to you for a minute?
Through the door she asked what's up?
Can you open the door?
Drago, let me call you back. She opened the door and asked what's up?
Let's go grab a bite to eat.
I already ate.
Well let's go do something.
How about going for a run?
Yeah, alright cool.
Gabriella changed into a pair of short shorts and a sports bra before strapping her I-pod around her arm.

She pressed play after locating Beyonce's Dangerously In Love cd. You ready she called out to Antonio?

Gordon can you listen for the phone in case the kids call. Antonio and I are going for a run.

Yes indeed he smiled as he passed her two bottles of water. By the time Antonio stepped outside Gabriella was at the curb warming up.

What the fuck you got on? Go put some clothes on.

Oh shut up and come on you jack ass she said as she took off running. They ran 5 miles before walking it out for 2 miles and then winding down at the entrance of Tago's driveway.

Tago's accountant Rhett Lawrence stood at the end of his Lincoln and smiled as Gabriella walked up.

Gabriella he said as he hugged her, Good to have you back. How have you been?

Great Rhett, how about you?

Fantastic, who's the gentleman?

Rhett this is my friend Antonio. Antonio, Rhett Lawrence Tago's accountant and lawyer. They shook hands. Gabriella asked Rhett Was being in Aruba for a year as relaxing as they say?

Yes indeed he laughed using her words. You really should vacation there some day.

Perhaps I should. What brings you out this way?

Unfinished business.

Please let me shower and I will meet you in Tago's office. Let Gordon know if he can get you anything.

What's up Antonio asked?

I'm not sure yet.

Rhett explained to Gabriella that Tago had several businesses that she had not been aware of. The companies have been basically running themselves and the accounts are getting out of hand. He wasn't too sure what to do with all the revenue.

What did you do in the past Gabriella asked?

I invested a little here and there, bought property, a number of things but all this was advised by Tago. I wasn't too sure how you wanted to handle it.

If it ain't broke, don't fix it. Continue to handle things as you would in the past. Tago trusted you to do it right all these years. Why should we switch it up now? Well let's go over the figures so you know exactly what you got coming in. After spending 2 hours going over the books Gabriella had numbers dancing around in her head.

She tried to spend as much time with Alejandro as she could because they would be leaving in a couple of days but there was so much to do at the house. Drago was constantly in her ear and Antonio constantly on her back. She was able to leave the house around 6AM the morning they were leaving and go to Alejandro's. He was just getting home from a night at the strip club.

Well damn Bonita, it's good to see you baby. He kissed her lips, sucking on her tongue before pulling her into his arms. How long I got you for?

A few hours. My flight leaves at 1 and I need to be back by 11. He bit his bottom lip as he starred into her eyes and asked How we gone do this? Come snuggle with me. They removed their clothes and snuggled up in bed.

Gabi

Yes Alex

When am I gone see you again? I gotta wait till you come back to New York to see you?

You're welcome to come to my neck of the woods. Just know that you can't stay the night at the house and I'm not ready to bring you around the kids yet in that sense. But we can get out and go places, maybe get a room here and there.

How long I gotta wait for you to get back to come through?

Whenever you want to come. Keep in mind I'm a mother. I have responsibilities and I stay on top of all that.

Where you work at?

I'm an editor and an author so I work from home.

That's what's up. Let's get some sleep. I'm tired than a muthafucka Ma.

When they woke up Alejandro had a sad look on his face.

Damn, I miss you already.

Aww she said as she kissed his lips. I've been thinking.

About what? Moving back to New York to be closer to me?

Moving back has crossed my mind a time or two.

What's the hold up?

Too much on the kids, all this back and forth.

Ever asked them what they thought?
Not as far as moving back to New York but I know they want to be with me.
So it don't matter where you at, they good. I'm sure the rest of the family would prefer them and you to be in New York. I know I would.
I will keep that in mind.
Oh yeah, what was you about to say?
I'm going to try to get up here every other weekend and any time the kids are out of school so I can come visit Adrianna.
She would like that.
I miss her.
I know Ma, me too.

Isabella asked Mommy
Yes baby she said as she braided her hair into micro braids.
I want to go back home.
To stay she asked?
Yes but I want you to come too. I miss my family, my friends and I just miss home.
Me too Mommy Fernando said as he leaned into her side. I miss my house. I miss my Daddy.
Aww babies she said as she held them and cried.
Antonio called after the kids had gone to bed. What you doing he asked?
Ironing the kids clothes for tomorrow.
Feel like some company?
I don't care.
Damn alright. Need me to pick up anything?
No. I'm good.
That night Antonio told Gabriella he had met someone. She had suspected it so she wasn't trippen.
She asked how long has this been going on?
We been kickin it here lately.
Gabriella got up poured herself a shot of Grey Goose and passed one to Antonio. So what's up? You sound like you got a lot on your mind Antonio said to Gabriella as she took a seat beside him.
As if you telling me what you just told me wouldn't shut a bitch up she laughed.

Good To Have You Back

Gabi
No need to explain. I'm good.
Are you? Really?
Yes, I let go when you told me you wanted to chill but I'm glad you were man enough to tell me how you felt and I respect you more for that.
But what's on your mind? You sounded like this before I told you what I told you.
The kids want to move back to New York.
And you too?
Yes, I was worried about how that would make you feel but I guess it really doesn't matter now. So when the school year is over we'll be moving back.
Wow that's only 2 months.
Not like I have to do much. We have a house in New York already and I can put an ad in the paper to rent this out so I'm good.
You sure about this?
Yeah

That night Gabriella prayed about her move some more, about the kids, Antonio, Alejandro, Adrianna, Drago. She wondered how Tago would feel about her moving back to New York after all this time. And since they were moving into Tago's house how would she handle situations with Alejandro if things got serious between the two of them which she had no doubts would happen.
She called Drago the next day and asked him how he felt about them moving back to New York.
He asked you ain't doing this shit cause of that nigga are you?
No, come on now you know me better than that. I was thinking about this long before he came back into the picture.
And what made up your mind?
My kids, they wanna come home.
Well that's what's up Bella. You talk to Antonio?
Yeah
What he say?
As if you don't already know.
You straight though right?
Yeah I'm good.
What's up with you and this other cat? Where you know him from?

He's my friend Adrianna's brother.

Y'all used to mess around?

Yes, back in the gap.

My brother knew about him?

Your brother tried to kill him but only because I was in love with him. Your brother was all over the place having babies, bitches calling the house and Alejandro well he's…he's been the perfect gentleman.

You tell Antonio about him?

No, I didn't think it mattered at this point.

So when y'all coming home?

One week after school is out, first week in June.

Cool, I'll let Uncle Juan know that way we can be there to help you pack and move.

Drago I need you to stay at home. You don't need to be gone any more than you already are.

Come on now, you my fam. Natasha understands that.

Yeah but I don't need you to come to Georgia Lil Bro. Just be ready to help unload the truck when we get to New York.

Alejandro called damn G I didn't take you for the type to put it down on a nigga and then shoot him a ghost. What's up? You done put it on me, got me over here going in circles and shit.

She smiled, you're so crazy.

Nah for real, what's up?

I'm moving back to New York.

When?

As soon as schools out here.

Already, you know I'm about to put that ass on lock right? Ain't nothing standing in our way now.

Chapter 8

The next 2 months flew by so fast that the house was packed up in a moving truck and ready to head to New York. Antonio stood beside Gabriella and said Gabi you take care of yourself and them kids.

Tony you act like I ain't gone never see you again.

He had a look on his face that said she wasn't far from the truth. You got something you wanna say to me she asked him.

Can we go somewhere and talk?

Antonio what is this about?

I think you should sit down.

Antonio get to the fucking point.

I lied to you.

About what?

About everything

She bit her lip and asked what are you talking about?

I'm Oscar Antonio Ortiz, a federal agent.

Gabriella gave him the dirtiest look. Tago wanted to make sure you were protected at all times. That's what I was here for. I knew Tago long before you mentioned him.

You lying son of a bitch she screamed as she hauled off and slapped him. Uncle Juan got out of the truck and asked what's going on as if he didn't already know.

So everything was a fucking lie?

Not everything. Gabi I fell in love with you.

Liar

No, I did but I wasn't supposed to. I pulled back because it's against policy. If I got too involved I couldn't make sound decisions so I lied about meeting someone else. I left that night because I didn't want to go that far with my lie, although I could have.

Gabriella felt like such a fool for believing all the bullshit he'd fed her. She got inside the moving truck slamming the door behind her and facing the front as Uncle Juan got in on the driver's side.

She asked Uncle Juan Is Tago really dead?

Yeah baby, that part is true.

You knew about this?

Found out during the funeral.

Drago know too?

No.

I can't believe this shit.

Alejandro called and asked where you at baby?

30 minutes away.

Can I come through?

Yeah that's cool.

Uncle Juan I don't feel like unpacking tonight so if you could just pull the truck around back and close the gate I'll get to it in the morning.

You sure?

Yes sir.

Alejandro parked in the circular driveway stepped from his Mercedes and rang the doorbell. Gabriella answered it in the same t-shirt and sweats she had worn on the drive from Georgia.

Hey she said as she walked outside closing the door behind her.

Hey? That's all I get? You gone have to come better than that. He turned her around to face him and kissed her lips. You didn't miss me he asked?

Of course I did.

What's with the Hey? Talk to me.

Antonio was an undercover federal agent.

What? Get the fuck out of here.

Tago wanted to ensure my safety when Ramero got out of jail so he hired Antonio well Oscar Ortiz to protect me. All these years I thought he was just some guy that was really feeling me when he was just doing his job.

Don't trip Ma. I'm glad the nigga wasn't really feeling you. Then I'd have competition.

She smiled You're a mess Alejandro.

She was falling for Alejandro but at the same time tried her damnest not to fall so hard, so fast. As if that mattered, once you fell one of two things could happen. You fall in love to stay in love or you get your heart broken. Gabriella had experienced more of the latter than she cared to admit. She tried to be at a level where she could handle whatever the outcome may be. She tried to accept the good and not search for the bad. At times she wondered if maybe she was too cautious. Alejandro confirmed it when he said you're just looking for something to happen. Stop searching and just go with the flow, right now things are good. Let me be good.

6 months after moving back to New York the two of them aren't sneaking around anymore but at the same time Gabriella won't let him come to the house or spend time with her and the kids. That bothers Alejandro because he's trying to be a major part of her life, not just a temporary fixture and she's keeping him away from the most important part. Conversations about this topic cause many arguments. On this particular day he invited her and the kids to his mother's for dinner and the family reunion the following weekend. She said Alex I don't know if we're ready for that yet.

You've got to be kidding me Gabi, when do you think you will be ready? The kids know me, they know my Mom. Maybe they don't know about you and me but that's only because you don't want them to. We been at this for over a year now. I'm sick of hiding shit. What the fuck are you trying to hold on to? When Gabriella took too long to answer he asked Oh you ain't got no come back for none of that huh? Wow, man you know what? I'll holla.

He hung up the phone in her face. She tried to call back but he wouldn't answer. She mentioned it to Drago because he wanted to know why she was so upset. Bella shit I'm with him. If this nigga really feeling you like you say he is no wonder it's bothering him. That would bother the hell out of me too. A whole year sis and the nigga ain't been to the house or spent time with you and the kids despite the many times he's offered. And you really feeling this cat? Either you lying about feeling him or you trippen off something else. So what is it? If you're worried about Tago he's dead Gabi. You need to move on with your life. If Alejandro makes you happy then let him. You deserve it, it's what my brother would want. It's what we all want, you to be happy. Quit beating yourself up over everything. Take that picture of you and Tago down off the walls. It doesn't mean you don't care and it doesn't mean you're disrespecting him. It means you're moving on. You were gone long before he passed away and that's nobody's fault but his own. Don't deny yourself happiness and don't punish Alejandro in the process. I've seen the way you light up at the mention of his name, at being with him. You want to lose out on that for some memories you will hold on to forever regardless of the outcome? Gabi, Tago ain't coming back. Make yourself happy. The kids want you to be happy.

Gordon walked in on her crying at the kitchen table and asked Bella, what's going on baby?

I'm in love.

Smiling Gordon asked Well okay, what's with the tears. Women in love aren't crying. Talk to me.

We had an argument.

About?

Silly stuff. He invited me and the kids to his Mom's for dinner tonight and his family reunion.

Okay, I don't see anything wrong with that.

I haven't officially introduced him to the kids as my boyfriend. He hasn't been around the kids but they know him from way back when and…

So what's the problem Bella?

I keep thinking about Tago and…

Bella, babygirl it's time you let go. Tago's gone and if anybody wanted you to be happy it's him.

But Gordon, what about the kids?

What about them? If this man really loves you he will love the kids just the same. I'm not worried about that.

Well what are you worried about?

Tago

Again Bella, you gone have to quit thinking about Tago. When he left those kids to you…

Tago left the kids to me?

Yes, isn't that why you have them?

No, I always thought Drago gave them a choice. The two of us agreed…

Good To Have You Back

Bella, Tago left specific instructions for you to have the kids. Drago didn't think it would be fair to you for Tago to put the kids off on you so he wanted to see what your take was on the situation and how the kids felt about it. Drago said he never mentioned the will to you. You never even asked for one. Your main concerns were the kids and whether or not Tago had a proper burial.

I don't care about anything else. If I had to take the kids with just the clothes on their backs I would have.

And Tago knew that. He knew you didn't care about his money. He knew that regardless of what you did and who you did it with you would always look out for the kids. You always have and he knew you always would. I agreed with him.

Gabriella sat the kids down and explained to them that she and Alejandro were dating and that he'd invited them over for dinner at his Mom's. She asked them how they felt about that.

You mean Alex Mommy Isabella asked?

Yes, Alex.

He's cute she smiled.

Gabriella smiled too, He is, besides that. What do you think of him?

For you Mommy, whatever makes you smile Fernando told her with a kiss to her right cheek.

Thank you baby she said as she hugged him close.

Yeah Mommy I'm with Fern on this one. If Mr. Alex makes you happy, then we're happy.

So would you two have a problem with him coming to the house sometimes?

Mommy Fernando said Can you please stop worrying about us and for once he asked as he cupped her face in his hands as he starred into her eyes Just do what makes you happy. Okay?

She bit her lip as a tear fell from her eye.

Fern you made Mommy cry Isabella fussed.

No, I'm okay.

Sorry Mommy.

No baby, don't be. You didn't do anything wrong. Your father used to do that to me all the time she smiled.

When they arrived at Lucia's Carmen escorted them inside with a bright smile, hugs and cheek kisses.

Look who's here she announced.

Lucia was in tears as she hugged the kids to her and then Gabriella. She asked their names, their ages, favorite subjects in school, sports, hobbies and everything you could possibly learn about a child.

Alex should be here any minute now. He told me about the conversation the two of you had this morning. I had a talk with him. Don't worry the two of you will be fine.

Alejandro held the front door open and Adrianna walked inside. Gabi she squealed with delight as tears ran down her face.

Hi Adrianna Isabella said with a smile.

Oh my Isabella, look at you. You're so big and pretty she said as she hugged her. And Fernando you're your father's twin. Man it's been a long time. Adrianna was so happy to be home and around family. Alejandro didn't speak two words to Gabriella but did greet the kids, even took Fernando out back to play football after dinner.

Don't worry Gabi he will come around. He's just stubborn as all get out Carmen told her.

Mrs. Lucia agreed with a laugh. Gabi knows, I'm sure.

Gabriella took Adrianna and Isabella out for ice cream at the Corner Creamery. Alejandro called.

Where are you?

Corner Creamery

Next time you decide to run off, tell somebody where you're going. Hurry up and get back here.

Alejandro she said before he disconnected the line in her face.

What's wrong Adrianna asked of the frown on her face.

Nothing, come on let's get you home.

Gabi

Yes

Can I go home with you and the kids tonight, please?

Yes, sure she smiled.

Alejandro stood on the front porch smoking a Black & Mild when they pulled up. Alex, Isabella said to him We brought you Butter Pecan ice cream cause Mommy said it's your favorite.

Thanks Isabella. He watched Adrianna laugh and talk with Gabriella, a way she didn't interact with anyone else. It was the side of her he missed most and Gabi being the angel that she is brought that out of her. They talked a good 30 minutes before making their way to the front door.

Gabi can I talk to you for a minute he asked?

Oh you're actually talking to me now?

Adrianna said alright big brother if you want her to stay around you better treat her right as she punched him in the stomach.

Ouch shit, okay he smiled as he pulled Gabriella close to him and kissed her lips. See we're making up. He deepened the kiss and held her close.

Get a room Adrianna laughed as she walked inside.

Thank you for coming.

Thanks for inviting us.

Look I'm sorry for the way I hung up on you this morning.

And a while ago.

Yeah a while ago too. I'm sorry, it's just that I don't want to settle for half of you. I want all of you. That's everything that is you, the kids included. I don't care that they're Tago's children. You're their mother, they belong to you and that makes them just as important to me. I want to be a part of your life forever, not just for now.

Okay, okay Alejandro. I had a talk with the kids, with Drago and I'm ready to move forward. Just please be patient with me, all this is new for me and at times it's overwhelming.

You gotta talk to me baby. You can't hold all this in.

Alright, alright I'm letting you in, don't let me down.

I won't baby. You have to trust me he said as he kissed her lips.

Adrianna is coming home with me tonight.

What? I haven't even been invited over and she comes home...

Calm your nerves, if you would like you can come too.

Can I?

Yes

I'll pass, I got business to take care of. Besides I'm sure you and Adrianna could use the time to catch up.

Adrianna's condition improved tremendously. She started spending more time away from the mental health center. Most of her time was spent at Gabriella's with her and the kids. Uncle Juan had just left with the kids traveling to San Antonio for a week to visit the Alamo, Riverwalk and a number of other important places.
So what are we going to do today Adrianna asked Gabriella as they straightened up the kitchen after breakfast.
I don't know. What do you want to do?
Miguel is having a pool party down at Tropics.
Oh yeah, is that what you want to do?
Yeah, I haven't been swimming in forever.
Alright we can go. I'm just waiting on Alex to come. I know if I leave before he gets here he will be all hot and bothered.

A couple of hours later Alejandro calls to let her know he's running a little late due to a problem with a connect. She tells him Okay, well just call me when you're on your way.
What you getting into today?
Me and Adrianna about to go to a pool party at Tropics.
Miguel's party?
Yes
Keep an eye on my sister man.
Alex come on now. You know I will.
Alright I'll hit you up in a couple of hours.

Gabriella and Adrianna were having so much fun kicking it with people from their past. Friends of both Tago and Pedro were present. Everybody was enjoying themselves.
Carlita Pedro's sister asked Adrianna, What you getting into later? You should come to Korbin's tonight and kick it with us.
Who is us?

Me, Porsha, Danielle and Alecia.

You know me and Porsha don't get along.

I'm not asking you to come because of Porsha. Just come kick it. You've been gone for a minute and I miss you.

Adrianna agreed to go out. Gabriella took her back to Miss Lucia's house around 7. Alejandro hadn't called back so she was expecting him to be pulling up any minute now. When 9 o'clock hit she dialed his number. He answered on the 4th ring with club music in the background.

What up G?

I was just calling to check on you.

I'm good baby. Just chillen up at Staxx's with the fellas.

Alright cool, well get at me later.

I will call you when I'm on my way.

Cool she said before hanging up. She dialed Adrianna's cell phone and asked what you over there doing?

Man, you must have been on the phone with Alex? I've been trying to call you. What's up?

I'm on my way to Korbin's with Alecia and Carlita. Alex just told Mom he probably wouldn't be over this way before morning so I figured he told you the same. You should come up to Korbin's and chill.

Does Alejandro know you're going to Korbin's?

Yes I told him, but I also told him I was staying with you tonight.

So he probably thinks I'm going too.

You know that's the only way he will be okay with me going. You really should come through.

Gabriella told Adrianna she wasn't feeling the club. She was a little upset with Alejandro standing her up but she wasn't about to trip. Eventually she decided to get out the house. She heads to Korbin's to keep a close eye on Adrianna. Gabriella's rocking a pair of skinny jeans and a fitted Gucci top with the matching Fedora and shoes. Her Fedora is cocked to the side and she's looking and feeling good. As soon as she steps up in Korbin's she makes her way to the bar for a Long Island Ice Tea. She scans the room for Adrianna. She had just taken a sip of her drink when she spotted Adrianna talking with some dude she recognized as a part of Tago and Pedro's crew. Whoever he was had been small time and didn't come around all that often so she couldn't remember his name. She made her way over in their direction just as Ricardo walked up on them. She could tell that Adrianna's posture changed and the expression on her face was one of fear.

Hey Adrianna managed to smile a look of relief when Gabriella walked up.

What's up she asked as she gave Ricardo a dirty look.

The guy asked Gabriella what's up? I'm BK from Brooklyn. I used to do business with your man's and them back in the days. You probably don't remember me.

I remembered your face but not your name. What's good?

How have you been holding up? Everything straight? You need anything he asked?

No I'm good. Thanks for asking.

Ricardo asked what you two doing up in here as he kept his eyes on Adrianna intimidating her.

Minding our own business Gabriella responded. Watch yourself she told him in an even tone breaking his stare.

What you mean, shit I'm just admiring her beauty. Adrianna knows what's up. Ain't that right Boo?

She started to walk away with Gabriella following behind her. What's up she asked?

I fucking hate him.

Don't let him get to you. Here sip this, come on she said as she leads the way to VIP. An hour later they're both feeling good courtesy of the drinks they had and the weed they smoked. They make their way down to the dance floor. After dancing to a few songs BK who had been standing talking to Carlita, Porsha and Alecia spots Adrianna and makes his way in her direction.

Damn Ma, did I say something to offend you he asked.

No, I'm sorry.

What's up with you and o'l dude?

He's my ex.

Y'all still kick it?

No, not at all.

So what's up? Can I get your number or what?

Yeah she said as she took the cell phone he held out to her and put her number in it. He hit the talk button to make sure she had given him the right number.

Porsha walked up and asked BK What's up with my drink as she rolled her eyes at Adrianna.

BK said Oh my bad homegirl, yo Ma he said to Adrianna you want to drink too? Come walk to the bar with me. She followed him to the bar with Porsha close behind. Porsha said I want a Cherry Vodka Sour.

What you want Ma he asked Adrianna?

A Hurricane.

He placed the drink order and posted up at the bar. He passed Porsha her drink and said Here you go Lil Mama before turning around and focusing his attention on Adrianna. This only pissed Porsha off. She rolled her eyes again before walking away. To Alecia she started talking bad about Adrianna. When Ricardo walked by she grabbed his arm and started up a conversation in hopes of making Adrianna jealous. Before the club closed she was trying to go home with him but Ricardo had already made plans. He took her number and asked for a rain check. Adrianna stood out front talking to BK while Gabriella chatted with Carlita and a few of Tago's homeboys. Adrianna said she was riding home with Gabriella.

When they pulled off in Gabriella's Bentley her phone kept beeping signaling alerts. She had missed calls, voicemails, text messages, all from Alejandro.

What's up she asked when she called him back?

You straight G?

Yeah I'm good. Just now leaving the club.

Adrianna with you?

Yeah we're on our way to the house.

Can I come through?

You on your way or are you already here?

About 20 minutes away.

Alright I'll see you when you get here, be careful.

You too baby.

Alejandro arrived a little after 5am snuggled up in bed with Gabriella once Mr. Gordon let him in. He slept until a little after 1 and only woke up then because Deuce was blowing up his cell phone. Deuce was calling because last night when they made it in they were chillen at the clubs and weren't handling business like they were supposed to. They needed to get shit in order and he felt like Alejandro had spent enough time bullshitten.

Alright my nigga damn. I'm on my way. Chill the fuck out he told Deuce.

When he walked into the living area dressed to the nines in Luis from head to toe he kissed Adrianna's cheek before kissing Gabriella's lips and saying I got some unfinished business I need to handle. I will be gone 3-4 hours at the most. When I get back let's get out and kick it. Cool?

Yeah Adrianna responded. Where we going?

Let me think on it. I'll hit you up and let you know. You straight G he asked Gabriella?

Yeah

Alright hit me on the hip if you need anything he said walking towards the front door.

Alejandro Gabriella called out.

He stopped, turned around and walked back into the living room. Yeah baby I love you.

Smiling he walked over to her kissed her lips again and said I love you too Gabriella.

He handled his business and arrived back at the house a few hours later. It was after 5pm.

Gabriella was grilling fajitas on the indoor grill when he and Deuce walked in.

Where's Adrianna he asked?

She went out with BK. Didn't she call you?

BK, who the fuck is BK?

A guy that used to get money with Pedro and them.

You mean Tago?

Yes

Alejandro had a pissed off look on his face as he whipped out his cell phone and dialed Adrianna's number. Yo, where the fuck you at he asked her. What I tell you man? Hell nah, fuck that. I don't know that cat. Get yo ass back over here and make it quick before me and you have problems he said before ending the call. He asked G, why the hell you let her leave?

Come on now, she's a grown woman. All I can do is find out who she's going with. Tell her to call me if anything goes down and chill the hell out like you should be doing.

Fuck that, we talked about this.

Calm down. I talked to Drago about him, found out he's cool people. He and Drago kick it on the regular. I would have been trippen too if Drago didn't vouch for him.

Vouch for who Drago asked as he came in. He dapped up Deuce and Alejandro before kissing Gabriella's cheeks.

Benito, BK

Oh yeah he's cool. He been feeling Adrianna since before she hooked up with Pedro. He ain't on no bullshit. Damn sis, I see how you do me. Can't even get invited over for dinner no more.

Whatever, you're hardly ever home. You know you're more than welcome to stay. I can put some more meat on the grill.

Yeah do that, need me to go get anything?

Where's Natasha?

I guess I will go by the house and scoop her up. What y'all getting into later?

You know they doing something at MGM tonight.

Oh yeah that's right Deuce remembered. Let's fall up in there and chill. Gabi you mind if I bring Estelle over?

Nah you know Estelle is good with me.

Alright we'll be back in 30-45 minutes he responded.

Me too sis Drago told her.

Alejandro was on the patio smoking a blunt. He was mad at Adrianna for not listening and mad at Gabriella for not taking him seriously. She walked out back with a glass of wine and passed it to him.

Thanks he mumbled while starring out at the pool.

Babe

Not now G, not now he said before sipping his wine.

She walked back into the house and finished preparing dinner. She had beef and chicken fajitas, flautas, Spanish rice, corn and refried beans. She wrapped everything up before going to the back to take a shower. She heard arguing while doing her final rinse and got out wrapping herself in a robe. As she walked into the kitchen Alejandro was yelling at Adrianna as if she was a child instead of talking to her like the 25 year old she was. He got all up in her face, that's when Gabriella grabbed him.

Calm down Alejandro.

He looked back at her bit his bottom lip heated and aggravated before the look on her face broke him down. He turned around to face her and said Alright G, I'm calm. Anything else you need me to do?

Come back here with me. I need help getting dressed she smiled. He smiled too as he followed her into the bedroom closing the door behind them. He pulled her into his arms kissing her slow and sensuously. He had just layed her down on the bed and untied her robe when his cell started to ring. He checked the caller ID and to her he said Hold up a minute while he rolled over laying on his back he answered What's up?

It had been a few days since he had been home to give it to Gabriella so she wasn't trying to wait any longer. She was unbuckling his belt and easing his pants down his legs then removed the rest of his clothes while he told the caller Say, I'll holla at you later yo.

They couldn't get in the groove because somebody kept blowing up his phone and the doorbell kept ringing. He told Gabriella, Don't worry. I got you baby.

Later on that night he ended up going to Baltimore to deal with an issue he had at one of his spots. From there he went to Virginia for 2 weeks to set up shop. Gabriella decided she wanted to go Miami so she mentioned it to Adrianna, Estelle and Natasha. She tried calling Alejandro to let him know but he was always too busy to hold a conversation. They enjoyed Florida so much that it became the thing to do at least once out of a month.

Chapter 9

Three months later the kids were out of school for the Summer and traveling with Uncle Julio and Aunt Janine so Gabriella had a lot of free time on her hands. Alejandro was still in and out of town. She planned to go to Las Vegas to chill. Adrianna was going too and had invited BK to come along, who in turn invited his homeboy Mark. They all kicked it together and had a good time. She let Mark know that she was already in a relationship so she wasn't looking to get caught up in any way and he respected that. Before the Summer was over Alejandro wasn't spending much time in New York because he was making that much money. Gabriella began to wonder if he even remembered their relationship exist. She was down in Florida again, hadn't heard from Alejandro in 3 days when he called with attitude.

Why you always running your ass to Miami? You fucking some nigga down that way?

For a nigga that ain't been home in months and that I hear from maybe once or twice a week you got a lot of damn nerve to be giving me attitude.

Answer my question.

What question?

What's up in Miami?

It's a nice chill spot.

You could have chilled in Jamaica. What's so special about Miami?

I see Jamaica all the time and everybody knows me. I just wanna get away and relax sometimes.

Yeah let me find out you fucking around and I'm gone do something bad to you. Straight up. But say, on the cool, I need you to pack up and head home. I'm here and I want to see you right now but I'm willing to wait a couple of hours.

She checked flights and couldn't find anything leaving that day.

You bullshitten right Alejandro asked?

No, the earliest flight they have is 5 o'clock tomorrow.

5am, take it.

5pm

Man you better call another airline and see what's up or me and you gone have problems.

She still didn't make it home until 9pm the next day. When she got there Alejandro had to help Deuce with an issue so he dropped her off at home and didn't come back until 3 o'clock the next day without even so much as a phone call. Drago and some of his homeboys were kicking it out back playing ball, smoking the good green and chillen.

Yo what up fam Drago asked as he dapped Alejandro up.

Shit ain't nothing, where my Boo at?

She and Adrianna went to DC with Natasha to pick up her brother.

How long they been gone?

Since about 10 this morning. Said they was on their way back about an hour ago. Should make it here no later than 7 or 8.

Tell her I said to hit me up as soon as she gets here.

Will do.

Natasha's brother Devon kept starring at Gabriella who had been asleep the whole ride. When he met her earlier he was mesmerized. Never before had he been at a loss for words. Not only was she beautiful but he could tell by the way she talked that she was educated. She was fine as hell too. Devon was all caught up.

Where we headed when we get to New York he asked Natasha?

We gone take Adrianna and Gabriella home and then go to the crib. I don't know about you but I'm tired. If you want to get out I'm sure Drago will be getting into something or you can always take the car and go wherever you want to go.

BK was talking about a party up at Kingz Dominion. You should come through. You know your way around right? If not, we could come through and get you.

Oh nah, I'm good. Thanks anyway. I'll see you up there.

Cool.

Natasha dropped Adrianna off first then said Gabi wake up woman. Yo ass been sleep the whole damn trip. Quit staying out all night partying she joked.

Yeah whatever Gabriella laughed. Can you stop at Wingstop so I can grab something to eat because I do not feel like cooking.

Yeah that's cool.

Where is Adrianna?

I dropped her off at Miss Lucia's. You know she trying to get to Kingz tonight for that party.

Alejandro gone fuck her up.
He still trippen?
All day, every day.
Well BK going so she straight.
Alex don't give a fuck about that. He still be trippen. I'm going I guess. Otherwise he would be trippen with me too. I haven't been to Kingz since I've been back. It's the shit now Gabi. You will have a lot of fun.
You should come too.
If Drago doesn't have plans I will go.
Alright well call me to let me know and I will pick you up.

She called Alejandro as soon as she got in but he was in New Jersey on a mission and said he would hit her up later. He also mentioned that he had a bone to pick with her.
What's this about?
We will talk.
Definitely
Around 11pm Gabriella was dressed in a halter top, a pair of short shorts and stilettos. Her hair was pulled up into a bun with Chinese chop sticks sticking out. She was pushing the Ashton Martin when she picked Natasha up. They stepped up in Kingz and mingled with the crowd. The club was packed and everybody was having a good time. Adrianna was posted up with BK and his crew. Devon spotted Natasha and Gabriella.
What's up?
Damn you fit right in Natasha laughed at him with his blunt hanging from his lips and two shots of Hennessy in his hands.
Just trying to get faded. Damn Gabi it's nice to see your eyes open he joked as he starred into her chestnut colored eyes wondering if they were contacts.
Nah playboy they're real. Everything about me is as real as it gets.
Already, let me buy you a drink.

They were big kicken it until some chicks started beefing. When Gabriella realized it was Adrianna she calmly walked over. One of the chicks she was beefing with was Porsha and some other chicks she didn't know.
What's up she asked Adrianna when she walked up.

That old skank bitch always running her damn mouth. I told her to do something. Ricardo walked up looked past Porsha at Adrianna, then Gabriella noticing the pissed off expression she wore he headed in their direction.

To Adrianna he asked What's up?

Yo chickenhead about to get beat the fuck up.

Say hold that down, you know that hoe ain't talking about doing nothing. She just jealous cause you getting all the attention.

Adrianna smirked before saying Whatever, you better tell her to watch herself.

Let me buy y'all a drink he smiled.

Nah we good Gabriella spoke up.

It's just a drink, chill.

That's alright. Come on Adrianna, let's move around she said as she walked off.

Devon asked Natasha What's up with that?

That chick Porsha and Adrianna ain't never got along. O'l dude that walked up used to fuck around with Adrianna. Had her head so fucked up she was in a mental institution. I still don't know what happened with that.

Gabriella look like she about to set it off up in here he laughed not thinking she would take it there because she was too pretty to be fighting.

A little while later Ricardo stepped to them again. Gabriella continued to brush him off.

Nah Sis, Adrianna tells her. He good. Have a seat. She ordered drinks and Ricardo got comfortable. Porsha and her crew are pissed off as they watch from across the room. So is BK but he figured Adrianna was only trying to get under Porsha's skin. She meant no disrespect to him.

Gabriella, Ricardo said to her It's nice to have you back Ma.

Thanks she said as she fired up a blunt and looked out at the crowd. Her cell phone buzzed on her hip just as Porsha walked up and rolled her eyes before saying to Ricardo I need to talk to you for a minute.

So, talk he tells her calmly while sipping his Grey Goose.

Alone.

I ain't trying to lose my spot. I will holla at you later.

What you dissin me for that bitch she asked as she glared at Adrianna.

Adrianna told her It's Ms. Bitch to you. Yo Ric gone ahead and deal with that hoe. Yo spot will be here when you get back.

Hoe, I got yo hoe Porsha said loudly drawing attention to her crew and the crowd in close range.

Adrianna said Like I said if you wanna do something hoe as she stood up and mushed Porsha in the face. Gabriella was already on her feet letting anybody know they could get it. Adrianna was beating the shit out of Porsha so one of her homegirls wanted to get in on it. Gabriella knocked her out before she could even get in good. Pretty soon Natasha and Carlita was involved and the other chicks were getting stomped. Ricardo was trying to break it up but BK, his boys and Devon told him to fall back. The bouncers broke up the fight put Porsha and her crew out the club and told Gabriella Yo G, chill out. Good to have you home. By the time she made it out the club Alejandro had heard about the fight and assumed they were beefing with some chick over Ricardo. Whoever gave him the story had no idea why they were into it. He was heated and going off on Gabriella and Adrianna as soon as he walked through the door with Drago, Deuce and Drama his little cousin. Adrianna was trying to explain what happened to Alejandro who was in no mood to listen. He took what he heard and ran with it. Gabriella let him bitch until he got tired of talking and asked her Oh you ain't got shit to say huh?

Oh you wanna ask questions now? That should have been the first thing you did when you walked through the door nigga. Don't come up in here with attitude about something some bitch done told you. That hoe don't know shit about me. Tell her the next time she want to run and tell something get her muthafuckin facts straight. And you, don't say shit else to me until you're ready to apologize she said as she walked to her bedroom slamming the door behind her really pissed off.

Drago and Deuce were like Nigga I told you not to come over here with that shit. Drama asked Adrianna Say, what went down at the club cuz? No bullshit. Adrianna told him what happened in detail and he was like This nigga wildin out like his girl fucking around on him or some shit.

After hearing Adrianna's story and calming down he walked to the back and knocked on Gabriella's door. Yo G baby, let me holla at you for a minute. Ain't you got business to take care of? Go do that. Ain't that what you been doing?

Open the door, let's talk.

I don't want to talk to you. Go lay down somewhere and calm your nerves.

My nerves is calm. Open the door so I can lay down.

The next day while up at the park chillen Gabriella spots Diana the chick that told Alejandro what went down at the club. She approached her to set her straight. It was the same chick that pushed the Corvette back when she first started coming back to New York.
Yeah it's me she smirked. I'm still around. You better ask Alejandro about me baby cause I ain't going nowhere. He can't make money without me. I'm his supplier. We see each other on the regular. But don't trip Ma, it's all good.
When Alejandro called her later she said I need to talk to you now and it's in your best interest to get here and get here quick.
G, chill out. Where you at?
On my way to the house.
Alright I'll be there.

What's up with you and Diana, don't feed me no bullshit.
She's my connect. She supplies everything to me on the low, sometimes I ain't even gotta come out my pockets.
Just your pants huh? And I guess that makes it all gravy for you?
Nah I'm just trying to get this money. I ain't feeling the broad or nothing like that yo. I'm just doing what I got to do.
If the shoe was on the other foot would you be cool?
Hell nah but there ain't no chance in hell you would have to get down like that. She supplying major weight, that's why I fuck with her.
I suggest you find a new supplier or find yourself a new girlfriend.
What? Come on G you trippen. Ain't nobody serving weight in my range but her. If it was that easy I would have quit fucking with her a long time ago.
Alejandro if you needed a connect I could have put you down with one a long time ago if only you asked.
I ain't know you fucked around like that yo. What you need with a connect?
He's a good friend of mines.
What the fuck you mean? What kind of friend?
The kind I don't have to fuck to do business with she glared at him. Now do you wanna meet him or not?
Nah, I'll figure some shit out.

She knew that he was skeptical about her relationship with the connect, any involvement between Gabi and an unrelated male caused him to be insecure.

Things between him and Gabriella were shaky now.
Miss Lucia asked Adrianna is your brother home yet?
No, can't even remember the last time he's been here.
Just then he walked through the door and asked what up fam? Fernando and Isabella were with him.
Hi Gran, Hi Auntie they smiled.
Hi babies, where's your Mom?
In Florida Isabella smiled.
Again Miss Lucia asked
Alejandro frowned up wondering again why she felt the need to spend so much time in Florida.
Adrianna said Maybe if your son spends more time in New York she wouldn't have to go to Florida.
Miss Lucia frowned up knowing Adrianna only said it to piss him off and it worked.
What the he... looked around at the kids and said Y'all gone on out back to play. Focusing back on Adrianna as they left the room he asked She fucking somebody down that way?
Alejandro his mother fussed.
Sorry Ma, Adrianna answer my question.
No but if she was why would you be mad? You got chicks all over the place.
What she keep going to Miami for?
She's working.
Doing what?
Modeling
Since when?
Since her second trip down there.
Why she ain't never told me about it?
Because she was just auditioning and nothing was definite.
And now?
They want her bad enough to put her on the cover of King Magazine, Sports Illustrated, Total Package and others.

Oh yeah, all this without discussing it with me.

Do you ever discuss anything with her? And knowing you she's probably tried to tell you a million and one times but you're always "handling business" and never at home. I'm surprised she hasn't given up on you by now.

Adrianna walked out back with the kids.

You know she's right son Miss Lucia said to him. You need to start spending more time at home and less time in those streets. Ain't that much business in the world to keep you away from your family. If you don't straighten up Gabriella will be gone for real. All that she said went in one ear and out the other because everything else came second to making money. Gabriella ran into Devon while in DC for a photo shoot once. They kicked it. Neither of them got out of line. He knew she had a man and she knew he had a woman. Their vibe was on point and they held some of the longest conversations. She started doing a lot of work in DC, and they in turn spent a lot of time together.

On this particular trip she had brought the kids along. They had been dying to know what goes on at a photo shoot and they got tired of Mommy leaving home without them. After the photo shoot they went to a pizza spot and ran into Devon the same time Alejandro called Gabriella's phone. Isabella answered it while Gabriella stood at the counter talking to Devon. The kids knew he was Natasha's brother so they didn't think much of the questions being asked by Alejandro about what Devon was doing there. He didn't trip about that but still questioned it. Then one time he arrived back in New York around 2 in the morning fell up in the club Degreez and spots Gabriella in deep conversation with Devon. They were laughing and joking around while taking sips of champagne and smoking a blunt. He kept his eyes on them with a hard look on his face. Devon gets up after saying something to Gabriella and walks off to the bathroom. They're both smiling and making googly eyes at each other.

Alejandro steps up and asks What the fuck is that all about?

What she asks annoyed. Hello to you too Alex.

Let's go he tells her.

Go where?

Home, what the fuck you mean where?

Can we wait on Devon to get back so I can let him know I'm leaving?

What for?

Cause I'm supposed to ride with him.

Oh is that how you doing it?

Don't even trip. I rode with Natasha and she ended up leaving early. I wasn't ready to leave so he offered to take me home.

Devon walked up and asked what up man as he got ready to dap up Alejandro who in turn gave him a dirty look.

Devon, I'm leaving. Thanks for the drinks. You be safe.

No doubt, you too.

She walked out to the car with Alejandro not too far behind her. Some chicks tried to holla at him but he clearly was not in the mood. Deuce stepped from his AMG and said Wassup to Gabriella before asking Where y'all running off to?

What's up he asked of the pissed off expression on Alejandro's face.

We on our way to the crib. I'll get at you later man.

Alejandro pulled away from the club just as Gabriella's text alert went off. A message from Adrianna asked You up? She replied back Yeah, what's up?

Alejandro asked What the nigga texting you now?

She dialed Adrianna's number and asked What's up?

Can you come pick me up from BK's?

Everything alright?

Yeah she lied. Where you at?

Coming from Degreez. What's up with you?

Me, what's up with you? You sound aggravated.

Your brother's here.

Oh about damn time he decides to come home. Where he at?

Driving, right here beside me.

Don't tell me he trippen already.

You know how he do. So what's going on?

Nothing that can't wait. We will talk later.

You sure you're okay?

I'm good, was just worried about you but I will call you tomorrow Sis.

Alright, good night Adrianna.

I love you.

Love you too woman.

What's up Alejandro asked?

Nothing, she was just checking on me.
Why she ask you to come get her?
Probably because she didn't want me to spend another night home alone.
Yeah right. What's up with you and that nigga?
You mean Devon?
You know who the fuck I'm talking about.
Ain't nothing up and lose the damn attitude. If anybody should be pissed right now it's me. You haven't been home in weeks.
Oh and that's reason enough for you to be skinning and grinning all up in another nigga's face huh?
With all that you out here doing I could be doing more. Don't tempt me.
He bit his bottom lip as he pulled up to valet in front of his building.
Alejandro good to have you home. Gabi, always a pleasure to see you.
Hi Rueben. How's Destiny?
She's a beauty, next time you come through I will show you pictures.
Okay, you have a blessed day.
Who is Destiny Alejandro asked as they walked towards the elevators.
His Shitzu puppy. Isabella decided she wants one too.
Where my kids at anyway? While you out running the streets all night
Whatever. They're with your Mom.
They took the elevator to the 20th floor, stood in front of 20107 as Alejandro unlocked his door. As soon as it closed he started up again.
Alex can we please not argue, at least not right this moment anyway? I just need you to fuck me and fuck me good.
Oh yeah, is that all you want?
At this moment, yes she said as she kissed his lips. He got lost in between her thighs, forgot all about Devon and the questions he wanted to ask. Instead he made love to her but she kept telling him to fuck her harder so he did until they both lost count of the number of orgasms they had and fell off to sleep. The next day he woke up around 2 in the afternoon to find the spot beside him empty. He thought Gabriella might have been in the bathroom, the living room or the kitchen but she had left around 10 o'clock that morning to go home and shower before picking up the kids and taking them skating. After that they decided to go to the mall.
Alejandro picked up the phone dialed her number and asked Where you at?

At the mall with my kids. Where are you?
At home, you couldn't wake me up?
Didn't want to, you were sleeping so good. I figured you needed your sleep.
How much longer y'all gone be at the mall?
Another 45 minutes to an hour. Why, what's up?
Come through and scoop me.
Not if we have to be on your schedule. Hell no.
I'm not working today. Come through here and get me. I wanna see my kids man. Quit trippen.

Chapter 10

Fernando had asked the million dollar question the other day. If they could call Alejandro "Daddy". True enough they had been in New York for at least 3 years now and Alejandro referred to them as his kids to any and everybody. Gabriella didn't know what to say about the question. On one hand she felt like it was wrong because it somehow disrespected Tago. On the other hand the kids knew who their real father was but they wanted to refer to Alejandro as Daddy because with Tago gone he was the only father figure they knew. The question bothered her so much because she didn't have the answer to it. She decided to go visit Tago's grave. She arrived dressed in a pale yellow Chanel pant suit with flowers in her hands. She talked to Tago about the kids, how they were doing in school, what extracurricular activities they were involved in and a number of other things before getting down to the reason for her visit. She had just asked the question when Drago and Uncle Juan pulled up.

Bella, what up? Didn't know you would be here Drago said as he bowed to kiss her cheeks.

Hey lil bro, Uncle Juan. Just came out to talk with Tago about the kids.

About them calling Alex Daddy Uncle Juan asked?

Yes, how did you know?

Isabella asked me if I thought her father would be mad if they did.

She asked me the same thing. In fact Fernando asked a few days later Drago admitted.

Well what did you tell them?

Tago would be cool. The way I see it as far as they go Alejandro's handling things the same way Tago would if he was alive. The kids love him and he loves the kids, no doubt. So if they want to call him Daddy it's cool with me. He already claims them anyway so I see no problem with it. And I see now that as much as he and Tago stayed into it he ain't never talked bad about him to anybody. He tries to let the kids know as much about their father as we do and that's what's up Drago said with a smile.

And Uncle Juan, what do you think?

I say he is Daddy and if everybody is cool then I'm cool.

But what Gabriella asks?

What do you mean but what?
I know you. I hear a but in your comment. What's that about?
Nothing concerning the kids.
Well what is it?
Alejandro is more like Tago than he cares to admit.
How so?
They're both too blind to realize what a good woman they have. I just hope Alex gets the picture before it's too late.

Devon called Gabriella to invite her to an All White Affair one of the record labels was having in New Jersey. Natasha, Drago, Deuce and Estelle would all be going along and he needed a date. He had originally requested tickets for both Gabriella and Alejandro but was told Alejandro wouldn't be able to make it.
Come on Gabi quit trippen. I know you got a man. I ain't even trying to come in between that. I wanna chill with you. I know you like to party and I need a date. I want it to be you, so what's up? You down or what?
Yeah I'm good but how about I meet you at the party? You know Alejandro will be trippen if I ride with you.
No doubt, it's all good. However you want to roll. I just need you to be there.
I will, 8 on Friday.
Yeah you can make it right? The kids straight?
Yes but do you mind if I invite Adrianna and Benito?
Nah that's cool, the more the merrier. I will put them in you and Alejandro's place.
That night Gabriella mentioned the party to Alejandro with the intention of letting him know she would be attending with Devon but he was like That's what's up G, gone on and handle your business. Let me hit you back he said just as some chick walked up and said Ay Papi I see I'm right on time huh?
Gabriella no longer felt bad about getting all dolled up to attend the party. In fact she felt incredibly sexy when the final touches were completed. She rocked a white linen dress that stopped mid-thigh, a pair of stiletto heels that really set off the dress while her hair cascaded past her shoulders in soft, beautiful waves. She arrived at the party in her Bentley Coupe and received compliments from anyone she came in contact with whether it be man or woman.

Bella Drago smiled as he kissed her cheeks while hugging her close if you don't stop looking so damn good Alex gone have some problems. Shit no wonder my brother was always trippen.

Smiling she said thanks for the compliment D. Where is everybody? I see you looking all dapper she said as she brushed his shoulders off.

Oh you know big brother taught me well. Everybody's in VIP.

And you're down here trying to see what you can catch.

What makes you think that he grinned?

Your brother used to do the same shit. Since he taught you so well I'm guessing I'm right?

Yeah he laughed.

Wanna know what I was doing in VIP while Tago was downstairs flirting with other women?

What? Sippen on the finest bubbly and looking pretty?

Besides that, it's natural for me.

No doubt, so what was you doing Sis? Tell me he smiled.

I was up in VIP flirting with any real nigga that wouldn't have a problem being my side piece and wouldn't throw salt in my game fucking up what I had with Tago.

Damn Sis that's fucked up. I didn't know you got down like that he said with the smile now gone from his face.

I don't, just knew that I could if I ever wanted to.

Tago ain't know that shit. He would have been ready to kill somebody.

Right, same way I didn't trip off the shit he did.

Why? Why you telling me this?

Because Natasha's just as smart as I am. I'm quite sure she's figured you out by now. You two have been together for 8 years and have kids together.

You trying to tell me Natasha fucking...he said with attitude?

Drago that's not what I'm saying.

Well get to the fucking point Sis. You're starting to piss me off.

Don't let there be opportunities. Natasha is a damn good woman. You know that but at the same time like Tago and Alex you tend to forget that the grass ain't always greener on the other side.

I hear you Big Sis.

Don't just hear me Drago. Get your ass upstairs and give your girl some attention before another nigga sets out to take your place because you're not on your job.

What up Queen G Devon asked as he walked up carrying two champagne glasses. He passes her one, hugs her close and kisses her cheek. He stands back, licks his lips and smiles before biting down on the bottom one all the while keeping his eyes on her.

Hi Devon, nice suit.

Man if you was single I would be all over you right now he admitted. She laughed. They mingled with the rest of the crowd. Everybody enjoyed the night. Photographers were snapping pictures and the party was a success. When it was all over with Gabriella thanked Devon for inviting her, left out the club the same time as Drago and Adrianna. She made sure Adrianna and BK arrived at his place safely and then Drago and Natasha followed her home. They stayed up talking a long time about different things. Once they left Gabriella tried calling Alejandro. She had called a few times earlier but he never answered. Now his calls were going straight to voicemail. She left a message Alex, call me. I just want to know you're okay. He never bothered to call her at all, not that night or even days later. A whole week passed by with no conversation and finally she asked Adrianna Did your brother say anything about when he would be home? He's here now. He took Issy and Fern shopping.

Okay.

What's going on with you two?

Why do you ask?

He's been here for at least 3 days and not once has he mentioned your name or said he was going to your place.

He hasn't said anything to me about what's going on. I've been blowing his phone up all week.

When Alejandro got back Adrianna asked Alex what's up with you and Gabi? Why, she ready to see other people or has she been doing it and you want to let me know?

What are you talking about?

What do you mean by what's up with me and Gabriella?

You haven't been over there since you've been home and you're not answering your cell when she calls.

And?

I wanna know why.

Cause I just ain't. I'm grown and I pay my own bills.

Miss Lucia walked into the kitchen and said That might be good enough for her but it ain't good enough for me. So tell me what's the problem?

Why don't you go ask her? She told you this much he asked in a huff.

She ain't told me nothing. Like Adrianna said you're avoiding Gabi and I wanna know why, now.

This is why he said as he tossed some pictures on the table. All the pictures were ones of Devon and Gabriella posing for the camera, in the middle of a conversation or dancing together.

That's from the white linen party Adrianna admits.

Gabi is so beautiful.

Ma, go ahead with that shit. She all hugged up with another nigga and all you can say is she fucking looks beautiful.

Alejandro you watch your damn mouth.

Sorry Mom.

You're upset over nothing. They're not even hugged up. These are all innocent pictures.

Yeah I would have thought that too if her and the cat didn't spend so much time together.

Well Adrianna added in, If you would spend a little time at home she could spend all her free time with you but obviously "work" is more important.

Adrianna her mom fussed…

Well…

She's right his Mom admits. Have you asked Gabi about the pictures, about why she and Devon spend time together?

Hell nah, it's obvious she trying to get with him. Let them do what they do.

You're so stupid Adrianna fusses Gabi doesn't want him. She just kicks it with him every now and then because they're friends. It's usually a group thing just like this white linen party. I was there, BK, Drago, Natasha, Deuce and Estelle. Why ain't none of them in no pictures?

You need to ask the person you got them from that question. We all took pictures and majority of the ones you have we were in. Why we're missing from the shots is puzzling. Where did you get these from anyway?

Does it matter?

Hell yeah cause you bout to trip with Gabi over some bullshit.

You ain't got no pictures from that night?

Not here but at BK's. I know Gabi has copies of all of them because the photographer wanted her to let him create a portfolio for her. He said he would email the shots so she could see the quality of his work.

Call her and have her email them to you.

Nope, I already seen them. How about you take the kids home, go see her and ask for them yourself.

Man she gone cuss my ass out.

You deserve it Miss Lucia laughed. You're so damn smart sometimes Alejandro you're stupid. You're going to end up just like your father, like Tago even. All over dumb shit. Is that really what you want?

Gabriella was painting the living area when she heard the kids come in with Alejandro and Drago. Mommy they squealed as if they hadn't just seen her yesterday.

Ooh Mommy this color is so pretty. Can my room be this color too, please Isabella asked?

Sure baby. Did you guys have fun at Gran's?

Yes, Daddy took us shopping and we got to pick out whatever we wanted. I got the new Dragon Ball Z game and man it rocks Mom Fernando was excited.

Good baby she said as she stepped down off the ladder after finishing the last of her painting. What's up she asked Alejandro without looking at him long. She was pissed to the point of wanting to cuss him out. Drago knew she was pissed by the tone of her voice and the look on her face. He kissed her cheek and said I came by to help you clean the shed but if you want to wait I can dig it.

No come on, let's get this over with. I still have so much to do. She told the kids she would be out back and to listen for the door because Mr. Gordon had the day off. Alejandro made his way into her bedroom in search of the pictures. He found them on the desk in her office in plain view. Just as Adrianna said all the pictures included everyone as a group. Yolanda had obviously cropped the

Good To Have You Back

photos to look like just Gabriella and Devon were in the picture. He had been avoiding her all week because of nonsense.

It took hours for them to get the storage cleared out and Gabriella had tons of boxes she would need to go through. They were taped shut so she had no idea what was inside. Drago decided to take the kids home with him. He knew Alejandro had been pacing back and forth to the back door since they had stepped outside. He figured they needed to talk but wouldn't do so in front of the kids.

Bella Drago called to the back of the house when he heard the shower shut off. Yes sir.

I'm taking the kids with me. Cool?

All night she asked?

Would it be a problem if it was?

Yeah because I would like for them to be at home tonight.

Alright Sis, I got you. I will just take them for a few hours. We will call when we're on our way back.

She walked from the back in a robe as she hugged and kissed the kids. Y'all be good.

After they left she stood at the front door until they pulled off. She had just closed the door when Alejandro walked up on her and said I missed you G.

Yeah right she said as she moved around him. Now that I know you're okay you are free to go back wherever you came from. She kept walking into the bedroom slamming the door in his face just as he walked up on it.

What's going on Mr. Gordon asked as Alejandro stood at the door 30 minutes later.

G ain't talking to me.

You see how she felt when you weren't talking to her. At least you know the reason why. What was so bad that you couldn't answer when she called?

Man Gordon I got some pictures that had me trippen.

From the white linen party?

Yeah, how did you know?

I saw them when Gabi brought them home. She's beautiful he said with a smile. Do me a favor.

What's that?

Treat her like she deserves to be treated or leave her the hell alone so someone else can. She has been through enough. You know that as well as I do.

G, can you open the door baby? I just wanna talk to you.
You're talking now.
I need to see your face.
You just did, say what you have to say.
I'm sorry.
For what?
For not calling you, not coming home, not answering when you called.
Don't you know I was worried sick about you?
I'm sorry.
Why?
I just told you why.
No, why did you do it? Were you with someone else?
Alejandro didn't confirm or deny it, instead he says I saw the pictures from the party and I tripped out. You and Devon seemed a little too cozy for my taste.
At least we aren't fucking, it was just pictures.
I admit I was trippen for all the wrong reasons.
Especially considering what you do on the regular.
Look, I'm sorry.
Don't be. How about you and me just be friends? The kids can still call you Daddy. You can come get them whenever you like but you won't have no obligation to me. And I won't be sitting around trying to figure things out.
You're kidding me right? I told you I made a mistake. I apologized.
Yeah well I've accepted too many of your apologies thinking things would get better. Maybe for you they have but for me they haven't. So I think it's best that we just chill for now and if the opportunity presents itself again maybe we can go at it with everything. But if it doesn't at least this way we can still maintain our friendship.
Alejandro was aggravated. He left the house pissed off. After a couple of hours he calmed down and hoped that once Gabriella calmed down things would go back to normal.

Mommy Isabella yells out as she walks in the door from school. Daddy's coming home today.

Good, where's your brother?

Right outside with Herman and Montrell talking about video games.

Do either of you have homework?

No, I did mines in class and Fern didn't have any. Mommy is it okay if Daddy stays for dinner?

Sure baby, if he has that kind of time, that's fine.

Alejandro rang the doorbell 3 hours later. Gabriella answered it in a pair of capri sweat pants and a tank top. Her hair was pulled back from her face yet down about her shoulders in long waves.

What's up Alejandro asked as he starred at her while biting his lip.

Hey, come on in. Dinner is almost done. The kids are over their friend's house she said as she turned to head in the direction of the kitchen.

Damn G, can I at least get a hug? Why you be acting like you don't know me when I come around? He sounded really offended which was the only reason she stopped to turn around. She hugged him, tried to make it brief but Alejandro wrapped his arms around her and wouldn't let go. Looking into her eyes he admits I miss you G. Why don't you let me come home?

Almost 2 months had gone by since Gabriella decided the relationship wasn't working out. While she transitioned smoothly Alejandro was having a hard time dealing with it.

Isabella walks in the front door followed by Fernando and screams Daddy you're home. Alejandro plays around with the kids until Gabriella lets them know that dinner is ready. They all take their seats at the table. Fern blesses the food.

They enjoy dinner and conversation for the next 2 hours. The kids want to go to the movies. Alejandro asks Gabriella You wanna come kick it with us?

No I already have plans. I figured the kids would be going home with you.

And where you going?

Out to a salsa club in Jersey City.

With who?

Devon

Oh yeah? Kids, let's get going.

During the movie all Alejandro could think about was what Gabriella was doing. When he and the kids got to his house it was after midnight. The kids showered

and stayed up watching Cosby show reruns while he lay in the bed in the dark.
He picked up his phone and text Gabriella. *Still out and about?*
Gabriella's cell phone battery had died and since the kids were with Alejandro
she wasn't worried about anything. She was having a good time with Devon at
the salsa spot. Around 2am she arrived home, showered and got in the bed
before picking up the house phone to check for missed calls. The light was
flashing alerting her that she had voice messages. They were all mostly from
Alejandro trying to find out where she was. His last message was left right at 2
telling her to call him when she made it home. She dialed his number and said
Hey, I'm home.
Alejandro looked at the clock saw that it read 2:45am, checked his attitude and
asked *Did you enjoy yourself?*
Yeah you know how much I love to dance, especially salsa.
Why don't you let me come pick you up and stay the night with me and the kids?
That's okay. I'm good. Just got out the shower. I'm about to lay down.
Mr. Gordon there?
Yeah he's watching Murder She Wrote and eating popcorn.
Alright, can we get together for lunch tomorrow?
That's cool. What time?
Around 1, that good for you?
That works.
Gabriella fell asleep shortly after she disconnected the call. It took Alejandro a
good hour to go to sleep.

When they met for lunch Gabriella was expecting to see the kids but they
weren't with him. *Where are my kids?*
With Adrianna, that okay with you?
*Yeah, that's cool. When you mentioned lunch I assumed you meant the four of
us.*
Is that the only reason you decided to come? You can't enjoy lunch with me?
No, that's not what I was saying. I just expected the kids to be here.
Their waitress came over to take their orders. Once she left conversation started
up again.
You and Devon seeing each other?
We kick it but no, it's nothing like that.

Can I come back home now? I can't take this shit.

I don't think we have been apart long enough. There's no use in us getting back together if you're going to be doing the same old thing.

I'm done with that shit. Whatever I have to do to come home I'll do it.

Okay, how about you be patient.

Patient? 2 months is patience, anything more is unnecessary.

How you figure?

Cause it has gone on long enough. The kids want me home. I wanna be home.

You're never at home Alex.

Look that was in the past. I'll be home now.

For how long? Enough to pacify us all before you're on the road again?

No that's not what I mean. Can we just try this again?

No, I'm not ready.

What do you mean you're not ready?

I think we should give it some more time. I don't want to go into another relationship dealing with the drama your street life brings. I can't take it.

So you want me to give it all up?

Alejandro I want you to do what makes you happy just like I need to do what makes me happy.

Chapter 11

Alejandro did start to spend more time at home. Gabriella was gracing the cover of almost every magazine known to man and featured in many of the new R&B videos. She was really doing her thing in the modeling industry which at times required lots of traveling and frequent party going. It seemed like the more Alejandro did to get right the more she seemed to be doing wrong. He called her phone around 5pm one day, it went straight to voicemail. He left a message telling her to call back. In between 5 and 9pm he'd called at least 15 times still getting voicemail. When she did finally call back he was pissed.

You need to get your muthafuckin ass on the next flight to New York.

What's going on?

My daughter is sick.

You take her in to see Dr. Mitchell? What's wrong with her she asked while powering her cell phone on to call her travel agent. Alejandro fussed in her ear while she conversed with Bonnie about available flights. She arrived at Alejandro's, used her key to get in to avoid waking the kids with the doorbell. She found them all asleep in Alex's living area with the TV still going. She kneeled down to kiss Fernando before making her way to Isabella. She was warm. Alejandro woke up starring at her just as Isabella's eyes open and she says Mommy.

Gabriella made Isabella take a bath in Vapor Rub before rubbing her body down with alcohol to take her fever away. She fixed her a bowl of chicken noodle soup and cuddled on the couch with her watching What's Happening Now. It was a little after 6 when Gabriella fell asleep. Fernando and Alejandro made breakfast before heading out the door to the basketball court.

Gabriella asked Isabella, Issy is there something you want to talk to Mommy about?

I miss you. I wish you didn't go out of town all the time. I need you to be home like you used to be, so does Fern.

Why didn't you just call me and say that?

Because I didn't want you to be mad at me.

Issy I wouldn't be mad. I'm not mad now.

Good To Have You Back

Isabella was asleep when Fernando and Alejandro came back. Gabriella was up cleaning up Alejandro's condo, the few little things that were out of place and the dust that needed to be removed from almost every inch of the house. It was Pine Sol fresh and super clean when she finished. She was standing in the kitchen cooking steaks, baked potatoes, corn and broccoli and cheese rice. For dessert she decided to make strawberry cheesecake.

Mmm...smells good.

Don't be coming in this kitchen dripping with sweat, smelling like a wet puppy. Ugh gross she said as she backed away from him.

Oh you wanna front, ain't like you ain't never been all up on me sweat and all. He pinned her body against the counter with his body pressed against her, hands on either side of her. He starred into her eyes and asked You don't miss me, not even a little bit?

Yeah maybe just a little bit she smirked. She kissed his nose before embracing him slowly. He rested his head on her shoulder while hugging her back. The two of them stood there like that a good ten minutes before Fernando walked into the kitchen.

Mommy A Low Down Dirty Shame is coming on in an hour.

Thanks baby, go take your bath. Hurry up. Don't be like your Daddy all up on people smelling stank. She wrinkled her nose and attempted to push Alejandro away from her. He picks her up in his arms and tells Fern Keep an eye on the food and listen for the door. Me and Mommy about to take a quick shower okay? Okay Daddy.

I'm not taking a shower with you.

Like hell you ain't. He carried her into his bedroom, closed the door behind him. They didn't shower together because Gabriella refused to.

A couple of nights later he comes over around 9pm. Gabriella is dressed in a short red nightie from Vickie's looking damn good. Before the door closes good he picks her up in his arms kisses her lips and snuggles into her. It's not long before they're making love in the hallway of the house. They hear the beep beep of the alarm and make a mad dash for the bedroom. Drago knocks on the door and asks Sis can I holla at you for a minute?

She pulled the strings of her robe tight before opening the door and walking out, closing it behind her. Yes lil bro, what's going on?

Remember that conversation we had at the white linen party a while back?
Yeah why, what's up?
I think Natasha's cheating on me.
Why?
She don't be hitting me up like she used to. She don't care that I stay out all night or that I take these long trips and she's always on the phone when I come through the door. She ain't said more than two words to me all day.
Natasha left Drago, not temporarily but for good. She filed for a divorce after finding out some chick was pregnant with his twins. 6 months passed by and he was losing his mind literally. He spent most of his time in the streets fucking chick after chick thinking they would help ease his pain and make up for Natasha. They didn't even come close. He started getting too relaxed in his responsibilities on his street pharmaceutical job and ended up doing a little time in prison.

Alejandro called Gabriella and asked Baby you need me to pick up anything while I'm out?
No, I made nachos and tacos.
Alright I'm on my way. Natasha call yet?
No and I'm really worried about her. I called Devon, left a message asking him to call me back.
Calm your nerves baby. You know she's probably just enjoying herself.
When Devon called back it was a little after 11. Yo Gabi sorry for calling you back so late Ma. What's up?
Hey D, have you heard from your sister?
Yeah she called earlier this week, said she was moving to Cincinnati with Maleek.
What? Are you serious?
Yeah she said they bought a house about a month ago down that way and they were bouncing.
D, by any chance did she mention the kids? I haven't heard from her all week and she was supposed to pick them up on Saturday. It's Friday, a whole week later and I haven't heard from her.
Damn, did you call her?

Yes, once or twice. I mean I wasn't trippen about them being here, just wanted to make sure she was okay.

Let me call her. You mind if I hit you back?

No, that's cool.

Around 12:45am he calls back while she and Alejandro are lying in bed watching recorded episodes of Grey's Anatomy. She gets out of bed because Alejandro was dozing off and she didn't want to disturb him. She and Devon spent at least an hour on the phone talking about Natasha's plans.

Yo G, who you on the phone with?

Devon

At 1 o'clock in the morning? Say tell him you will get at him later before you and me have problems.

D, can I call you back tomorrow?

No problem Ma, good night. Tell Alejandro I said what's up.

One o'clock in the morning? The conversation couldn't wait till daylight?

Alejandro don't start Papi. I'm not in the mood for bullshit.

What's up?

Natasha moved to Cincinnati with Maleek.

Okay, that's just a couple hours away. No big deal.

She moved without bothering to mention it to me and she hasn't called about the kids at all.

Quit trippen, maybe she's getting everything situated. She will call.

Weeks later Natasha calls all bubbly as if her kids or the fact that Gabriella hadn't heard from her in weeks was the furthest thing from her mind. She talked so fast the first 30 minutes that Gabriella couldn't get a word in.

Finally Gabriella asked Bitch, have you lost your muthafuckin mind?

What? Oh no, I'm just chillen trying to make it without Drago.

Trying to make it? Please. You know that's the last thing you had to worry about. You've been gone for over a month. You have 6 kids Natasha. You can't just run off without a care in the world.

Can you just watch them for me for a few weeks? We're almost through over here.

Are you high?

A little she laughed, how can you tell?

Off what?

What do you mean off what?

Natasha what are you high off of?

Damn Gabi since when did you become my mother? You interrogating me and shit. Wanna give me a drug test too?

Natasha showed up for the kids high. She didn't look herself. Luckily the kids were not around to see her because she looked that bad. Gabriella tried talking to her in a civilized manner. When that didn't work she got downright ugly with her. Gabriella refused to allow Drago's 3 kids to go with Natasha. She wanted to keep the other 3 but Natasha was adamant about taking them with her though she didn't seem the least bit concerned about the other half. She couldn't understand why until Devon flew in from DC to have a talk with her after she told him what was going on. Alejandro was in Virginia with Deuce looking into opening up a barber shop. She tried calling to talk to him but got frustrated with his voicemail and gave up.

Devon arrived dressed to impress in a business suit having left work in a hurry. Wass up he asked as he embraced her briefly before asking Where's the fam? In the family room watching Jackson 5. Come on back. Mr. Gordon you remember Devon, Natasha's brother.

Mr. Gordon shook his hand and asked Can I get you anything? A drink, a snack, a meal?

A meal and a drink sounds good.

Gabi prepared roast, mixed vegetables, black eyed peas and candied yams. Anything you do not like or anything you would like to add?

Everything sounds good, I will take a lot of everything. Hot sauce and cornbread if you have it.

Coming right up.

Mr. Gordon we will be out on the patio. Please look out for the kids and if you need anything come get me.

I have everything under control Bella. Would you like a drink? Perhaps a non-alcoholic beverage?

A Hennessy

Straight up he asked with a frown?

Please, in fact bring me two. To Devon she asked would you like a drink as well?

Cognac on ice with a little Sprite if you have it.

Bella I really don't think you should...

Okay Mr. Gordon a Ginger Ale please.

He smiled Coming right up.

What's up? You got something you wanna tell me?

I'm stressed out and Drago is starting to ask questions. I tried keeping everything from him so he wouldn't stress about it too but he has been talking to someone who obviously knows more about what's going on than I do.

What do you mean?

I didn't know your sister knew Maleek long before we saw him in Vicksburg. This whole time I assumed he was some cat she was feeling and hooked up with out of the blue. Now I'm hearing that her oldest kids are all his and that she was supposed to marry him before he went to jail. Is there any truth to that?

Yeah she was all caught up on that nigga before Drago came into the picture. I didn't say anything because I thought everybody already knew. I don't like the cat but shit she grown and I can't tell her shit he said as Gordon walked out with a tray.

Thanks Gordon. Devon your sister is on drugs. What drug or drugs I'm not sure but when she came to pick up the kids she was all skinny. She didn't seem like herself at all. Has she ever ran off like this before?

Anything goes when she's with Maleek. There's no telling what all she's into right now. She used to do heroin back in the days. When he got locked up she went into rehab, got herself cleaned up and was good until she hooked back up with him.

Damn

What's Bro saying?

He wants to know what the hell is going on and shit...

Gabriella went to visit Drago ready to tell him as much as she knew though she didn't want to.

Yo Bella what's up Sis? You glowing. What's the business? You got something to tell me he asked as he hugged her and kissed her cheeks. Where are the kids?

The kids are with Adrianna and BK at Miss Lucia's.

Okay so what's good he asked with a smile. What's the news?

Gabriella frowned up and said It's not good D.

Aww come on Sis you know I wouldn't get mad if you told me you're pregnant. I mean shit I've been waiting all this time to hear it.

Pregnant? Me, no.

What? You getting thicker, your hair and nails growing. Stop playing, spit it out.

Drago I'm serious. I'm not pregnant.

You been checked?

No, for what?

Seriously Sis you might wanna go holla at your doctor.

Shut up.

He smiled, On your next visit or maybe in your next letter you will be telling me we're about to have a new addition to the family. But yo you gotta go see the doctor first or at least take the kit or something. So what brings you here today during the week?

I came to talk to you about Natasha.

Man, fuck her. I ain't stuttin that broad. Let her do Maleek.

Drago she's on drugs.

Heroin her preferred drug. Yeah she said she and Maleek used to get down. But yo that's on them. Where my kids at? Fuck that trick.

I have the kids.

That's what's up. Good looking out Sis. I know having 8 kids is a lot to deal with.

5

Huh?

I only have 5.

Where's the other 3?

She took them.

Let me guess, hers and Maleek's?

Yes

I ain't trippen yo, it is what it is. I mean I wish they could stay with you cause I love them just the same and I want them to be taken care of but shit, they got a daddy. What else is up? What Bro up to?

He's in Virginia a lot. Says it business but I don't know.

What don't you know?

He's in Virginia 3-4 times a week.

He still coming home every night?

Yes

Well why you trippen? He fucking up at home?
No
Alright then let that shit go yo. I'm about to be an Uncle. That nigga gone have to chill the fuck out anyway.
Drago I'm not pregnant.
Yeah right, and your name ain't Gabriella Pennington either he said as he kissed her cheek. On the real Sis go see your doctor. Prenatal care is imperative. Gone handle up.

Once back in New York Gabriella headed to her doctor's office determined to prove Drago and Mr. Gordon wrong about her pregnancy. She walked into her doctor's office signed in and took a seat. Adrianna text and asked How did it go with Drago?
She replied back Better than I expected. He's worried about the rest of the kids of course.
Adrianna said That's to be expected.
The nurse called Gabriella back to check her height, weight and other issues before having her pee in a cup. She then got her situated in a room to wait for Dr. McCoy to arrive. As soon as she walked in with a frown Gabriella feared that everyone knew what she refused to believe. Instead Dr. McCoy told her that she was under too much stress, suggests that she takes it easy. Maybe take a vacation. Her blood pressure was high as well. Gabriella arrived home around 3:45pm and started to prepare dinner. She decided to make spaghetti, fried chicken, a salad and garlic bread. She powered her cell phone back on and immediately dialed Adrianna to let her know she'd made it home. Alejandro and the kids came in through the front door.
Hi Mommy. Hi Auntie.
Hi babies, how was school she asked all 5 children before hugging and kissing them.
They had so many questions and comments that a good 45 minutes passed before the kitchen was clear and Alejandro asked through clenched teeth Where the fuck you been all day?
I went to go visit Drago and…
During the week?

Yes I had to tell him what was going on so he would stop worrying. He's hearing all kinds of shit in prison.

And you couldn't make it back in time to pick my kids up from school?

After I got off the plane I had a doctor's appointment.

For what and why couldn't it wait for another day? Why you call Adrianna an hour before the kids get out asking her to pick them up? You ain't said shit to me about going to see D or no damn appointment. So what's up?

Mommy Fernando asked as he entered the kitchen Is the food almost ready?

Yes baby, go tell everyone to wash up. Everybody finished their homework right?

Yes maam.

When he left the kitchen she busied herself fixing plates. Alejandro watched her closely waiting on an answer.

Gabriella he said as the doorbell rang. He expected Gordon to get it but it kept ringing.

Can you get the door please Gabriella asked? Gordon is off today.

When Alejandro answered it was Devon and Natasha's other 3 kids.

What's up he asked as he dapped up Alejandro who wore a pissed off expression on his face.

What's up Alejandro mumbled. To the kids he played and joked with.

He showed Devon where the rest of the kids were, told him that he and Gabriella were in the kitchen and they were about to have dinner.

Devon's here.

Shit, I forgot he was bringing the kids over.

You forgot to tell me too huh?

Baby please.

What the fuck was the doctor's appointment for?

Why do you have a goddamn attitude?

Answer the muthafuckin question he glared through clenched teeth again.

I thought I was pregnant, or everyone else thought I was and I was just trying to make sure she told him as everyone walked into the kitchen. She hugged and kissed the kids while asking questions before hugging Devon and thanking him for bringing the kids. She prepared more plates as everyone gathered around the big family table. They talked about a little this and that throughout dinner. After the kids finished they returned to the family room and the adults made their way out to the patio. Alejandro fixed Cognac for himself and Devon and grabbed a bottled water for Gabriella.

Devon told them he was adopting the remaining children and would be moving to New York in a couple of days. Gabriella left the two of them on the patio while she prepared the kids for bed, tucking them in and singing them to sleep. She made her way to the bedroom after saying good night to the men and got into the shower. She lay in bed starring at the ceiling until Alejandro walked into the bedroom.

G, wake up baby he said before flipping on the lights.

I'm awake.

You alright he asked as he got in the bed kissing her lips.

Yes

Why don't you sound like it? And your facial expression is telling me something different. So what's up?

I'm…

You're worried about something. What is it?

5 kids Alejandro? They're wearing me out.

We straight baby, quit trippen. I got you.

Drago's children spent time with various family members throughout his prison stay.

Chapter 12

After Drago's release from prison he tried to go legit for a short period of time. He had most people fooled, those closest to him knew it was just a front.

Alejandro Diana called out while he was in the shower. Your cell keeps ringing. He was too caught up in the shower and his music to hear anything going on outside of the walls of the bathroom.

Diana picked up his phone saw Bella as the person that had been calling and frowned up. When his phone started to ring again she hit the talk button and walked out of the bedroom just as Alejandro stepped out the shower.

Yo Dirty he yelled out, get me a dry off towel. When she didn't respond he yelled out Diana, I know you hear me. Quit bullshitten.

She walked into the bedroom with a dry off towel and two glasses of wine. Did you hear me she asked?

Nah wassup?

Your phones been ringing.

He picked up the phone saw all the missed calls from Gabriella and quickly dialed her back while motioning for Diana to keep quiet.

My bad G, wassup?

Daddy it's me Fern. Are you still coming home today?

Yeah I will be there in a couple of hours. You gone wait up for me?

Yes sir, Mommy said I can stay up as late as I want.

Where is Issy?

Staying all night with Carmen's daughter Roxanne.

Where is your Mom?

She and Auntie went out with BK and his friend somewhere.

They didn't say where they were going?

Mommy just said she would be home by 1.

How long she been gone?

Since about 5 o'clock. She was going to get her hair done and I think to the mall.

Alright son, I'll be there in a little bit. Don't lock the top lock.

I won't.

Where you headed Diana asked when he started to get dressed.

About to go to the crib.

Why can't you at least stay a few more hours?

Nah I'm about to go chill with my son.

As soon as Alejandro walked out Diana's door he called Gabriella's cell phone.

Yes sir Fernando answered.

Your Mom back?

No sir, she left her phone here. She switched out purses and forgot to grab it.

Are you on your way?

Yeah I will be there shortly. Hang tough alright?

Alejandro hung up and dialed Adrianna's number.

What up Alex she answered with loud music in the background.

Yo what you up to?

Chillen, what you up to?

G with you?

Yeah she here.

Put her on the phone.

She in the bathroom.

Bullshit, put her on the phone man.

She in the bathroom Alex. I will tell her to call you when she gets out.

Nah fuck that. I will wait.

Gabi my brother wants you.

Hey Papi what's up she asked as she took a seat?

I'm on my way to the house.

Okay

I should make it there in a couple of hours.

Alright.

He took that to mean she would be there when he got there or if not already there she would at least be on her way. He was playing Madden 2011 for a good hour with Fernando when his cell phone rang.

Damn my nigga where you at? At some chicken head's crib?

Nah playing Madden with my son.

Oh that's what's up. You giving Gabi a break?

Something like that. Why, what's up? Where you at?

Kingz Dominion, everybody and they mama out tonight.

Good To Have You Back

Oh yeah?
Yeah just ran into Adrianna and BK.
My girl with them?
Yep, saw her too. That's why I called.
What she up to?
Shit, nothing just chillen.
What you call me for?
Cause you stay fucking around in them streets too much to come kick it with your peoples. Every time I see Gabi she by herself. Yo that shit ain't cool man. Gabi supposed to be on her way home. If you run into her again tell her I said to get at me ASAP.
Will do. I take it you in for the night?
Yeah.
Alright, cool. Get at me in the noon day.

Yo Gabi Alex said to holla at him.
Where was he?
At the house playing Madden with Fernando Marko told her.
Alright, thanks.
What's up Adrianna asked?
Alex is home.
Already? He must have been here when he called.
Ain't no telling with him.
I guess I will see you some time tomorrow.
We still going to see Jesse?
Come on now be for real. Alex ain't about to let your ass out of his sight. You can hang that shit up. And yo ass ain't gone want to go nowhere.
Whatever, call me tomorrow.
I will. Love you Sis. You be careful.
You too, love you back.

When Gabriella pulled into her circular driveway Mr. Gordon was out smoking a Black & Mild. He opened her car door.
Enjoy yourself he asked?
Yes it was okay.

Good To Have You Back

Alex is home.

Yeah I know, he called.

I made some waffles and fruit for you. Figured you might be a little hungry.

Thanks Gordon, you know me. I thought about stopping at the Waffle House.

Where is everybody she asked as she walked inside to all the lights out on the right side of the house where all the bedrooms and the game room was.

Fern fell asleep about an hour ago and Alex just went into the bedroom.

Gabriella took a seat at the bar and ate her waffles while talking with Mr. Gordon about a family vacation.

Alex called out Mr. Gordon Gabi ain't...he spotted her seated at the bar and said How nice of you to join us.

Hi babe she said as she accepted the kiss he offered.

Took you long enough to get here.

The club stays open until 4am, had you not been here I would probably have stayed a little longer.

You told my son you would be home by 1.

Okay, so it's 12:45. I'm on time.

Quit running off leaving your cell phone. I shouldn't have to call other people to get a hold to you.

I was at the club before I even realized I didn't have it.

Were you in that big of a rush to get there?

Just wanted to get out of the house.

When Issy coming back?

Next weekend.

Y'all didn't ask me if she could stay that long.

She called to tell you but of course you didn't answer. Besides you know she's in good hands.

I don't doubt that. Just ain't seen my baby in a couple of weeks.

And who's fault is that?

Mine Alejandro said as he kissed her cheek.

Mr. Gordon said Good night you two. I'm going to bed. See you in the morning.

You plan on coming to bed any time soon?

Yeah in a little bit. After I go through this mail.

Can't it wait?

For what?

I got a problem I need you to solve.

It will have to wait.

What he asked in disbelief.

With Fern and Mr. Gordon here and you having been gone for so long I can't keep quiet.

Alejandro smirked Well you got to cause I need you.

Hold off until morning. Fern's going to Drago's and Mr. Gordon is going on vacation.

Man you trippen. I'm getting me some tonight, as soon as your ass gets in bed. He was true to his word. With Maxwell's latest cd playing loud enough to drown out the sexual sounds they made the two of them went at it nonstop until a little after 4 in the morning before falling off to sleep snuggled up in each other's arms.

Gabriella opened her eyes slowly adjusting to the sunlight coming through the opened shutter blinds. She glanced over at the clock 10:39am. Alejandro wasn't in bed and she'd concluded that he more than likely had already left the house. She sighed as she shook her head and slid out of bed with a stretch high above her head. She brushed her teeth and washed her face before putting on a robe and going in search of Fern. The house was empty. Even Mr. Gordon was gone. She looked around for a note, checked her cell phone for missed calls and realized it was turned off. She dialed Alejandro's cell from the house phone. It rang twice before he picked up.

Alex, where is Fern?

Just dropped him off at Drago's.

Did he eat breakfast?

Yeah Gordon hooked him up before he left.

Did you pack Fern's bag or did he do it?

He packed it but I checked it. He good, he got everything he need.

You on your way back to the house?

Yeah I'm about to pull up in a minute. You need anything while I'm out?

No, I'm about to cook breakfast. You want some?

Nah, I'm good.

Alejandro made it home, got his hair braided, took a shower and left again. He said he would be home by 7 so he and Gabriella could go to the movies and out to eat. When 7 came he called to say he was in the middle of something, suggests that she chills with Adrianna until he gets done. When he's finally through handling business its 11pm. He apologized that time got away from him and he had a whole lot going on.

What are your plans for tomorrow he asked Gabriella as they lay in bed together after having sex.

Going to Jesse's with Adrianna.

For what?

Been a while since we've seen him. Just going through to check on him.

How long y'all plan on being out that way?

Not sure, all depends on what's going on.

Let's try to hook up when you get back.

Jesse had some friends over playing Dominoes and smoking blunts when Adrianna and Gabriella pulled up.

Yo Jesse you got company Dale said as he glanced out at the Lexus jeep parked at the curb.

Who the fuck is that he asked as he slammed a Dominoe down on the table.

Fuck if I know nigga, this your crib. Give me fifteen Star he called out.

Whoever it is pushing New York plates Morris said as he stood up from the table. Two chicks stepped out and Briscoe was like Goddamn my nigga, fuck trying to figure out who it is. Let's go get to know them.

Jesse got up from the table with a smile and opened the door just as Adrianna was about to knock.

Diamond Princess what's really good he asked as he hugged her for a long time.

Hey Jesse, long time no see. How have you been?

I'm still breathing he laughed. Who you got with you he asked as he looked at Gabriella closely. Well if it isn't Queen G, man I ain't seen you since Fern was born. Where the hell you been hiding out at?

Gabriella also hugged him. I wasn't hiding, just had to get away for a while. So you back now? For good?

Yes

That's what's up. Y'all come on in, have a seat. Y'all want something to drink, eat or smoke?

Adrianna asked for smoke and drink. Gabriella said I'm good.

Jesse introduced them to the crew and they kicked it a while before getting out and cruising the Ave to holla at some people from back in the days.

It was 5 o'clock when Alejandro called Gabriella's phone. Wassup he asked?

You decided what you want to do yet?

Don't matter to me.

You made it home?

No, we're still in Jersey.

Goddamn, all day G? You left the house at 9 o'clock this morning.

We just chillen with Jesse.

You need to be making your way back here.

Why, you at home already?

Nah but I will be by the time you get here.

So where are we going?

I will figure it out. Just hurry up and get home.

An hour and a half later Gabriella was dropping Adrianna off at BK's and dialing Adrianna's number by mistake while trying to call Alejandro.

I'm on my way to the house babe.

Alright be safe he said before his other line beeped.

When she made it home he wasn't there so she showered and washed her hair before putting on an Enyce dress and heels. She was trying to decide what to do with her hair when Alejandro called.

What you doing he asked?

About to put some curls in my hair. Where are you? You said you would be here when I got here.

Yeah I got caught up. I'm gone be a minute. Why don't we just chill at the house. You cook or I can stop and pick up something if you can wait an hour or two.

Alex

Before you start trippen I'm handling business with D and them. Had to move some shit around.

Everything okay?

Yeah, it will be.

Cool, I will see you when you get here.

You gone cook or you want me to get Deja's?
I will cook.
Already, see you in a little bit.

Gabriella prepared enchiladas, refried beans and rice & corn. An hour after she finished cooking she took a nap. When she woke up it was after 10pm. Alejandro hadn't bothered to call back. She called him, got his voicemail. She left a message that she was waiting on him. 45 minutes later she called again, still no answer so she called Drago.
Bella, what's up Sis?
Did you get everything in order?
Yeah, yeah I'm on point now. Alex hooked it up. What you getting into tonight?
Alex said he was dippin out to Brooklyn to check on Aunt Teresa.
Oh yeah, I didn't plan on doing anything. I'm about to lay down and get some rest.
Cool, well call me if you need anything.
Will do.

Alejandro didn't make it home until 5 o'clock the next morning. Though he tried to sneak in Gabriella was well aware of the time and only pretended to be asleep when he snuggled up beside her. Isabella called at 8. Gabriella was out running so nobody picked up. She kept calling back until Alejandro answered.
Hi Alex, where's Mommy?
Alejandro reached for Gabriella realized she wasn't beside him, glanced at the clock and said I guess she's out running.
Carmen is going to Miami to visit her sister Louisa. Can I go please?
You haven't been home yet.
Yes I have.
Not since I've been here.
Well, every time I get ready to come home you're never there. Fern's at Uncle D's and Mommy needs a break.
Why you say that?
Because she never has any time to herself.
With everybody gone she ain't got nothing but time.
Yeah, time to worry about us. I think Mommy deserves a vacation.

Where to?
Somewhere she has never been, a quiet, relaxing place. Why don't you ask her where she wants to go?
I will. So when you coming home?
I will tell Carmen to bring me home before she goes to Grandma's. Daddy you better be at home too.
What you mean? I am here.
You're there now but you always leave.
Well what time you think you gone be here?
In the next 2 hours.
Okay

When Gabriella came in from her run Alejandro had his back posted up against the headboard while he watched the news. Gabriella said Hey as she walked into the bedroom. She showered then came out drying her hair while wrapped in a bath robe.
G, come here.
What's up she asked as she stood on her side of the bed.
Not way over there, come over here.
She was on her way to his side when her cell phone started to ring. Hello she answered.
Hey Satin, no I'm up. You're good. Really? Sure I would love to. Just give me the details. Fern is with Drago and Issy is with Carmen. Summer time they're usually all over the place. Okay yeah I can do that. I will check into it and call you later on today. Okay? Cool.
What's up Alejandro asked?
Satin wants me to come to Phoenix to chill with her for a minute.
What's a minute?
A week or two.
You trippen. A week or two? Yeah right. Maybe a weekend, a couple of days but a week is pushing it.
Please, as much as you stay gone I know you aren't trippen.
Yeah I am. His cell rang, he took the call. It wasn't long before he was getting up out of bed showering and brushing his teeth preparing to leave.
What you got going on today?

I'm not sure.
I'll call you in a little bit so we can hook up, go to the mall or something.
Yeah.
Surprisingly he called around 1pm and they met up at the mall with Drago.

Isabella was with Gabriella and upset about him not being home when she arrived. Before the night was over with Isabella had plans to go to Miami. Fernando was going to visit Uncle Jesus in Chicago and Alejandro needed to make a trip to Kansas City, Missouri. He'd be gone at least 3-4 days. Gabriella booked her flight to Phoenix and was on a plane 2 hours after Alejandro left town. When she told him she was going he put up a fuss. Tried to talk her out of it but she had already made up her mind and wasn't giving in. She got settled in Phoenix at Satin's house. They caught up on each other's lives while sippin Ciroc and Nuvo. Alejandro called Gabriella around 8pm wondering why she hadn't called him all day.
Damn baby, you don't miss me?
Would it matter? You wouldn't come home if I did.
I got business to handle.
Figures.
What you doing?
Drinking
Is that why you all fly at the mouth?
Blame it on the alcohol.
Where you at anyway? Better have your ass at home since you getting toasted.
I'm in for the night, at Satin's.
What?
I'm at Satin's.
Oh yeah, thought we was clear on what I said this morning?
Alex you trippen for real.
Nah you trippen. Go ahead, have your little fun. Hit me up when you get home. Holla he said before hanging up.
Gabriella didn't bother calling him back. Even without the liquor she knew he was trippen, especially considering that he'd been MIA lately even when he was home. She decided that she was going to enjoy her trip and deal with him when

she got back. She spent quite a bit of time in the clubs and was surprised to run into Antonio and his homeboy Victor.
Gabriella
Antonio
Nice to see you. How have you been? How are the kids?
I'm good. The kids are great. They still ask about you, you know?
Tell them I said hello. What you doing out this way?
Visiting Satin.
Satin lives here now?
Yep
Oh Victor this is a good friend of mine Gabriella. Gabriella my homeboy Victor. And this is Satin, my homegirl. Satin you remember Antonio right?
Yes
And this is Victor, Antonio's friend.
Damn I bet the two of you can't keep them off you huh Victor asked?
Yeah, they're like hounds Satin laughed.

Antonio kept his eyes on Gabriella the entire night. He couldn't resist getting her off to the side and asking Can we go somewhere and talk?
Now she asked with a frown.
Doesn't have to be now but if I could just talk to you. I want to clear up anything you have running through your head about me, about the situation.
Really, after all this time? Why does it even matter now?
It always has.
Satin asked Gabi you ready to go? I'm hungry, craving some waffles.
Pancakes for me. Yeah let's go. Antonio it was good seeing you she said as she started to walk away.
Oh yeah, just like that huh? Wow
What?
I did just ask you a question.
How about tomorrow we meet for lunch?
When and where?

Victor asked Antonio where do you know Gabriella from?
A case I worked on.

What you mean? You met her while working a case or was she apart of it?
Both
Elaborate, I need details.
I met her while working a case.
Okay so what happened?
What do you mean what happened?
Why you ain't never hook up with her?
It's against policy.
Gabriella's a drug dealer?
Nah
Victor looked at Antonio like he was crazy. You keeping shit a secret. I ain't dumb nigga. You was really feeling her at one point so why didn't y'all ever hook up?
I don't want to talk about it.

A couple hours later Antonio couldn't sleep so he decided to go hang out in the Jacuzzi. Victor just so happened to be on the elevator when he got on.
Where you coming from Antonio asked him?
Hollering at this chick that works the front desk. What you up to?
About to go for a dip in the Jacuzzi.
What's up? You alright?
Man
Victor didn't pressure him. He just waited on him to get his bearings together and allowed him to speak freely.

I started out watching Gabriella because we thought she was the ring leader of a drug connection. Her ex told the FEDS that she was the master mind behind everything that was going on. He even told the cats he was in business with that she was the one who gave them up when all the while it was him snitching. Of course it took us years to figure that out. She got caught up in a lot of shit. She hooked up with Tago, got pregnant by him. Her ex and his peeps kidnapped her. Beat her up pretty bad. She never told Tago who did it because she knew he would retaliate. He didn't give a fuck about the FEDS being all over him. He was ready to go to war.
You was fucking around with Tago's girl? Are you serious?

Not while they were together. I ain't stupid. She and Tago split up and I went undercover to try and see what else she was into after she and Tago parted ways. Tago had no idea I was undercover so he hired me to keep an eye out for her. Not because he didn't trust her, he just wanted to make sure nobody fucked with her. She moved to Georgia, got herself together. Some dudes approached her one day. They didn't look like anybody I had seen her with before. With all she had been through I wasn't about to take no chances. I showed my face. Antonio remembered it as if it was yesterday.

Chapter 13

Alejandro was smoking a blunt while Diana was sucking him off. She had been trying to get a rise out of him for the past 20 minutes but nothing was working. Adrianna had called to tell him he was fucking up with Gabriella. While he tried to act like it didn't faze him it was all he could think about since they'd had the conversation. He was at Diana's now because she was hitting him off with his next shipment from her Cuban uncle. He kept fucking with her because he never had to pay for his weight, at least not out of his pockets. He'd pay her in sex every so often just to hold his spot but it was nothing serious. Diana used to be his main chick before Gabriella came back in the picture and shut all that shit down. At least she did for a minute anyway. When the connect he started working with to free himself from Diana was being watched by the Feds he had to go back to Diana to keep his empire moving. His relationship with Diana was business related and making money was important to him. Gabriella understood his hustle, not the involvement with other women but she knew how the game went. She knew Alejandro was at the top of his game in all of New York, New Jersey, Maryland, Virginia and surrounding areas. On one hand Alejandro wanted to be a family man, settle down with Gabriella and get married. He'd already legally adopted Gabriella's kids Fernando and Isabella. Fern and Issy belonged to Tago, Gabriella's deceased ex-boyfriend. Alejandro wanted to give them the world and everything in it because he had mad love for them. He had mad love for the streets too and the hustle was in him. Right now he was battling between the two.

Alejandro what's the matter baby Diana asked?

Nothing, go roll me a blunt.

Diana got up and left the den. Alejandro checked his phone. Out of all the phone calls and text messages he had sent Gabriella she hadn't bothered to return not one. He had spoken with the kids several times over the past few days. Whenever he asked for Gabriella she was always out. He was starting to think she was avoiding him for whatever reason. Could be the fact that he was supposed to be home a week ago, or that he cancelled the cruise they were supposed to take like he cancelled many other trips due to "business". It could be that she was fed up with the lack of quality time the two of them spent together lately or the many empty promises he had yet to fulfill. He told himself that he was about to take a break, get shit right at home and let his right hand man Deuce take over for a minute. Between Deuce and Drago he knew shit would be handled the right way. The argument he and Gabriella had before he left home this time was now replaying in his head.

Alex I'm going to Phoenix to visit Satin.

Why can't Satin ever come here? You've been to Phoenix at least 6 times in the past 6 months. What's up down there?

What you mean what's up there? Satin is and we kick it. Beats sitting around the house all day.

Get out and do something. Tell her to come here and y'all just chill. That way I won't be worried about you.

Worried about me for what?

Alejandro couldn't tell her that nobody was in Phoenix to keep an eye on her. In New York somebody reported her every move. In the beginning he cussed people out for calling him every time they saw her out somewhere without him but the more and more time he spent away from home the more shit he got involved in. Although he was doing dirt he was still madly in love with Gabriella and wanted to hold on to her. Making sure another nigga wasn't trying to take his place was important.

If some shit was to pop off here I got a number of people that could be on it in minutes. In Phoenix we don't have that security.

Security? What the hell do I need security for?

Come on now Gabi you know how the game goes. I'm major, the only way a nigga can get at me is through you or the kids. I ain't having that shit.

Alex you buggin. Last I heard nobody was against you. Everybody is for you and why the hell would I need security in Phoenix?

I'm not arguing with you on this one. You're not going. Call Satin and have her come here. I will pay for the flight.

Gabriella looked at him like he was crazy.

I'm going she said before turning to leave the room.

He caught up to her in the hall. *Look, I ain't bullshitten Gabriella. You ain't going.*

Whatever.

He grabbed her hand when she tried to walk away from him again.

This shits serious, you know that. So calm your muthafuckin nerves and listen to me. From now on these outside trips is out until I give you the okay. When shit die down you can go wherever you want to go but right now Phoenix is not an option he said in all seriousness.

His chirp went off on his cell phone. Diana was letting him know his package would be arriving soon. Usually she would have her brother make the call to keep confusion down but for whatever reason she made the call right then. Gabriella gave him the screw face because he had been denying involvement with her ever since she told him to find another connect.

He chirped back. Alright I will be through there in a minute.

By now Gabriella had walked off.

Yo Gabi he called out but she ignored him. Soon he heard a door open and the alarm beep. He walked to the front door thinking she had left out that way when he heard the garage going up. He rushed to the back of the house only to see the garage going down and Gabriella's Lexus gone from its parking spot. He chirped Yo Gabi bring yo ass back here. Quit trippen. It's not what you think. She ignored him, the chirps, the phone calls all went unanswered. It was after 1 in the morning when she finally came home. Alejandro was in her face before the back door could shut good. He was pissed off and cussing her out about not answering her phone and staying out all night. She attempted to walk past him without a word which aggravated him more. Fernando was sleep walking as he came into the kitchen where they were.

Alejandro did you just hear anything I said Diana asked him as she snapped him out of thoughts.

Nah, what's up?

Gina just called. I'm about to swing through there.

Alright, cool.

You coming.

Nah I'm about to shower and get a nap in.

You sure you alright?

I'm good.

He heard Diana's car leave the garage and the condo fell silent. He called home again, no answer. He called Fernando got voicemail on the first ring so he tried Isabella. She answered after three rings.

Hey Daddy
What's up babygirl, where y'all at?
Leaving our kickboxing class.
You and who?
Me, Mommy, Auntie and Leandra.
Where y'all headed? Where's Fern?
We're about to go to Coney Island. Fern is with Grandpa.
When did Grandpa get back?
Yesterday. Daddy when are you coming home?
Why, you miss me?
Yes, can you come home today please she begged.
I can't make it today baby, give me a couple of days.
You said that earlier this week and you're still not home.

Gabriella was stopped by a guy that grew up with Gordon (Grandpa). He stood there talking to her for a good ten minutes. Alejandro couldn't answer Isabella's questions from trying to hear the conversation.

Mommy Isabella called out Daddy wants to speak with you.

Gabriella accepted the phone but only because Isabella was passing it to her and she didn't want her to know that she was upset with Alejandro.

Yes she answered politely.
When you make it to the house I need you to call me back ASAP.
Are you hurt? In trouble?
Nah

Cool she responded before passing the phone back to Isabella. When they arrived home Isabella took her shower first and then Gabriella took hers. She put on her pajamas when she stepped out and looked at the huge bed she shared with Alejandro whenever he was home. She couldn't remember the last time they had sex and she was definitely horny. Alejandro was too busy to care about all that. He wanted to make love to her but by the time he made it home Gabriella was usually annoyed with him because of the length of time he spent away. She lay across her bed reading Diary of A Street Diva. A few chapters in she dozed off. Alejandro called the house phone, Isabella answered.

Where yo Mama at?
In her room.
Go take the phone to her.

Isabella walked into her Mom's room. Mommy, Daddy wants you she said when she realized she was asleep. Daddy she's asleep.

Wake her up.

No because she's tired. She's not even under the covers. She fell asleep reading a book.

She was supposed to call me back when she got home.

Yeah well she took a shower and fell asleep.

Wake her up.

Daddy

I'm serious Issy. I need to talk to her.

Mommy she said as she tapped her shoulder. Mommy, telephone. It's Daddy. Hello Gabriella said groggily.

Gabi

Yes

Good night Bella, sweet dreams. I love you.

With a sleepy smile she said good night Alex. I love you too. She was not awake, simply responding to a part in her dream where things were good between them.

Isabella smiled as she accepted the phone after covering her Mother up with the blanket.

Gabriella was set to leave for Phoenix on Thursday. Now that Gordon was home she knew the kids were in good hands and she didn't feel bad about leaving. She had put the trip off long enough by waiting on Alejandro to come home. He called that morning to say something came up and he would be gone a few more days.

Have fun Mommy Fernando told her as he kissed her at the airport.

Yeah Mommy and don't worry about us. Grandpa's here and we're in good hands. Besides, Daddy will be home in a few days too.

Satin picked Gabriella up from the airport. Hey woman, I thought you would never make it back down here.

I told you I would come as soon as I could Gabriella said as she hugged her.

That night the two of them decided no clubs. Instead they went to R.S.V.P Bar & Grill. While eating grilled steaks, chicken, shrimp and steamed vegetables they sipped a little wine.

Just then Antonio walked into the bar alone. Gabriella starred at him from across the room. He must have felt her stare because he glanced around right into her face.

What are you looking at Satin asked as Antonio walked up.

Ladies he said as he hugged them both. How have you two been?

Good Gabriella told him. How about yourself?

I can't complain.

Care to join us Satin asked or will your guest arrive shortly?

Raymond is coming supposedly. He's late as usual.

Well have a seat Gabriella tells him as she scoots over to make room for him. As you can see we have our own little buffet going here. She signaled the waiter for extra plates and more food. What do you want to drink she asked?

A Hennessy and Coke. Thanks. How are Isabella and Fernando doing?

Great. Fern will be starting middle school next year. He's excited. He will be in football, basketball, track and soccer. Isabella will be in the 9th and she's working with the school paper as an editor, volleyball, basketball and track. They're both making straight A's.

That's great Gabi. Any new pictures?

I have the family picture we took a couple of months ago.

I think I have their sports pictures Satin said as she pulled out her purse.

Before they parted ways Antonio and Gabriella exchanged numbers. That night she and Satin stayed awake talking until the wee hours of the morning. Satin is dating Antonio's friend Danny, things were getting serious. Gabriella was happy for her. The next morning Danny treated them to breakfast at Hanley's. Antonio joined them. Gabriella wore a halter top, a pair of shorts and lace up sandals. Her hair was pulled up in a high ponytail with a pair of sunglasses poached atop her head, face free of makeup. Antonio couldn't help but admire her beauty. He tried to keep from starring. When breakfast was over Antonio took a chance and asked Gabi can we talk? Alone, you and me.

Yeah that's okay. Satin…

Go ahead girl, call me when you're back at the house. You have your key right?

Yes, I have it.

Antonio held the passenger door of his Jaguar open until Gabriella was seated safely inside. He eased his way out of the parking lot and asked You want the windows down or the air conditioner on?

Windows down is good.

After a few minutes he asked So how have you been, really?

I'm okay.

Just okay? You look frustrated, what's going on?

Gabriella blushed, she was sexually frustrated but she wasn't about to let that cat out of the bag. Nothing, I'm alright. Everything is good.

You know you can talk to me about anything right?

Yeah I know, what did you want to talk about?

I just wanted to tell you how sorry I am…

Tony you don't have to apologize.

But I do because I mislead you and…

You lied to me, yes but you had good reason. You were doing your job and you just got caught up. I understand that part.

Do you?

Yes

But what?

I don't understand why Tago had you watching me even after everything was over.

He was worried about you, wanted to make sure you were safe.

Okay but couldn't you have did that from a distance? Why were you still watching me as if I was under investigation by the FEDS.

Truthfully I wasn't supposed to get close to you. You weren't supposed to know I exist. That day I ran into you at the coffee shop I fell in love. I didn't believe in love at first sight until then. I know I wasn't supposed to get next to you but I couldn't help myself. I tried to shake the feelings that I had but it wasn't easy. The more I tried to stay away the more I wanted to get to know you I couldn't just walk away. The case was over, Tago was gone and I couldn't…

I was mad at you at first, hated what you did to me. You broke my heart in a sense but at the same time I couldn't really be mad. I enjoyed being with you and over a period of time that's all that mattered. The more I thought about the situation the more I understood it and so I forgave you and I missed you.

Good To Have You Back

I missed you too Gabriella and I'm sorry for hurting you.

Okay, make this your last time saying you're sorry. So what have you been up to?

Nothing really, just trying to get settled here in Phoenix.

On a case?

Nah, I retired. Decided I'd had enough.

Really, wow?

Yeah, I'm 34. I spent 16 years working on the force.

So what are you going to do now?

Started my own PI firm, it's not much but I don't really need the money. I'm just doing it to keep busy. That and working with the Phoenix Boys and Girls Club as a youth counselor. I enjoy working with the kids, teaching them the rights and wrongs in life.

That's great Antonio she said with a bright smile. Issy and Fern still ask about you all the time.

You tell them you saw me the last time you were here?

No, because I knew they would want to see you or at least talk to you but I didn't have a number for you.

Well you do now, they can call me any time. You still with Alejandro? Heard he adopted the kids.

Yes we're still together. The adoption was finalized almost 2 years ago.

When did you get married?

I think we both like things just the way they are right now.

Antonio looked into Gabriella's eyes while stopped at a red light and said if you say so.

What about you? You meet any interesting women here in Phoenix?

I meet interesting women everywhere I go.

Okay well have you met anyone worth keeping around?

Yeah, have I kept them around? No

Why not?

Because I'm still comparing them to you and none of them measure up. They don't even come close.

Smiling Gabriella said you can't expect them to Tony. When God made me he broke the mold. There will be no other like me.

Yeah that's my bad. Should have realized what I had in you before it was too late. That way I wouldn't sit around thinking about what could have been.

Gabriella glanced over at him then starred out the window. They drove in silence some more before Antonio maneuvered the car into the parking lot of a park with a pond. He walked around to open her door, reached for her hand. Gabriella felt the electrifying tingle that shot through her hand.

She bit her bottom lip, shook it off and stood up.

Come take a walk with me he tells her having felt it himself.

While strolling along the trail they watched the ducks. Two ducks were kissing or at least it looked that way. It was so peaceful out.

Tony...Gabi...they both started at the same time.

You go ahead he told her.

Remember the night you left my house because you got that phone call, did it really have anything to do with another woman?

No, I just said that because it seemed like a logical explanation. There wasn't anyone else. I just didn't want to mess up the case, to do what Tago said was against the rules.

What exactly did Tago say to you?

He said I was only to follow you and make sure you were safe. I wasn't supposed to develop any kind of relationship with you. I definitely wasn't supposed to fall in love. Same rules with any case. For 16 years I never had a problem. I could meet countless women while working cases, some I even got involved with on a sexual level but when the case was over everything was over. I could walk away with ease and not look back. Not even once with you, I couldn't do that. I wanted to come back for you and the kids but you hooked up with Alejandro so I loved you from a distance.

You know when you got up out of my bed that night I wanted to slap you. Hell I wanted to slap myself. To this day I still beat myself up about it.

Gabriella laughed as her cell phone rang. Hello she answered?

Gordon was calling. Bella just giving you a heads up. Alex knows you're in Phoenix and he's pissed. You didn't tell me he told you not to go.

He did.

Well if you know all this is going on why...

Papi nothing's going on. He just wants to know my every move. He can't have people watching me in Phoenix the way everyone reports my every move at home. He hates that.

He sounds really upset Bella. Are you sure that's all it is?

Yes, if it was anything more do you think he would be away from home?

Good point. This is the first I've heard of it.

And it will be the last, trust me Drago and Uncle Juan would have told you if anything was going on even before I found out.

Okay well, I just wanted to be sure. You know he will be home soon right?

Yes I'm sure he will be…No I'm not coming home, least not until Wednesday.

Alright Bella, I will keep you posted.

Thanks Papi. Where's Issy and Fern?

Out back playing with Drago and the kids.

Drago's home?

Yeah he brought the whole crew with him too. He's so happy.

When everybody gets settled have them call me.

Will do.

As soon as she hung up Alejandro called. Yes she answered thinking there is no use avoiding him when he already knew where she was.

What I tell you man? You think this shits a fucking joke?

She listened to him rant and rave much like she does when he's off on his trips and calling home to let her know he'll be gone even longer. He would say I will get there when I get there. Chill out.

You need to find out when the next available flight leaves and get on it.

Alex

Don't Alex me Gabi. I'm not bullshitten. You need to be on the next available flight.

I will be home on Wednesday.

Keep fucking with me Alejandro warned before hanging up.

What's up Antonio asked?

Nothing, what were we saying?

Antonio starred at her a minute. I'm going to see Tyler Perry's I Can Do Bad By Myself tonight. You seen that yet?

No, Satin mentioned that she and Danny were going.

You're welcome to come with me.

Yeah that's cool. What time should I be ready? The mention of time made Gabriella take a look at her watch, the clock read 12:35, the sky was dark and the stars shined yet she hadn't paid attention until just now.

Let's say we go to the Studio Movie Grill that way we can get dinner and a movie. About 8:15, that too late?

No that's fine.

I better get you back. I'm sure Satin is worried about you.

Satin picked that time to call. Hey woman, did the two of you get lost?

No, we're about to head back now.

Everything okay?

Yes maam, just fine and dandy.

Okay, be careful. See you soon.

Chapter 14

Alejandro called Gabriella's cell phone a number of times while she was in the shower. 2 hours had passed since their conversation and he automatically assumed she was on a plane headed home. When Fern woke him up the next morning about going to play basketball he looked over at the clock noticed it was after 10AM. Gabriella's side of the bed was just as it had been when he came home the night before. Your mama here?

No, she's in Phoenix until Wednesday.

Where is Issy?

Making breakfast with Grandpa. Daddy are we going to play ball?

Yeah son, give me a minute. Go eat breakfast while I get dressed.

Yes sir.

Alejandro waited until Fernando had left the room closing the door behind him before picking up the phone and dialing Gabriella's cell phone number. She didn't answer.

30 minutes later Alejandro was up taking a shower when Gabriella returned his phone call. She spoke with the kids and Gordon before asking to speak with Alejandro.

Mommy, Daddy's still in the shower Fernando told her.

Alright, tell him I called. I'm about to leave now so I will talk to you guys later.

Love you Mommy.

Love you too baby.

Alejandro came from the bedroom in a tank top, basketball shorts and Jordan's. He grabbed a few slices of bacon, a glass of orange juice and took a seat at the bar.

Good morning Daddy Isabella said as she kissed his cheek when she brought her empty plate into the kitchen.

Morning babygirl, thanks for breakfast.

No problem. Mommy called while you were in the shower.

Oh yeah, what she say?

She just asked what we were doing. Fern talked to her the longest. Fern, what did Mommy say?

That she loves us and she will see us later.
Where was she at?
I don't know but she said she was leaving.
Good Alejandro said with a smile. You ready to go ball?
Ooh Daddy can I come too, please Isabella asked?
Yeah come on.
Grandpa, me and Fern are going to play ball with Daddy.
Gordon said I'm going shopping. Any special request?
Mommy said don't forget her banana pudding ice cream Isabella reminded him.
Grandpa can you get me some fruit snacks please and some snack size cheez-its that I can take with me?
Yes. Alex do you need anything?
Whipped cream, chocolate syrup, strawberries, mangos, kiwi, cantaloupe and honey dew melon.
Gordon smirked. Fern asked Daddy what are you going to make?
Something special for your Mama.
That's sweet Isabella smiled. You and Mommy need to spend some quality time together. It's no wonder we can't have a brother or sister yet. You're never home to make one.
I'm here now.
Yeah and Mommy is gone Fernando said as he shook his head while walking off bouncing the basketball. Alejandro and Gordon starred at each other.
Quit bouncing that ball in this house Fernando, Isabella yelled.
You're not the boss of me.
Fernando Alejandro said and he held the ball in his hands.
You know better Isabella fussed. I'm not your boss but right is right and wrong is wrong. If Mommy were here you would be in trouble.
Yeah, yeah, yeah. Why don't you go to the mall or something Fern asked in an annoyed tone.
Because I don't want to.
Well find something else to do. You don't have to follow us around.
I can go if I want to, Daddy said.
You get on my nerves always trying to…
I want to go with Daddy too Isabella said with a roll of her eyes.
Hey, hey cut it out Alejandro told them. We're all going. What is the problem?

She is always trying to go everywhere we go. I just want to hang with you Daddy Fern told him.

He's my Daddy too.

So...

Come on let's go Alejandro told them. To Gordon he said when Gabi gets here tell her I said to call me ASAP.

You're just going to play ball right Gordon asked confused. He was under the impression that Gabriella wasn't coming home until Wednesday and it was just now Sunday.

Yeah

Alright.

Inside the car Isabella and Fernando continued to argue back and forth.

Isabella, Fernando cut the bull. What's really going on?

I missed you and I want you to play ball with me because we haven't been able to in a long time.

Well Fern I missed Daddy too and maybe I just want to go so I can be near him. Sorry Issy.

Sorry Fern.

I'm sorry too Alejandro told them. I'm going to do better for real.

When Gabriella didn't make it home on Sunday Alejandro was pissed but sucked it up because he knew it was his own fault. If he would stay at home sometimes he wouldn't feel threatened whenever Gabriella was away from home. He called up Deuce and Drago for a late night meeting on Friday. Over Hennessy and fajitas he explained what he needed them to do to keep business afloat for the next few months. Anything that involved going out of town or being away for more than a couple of hours would be handled by one of the two. Drago already knew that Gabriella had been getting on to Alex about the amount of time he spent on the road. Alex had also mentioned to them Diana's chirp in the middle of their argument. They both knew she was probably pissed. They also figured Alejandro could use a break anyway since he was always on the go. Tuesday morning when Gabriella called home Alejandro answered the phone the same time Isabella did. Issy, I got it baby he said into the receiver. I will bring the phone to you when I'm finished.

Don't give it to Fern first Daddy because he always hogs the phone.
Alright babygirl, I got you. He heard Isabella hang up the phone. Gabi
What?
When you get home you and me gone have a long talk.
Alright. What about?
Ain't no need in getting into it right now. Have your fun. We will talk.
Cool, put the kids on the phone.
Alejandro pulled the phone away from his ear and looked at it. He got out of bed,
walked the phone to Isabella. As soon as she got it she and her mother started
talking nonstop for a good 45 minutes before Fern got the phone. After that she
spoke with Gordon. Each time their conversations were lengthy and ended with I
love you. She hadn't said that to Alejandro. He was hoping to get the phone
back before she hung up. Gordon sensed this but it was too late. Gabriella had
already hung up.
She's going for her morning run.

Later that day she called one of the kids cell phones a few times but didn't
bother to speak to Alejandro. He had no idea what time her flight would arrive.
Around 9 that night he called to ask her that but when she answered neither of
them could hear over the loud music playing in the background. He text her
Where you at? She replied back Palmer's. What's that he asked? A club she
replied. What time your flight arrive? 1:15 was her last reply for the night.
She was having way too much fun to be replying to text messages. She put her
phone back between her breast on silent and returned to the dance floor. She
and Satin didn't make it in until 7 the next morning. Gabriella would have
overslept if Danny hadn't come by to switch cars with Satin to take hers in for
new tires. Gabriella begged Gordon to pick her up from the airport because she
wasn't ready to face Alejandro. She knew he sounded calm over the phone but
he was still pissed off about her going to Phoenix after he told her not to. Gordon
managed to talk Alejandro into letting him pick her up. Isabella helped
unknowingly by asking him to take her and her friends to Adventure Landing.
Alejandro wasn't going to tell her no. Knowing that Gordon would pick Gabriella
up he agreed.

Bella Gordon said when he saw her. You're almost two shades darker. I thought I told you to stay out the sun?

Hi Papi she said as she hugged and kissed him. I missed you.

Missed you too.

Where is Issy and Fern?

With their father.

How did you manage? Is he mad?

He took the kids to some park. No, he seems pretty calm.

Really?

Yeah

He said we're going to talk when I get back.

I'm sure you will. He was pissed when he first found out you were gone. I have never heard him curse so much.

Not in front of the kids I hope.

No, you know Alex would never do that in front of the kids. They have no idea what's going on. I think Alex is starting to see what his being gone all the time is doing to everybody.

Why do you say that?

With you gone and Issy & Fern fighting for his attention...

Fighting?

Not so much as fighting in a physical sense but bickering like siblings do. They each want to spend some quality time with him alone and well he had to deal with that these past few days.

Gabriella came home, showered and got started on dinner. She made beef and chicken enchiladas, refried beans, rice and corn. She was standing at the stove when the kids walked in through the back door, all 8 of them followed by Drago and Alejandro. All she heard was Mommy and Auntie squeals for the next 20 minutes as everyone tried to get her attention. She was just as happy to see the kids as they were to see her. She sent them off to the back to get cleaned up for dinner.

Damn Bella Drago said as he hugged her and kissed her cheek You think you got enough sun while you was gone?

Shut up, I will be my own color in a couple of days.

What you cooking?

Enchiladas. Get your dusty butt out of my kitchen reaching into my pots.

Why I gotta be dusty he asked as he tasted a spoonful of beans while burning his tongue in the process of trying to be sneaky.

Unh huh, see that's what you get Gabriella told him as she popped him with a towel.

Alejandro walked up on her from behind hugging her before turning her around to face him. He kissed her long and hard while starring deep into her eyes. I love you G he said when the kiss was over.

I love you too Alex she said as she wiped her lipstick from his lips.

I'm still mad at you he reminds her.

I figured as much. You will get over it.

No doubt he said as he kissed her again while copping a feel of her behind. Damn I can't wait to get this he said as he pressed himself up against her showing her how bad he needed her.

I got you babe she told him with a smile just as the kids came back into the kitchen. As soon as we get some free time.

Gordon helped Gabriella fix the plates for the kids. Drago and Alejandro fixed the adult plates. They all sat in the family room watching A Time To Kill.

Later on that night Alejandro and Gabriella made passionate love. The illumination from the scented candles, the music, the fruit, whipped cream, chocolate syrup, toys and sexual activities kept them up until 6 o'clock the next morning. The door to their bedroom remained locked as Gordon fixed the kids breakfast and assured them that both their father and mother were still in bed asleep. Gabriella was the first to emerge from the room after 11 still in her bath robe bringing the fruit platter and other goodies back to the kitchen.

I hope all that noise the two of you made last night made me a grandbaby Gordon said while sitting at the table watching her as he drank a cup of coffee.

She blushed Papi, could you really hear us?

Hard not to the way you two were carrying on. Good thing the kids' bedrooms are on the other end of the house because they would have gotten an earful. Sorry she blushed.

Don't be. It's perfectly normal Bella. So, did the two of you talk?

No, not yet. Maybe he forgot about it she winked as she heard Alejandro in the family room with the kids.

I doubt it Gordon assured her.

Alejandro walked into the kitchen. Good morning Pop. Good morning baby he said as he kissed Gabriella's lips and accepted the coffee she passed to him as he took a seat at the table. She winked at Gordon again before turning around to fix Alejandro's plate. Just as she sat it down in front of him he announced Drago's coming to get the kids in a little bit. G, you and me got some things to do. A lot to talk about.

Gabriella mouthed Shit behind his back and Gordon laughed while pretending to read the paper.

In an hour the kids were dressed and ready for their outing with Drago. Gordon left to visit some friends. Alex and Gabi were sharing a shower.

Daddy Fern called out Somebody's at the door.

Alright, hold up he said with Gabi in his arms, her back against the wall of the shower with her legs thrown over his shoulders and his dick inside her. Gabi gripped his dick, loosened and gripped a few more times before they both had an orgasm.

G

Yes baby she asked as she watched him slip on a robe.

You still taking them birth control pills?

No, haven't been on them in a little over 6 months now. Why?

Trying to figure out why we ain't pregnant yet he said as he left the bathroom and then the bedroom heading to the front door.

What up Deuce he asked as he dapped him up.

Dymond and Desmond Deuce's twins were with him. Hi Uncle Alex.

What up he asked as he picked the 3 year old boy and girl up in his arms and hugged them with smiles.

Uncle Alex where's Auntie Gabi Desmond asked?

Back there taking a shower.

Where is Fern and Issy Dymond asked?

Isabella walked in and called out Fern, Dymond and Desmond are here.

Hi Double D she said as she kissed and tickled them. Fern was happy to see them.

Yo where's my love Deuce asked? I know y'all see me standing here.

Alejandro left them with Deuce and made his way towards the back of the house just as Gabi was coming out of the bedroom in a Miskeen dress, barefoot. He stopped her and pinned her up against the wall with his hands all over her. We gone fuck around and be in the house all day going at it he said as he kissed her lips.

The doorbell rang again, Drago this time. Go get dressed baby Gabriella told him.

After another hour the house was clear except for Gabriella and Alejandro. Alejandro was busy counting the money both Drago and Deuce dropped off. Gabriella was paying bills online.

The house phone rings Gabriella picked it up. It's Alejandro's mother, she wants to see her family today. Gabriella explained that the kids are with Drago for a couple of hours but that as soon as they got back they would all come over. They talked a good 30 minutes before getting off the phone. Gabriella's other line beeped before she put the phone down.

Adrianna was calling about some party one of her homegirls was having that night.

Alex is home chica and he is not letting me out of his sight.

Sure as hell ain't he said as he walked into her office. You ready baby he asked? We need to go by the bank. You got them other deposit slips ready?

Yeah. Adrianna call me on my cell phone in like 5-10 minutes.

Gabriella added the amounts that Alejandro had just counted and separated into her accounting book. She made out the deposit slips and finished up the last of the bills before gathering her purse and shoes following Alejandro into the garage. Today they were pushing the Bentley. They spend an hour at the bank getting their accounts in order before going to a furniture store to look for new furniture. They both agreed that after 3 years it was time to upgrade.

A few hours after shopping they stopped off at Chili's for lunch. Alejandro ordered a burger, fries, a side of chips and queso. Gabriella ordered a grilled chicken Caesar salad.

That all you want Alejandro asked Gabriella.

Yeah

You didn't eat breakfast.

I know, I wasn't hungry.

You alright he asked with a concerned look on his face.

Yes, I'm fine she said as she took a sip of her drink.

Over food he said Gabi I know I haven't been much of a father to the kids or a man to you with me being out of town so much and I want to say I'm sorry. I was out there trying to get money and was neglecting my family. I decided to take some time off. I'm going for anywhere between 2-6 months. I already let Deuce and Drago know to handle things in my absence. I won't be making any trips but I will still do what I need to do on a daily basis to keep things in order. He said all this in between bites of food and in the end was hoping Gabriella would be happy about his decision but her attitude was a bit nonchalant. She simply said Okay and picked over her salad. He was surprised that she didn't ask any questions or put up a fuss about his dealings with Diana. Since she didn't bring it up he never mentioned it. When he finished eating he asked You sure you're okay? You barely touched your salad.

I'm going to take it with me. I'm not really hungry for some reason.

Drago called said he and the kids were going to Uncle Juan's.

Drago can you bring them by Carmen's, their grandma wants to see them. We can meet you guys over there.

Cool Drago tells her.

They spent a good 3 hours at Carmen's before Deuce called Alejandro about an urgent matter. Since Drago had the kids Alejandro agreed to take care of it. He told Gabriella he needed to make a run but would be back before the night was over with. Gabriella used this time to go through Fernando and Isabella's closets pulling out the things they could no longer wear. She boxed up old toys and moved about the house in search of other items they didn't use. She had several boxes packed and in the garage when Alejandro arrived home. With a puzzled expression on his face he walked in and asked What's all those boxes for?

Just some old stuff that we don't need anymore.

Alejandro looked around and noticed that a lot of pictures, knickknacks and other things were missing. Pictures too he asked, where are all the family photos, the trophies?

I figured it would be best to clear all that out of the way, vacuum and dust before the new stuff gets here. That way the movers can move it wherever it needs to go.

Oh

Why you got that look on your face she asked as she starred at him a minute.

Nothing, it's been a long day. Let's go shower.

Let me finish this up and I will be in there.

Another shower and making love Alejandro was snoring softly while Gabriella couldn't sleep. She got up, poured herself a glass of wine and went into her office. She started reorganizing her files. When she did finally fall off to sleep it was after 5AM on the lounger in her office.

Alejandro woke up around 9 realized she hadn't been beside him for a while because her side of the bed was cold. He got up to use the bathroom, expected to find her in the kitchen cooking breakfast. No notes were attached to the refrigerator and all the cars were still parked in the garage. He called her name several times but she never answered. Finally he found her inside her office still asleep.

Yo G, wake up baby. Go put some clothes on. The furniture people just called. They're on their way.

Chapter 15

The first couple of weeks home Alejandro spent all his daily free time with the kids. If they weren't out playing basketball or football it was running or some other activity. He was also teaching both Fern and Issy how to drive. His nights were spent making love to Gabriella. Since he'd been home the two of them have been all over each other. He was waiting on Gabriella to miss a period, experience morning sickness; some indication that a baby was on the way. A month later and no signs of a pregnancy where Gabriella was concerned. She asked her gynecologist if she could still have children. Her doctor told her that she didn't see her previous miscarriages causing her not to go through full term and none of her pap smears came back abnormal. She suggests that Gabriella tries to monitor her ovulation and have sex when she was ovulating for a better chance of conceiving. She also gave other tips in which would help both her and Alejandro during this time. She spent a good 2 ½ hours at the doctor's office before returning home. There was a note on the refrigerator to call Alejandro ASAP.

She dialed his number. Alex

Where the fuck have you been? I done called you at least 50 times.

Calm down, I was at Dr. McGlothin's office.

For what, you had a goddamn pap smear earlier this year.

Will you stop all that cursing.

Gabi you gone make me fuck you up. I'm on my way to the house.

Okay, I'm about to get started on dinner.

Whatever.

When Alejandro walked in Gabriella was sitting at the breakfast nook enjoying a peach and her book Mistress of the Game while she cooked a dinner of smothered pork chops, mashed potatoes, broccoli and cheese casserole and fried cabbage.

What the hell you go to the doctor for he asked as he took a seat across from her. You lied to me about the birth control pills. You just recently had a prescription filled.

Bullshit, the last time I had a prescription filled I got a year's supply through mail order and the label is dated to show when it's supposed to be used. If you would have paid attention you would see that there are months' worth of packages that have never been opened she said as she got up and walked over to the stove. Once again Alejandro said in an even tone, What did you go to the doctor for today?

You just called me a liar. You need to apologize.

You ain't answered my question, for all I know you could still be lying.

Why would I need to lie about going to the doctor Alex? Why would I lie about anything?

Why didn't you tell me you were going? Why was it a secret?

It wasn't no secret and I didn't tell you because it wasn't important.

I'm gone ask you one more time, what did you go for? You have an abortion you didn't want me to find out about?

Gabriella turned around to look at him. Alejandro she yelled before saying in Spanish No I didn't have a goddamn abortion. Why the hell would you even think that?

We've been going at it for damn near a year now and…I mean shit…

Oh and what? Because I go to the doctor I have to be going for an abortion?

Alejandro I want a baby as much as you do, if not more. I don't know why I'm not pregnant. That's why I went to Dr. McGlothin to make sure there is nothing wrong with me, to make sure I can even still have kids she said as she turned off the stove and walked out of the kitchen down the hall into their bedroom slamming the door behind her.

Gordon came in with the mail and asked Where's Bella? Did she call yet?

Yeah she's here Alejandro said as he walked to their bedroom and attempted to open the door. It was locked. Yo Gabi, open up. I want to talk to you.

Leave me alone she yelled.

Look I'm sorry.

What happened Gordon asked in a concerned tone standing at the door beside him. Where was she?

At the doctor's office.

Gordon's eyebrows went up a notch, Everything okay?

Yeah, I guess.

You guess? What's that supposed to mean? Why is she upset with you?

I accused her of having an abortion.

An abortion, Gabriella please. You of all people should know how bad she wants a baby.

I know and we been trying for over a year, still nothing. I found all these birth control pills when she said she wasn't taking them.

She stopped taking them a long time ago.

Yo Gabi, open up Alejandro said as he tried turning the knob again.

Leave me alone she screamed out.

Come on son, give her a minute to calm down. Let's go have a drink.

Isabella and her friend Leandra came through the front door. Daddy, where is Mommy?

Man, what happened to Hi Daddy, hi Grandpa? What happened to the hugs and kisses Alejandro asked?

Sorry she said as she hugged and kissed them both. Now where is Mommy?

Back there in the bedroom.

Is she asleep?

Why don't you go check?

Before Isabella made it down the hall good Fern came through the door. Daddy, Grandpa you're both home. Does this mean Mommy isn't here?

She's here Gordon tells him. She's in her bedroom.

Good because I want to tell her something he says as he rushes to the back yelling out Hi Leandra.

Hi Fern she blushed.

Gabriella made her way into the kitchen after telling the kids to get ready for dinner. Fern's friend Ahmad was coming to stay over and Leandra was also staying. Gabriella kissed Gordon's cheek and said hi Papi.

Hi Bella, you and Alex go to the back and talk while I fix the kids plates.

I have nothing to talk to Alex about.

Gabriella

What?

Go on, I will bring your plates back in a little bit.

Alejandro was the last to enter the room so he closed the door behind him. Baby I'm sorry. When she didn't respond he walked up on her and wrapped his arms around her. He kissed her neck and asked you forgive me? The chirp on his

Good To Have You Back

phone went off. Diana's brother was trying to arrange an urgent meeting with the Cuban uncle. Yeah I got you man. I'll get there tomorrow some time. Cool. Everything okay Gabriella asked concerned.

I hope so, won't really know until tomorrow but fuck that. Are we okay?

Yeah we're good but you still owe me an apology.

I'm sorry baby, for real.

Later on that night they were seriously going at it. Alejandro was on the verge of an electrifying orgasm when Diana's brother called him again. He was letting him know that his flight leaves at 6 in the morning. Alright Alejandro said as he let go inside of Gabriella and said Fuck after releasing the chirp he rolled over and got out of bed. Gabriella lay there watching him get dressed. They both glanced at the clock. 4:15AM

He picked up his cell and left the bedroom after kissing Gabriella's lips and telling her to get some sleep. He phoned Deuce and Drago. They all planned to meet up at the airport. When he walked back into the room 30 minutes later he whispered G?

What she asked having watched him since he walked through the door.

I gotta make a move.

When will you be back?

Hopefully before the kids get home from school.

Anything serious?

Nah not like that baby, gone ahead and get some sleep. I'll call you when I get to where I'm going. I will tell Pop to get the kids up for school.

I can handle them.

I know but you need to get some rest babe. Pop will handle everything.

Alejandro I love you.

I love you too Gabriella he said as he kissed her lips.

As soon as Alejandro made it to Diana's neck of the woods they went straight to her condo. He had been home a month and a half so conversation between the two was limited, almost non-existent. The front room was dark because the shades were pulled close. In the bedroom he found Diana and another chick seriously going at it.

Alejandro I'm so glad you could join us she smiled.

What's up with the meeting?

This is it baby, the threesome you've been asking for.

Yo Dirty, I know you ain't get me out of my bed at 4 in the morning for no bullshit.

No, this is what I needed you for. I couldn't wait and I figured I would make it worth your while.

Say he said to the other chick Get up out of here. Let me holla at Dirty for a minute.

The chick removed her head from between Diana's legs and left the bedroom naked.

Yo when I called you what did I tell you he asked Diana?

I know what you said but baby this ain't work and I figured you would enjoy this.

Alejandro's cell phone rings he notices the house number and motions for Diana to be quiet.

Daddy Fernando says when he answers.

Yeah son, what's up?

Remember you are supposed to have lunch with me today.

Yeah I ain't forget. I will be there.

Okay. Issy wants you. I love you Daddy.

Love you too son.

Daddy you promised you wouldn't be going out of town for a while Isabella reminded him.

I know babygirl, I will be home no later than 11

Tonight? You're supposed to have lunch with Fern today.

I will be there alright?

Daddy if you're not here…

I will be there Issy. Where is your mom?

Packing our lunch.

Where is Grandpa?

Warming up the car.

Alright I'll see you when you get home from school.

Can we go to Cavallo's today please?

Yeah let everybody know so Moms and Pops don't cook dinner.

After hanging up he told Diana Get me on the next available flight ASAP.

Can we at least finish what you came here for?

I didn't come here for bullshit. I came to handle business. Get on the muthafuckin phone and get 3 flights back to my neck of the woods now he said as he walked out the room slamming the door behind him.

Yo where Deuce Alejandro asked when he walked into the living room.

Back there hollering at o'l girl. What's up? We handling business or what?

Nah that bitch had us coming out here for nothing. Yo Dirty get yo muthafuckin ass out here.

Yeah she asked.

You gone pay me for my time too. You gone pay Deuce and Drago for coming with me. Don't let this shit happen again.

Well damn, excuse me for trying to get a little bit of your time. My bad.

He glared at her as she left the room. She transferred $45,000 into his business account and had their return flights set to go. Alejandro left out the door without another word.

Yo Alex Drago said to him on the way to the airport. You better put that hoe in check. She pulling stunts like this ain't no telling what else she will do.

Another month passed Alejandro has rejected all of Diana's calls and blocked her text messages from coming through. She knew he was pissed but ignoring her was pissing her off. She started calling their house phone hanging up. Luckily Mr. Gordon had always been the one to answer.

Who was that Alex asked Gordon as they sat in the game room watching the game.

Unknown name, been happening a lot lately.

What they say?

Nothing just hung up.

Alejandro assumed it was a telemarketer and didn't think much of it until one day Isabella answered.

Daddy a lady is on the phone from Cuban Connections and she wants to speak with you. Are you available?

Yeah I will take it in my office. Give me a minute.

As soon as he heard Isabella hang up he told Diana Look you dumb bitch quit fucking playing with me about my family. Don't call my goddamn house again.

I suggest you come see me before the week is out she hissed before hanging up.

He ignored her. Sunday she called while the family was having breakfast and then again during dinner time. Monday a package was delivered to Alejandro from Cuban Connections that included soiled panties, empty condom wrappers and pictures of naked women. Luckily Alejandro opened his own mail because Gabriella refused to open anything that didn't have her name on it. She had thousands of letters that came in Tago's name that included checks written out to him before he died. It wasn't until recently that they found this out after several business associates contacted his lawyer about the checks not being cashed. Alejandro was heated. He and Gabriella were supposed to go out dancing that night.

Yo Pop let Gabi know I had to make a run.

Why don't you call her son, it will sound better coming from you?

She will hear the frustration in my voice. I don't want her to worry.

What's going on?

We will talk later, it's nothing I can't handle Pop.

Hours later Gabriella makes it home. Gordon tells her about the run Alejandro had to make. She's upset but feels that it must be important or else he wouldn't have left. Gordon took the kids out for pizza. Gabriella enjoyed a nice hot bubble bath. She was waiting on Alejandro to call. When the phone rang she rushed out the bath tub to answer it.

Gabriella I'm so glad you answered. I've been trying to reach you for weeks now.

Who is this?

You remember me, Alejandro's friend with the red Corvette. I just wanted to say thank you for letting him come over to unclog my pipes. He's such a big help she laughed. He should be here any minute now I'm sure. It's been backed up for so long I wouldn't be surprised if a baby is caught up in there somewhere she joked. Oh my, someone's at the door now. Maybe that's him. Alejandro is that you baby?

Yeah it's me. Open the goddamn door. Fuck you got all the locks on the door for?

My bad baby. Girl let me call you back. My man is home she said before hanging up.

Gabriella hung up and dialed Alejandro's number. He didn't answer. When she sent him a text he didn't answer. When she hit him 911 he called Drago.

Bro, call your sister for me. She hit me 911.

Drago knew where he was and knew what to do. He hung up with Alejandro and dialed Gabriella.

Bella

Yes she asked in a clipped tone.

Can you braid my hair?

I'm not in the mood D.

Please.

No, I will call you back she said disconnecting the call.

Drago dialed Alejandro. She's pissed about something.

Alright let me call Pop and see what's up. Go by there for me.

When Alejandro called Gordon, Gordon told him about the phone calls he got this morning from Cuban Connections from a lady by the name of Diana.

Gordon had heard enough arguments between Alejandro and Gabriella to know who Diana was.

Alejandro hauled off and slapped Diana. He ended his call and started fighting with her. When it was all over with he told her I'm through fucking with you. From now on watch how you come at me he said as he packed the things he had at her place and walked right out the door. He dialed Diana's brother's number.

Yo Dante' put me in contact with your uncle Corleone ASAP.

Alright, I got you.

By the time Alejandro made it to the car his cell phone was ringing. Corleone this Alejandro. From now on if we're to be business partners it's you and me. What's going on?

I'm through fucking with Diana. I suggest you have a talk with her before she causes problems in our association.

When Alejandro made it home he walked in the house and into the family room. Gabriella come here. Let me talk to you for a minute.

Gabriella stood up with a roll of her eyes and walked past Alejandro into their bedroom. He closed the door behind him and said baby I'm...

Alex save it. Your bitch called here today to let me know you were on your way over. In fact I was on the phone with her when you walked through the door. So save your tired ass stories for someone else she said as she left the bedroom. He walked out G, let me explain. It ain't what you think.

When I asked you if you were still messing around with her you said no.

I ain't been messing with her, not like that.

Bullshit she yelled.

Alejandro snatched her arm and pulled her into the bedroom. Look I said it ain't what you think. Calm the fuck down. That bitch just trying to keep shit poppin off over here.

If you weren't fucking around with her Alejandro she wouldn't have no reason to call here.

Mommy Fern called out from the door.

Yes baby

The movie is on.

Okay I'm coming. Did you pop the popcorn?

Yes maam. Daddy are you coming too?

Yeah son he said as Gabriella snatched away from him and walked into the bathroom. She closed herself up in the bathroom and slid to the floor as the tears started falling down her face. She ignored Alejandro's constant knocks on the door. She pulled herself together took a long hot shower, washed her hair and changed into her night clothes. She made her way out the bedroom into the family room which was dark except for the TV. She took a seat on her lounger. The kids were on the floor with Alejandro who kept starring at her right along with Gordon. Isabella got up and lay on the lounger with her mother.

The kids had Friday, Monday and Tuesday out of school. Alejandro was going on a fishing trip with Gordon, Drago, Deuce and Uncle Juan. Gabriella decided to take the kids to Phoenix. Satin wanted to take them to Speed Zone for the night. Antonio was there with some kids from the Boys and Girls Club that made A's and B's on their report card the last 6 weeks. Fernando was the first one to notice him. Antonio he screamed while running in his direction. Isabella wasn't sure if it was him or not. When she realized it was she ran over to him. Gabriella bit her bottom lip, looked over at Satin and shrugged her shoulders. Before they made it to Phoenix they talked about whether or not the kids should be able to see Antonio. Satin felt like they should because the kids missed him and he missed the kids. Gabriella was against it because she didn't want no issues with Alejandro when he found out Antonio lived in Phoenix or to even know he'd been there. He would automatically assume that was the reason Gabriella often came to Phoenix. There was enough drama in the Pennington, Diaz, Solera household. It was too late now that the kids saw him it would be hard to keep them from contacting each other. Antonio walked over hugged both Satin and Gabriella before introducing the club kids to everyone standing around. The kids played until 1 o'clock that morning before returning to Satin's with plans to meet Antonio for breakfast. Their 4 day trip was spent with Antonio doing a little of everything. Before leaving to go home Gabriella told them You know your father...

We know Mommy Fernando said, we won't mention that we saw Antonio to Daddy.

She breathed a sigh of relief.

Antonio was over at Satin's having dinner. Danny invited him over because he needed a home cooked meal. Satin was cooking beef tips and rice, mashed potatoes, cabbage and corn on the cob. Fernando called Satin to let her know he got all A's on his report card. When he heard Antonio's voice he wanted to speak with him. This became an everyday thing for the kids to speak with Antonio. Uncle Juan's fiancé Carlita was leaving Pennsylvania to move to Long Island so Alejandro was helping them move. Aside from that he spent quite a bit of time meeting with Corleone to set up a new way to handle business.

So he spent a lot of time away from home.

Fernando and Isabella wanted to spend their Spring Break in Phoenix with Satin, of course they knew they would also get to see Antonio. Gabriella didn't mind them going but she told them to discuss it with Alejandro before flight arrangements were made and they got their hopes up. They must have called Alejandro after school one day because when he did make it home the first question he asked Gabriella was I guess you going to Phoenix too with a hint of attitude.

No she said without looking up from the book she was reading. I hadn't planned on it. Why?

Was just wondering. I'm cool if you cool his voice calmed a bit.

I know they're in good hands. Just wanted to make sure it was okay with you. What's for dinner tonight?

I hadn't planned on cooking. Fern is going out with Herman and Issy's staying with Naomi for the night.

You want to go grab a bite to eat.

No

What you gone eat?
Me and Adrianna are going to Studio Movie Grill
To see what?
Jennifer's Body
I wanted us to go see that tomorrow.
Yeah, well we're going today.
Good, what time we leaving?
Gabriella removed the book from her face and said You're...just as Adrianna chirped. BK's back in town. He's going to the movies too. See if Alex wants to come. If not I will have BK call somebody. Gabriella rolled her eyes and started reading her book again.
So what time we leaving?
Movie starts at 9:15
Cool, can I get you to trim me up baby?
I will do it before you shower.
I'm ready now if you don't mind.
You will have to wait. My book is at a good part and I don't want to stop.
What you reading?
Dutch Trilogy.
By Teri Woods?
Yeah
Alejandro came and sat down beside her noticed that she had just started. What I miss he asked?
She passed the book to him and got up. I'm going to take my shower, have at it. When she stepped out the shower Alejandro sat atop the bathroom counter in just his boxer shorts. The clippers were plugged up and he was ready. She wrapped the towel around herself and walked over to him as he got down. He picked her up in his arms and sat her atop the counter. She lined him up, shaved his beard and mustache before passing the clippers back to him.
Thank you Alejandro told her with his hands planted firmly on either side of her as he tried to kiss her lips. She turned her head away and tried to get off the counter. He held her in place.
G this shit been going on long enough. My dick harder than a muthafucka. You gone deny me that? He looked deep into her eyes. She could no longer hold off on the sex. She figured I will give him that even if he can't get nothing else. She

kissed him hard, eased his boxers down and opened her towel. They skipped the four play and went right to the sex. Straight fucking. Alejandro couldn't get enough. He wanted to go at it all night but Gabriella remembered the movies. As they got dressed Alejandro watched Gabriella licking his lips. By the time Adrianna and BK arrived the two were dressed and ready to go. The movie was good and scary. Before it was over Alejandro got a call from Deuce about some business so he had to roll out.

Chapter 16

Sis, let's fall up in Cocoa's.
What's going on up there?
I don't know, that's what I'm trying to find out.
It's cool, can't stay too long. Gotta get the kids ready for Phoenix.
Oh Alex gone let them go?
Yeah he said he was alright with it.
But he don't know Tony there right?
No, the kids are going to Satin's. Of course they will see him while they're there.
You bet not let Alex know, he gone flip the fuck out for real.
I know and the kids know too.

Gabriella went home, showered and changed into a pair of snakeskin Prada pants with matching stilettos and a fitted top that hugged her frame. She rocked her hair in a ponytail with big hoop earrings, a little makeup and was feeling good. Isabella was gone for the night and Fernando would stay home with Grandpa and Ahmad. Alejandro said he didn't know how long he would be out or if he was going to get into anything.

Damn Big Sis Adrianna smiled as she looked her over Bro better watch out before you get took.
Whatever, why yo ass ain't ready?
Fucking around with BK.
Well hurry up, I told you I can't be out all night.
Alright, alright while I finish up can you pick me out some shoes to go with this outfit?
Pick another outfit. I'm not feeling this. Why you trying to be all covered up and shit?
You know BK be trippen just like Alejandro. He see you in those painted on pants with your ass all poked out he gone be on you.
Alex said he was handling business. Only way he coming to the club is if somebody start running they mouth, but if he does who gives a fuck, really?
Ah come on now, quit frontin. You know you love him.
I do, no doubt but right now I'm pissed at him so he gone take the shit I'm dishing out.

Cocoa's was poppin and before long it was like 1 in the morning. Alejandro and Deuce walked up in the club. Some chicks were giving him info about where Gabriella was in the club. The same chicks had been the ones hitting him up with texts letting him know her every move. Before he could reach the area where Gabriella was Diana and her homegirl Chyna walked up.

Damn Daddy can we kick it for old times sake Diana asked

Alejandro ignored her so she followed behind them. She kept grabbing at him until he turned around and said Bitch I...Deuce said Slow up there Bro. Here come Gabi now.

As they watched Gabriella and Adrianna walk down the stairs some dude stopped Gabriella by calling her Tago's Queen. She smiled as she hugged him close.

How have you been? I thought you...

Yeah I've heard the stories. I moved away for a minute but I've been back for almost 4 ½ - 5 years now.

I heard about T, sorry I couldn't make the funeral but you know when you on the run you gotta lay low till shit die down.

Yeah I know.

I miss my nigga though. How are you Ma? You looking fly as usual. Where the kids?

How they doing?

We're good, they're getting big as ever.

Yo if you don't mind, take my number.

Just as Gabriella pulled out her phone Alejandro walked up. He mugged first Tyren and then Gabriella. Tyren mugged back. Being that Tago and Alejandro stayed at each other's throats over Gabriella back in the days. Tyren ran with that beef then too.

Sensing the tension Gabriella said Hey baby as she kissed Alejandro's lips. Tyren you remember Alejandro. Alejandro this is Tyren.

Tyren feeling Gabriella extended his hand to dap up Alejandro. Alejandro looked him over then dapped him up. GP take my number and hit me up.

Tyren and Tago were like brothers. Drago obviously had no idea Tyren was in town because they would definitely be together up in some club. Once Gabriella had his number Alejandro took one look at her and walked off. He just so happened to be headed in Diana's direction.

Gabriella called out his name, when he didn't stop she grabbed him but he shook her loose and kept it moving.

Gabi let him cool down Adrianna told her. You know how he gets sometimes. He will be alright in a minute. Come on let's go get another drink. Gabriella fired up a blunt.

Once seated at the bar she spotted Diana dancing near Alejandro but not up on him. She sipped the last of her Hennessy and got up. Before Adrianna could stop her she was headed in that direction. Deuce saw her coming. She walked right up on Alejandro and said Let's go.

Where we going?

Don't try to play me.

Oh you mean like you did by putting another nigga's number in your phone right in front of me?

You act like he's just some nigga off the street.

To me that's all he'll ever be and that shit's disrespectful yo. Get the fuck out of my face before I do something to you he said in a huff.

Gabriella's facial expression went from shock, anger and then a smile as she got all up in Alejandro's face. You wanna know what's fucking disrespectful yo, having yo bitch call my goddamn house. Now that shits disrespectful. You can't do shit to me that hasn't already been done she said as she grabbed his nuts and through clenched teeth she told him Don't ever fucking threatin me again. She put the doobie into his drink and told him Now get the fuck up before I act a goddamn donkey up in here on you and your bitch.

Alejandro starred into her eyes and asked What, you done grew nuts or something? You holding?

Fuck with me she told him as she turned to walk off.

Alejandro bit his bottom lip as he watched her walk away. Yo I'm out.

You are such an ass Adrianna told him in annoyance.

You rollin with us or with Deuce?

With you, hopefully I can help save you from this mess you done created.

Laughing as he started walking he said I'm straight. I'm fucking G up when I get home, for real yo. She got me fucked up.

Deuce walked behind him and said chill out my nigga. You know Gabi don't even get down on no bullshit. Tago and Tyren was tight. That nigga just as much Fern and Issy uncle as Drago. That's all that shits about.

Miss me with that bullshit, that nigga called her Tago's Queen. Fuck that nigga, she belong to me now.

Yeah and you know that Adrianna told him, so why are you trippen?

That nigga used to beef with me like I was fucking his girl yo. That shit don't just die down like that.

Alejandro you know how it is. That's just like me beefing with the niggas you beefing with but fuck it when it comes to the kids its one love my nigga Deuce told him.

Right Adrianna said as they stepped outside. Diana and Chyna were standing talking to Gabriella. Diana was doing all the talking and Chyna was standing there as if she was Diana's bodyguard or some shit. Nobody could hear what was being said.

Gabriella hauled off and punched Diana, without saying a word she dropped more blows. Chyna got punched in the mouth before Adrianna or anyone else could break the fight up. Alejandro, Deuce and Adrianna held Gabriella while 2 bouncers held Chyna and Diana. They thought everything was calm and cool so the bouncers let Diana and Chyna go. Alejandro and the crew started walking away. Diana pulled out a box cutter and ran up on Gabriella screaming. Gabriella moved just in time to avoid getting slashed. This made her madder than she already was so she went at Diana like a beast and had her laid out in no time. Using the box cutter Diana attempted to cut her with she slashed her face until she spelled out Gabi in big letters. Her face was a bloody mess but she would live. Gabriella spit in her face and told her Bitch find you somebody else to play with cause I'm not the one. She hauled off and punched Chyna again too this time knocking out some of her teeth and splitting both her top and bottom lip with the ring she wore.

Alejandro tried to grab Gabriella but she snatched away from him and hopped in the driver side of her Bentley. Adrianna hopped in the passenger and they pulled off. Alejandro got in the car with Deuce, tried calling Gabriella but she wouldn't answer. He called Corleone about the incident, said that once he got Gabriella straight he would give him a call back. Drago had heard about the incident and was calling Gabriella and Alejandro's phone.

Yo Bro what the fuck happened Drago yelled?

Man, G just got into it with Diana.

I heard she carved her name in the bitch face. How this pop off?

Man we was up at Cocoa's and Diana was running her mouth as usual. I don't know what the fuck she said but G was already pissed off when she approached her. You know G is normally the one to keep a cool head but shit...Alejandro was at a loss for words.

You and Bella into it?

Man, yeah something like that. I was trippen off Tyren giving her his number.

Tyren, you mean ACE?

Yeah

You know ain't shit going down right. That nigga's family for real yo.

When Deuce pulled up in front of the house Gordon was out front smoking a cigar.

What the hell happened he asked as soon as Alejandro was close enough to him.

G got to fighting this chick at the club.

What chick?

Diana he said as he looked off.

Gordon put out his cigar and walked back inside. Fuck, Alejandro yelled out.

Gabriella snatched open the door and told him get your ass in here and quit doing all that damn cussin. Your son is still awake.

Yo G let me holla at you for a minute.

Alex, not now. Your son is up waiting for you. Fix your face and come in. Deuce you might as well join the party.

Alejandro asked You alright.

Me, hell yeah I'm good. You should have been asking yo bitch that.

Daddy Fernando yelled when Alejandro walked through the door.

What up son, it's like 3 in the morning. What you still doing up?

Waiting on you and Mommy to get home. I thought you was out of town again.

Nah, I ain't going nowhere. Where's Ahmad?

Asleep, he couldn't stay awake.

You barely standing yourself. Gone and go get in the bed. We in for the night.

Okay good night Daddy, good night Mommy. Good night D. Love you guys Fernando hugged and kissed Gabriella before leaving the room.

She walked into her bedroom closing the door behind her. Drago came in shortly after she stepped in the shower.

Where my sister at he asked?

Back there taking a shower.

Man I seen pictures of yo girl face, you know that shits permanent right? She gone need a whole new face if she want that shit to go away. I told her to chill the fuck out when she started calling the house. I knew Bella wasn't taking shit lightly. Only reason she let it ride is because of business. If Diana had of played her part shit would be cool but...

Corleone gone be on some bullshit yo Deuce announced.

Fuck that shit, I'm probably about to get put out, lose the best thing to ever happen to me Alejandro said seriously.

Gordon interrupted, No. You're good for now. She would have had your shit waiting for you at the door. With Gabriella you have nothing to worry about but Corleone is going to be a problem. Business or no business if he fucks with Bella I'm going to rip him apart.

Ah nah Pops you know I ain't even gone let it go down like that Alejandro said as his cell rings. It was Corleone, Diana's brother and another uncle all pissed about Diana's face. She would need plastic surgery to patch up Gabi's art work and nobody was feeling that shit.

Yo, I told you to tell Diana to chill the fuck out. I knew what Gabi was capable of. That's why I told you Diana don't want to fuck with her, no bullshit.

The other uncle was telling Corleone not to do business with Alejandro anymore. Corleone argued that 75% of his income was Alejandro's profits. He would take a major loss cutting him loose and that's the only reason he wanted to keep him around.

Man you know what, I ain't got time for bullshit. Fuck it I'll get it how I live. If this how you handle business I don't need to fuck with you no way. Keep yo shit, I'm good. Just remember you paid in full Alejandro said before hanging up. To Gordon, Drago and Deuce he said I'm going to bed. I need peace. Y'all niggas hold it down.

He continued into the hallway and to his bedroom. He was surprised that the door wasn't locked. When he walked in Gabriella was drying herself off. He closed the door behind him.

Look G

I don't want to talk about it.

Alright.

Alejandro showered a long time and stepped out. Gabriella was standing at the door with his phone in her hand. Your phone is going bananas. Corleone said to call him ASAP.

Fuck him.

Ain't that…

Yeah but fuck him. I will figure this shit out.

Don't stress babe, definitely don't lose no sleep she said as she kissed him slow and passionately. Put her sex game down on him to put his mind at ease. She had him knocked out in no time. She walked into her office and made a phone call to an old Columbian friend of hers and Tago's. She would be flying out to meet with him in a couple days.

She told Alejandro Baby we need a vacation.

We do but Bae, I gotta get shit up and running before I make any moves.

Shit is up and running, you just came back.

Yeah but how long you think that gone last? We got bread but other niggas gotta eat too. I ain't trying to come out my pocket you feel me?

I got you, can we just take this trip and…

Gabi come on now, I don't have time for…

Alejandro we're taking this fucking trip so don't give me no bullshit. I already made reservations. Whatever you had planned, cancel it.

Where the fuck do you get off telling me what to do? I wear the pants in this relationship. I got the balls, not you.

I respect that she smiled but right now I want what I want. This is one of those things thats non-negotiable so I suggest you do what it takes to make it happen. You feel me yo?

Alejandro bit his lip and said Goddamn I love you woman, for real.

See how easy that was she asked as she kissed him back. I love you too. I promise you won't regret it.

Alejandro would remember this trip forever because Gabriella had way better connections than Diana and put him down like a nigga that knows his shit. He couldn't deny that Tago taught her well.

Good To Have You Back

Chapter 17

*Yo Alex you better get yo shit together. No more bitches, no trips, no…
I got you baby he smiled. I promise you I got you no doubt.*

*When they arrived home from their trip Alejandro went straight to work getting things in order. He and Gabriella talked about him leaving the game and getting more involved with the legit business they already had open.
I feel you baby, I'm going to work it out he told her.*

*4 months later the beef Corleone had in behind all the money he was losing had him going crazy. He'd made several phone calls and trips to New York to settle the issue with Alejandro. Business was better than ever for Alex, Deuce, Drago and Tyren as well their other team. More money was being made and nobody had to deal with bullshit to keep the connect bringing product. For Alejandro there was no going back to Corleone. In his eyes he felt like right was right and wrong was wrong. If the shoe was on the other foot Corleone would expect Alejandro to continue business like normal. Things shouldn't have come to an end the way they did, especially considering that Alejandro warned him about Diana's drama long before shit got ugly. Now he was blowing up Alejandro's phone, offering better prices, apologizing, the whole nine.
Between Alejandro, Gordon, Drago, Deuce, Tyren and uncle Juan they watched Gabriella and the children like hawks. Everybody knew that the only way to get to Alejandro was to fuck with his family. What Corleone and Diana didn't know was that if they fucked with Alejandro's family his crew would be hell on them by themselves. With Tago's crew joining forces which would definitely happen shit would be deadly no doubt.
Tyren got tired of Corleone and his bullshit. He wasn't the type to exchange threats. He would get the job done whatever that meant. To get back at Alejandro Diana used Tyren. She hooked up with him and flossed him in Alejandro's face. Tyren used her to get to Corleone and her other uncle. He wanted to get in good with them so he could slide right through and handle his business.*

Alejandro was out back playing ball with Fernando and some of his friends when Gabriella stepped out. Alex I'm taking Issy to the mall.
I'm rollin.
That's okay. Papi's going.
Alejandro walked up on Gabriella hugged her close and kissed her lips. You keep your eyes and ears open.
I know Alex.
Don't worry about dinner. I'll handle it.
But I thought you had to be somewhere at 3 and wouldn't be back for a while.
I do but I can handle dinner baby.

Alejandro received a phone call from Diana saying that she and Tyren were about to get married.
Congratulations Alejandro told her with a smile.
That wasn't the response she was hoping for. She wanted him to argue that the two of them were meant to be together and that she couldn't marry Tyren. I'm taking him to meet my uncles in a couple of days and then we will leave there and get married.
Everything went according to her plans. Tyren met the uncles and the other family members, they liked him instantly. Tyren almost felt like what he wanted to do would be way too easy. Before the wedding was supposed to happen they wanted to have the traditional bachelor and bachelorette parties. For Tyren this was the perfect opportunity to kill two birds with one stone. He had 2 sets of twins come down to perform at these parties. They were all assassins and would get the job done without error. The night of the party he kept telling Corleone something didn't feel right.
You're just getting cold feet. You will be alright Corleone laughed as he slapped him on the back. Once you join the family you will be rich and well taken care of. Can't get no more right than that. You do love Diana right?
Yeah I love her with all my heart but I've been having a bad feeling about all this since I got here. Not sure what that's all about.
Let's go have some drinks and fuck some bitches. You'll be alright.
By 2AM the party was well under way and by 4 the twins had completed their jobs. They pulled a body in to serve as Tyren's before setting the place on fire.

Good To Have You Back

Teach these cock suckers not to mess with my family. Tyren had been successful in getting rid of everybody in Diana's family that knew anything about him. He used the name Thomas Pentel and everybody around the way referred to him as plain old T. He returned to his neighborhood with no issues.

Alejandro walked into his bedroom around 3 o'clock one morning prepared to apologize to Gabriella about staying out so late when he realized she was not in bed. The TV was on in the family room so he assumed that's where she was. When he reached that area he saw Gordon watching Night Court and eating fresh vegetables.

What's up Pop?

Hey son, how's business?

Everything's good he said as he took a seat.

Gordon passed him a bowl of fruit. Alejandro took a few strawberries. Guess you're wondering where Gabi is huh?

Yeah, she out at some club?

No, Satin's mom passed away this evening so she went to Georgia to help out with the funeral arrangements. She tried calling you only a million times and finally gave up. Your voice mail was full too.

Where my kids?

In the back, asleep.

Alejandro got up to check on Isabella and Fernando before grabbing the house phone and dialing Gabriella's number. Hello she answered on the first ring.

You alright Alejandro asked?

Gabriella said I'm good as her eyes adjusted to check the time. Alex, is everything okay at home?

Yeah everything's cool. Just you ain't here.

Okay well I will call you in the morning. Good night.

G he called out just as she hung up. She shut her phone off after that and rolled over to go back to sleep. Alejandro tried calling her again several more times and got pissed off when she didn't answer.

Son, go to bed. She's not going to answer. She's probably tired. They drove to Georgia from here so I'm sure they're just now going to sleep.

Who all with them?

Just her and Satin.

Satin don't have no brothers and sisters?

A brother that's younger and a sister that passed away a few years ago.

Did G say about how long she would be gone?

No, but I'm assuming long enough for the funeral and a day or two afterwards.

Why, you need to leave town? I got the kids.

Oh nah Pop, I'm at home for a minute. Just not used to G being away from home.

We will be alright, it's only a couple of days.

2 days later Gabriella had just finished helping Satin with the funeral arrangements. The two of them were on their way to dinner when Danny called. He said his flight had arrived and he needed directions from the airport to the house.

We will pick you up Satin told him. We're only about 5-10 minutes away.

When they arrived at the airport Antonio was there too. Gabriella couldn't take her eyes off of him. He was dressed in a cream colored Christian Audiger fitted shirt that showed off his muscles all over and a pair of Christian Audiger jeans. Gabriella was starring so hard that Satin had to remind her to pop the trunk.

Gabriella bit her bottom lip. What's going through your head Satin asked?

Man I sure know how to pick them she laughed.

Yeah you do Satin smiled as Danny and Antonio got in the back seat of Gabriella's BMW 750i

You guys eat yet Satin asked?

No, was hoping we weren't too late for dinner.

We were actually on our way there.

After dinner Satin showed Antonio to the bedroom he would be sleeping in which just so happened to be right next to Gabriella's. The two of them would share bathrooms during their stay. While Satin and Danny went into Satin's old bedroom closing the door behind them Antonio and Gabriella argued over who should take their shower first.

You go, it's cool she told Antonio.

Ladies first.

I'm excusing that at least this one time.

Smiling Antonio told her Don't get mad if I use up all the hot water.

Please don't. I will be highly upset.

I know, that's why you should go first.

I need to call home before my kids go to bed. They had games earlier so I didn't get to talk to them.

Cool. I will leave you some hot water. Tell the kids I said hi and I can't wait to see them again.

Will do.

By the way, I've been meaning to talk to you about that.

What?

Gone ahead and call the kids. We will talk later.

Gabriella called home first spoke with Isabella about her classes and somebody she had been interested in since 3rd grade, a guy named Victor. She went on and on about how cute and well - mannered he was. She asked if she could go out to the movies with him.

You know your Daddy is not going for that, especially without persuasion on my part.

I know, that's why I was going to wait till you get back.

Maybe we can invite him and his family over for dinner one night. Otherwise Alex is definitely not going for it. I can just hear him now throwing a fit.

He might not even agree to the dinner. Daddy can be so crazy at times.

Not crazy, he was a boy once and he's trying to keep you from going through all that he put some poor little girl through.

Well I don't think Victor's like that.

What makes you so sure?

He's nice, he opens doors, carries my books and all. Mommy he even buys my lunch sometimes.

Why would he buy your lunch? You always have plenty money.

I know but he always wants to buy me lunch and he brings me poems, writes letters and…

Wow, does he make good grades is what I want to know.

Straight A student Mommy and he also writes for the school paper. He tutors for the Big Brother, Big Sister program and he's active in church.

Wow, he's quite a character to be so young, but that's great Issy. Your Daddy and Uncles should be cool with him.

If Grandpa like him I think Daddy will too.

Grandpa has met him?

Yes, Victor walked me home today and Grandpa was out front watering the yard. I didn't even have to introduce them. Victor walked up to Grandpa, introduced himself. Grandpa seemed impressed. You will be too Mommy.

Okay well I should be home in a few days. We will set it up for Sunday if you think that will be okay.

Sounds good to me. Okay I have to go finish my chores before Oscar the Grouch gets here.

Who is Oscar the Grouch?

Daddy, ooh Mommy I so wish you would come home. Daddy is so mean when you're not around. He fusses about everything and when we ask to go somewhere the answer is always no or we can only leave for 2-3 hours if that.

Well it is a school night Issy. You know the rules.

Mommy I asked if Fern and I could go to the movies, even take Ahmad along with us to see Cloudy With A Chance Of Meatballs in 3D and he was like No, why can't you watch it at home. Well duh Daddy it is a new movie. So I asked if he or Grandpa or both wanted to come with us. He said he hadn't said whether or not we could go and then said he didn't feel up to it. He hasn't felt up to anything since you've been gone. He misses you Mommy.

Can I talk to Mommy now please Fern begged?

Yes, good night Mommy. I love you Isabella told her.

Good night Issy, love you too baby. Sweet dreams. Don't forget to call me in the morning before school and ask Victor about dinner on Sunday.

Okay I won't. Here Fern, our incredibly beautiful, most amazing Mommy would like to speak with you now.

Hi Mommy, I miss you.

I miss you too baby. How was school today?

Great. I got A's on all my test and my teacher is supposed to send you an email about me tutoring other kids on Tuesdays and Thursdays.

That's great Fern, sure you can do it if you want. How many kids will you tutor?

2-3 a day on Math, Science and Spanish.

Good, that will sharpen your skills. When will this start?

Next month on the 5th.

Okay, how was your game? Issy said you guys did a great job.

We did. The score was 28 to 24 and Mommy everybody played so good. Daddy taped it so you can watch it when you get home. And Mommy I got the MVP award.

Congratulations baby, I'm so proud of you.

Mommy I did everything you told me to do and it worked he squealed. I told them we have to wait till you come back to take pictures. I want you to be in the newspaper with me, okay?

Okay baby Gabriella smiled through tears.

Okay Mommy Grandpa wants to talk now. I have to finish my chores before Robocop gets home.

Robocop Gabriella laughed, what's with all these names? Your sister calls him Oscar the Grouch.

Mommy I know Satin needs you right now but the sooner you get home the better. Trust me. I love you Mommy. Here's Gramps.

Bella

Yes sir, how was your day?

My day was good. How was yours?

Demanding but we finished all the arrangements.

That's good. I know it's a lot of work but somebody's gotta do it. How's Satin holding up?

She's better. Well off and on which is to be expected. Danny got here earlier so between the two of us we try to keep her uplifted.

Yeah things will pan out after a while. She will be alright.

I was thinking about spending some time with her in Phoenix.

Not such a good idea. I don't think Alex can deal with you being away any longer.

I heard stories; Oscar the Grouch and Robocop.

He's taking all of his frustration out on the kids. If you would just talk to him maybe he will calm down.

Papi we talk every day.

Yeah for 5-10 minutes at the most. When's the last time the two of you just...just talk and not argue? Don't think about whatever arguments you were having or intended to have before you left. I know the two of you miss each other, just say it and go from there. No need in making the situation any worse by acting ugly towards each other. It's not good for either one of you, not good for the kids and not good for me. I'm getting too old for this nonsense. I feel like I'm playing referee here at the house sometimes.

Pop did G call Alejandro asked when he came in through the back door.
Yeah son, she's on the phone now. You want to talk to her?
When you finish up, tell her I would like a moment of her time if it's not too much to ask.
Here, I'm finished. Bella, I love you. Good night baby.
I love you too Papi. Good night and I will try, okay? With this phone call I will try. Okay.

Hi baby she said when Alejandro got the phone.
Wassup, how was your day?
Sad, informative and kind of depressing but I'll live. How was yours?
About the same, just got word that Diana and her family was killed he sad sadly.
Oh my God Alex, what happened?
They say a fire but that just don't make sense to me. Everybody in the house burned up.
What started the fire?
Faulty wiring supposedly.
Man, I'm sorry to hear that she said sincerely. When's the funeral going to be?
Saturday.
I should be back by then. Need me to do anything?
I'm going to the funeral. Not on no disrespectful shit but because…
I understand Alex. Believe me, I do. If you need me to do anything just let me know.
After that conversation with Alejandro Gabriella felt emotionally drained. She took a long hot shower, washed her hair and then walked into the kitchen in the dark for a glass of warm milk.
I see you still like walking in the dark Antonio responded as he flipped on the light switch when he entered the kitchen. He glanced at her and asked You alright?
Yeah I'm okay.
What the kids up to?

Issy has her first crush and Fern got MVP in basketball.

What Issy doing crushing? Me and her gone have a long talk.

Come on now, she's at that age.

Yeah whatever, I say wait until she turns 21.

21, are you serious?

As a heart attack. You think differently?

She's a teenager. She's at the age of exploration. You can't shelter a kid at this point. All they will do is rebel and I personally don't want to see the outcome of that.

Yeah I guess you have a valid point. Just hard for me to picture it. I mean what…Antonio paused realizing that he was putting himself in a position he wasn't in. Sorry.

It's okay. I know what you were going to say. I know Alex is going to have a fit. Not to mention Drago and Tyren.

Fern have his picture taken yet?

No, he wants to wait till I get back so I can take it with him.

Cool, make sure you email me the information.

I will.

You going to bed now?

Yeah I'm tired. I will see you in the morning.

Breakfasts on me.

You're a guest.

So are you. Good night Gabi.

Good night Tony. Sweet dreams.

Same to you.

That night Gabriella was in Antonio's dreams just as she'd been since he left Georgia, only this time Gabriella was having the same dream. Somehow he could feel it. The two of them were having dinner at Joy's in Phoenix, afterwards they decided to take a walk. While walking and talking they got caught up in the moment and started kissing.

Gabriella woke up out of her dream when Alejandro popped into her head. She tried calling his cellphone but it just rang and rang. She glanced at the clock on the digital cable box and realized it was after 3 in the morning. She got out of bed to go into the bathroom and ran into Antonio coming out.

My bad he said when he bumped into her. Next thing they knew they heard both Satin and Danny moaning as the headboard banged against the wall.

Damn Antonio laughed, Danny Boy handling his business.

Whatever, sounds like Satin is doing the damn thing Gabriella smirked when Danny kept saying Goddamn baby, ooh shit, fuck, ooh, ooh.

Gabriella went into the bathroom to relieve herself. Once her business was done she tried calling Alejandro again in hopes that the two of them could have phone sex but Alex didn't answer. She left the bedroom once again, blunt in hand she made her way out to the back porch. She fired up and took a seat on the porch swing. Though it was raining she still sat there. When it started thundering and lightening Antonio opened the patio door and said Come on Gabi, let's go to bed.

She looked back at him wondering Is he thinking what I'm thinking?

It's pouring down out here Ma. Come on.

She pulled on the last of the blunt until lightening lit up the sky and thunder roared scaring her a little. Okay, Okay I'm going in.

Antonio had the TV on in the family room watching Tryin' To Sleep In The Bed You Made

Mind if I join you she asked?

Of course not, have a seat. Get comfortable.

She took the seat he had been sitting in without knowing. You comfortable? You need anything he asked?

A blanket, it's a little chilly in here.

That's cause you're wet.

Gabriella bit her bottom lip thinking of how true that comment was.

Get up, go change.

Yes sir, anything else?

Antonio looked at her and turned his head away not wanting her to read his mind. She took that as an insult and walked into the bedroom she was sleeping in. She changed into a long sleeved UCLA t-shirt and a pair of tights. She pulled her hair up into a ponytail and walked back into the living room. Antonio had gotten comfortable in his original spot.

Gabriella looked at him with her hands on her hips. Can I have my seat back please?

Your seat? That was your seat because you sat in it before I could get back to it.

Can I have my seat back?

Nah, I'm comfortable.

Please she asked as she stood right in front of him.

Slowly he stood up and allowed her to have his seat. You need anything he asked?

That blanket I asked for earlier.

Anything else?

Some caramel popcorn would be nice.

He smiled as he turned to go into the kitchen. He popped her popcorn, fixed a glass of water, grabbed some cantaloupe for himself before returning to the dining area. He handed her popcorn and water to her. He sat on the floor in front of the TV and got comfortable. The movie was very interesting. The two of them read the book together a few years ago.

Man that was deep Antonio said as he stood up to stretch. When Gabriella didn't say anything he turned around to look at her. She must have fallen asleep while the credits were rolling. He watched her a minute before picking her up in his arms and carrying her to the bedroom.

Tony she mumbled.

Yeah baby

Thank you.

No problem Ma he said as he lay her head down on the bed. Good night.

Chapter 18

Gabriella returned home the day after the funeral. She took pictures with Fernando, had lunch with Issy and ran a couple of laps with Gordon. By the time she was inside the house she changed a few rooms around, took a hot shower and got started on dinner. She was cutting up sweet potatoes when Alejandro, Deuce and Drago walked through the garage door.

Well damn baby Alejandro said with a smile So nice of you to come home. He picked her up in his arms and kissed her lips slow and passionately. I missed you he said sincerely.

Missed you too babe.

What up Bella Drago asked when her feet were on the floor again. He hugged her close, kissed both her cheeks.

Deuce gave her a big bear hug and asked Can I stay for dinner? My mama ain't cooking.

Alejandro laughed Your mama ain't never cooked.

I know right Deuce laughed. My woman don't cook neither. Only time I get a home cooked meal is when I'm over here. Gabi look I will put in on the groceries, buy pots and pans, whatever you need me to do.

You're cool Deuce as long as you wash your hands first.

Where's the rest of my fam?

Fern is with Ahmad at a debate and Issy went out with Ashley to the mall.

It's getting late Alejandro said as he looked at the clock.

It's barely 7 o'clock Alex. Go take a shower and get cleaned up.

I got something to get into later.

Can't it wait?

For what?

For me, I just got home.

Nobody told you to stay gone so long.

Nobody ever told you stay gone that long either.

You know I'm handling business.

Alright Alex, whatever.

What you mean whatever? You act like you don't know what time it is. Don't start trippen off me. You're the one who left here without talking it over with me first.

I tried calling you before I left.

That's beside the point G. Miss me with that nonsense. You knew me and you was gone have problems as soon as you got back.

Okay Alex

Don't okay Alex me he fussed.

Isabella came in with a few shopping bags talking before entering the room.

Mommy I bought 2 pairs of jeans and 6 shirts with 3 pairs of shoes, one of them boots, all for less than $300

Good Issy, go get cleaned up for dinner baby.

Hi Daddy, hi Uncle Drago and Deuce.

You just hit me up for $500 at the mall yesterday when you bought all that stuff. Where did you get another $300 from?

Mommy she smiled.

$800 in 2 days Issy?

That's cheap. When I go shopping with Auntie we spend a good $1500 in a couple of hours Isabella laughed.

You can't go to the mall with your Auntie anymore unless you're spending her money he laughed too. Go get cleaned up.

Drago and Deuce were now in the family room watching an episode of The Game.

Gabriella was standing at the stove making sure her sweet potatoes didn't stick to the skillet. She was hoping Alejandro had finished with his temper tantrum. He was just about to start back up again when Fernando came in with Gordon.

Hi Daddy Fern said as he hugged Alex.

Hey, how did the debate go?

I think I want to be a part of the debate club now.

That's good son. I think you will be great at it. What do you plan to give up to take that on?

I haven't thought about it yet.

What days are the debates usually held on Gabriella asked?

Tuesdays and Thursdays

Well you're already committed to tutoring on those days baby, at least until schools out.

Yeah so I was thinking about starting up next year and maybe dropping a sport.

It's up to you son, as long as you aren't dropping a class it's all good Alejandro tells him. Go get washed up for dinner.

What's up Pop Alejandro asked as Gordon washed his hands and set the table. We're having company. Drago and Deuce are here.

Anybody else joining us?

No, that's all Gabriella said as she removed the roast from the oven just as her cell phone rang.

Hello she answered. Yes Lawrence this is Gabriella. Okay, everything is fine. I'm glad you called. I wanted to talk to you about investing.

Alejandro cleared his throat. Gabriella ignored him. As everyone came into the kitchen she left out after asking Papi, do you mind fixing plates while I take this phone call?

Go ahead Bella

15 minutes later dinner is out on the table and Gabriella is still on the phone. The rule is that as long as everyone is in the house they all sit down for dinner together. Alejandro told Fern Go tell your mama we're waiting.

Fernando did as he was told. Gabriella told him okay baby. Go ahead and start prayer. I will be there in just a minute.

Okay. Fernando walked back to the table took his seat and said I'll say grace. Alejandro said Hold up a minute as he tossed his napkin on the table and got up. He walked into the office, tapped lightly on the door and said we're ready to eat.

Okay, I'm almost finished.

Come on now, that shit can wait.

Alex

Gabriella

Okay Lawrence, yes email me what you have so far and I will get back with you no later than Friday of next week. Thank you. Always, my pleasure. When she hung up she looked at Alejandro and said That was rude.

Come on let's eat. Everybody's waiting on us.

She placed her cell phone on the desk top and walked out ahead of Alejandro. He smacked her on the ass much harder than what she was used to. Shit Alex. Oh it's like that? A nigga can't touch you now?

Quit trippen, you just hit me hard that's all.

Yeah whatever.

She turned around and said Alex

Let's eat he said as he walked right past her into the kitchen. Fernando, go ahead he said once Gabriella was seated.

Fernando lead them in prayer and everyone got quiet as they ate. The food was too good for words.

After dinner Gabriella sat down to braid Isabella's hair into zigzag cornrows while Fernando and Gordon played a game of Chess. Alejandro, Drago, Deuce and now Tyren who had come by after dinner sat out back talking for a good hour. When Alex came inside he said G, let me holla at you for a minute.

She really didn't want to get up but sensed that it was important. Issy baby get up for a minute, stretch your legs. In fact why don't you go take your shower.

Yes maam

Gabriella followed Alejandro to their bedroom where he closed the door behind her. I'm about to dip out to PA for a few hours. Don't leave town while I'm gone.

Whatever Alex, you act like I just dipped off. It was an emergency and I tried calling you.

Like I said don't leave while I'm gone. I should be back before the kids get up for school.

Gabriella starred at him.

What? What's the problem?

Alex do you really have to go tonight?

G, come on now you ain't new to this. You know how the game goes. As he was talking he changed clothes right before her. She walked over to him and wrapped her arms around him from behind.

What he asked?

I missed you.

Yeah right, gone go finish my daughter hair.

She's in the shower she said with her arms still wrapped around him.

Alright let me get dressed he said brushing her off.

Well damn Alex fuck you too she said as she walked out of the bedroom.

G, come here he called out as he put on his pants. She ignored him. Gabriella bring yo ass back here. Still she ignored him. He finished putting on his clothes and got his cell, money and keys together and called out to Gabriella again. This time when she didn't respond he walked into the family room and leaned over to kiss her when she turned her head away from him.

Oh it's like that he asked. Cool he said as he put a hat on his head. He kissed Isabella's cheek, dapped up Fernando and said alright I'm out. I will be back later.

Daddy what's later? It's already almost midnight Isabella confirmed.

I'll be here when you get up in the morning.

Thought you weren't going out of town.

Who said I was going out of town?

What other reason do you have for staying out all night during the week? Isabella Gabriella said with a gentle squeeze of her shoulders.

Issy never forget that I'm grown. I tell you what I want you to know when I want you to know it and that's that. Like I said I will be here when you wake up in the morning and that's all that matters.

I wasn't trying to be smart Daddy. I just wanted to know.

I'm going out of town for a couple of hours, just around the block. Cool?

Yes

Now get up and give me a hug.

She stood up and hugged him. He kissed her forehead and said Sorry. To Fernando he asked you cool?

Yeah I'm good Daddy.

You and Pops keep an eye on my girls while I'm gone alright?

Yes sir. Check mate.

Alejandro smiled, alright Pops I'm out. Hit me on the hip if you need to. Yo G, you and me gone have it out when I get back.

She paid him no mind as she continued to braid Isabella's hair.

Gabriella had trouble sleeping that night. She dozed off for a good 20-30 minutes but woke right back up. She called Alejandro's cell. His phone rang a good 5 times before his voicemail came on. She hung up and text him. Everything alright? He replied If it wasn't you would be the first to know. Get some sleep.

When it was time to wake the kids up the next morning Gabriella was still wide awake. She was on her way down the hall to the kids' bedrooms when the alarm beeped twice letting her know a door had been opened. Alejandro walked into Fernando's room and said Get up son. Isabella's shower was already going. She had an alarm clock in her room.

Good To Have You Back

Good morning Alejandro said as he walked past Gabriella headed straight for the shower. I brought breakfast he said as he dropped his clothes in a pile at the entrance of the bathroom. Gabriella stood in the doorway of their bedroom watching him while biting her lip until he closed the door.

Gordon asked you need me to make breakfast?

Alex said he brought something.

Where is he?

Taking a shower.

Gordon had a puzzled look on his face before saying you look like you could use some sleep.

I'll settle for a cup of coffee Papi. I have so much to do today.

Like what? Need my help?

Yes if you could take the kids to practice. I will pick them up from school but I need to meet with Lawrence at 4:30. If you could do that and cook dinner I'd greatly appreciate it.

No problem, anything else?

No Papi, thank you. I can handle the rest.

Why don't you join Alex in the shower?

I guess I will.

I will have your coffee ready.

Okay.

Gabriella walked into the bathroom stepped out of her clothes. Alejandro asked What's up as he opened his eyes a little while water ran over his head. Gabriella opened the shower door and got in.

Damn G, thanks for letting the cold air in he said as he opened the door and got out.

She stood there until he grabbed a towel, left out the bathroom closing the door behind him. By the time she showered and dressed the family was seated at the breakfast nook eating their breakfast. Alejandro was laughing at some joke Fernando was telling.

Good morning Mommy Isabella said as she got up to hug her. You look like crap.

Gee thanks Issy.

Mommy why did you keep getting up in the middle of the night Fernando asked.

She couldn't sleep Isabella answered for her.
Alejandro glanced at her briefly before taking a bite of his bacon.

Gordon asked, You want breakfast Bella?
No Papi, I'm fine. Just coffee, thank you.
What time are you leaving Gordon asked?
I'm heading out when I take the kids to school. I'll fix dinner after school.
Everybody cool with enchiladas? There is no more leftovers.
Where you going Alejandro asked?
To the bank and a few other places.
A few other places like where?
To look at a few buildings over on Hightower Blvd.
Oh yeah, what's up over there?
Looking to expand Computer Networks so we need a bigger building.
When did you decide this?
Been thinking about it for a while.
Wow, I guess talking it over with me was unnecessary huh?
You had a lot going on and I figured I could take care of it without bothering you.
Alejandro bit his bottom lip and said I will be joining you this morning.
Okay that's fine.
Gordon watched the two of them out of the corner of his eye. He placed the cup in front of Gabriella along with 2 slices of wheat toast and strawberries.
Thanks Papi
I will take the kids to school. You two get it together.
As soon as the garage closed Alejandro started up about Gabriella handling financial matters without him. He asked her if she was sneaking off to meet with Lawrence.
Why the hell would I sneak off to meet with him? He's my finance lawyer.
Yeah and let me find out there is something else going on.
Alejandro I have nothing to lie to you about.
Good, go get dressed so we can get down to the bank before it gets crowded.
Gabriella rolled her eyes as she finished off what little breakfast she had.
In the Benz on the way to Wachovia Bank Satin called. She was telling Gabriella about all the insurance policies, bank accounts and creditors she would need to get a hold of to notify of her mother's death. All this was too overwhelming for

Satin. Gabriella told her she would handle it. Look Satin I have some errands to run this morning but I'll give you a call between 3 and 4:15 and we will talk. No problem girl, anything I can do to help.

No sooner had that call ended Drago's baby mama Janaye was calling about financial aid paperwork and assistance in her Accounting class. Again Gabriella agreed to help. Adrianna called wanting her hair done and she agreed to that.

Yo did it ever occur to you to leave some time open for family?

Last I checked they are family.

I mean in your own damn house. You making all these plans like you ain't got other responsibilities and shit.

Alex please don't start with me this morning. I'm so not in the mood for bullshit right now she said as she stepped into the bank and was immediately greeted by Raymond Winchester.

Good morning Mrs. Diaz, Mr. Solera

Before Gabriella could correct him just as she always did Alejandro said it's Pennington. Gabriella Pennington, if it changes to anything it will be Solera. Don't get it twisted.

I'm sorry Mr. Winchester said with a smile, She corrects me every time we meet and for some reason I never can seem to grow out of it. Have a seat here in my office. Would the two of you care for anything to drink?

Gabriella replied No thank you as she looked to Alejandro.

I will take a Hennessy straight up if you got it.

Mr. Winchester laughed, I will take a Cognac myself. Unfortunately they don't allow drinking on the job. It's coffee, water, tea or pop.

Nah I'm cool. Let's get down to business.

Mr. Winchester tapped a few keys on his keyboard and said your companies are all doing extremely well. I think the decision to expand is wonderful. I hear you're looking into Jersey, Baltimore and Pennsylvania in the near future. That's great. I have relatives in Pennsylvania that I always order equipment for and take up there to them when I'm going to visit.

Yes a number of customers have inquired about opening a store there. This past year I have received so many letters on expanding and I just feel like it's time we branch out.

Well here's what we've done so far and here's what we're looking to do in the next 6-12 months Mr. Winchester said as he showed them printouts. After 2 ½ hours of slides and discussions of financial matters their banking business was complete. Gabriella had received an email from Lawrence and the business realtor on additional properties ready for viewing.

Where to now Alejandro asked?

I guess we can start in PA first and get it out of the way.

PA, you're kidding right? We ain't going to PA today.

Alex I have business to handle. If you don't want to go I can drop you back off at the house.

You ain't dropping me off nowhere. I'm saying, what's in PA?

A few buildings that I'm looking into.

In PA, right now?

In PA, NJ, MD if we get on the freeway now we'll be back right on time to pick the kids up.

I'm saying though G, why PA?

Why not? There's a lot of potential in the business district. Computers and networking are a necessity. Why not PA or anywhere else? Isn't that why you branched out? To make more money? Well I'm branching out for the same reason.

Next time you have a crucial idea in your head like this one, let's talk it over first. I don't care how busy I am, we should have discussed this.

Alex I agree we should have discussed it but baby you have to agree that PA is great for expansion, especially right now with the property going for little or nothing.

I think it's too far out. Who gone run it? How you gone keep up with everything? You ain't finna be running back and forth to PA, or none of them other places 2-3 times out of a month or even once a month. If that's what you had in your head you can kill that thought right now.

I figured the first 3-6 months I'd have to make frequent trips to make sure things are going the way they should be but once things get under way we're good.

Yeah we definitely should have talked this over G. It ain't happening.

What's not happening?

You going out of town all the time, I'm not with that shit. Straight up.

Alejandro I could see if I was going off bullshitten but this is business. Like you say it's going to keep money in the bank and I'm gone make it happen.

Drop me off at Deuce's. Hit me up when you get back he said as he dialed Deuce's number.

Yo Deuce I'm coming through without my ride. You got me? Already. Alex

G, do you. Obviously what I say don't matter no way.

You know that's not true. I just don't understand your argument.

What, saying it's not a good idea ain't enough?

Hell no that's not enough. Not in this case when I have cold-hard facts that say it's the best idea yet.

Alright G, whatever man. Gone go handle your business he said as he turned Gucci Mane's latest CD up drowning her out and ending the conversation. 20 minutes later he pulls up in front of Deuce's and says Hit me up when you get back. He steps out the car without looking back.

Ugh he's really starting to get on my nerves.

Gabriella liked the 2nd building she viewed in PA, the 5th in Maryland and was undecided in New Jersey. She ended up getting stuck in traffic on the way back and tried calling Alejandro a number of times to have him pick up the kids but he wouldn't answer. She called Gordon and without question he said I will handle everything. You drive safely Bella.

She made it home or back to her city in just enough time to meet with Lawrence to discuss her findings. Alejandro blew her up throughout their entire 2 hour business meeting. Even after she spent 30 minutes telling him what was going on. He argued that she hadn't been home all day and 7 o'clock was fast approaching. He complained that the kids had homework, practice and chores to do. She argued that Issy and Fern knew what needed to be done and when. Gordon was there if they needed help. In the end he hung up in her face which only frustrated them both even more. By the time her meeting with Lawrence was over she was boiling hot and ready to let Alejandro have it.

When she got home she talked with the kids a while before asking Where's your Daddy?

He said he would be back later Fern replied.

Mommy he said it would be tonight though Isabella added and he's not going out of town.

You guys finish your homework?

Yes maam, Daddy and Grandpa checked it. Daddy signed all the paperwork.
What paperwork?
Just PTA, field trip forms, talent show and…
Let me see those papers. Issy go tie your hair up baby.
Mommy, Satin called. She faxed you some information. There are about 32 pages worth of stuff.
Okay Gabriella said as she picked up the phone and dialed Satin's number.
Satin answered out of breath. Hey woman. I hope you don't mind but I faxed everything over to you.
No it's cool. I'm glad you did. I had so much going on. Sorry I didn't get to tell you.
Oh it's fine, Gordon told me. I will call you back in the morning girl. Danny and me trying to go half on a baby.
I ain't mad at you sister. Do the damn thing.
Good night Gabi. I love you.
Love you back Satin.
Adrianna walks in with her friend Samantha. Hey family she said with a big smile. Fernando and Isabella rushed over to her with hugs and kisses.
Hey sissy pooh she said to Gabriella as she hugged her long and hard. You okay?
Yeah I'm alright. How are you?
Better than I was before.
Amen Gabriella said with a smile. Y'all give me a few minutes to get my babies settled and I will be right back. Help yourselves to the kitchen.
What you cook?
Gordon made enchiladas.
Mmm…yum, yum. Adrianna fix me a plate girl.
You better be glad I like you, you cow.
Both Gabriella and Samantha laughed as Gabriella left the room to check on the kids. They were in the family room with Gordon watching House of Payne.
Hi Papi she said as she leaned down to kiss his cheek.
Hey baby, how did it go today?
Long story, we will talk later.
I will get the drinks ready.
Good because I need something strong, not fruity.

Good To Have You Back

Kids I'm about to get started on Auntie's hair. Y'all need to be in the bed by 10.
Yes maam
Bella, did you eat?
No and my stomach sounds like a rumble in the Bronx. I know if I don't get
started on Adrianna now it won't get finished tonight. If I eat it won't get started
at all. It shouldn't take me but an hour and a half.
I will have your plate ready. Can't drink on an empty stomach. In fact I will make
warm tea instead.
Papi
I'm thinking about the future. You know, what you and Alex promised me you
were working on?
Only thing Alex is working on right now is my nerves.
Gordon said Get out of here and go do hair. We will talk later.
45 minutes into braiding Adrianna's hair Alejandro comes in. He stops in the
family room to talk to Gordon and the kids before bypassing Gabriella, Adrianna
and Samantha altogether.
Well damn Big Bro, hello to you too Adrianna yelled out. I didn't sleep with you
last night.
What's up he asked when he walked back into the room kissing Adrianna's
cheek. He asked What up yo simmity Sam?
Hey Alejandro, thanks for looking out for my Mom the other day. We really
appreciate it.
No problem Sam, anything I can do for the fam, I will. He left the den and walked
into the kitchen. He fixed himself a plate and was headed towards the game
room when the doorbell rang. Drago came in said Hello to everyone, offering
hugs and kisses before fixing his own plate and going into the game room. A
good 2 hours later Adrianna & Samantha were gone. The kids and Gordon were
off to bed and Gabriella had just stepped out of the shower. She'd heard the
doorbell ring several times but assumed Alejandro or Drago would get it. When it
continued to ring she threw on her robe tying the strings tight and walked down
the hallway towards the front door. She understood why the guys couldn't hear
anything. The TV was extremely loud. When she answered the door it was
Tyren.
Hey Ty, come on in. Foods still out in the kitchen. The guys are in the game
room.

Good To Have You Back

You alright sis?
Yeah I'm good. How about you she asked as she locked the door.
Superb
Gabriella walked into the game room and asked Y'all mind turning that down? They could see her lips moving but had no idea what she was saying. She walked towards Alejandro, grabbed the remote and lowered the volume. The kids have to get up in the morning.
My bad Alejandro said as he eyed her seductively.
Ty is here.
Alejandro said get your ass back there and put some clothes on. Fuck you doing walking around in your robe anyway?
If you two would have answered the door I wouldn't have had to rush my shower. You knew he was coming. You should have been listening for him.
Man, go put some clothes on.
I'm going to bed anyway. Good night she said as she kissed his lips before he could speak.
Good night lil bro. Are you staying here tonight?
Nah, I'm dippin as soon as the game goes off.
Alright, be careful.
Damn sis Tyren asked You going to bed already?
Yeah I had a long day. Good night guys.
I'm waking yo ass up when I come to bed Alejandro told her.
Good, I need you to.

She assumed Alejandro meant he was waking her up for sex when he made that comment but when he shut the door and flipped on the lights the first thing out of his mouth was Yo G wake the fuck up. You and me got a serious problem we need to discuss.
I was thinking the same thing she said as she removed the comforter from on top of her exposing her naked body.
Hold that thought he said as he removed his clothes. What's up with the buildings?
I saw a lot of good ones today she said as she watched him undress while playing with herself.
And?

And I'm still going over the details. Come here Daddy, can we talk about this later?

Hell nah, we bout to talk about this shit now.

She ignored him as he came to his side of the bed she stood on her knees to kiss him. He allowed the slow tongue kiss but when her hands started to caress his body although his dick stood at attention he held her arms in place.

G, all bullshit aside. I'm serious. Why didn't you discuss this expansion thing with me? We talking millions of dollars which means you done thought this shit out over a period of time and not once did you think to bring it up to me.

Alex you were never home when I started really trying to see how things would work. When we did finally get together we had so many other things going on and you, yourself had a lot of issues so I didn't want you stressing over nothing. You got shit all figured out huh?

Yes and we can discuss it in depth later but right now I need you.

Oh yeah, well that's too bad. You see, I got a lot going through my head right now. Why don't you handle that by yourself like you do everything else, Miss Independent he said as he got in bed pulled the cover over his head and turned his back to her.

Alejandro

Go to bed Gabi, we have to get up early in the morning. Band practice starts at 7 he said as he shut off the night light as if she wasn't butt naked and horny as hell. Gabriella thought it was a joke until Alejandro started snoring lightly a few minutes later. She wanted to strangle him. She hit him with a pillow instead but he was out for the count on the far side of the bed as if he didn't really want to be near her. By the time the alarm clock sounded the next morning the two of them were snuggled in each other's arms. Alejandro's dick was hard as a rock and poking Gabriella's backside. He put himself inside her and woke her up with 2 good strokes that had her body trembling.

Fernando knocked on the room door and said Daddy can you help me?

Yeah son, here I come he said as he pumped hard 3 times and busted a quick nut. He tapped Gabriella's ass before getting out of bed and asking Did I hit it just right that time?

You hurry up and get back in here to finish what you started.

What? I'm through, get up and go get breakfast ready. I got the kids he said as he left the room. Gabriella screamed into the pillows surrounding her before getting out the bed and going to the shower. Just as she stepped out Isabella knocked on the door.

Mommy

Yes baby?

Don't forget Fern and I are going to Angelique's house for a little while after school today. Mrs. Pedro said she would bring us home by 9.

Gabriella opened the door and asked you still have cash on you right?

Yes, Daddy just gave us a hundred bucks.

You guys are dressed early.

Yeah Grandpa is taking Carmen to breakfast and Daddy's taking us to school. He said he was meeting with Mr. and Mrs. Wells to discuss business. She kissed Gabriella's cheek and said I will see you later Mommy.

Fernando came in and rushed her hugging her close. Good day Mommy.

Smiling she hugged them both. You guys have a good day, Mommy loves you.

We love you too Mommy.

Go tell your Daddy he better not leave out that door without speaking with me.

Alejandro was already parked out front with the car running waiting for the kids when Fernando told him what she said. He replied Oh she will be alright.

Gabriella dialed his number and asked What's up?

You plan on coming back any time soon?

Nah, I probably won't be back until 12 or 1.

Well thanks for letting me know.

Why, you need something?

Yes, I need you.

You had me this morning remember he asked with a smirk remembering her moans.

Wow you lasted all of 10 minutes.

It was a quickie, they're supposed to be quick. What you trippen off of?

I'm horny as fuck.

Oh yeah? Why don't you use that thing you got in that brown bag the other day.

My rabbit?

Yeah whatever the hell it's called.

I got that for when you're not here.

Yeah well I've been at home for a minute, so what you really get it for?

I ordered it a while back and because it is so popular it was on back order.

Alejandro's other line beeped. Sherrie popped up on the screen. Say let me hit you back in a little bit he said before answering the other call.
What up Sunshine?
Hey good morning, you busy?
Never too busy for you baby.
Kids at school already?
Yep, just dropped them off.
Will I see you today?
I'm gone try to make it but I can't promise nothing.
Why don't you come stay the weekend with me?
I will see what I can do. Gotta get my kids situated first.
Okay well I'm on my way to work. If I get some free time I will call you later.
You better make time for me. I make time for you.
I got you Boo.
Alejandro hung up with a smirk. Sherrie was the new chick he was messing with. She worked for UPS as a district manager and could move packages the legal way. Plus she would be the least suspected being involved with drugs coming from such a prominent family. She would do any and everything Alejandro asked as long as he made frequent trips to visit her and hit her off with the long john every now and again. She even knew about Gabriella but didn't care as long as the sex was good. He knew he wouldn't have no problems out of her the way he did with Diana approaching Gabriella on some bullshit. He told her about what happened to Diana and Sherrie was scared shitless. When Drago called later that day to say him and Tyren were taking a trip to California to visit some relatives Alejandro figured he would use that as an excuse. He knew Gabriella wouldn't ask Drago if they were together so he was cool. When he got home around 1:45 Gabriella was working out on the weight bench with her I-pod headphones in her ear. He walked up to her removed one and said I'm going to Cali for the weekend, cool?
I guess.
What you mean you guess? Kids are spending the weekend with Angelique and Cesar so you have the house all to yourself. Gordon is going to Florida with Carmen.
Okay she said with a sigh before putting the ear piece back in her ear and continuing her workout. She finished up a good 30 minutes later. Alejandro was

in the bedroom on the phone. When she walked in he said Hey let me hit you back in a little bit. He disconnected the call and asked Gabriella What you cooking today?

I was thinking we could go to Barney's.

The kids are staying all night at the Pedros'.

Well damn thanks for making sure it was okay with me.

I figured you could use some free time to handle all this business you got going. What about their clothes?

I gave them $600 a piece. They're supposed to be going to the mall.

Gabriella walked into the bathroom and turned on the shower. By the time she got out her cell phone was ringing. Alejandro was calling to let her know he had stepped out and would hit her up in a couple of hours. It was Thursday and the kids were out of school for fair day on Friday. Gabriella spent the rest of the day closing out Satin's mom's accounts. Alejandro hadn't made it back or called so Gabriella fixed herself a small salad and watched Desperate Housewives.

It was almost 8 o'clock when Alejandro called to ask her to pack a bag for him to go to Cali because they were about to leave out in a few hours. She didn't argue. She called Gordon to make sure he didn't have plans to leave town over the weekend. Then she called Satin to see if she had plans. By 9pm her flight to Phoenix was booked for an 11pm departure. Alejandro showed up at 9:15 to grab his bag. He kissed Gabriella's cheek and simply said I will call you when we get there.

Alright, be careful Alex. I love you.

Love you too G he said on his way out the door.

Chapter 19

Gordon asked as he put Gabriella's suitcase in the car Does Alex know you're going to Phoenix?

No and I'm starting to think Alex could care less about what I'm doing.

Why do you say that?

His whole attitude towards me has been messed up since I got back.

Well he will get over it.

Yeah I hope so she said without much hope.

So what happened yesterday with the expansion thing?

I've already decided on majority of the properties. Alex seems to think Pennsylvania is not a good idea.

PA, why not? I say business will do great there.

Yeah, me, you and everybody but Alex. When I told him about it his whole attitude changed, as if it wasn't already bad enough.

Well what reasons did he give as to why it's not a good idea?

That's the thing, he didn't have a real reason or at least not one that he cared to share. He just said it's a bad idea and I should listen to him. When I disagreed he decided he wanted to be dropped off at Deuce's house and his attitude towards me is even worse now than it was when I got back from Georgia.

Well going to Phoenix won't do nothing but piss him off even more.

He's just going to be pissed. Supposedly he's going to California with Drago and Tyren. He didn't tell me until today. The kids are spending the entire weekend with the Pedro's'. He even okayed that without so much as a phone call. Then had the nerve to ask me to pack his bag like he didn't walk out of the house this morning as if he lived alone.

I don't know what's gotten into you two but you better get it together quick.

When Gabriella arrived in Phoenix she called Gordon and the kids to let them know she made it. She got settled at Satin's, showered and dressed for a barbecue at Danny's. The crowd was a mixture of races. Everyone was laid back and cool to the point where the night flowed with no error. A lot of the men saw Gabriella alone and tried to hit on her, even the women gave plenty comments. She was so happy when Antonio arrived that she walked over to him as soon as he walked through the back gate. A group of guys were chatting it up with him when he noticed Gabriella.

Gabi he smiled, I didn't know you were in town as he hugged her.

Just got here a couple hours ago. What took you so long to get here?

Had I known you were here I'd have gotten here sooner. I was just laying around the house in one of my antisocial moods.

Well I'm glad you decided to come out of it. Protect me she said as a guy walked up smiling in her direction. He had been asking her questions since she had arrived. When she said she was in a relationship that didn't change his outlook on things.

Hi Norris, this is my fiancé Antonio.

Antonio shook his hand, nice to meet you man.

Norris didn't know what to do or say. Antonio took Gabriella's hand and guided her to a sitting area. He laughed, it's not really that bad is it?

Yes she said as she pulled her seat closer to his to let everyone know or at least make it appear like the two of them were together.

You shouldn't look so damn good.

Gabriella blushed, well hell it's not like I try to. I'm wearing jeans and a t-shirt, no makeup and my hair is in this funky ponytail.

And you still look beautiful. You really shouldn't look so good.

Sometimes I wish I can turn it off, like now she said as an older gentleman walked over and said I see your fiancé has finally arrived.

Yes she smiled, Antonio this is Mr. Gibbs. Mr. Gibbs this is my fiancé Antonio. The two of them shook hands. Mr. Gibbs complimented Gabriella a number of times and even openly continued his flirting. All the while telling Antonio what a lucky man he was to have found such a beautiful woman.

Danny's barbecue ribs were fall off the bone, finger licking good. Gabriella couldn't seem to get enough of them. Satin wasn't much of a cook so originally they planned to get their sides from the super market but Gabriella ended up making potato salad, baked beans, fried cabbage and grilled corn. She even put fish and shrimp on the grill. Surprisingly when the barbecue came to an end everyone stuck around to help straighten up. Alejandro hadn't bothered to answer any of the calls Gabriella made to his phone throughout the day because everywhere he went Sherrie went. She seemed clingy but he would nip that in the bud before it got too out of hand, right now he just wanted to make sure everything was in order. He knew Gabriella would be pissed when he did finally return her call so he tried to think of an excuse.

Meanwhile Drago called Gabriella, they spoke for a good hour in which she talked with other members of Tago's family. Everybody wanted to know when she and the kids would come visit. When Tago was alive he didn't fool with his Mom's side of the family because they were always in his pockets. The only time he would hear from them was when they needed something. Isabella and Fernando knew that side of the family exist but had not had any interaction with them. Drago had always been close with his Mom's side since he lived there prior to moving to New York whereas Tago left California to live with his Uncle Juan when he turned 13 because his Mom spent most of her time running the streets. Gabriella remembered the rare occasions in which she met some of that side of the family, none of them were pleasant. Bad vibes is all she ever got so she wasn't in a big hurry to spend any real time with them. Most had shown up at Tago's funeral to see what they could walk away with. In the years since his death not once has anyone bothered to try and build a relationship with Isabella or Fernando. Gabriella felt the conversation was pointless and Drago sensed that. Once they wrapped that up he started talking about other things.

Drago asked Did you and Alex decide where to post up at in PA? I heard y'all plan to be out there a lot with the expansion and all.

I went to view some property the other day and I pretty much made my decision.

A house or condo?

Huh she asked puzzled.

I'm guessing a condo right since the kids won't really be there.

Drago we're not buying a house or a condo. We're looking for a building for Computer Network. What are you talking about?

Oh he paused for a long time…I thought y'all would chill there sometimes. You know, until business is solid. Quickly he changed the subject. While Gabriella didn't make a fuss over it she did save the conversation to memory to replay later. When she asked Is Alex getting along with everybody Drago's initial response was Huh? Then he said You know Alex, he cooler than a fan. But sis, I'll hit you up tomorrow some time. I'm about to go to this club he said before blowing her a kiss and telling her he loved her. The entire conversation gave Gabriella plenty to think about. She was so deep in thought that she hadn't heard Satin speaking to her.

Gabi, Gordon's on the phone.

Hello, Gabriella said when she answered. No I didn't request anything. Maybe Alex did. You probably have a better chance of reaching him than I do. He's not answering my calls. I've called him at least 5 or 6 times since I've been here. Okay, well call me back to let me know what he says.

Gordon called Alejandro. He heard a woman laughing in the background.

Hey Pops.

Son, did you order from Schwan's?

Yeah, man I forgot all about it. It's like three hundred dollars worth of food, right? Tell Gabi to go ahead and pay for it. Where she at anyway?

Gordon purposely ignored the question. The other line is beeping.

Alejandro realized he hadn't spoken with the kids all day and decided to call Isabella's phone. When Isabella didn't answer he called Fernando.

Daddy its' about time you called.

Why didn't you call me?

I tried but kept getting a busy signal.

My bad son, how was your day?

Good, I got an A on my History test.

That's what's up. Where's Issy? Why she ain't answering her phone?

She dropped it in the rain today. Mommy said she would have to wait until she comes back to get a new one.

Come back from where?

Phoenix.

What's Issy doing in Phoenix?

Not Issy. Mommy is in Phoenix.

Oh yeah, when did she leave?

Early this morning. How's California Daddy? Are we ever going to get to go there?

Yeah son Alejandro said as he stood up from the sofa, grabbed a Black & Mild and stepped out on to the patio. Fernando put Isabella on the phone.

But Daddy, I...

Fern

Okay, okay. Issy, Daddy wants you.

Yes sir Isabella asked when she answered.

What happened to your phone?

I was running to the car after school and dropped it in the rain. It was in a big puddle of water so now it won't work.

So why didn't you go get a new one?

I will, Mommy said I had to wait.

Wait for what? Where is your Mom?

She went to Phoenix this morning she sighed.

Alright let me call you back. Stay by the phone.

Daddy

I will call you back he said before hanging up and dialing Gabriella's number. Of course she wouldn't answer after the times she'd called him. He called Isabella back and said Call your Mama on 3 way.

If you just called and she didn't answer she's not going to answer for me either she lied.

Call Satin's on 3 way.

Isabella did what she was told. When Satin answered she said Hi Satin can I speak with my Mommy please?

Sure Issy is everything okay?

I don't know she answered honestly.

You're not hurt or anything right she asked while walking the phone into the bedroom Gabriella was sleeping in. Gabriella had fallen asleep while reading Section 8 by Kwan. That sister was wore out from the days' events.

Gabi, wake up. Issy's on the phone.

What's going on Gabriella asked when she answered.

Mommy…

Gabriella hang up and call me right back Alejandro said with attitude.

Isabella tried to speak. Alejandro told her to clear the line.

Gabriella called him back after speaking with Isabella and assuring her that she wasn't in trouble. Gabriella hadn't told the kids not to tell Alejandro that she was in Phoenix because she didn't want them lying to them. Isabella was afraid Alejandro would be upset which it was obvious that he was. Gabriella was trying to figure out who gave a shit when she dialed his number.

Yes Alex she said before glancing at the clock and noticing it was after midnight.

Fuck you doing in Phoenix? You ain't told me shit about going nowhere. We had this conversation already.

Alejandro I came to Phoenix because I wanted to. I called you a number of times.

That was after your ass had already left home.

It really doesn't matter seeing as you didn't have too much to say to me anyway. You need to be on the next flight headed home.

Please, my flight leaves here Sunday at noon. I will see you when I get home, if you're there. Anything else you and me need to discuss?

Yo G, I ain't bullshitten with you.

I'm not bullshitten either Alex. Why is it that every time I go somewhere you got something to say but you make plans without letting me know all the time. I'm not going through this with you tonight. Call me in the morning. I love you. Sweet dreams.

Alejandro thought for sure Gabriella had put the phone on mute in an attempt to piss him off and get back at him for not answering the phone. When the recording said *If you would like to make a call please hang up and try your call again* he got aggravated. He tossed his Black & Mild and walked back inside. To Sherrie he said *I gotta go check on my kids. Will you take me to the airport?*

Sure, everything okay? Do you need me to do anything? Check flights or something?

Yeah check flights to Phoenix. I need to be on the first one out.

Okay calm down.

Sherrie booked a flight for him while he showered and changed clothes. Alejandro called Gordon to get Satin's address. When Gordon didn't answer he had Sprint track her down using Family Locator. He put the address in the navigational system of his phone while on the plane. By 7 o'clock the next morning he was knocking on Satin's door even more pissed off than he was before. Satin answered the door dressed for the day in a tank top and shorts. *Hey Alejandro, come on in. Gabi is still in bed. You can come back here* she said as she showed him to the room. *I didn't make breakfast because I knew she wouldn't be up no time soon and I'm on my way out the door. If you want something help yourself.*

Thanks he said as he opened the bedroom door then closed it behind him. He heard the garage rising as Satin pulled out.

G, get yo muthafuckin ass up. Let's go.

Gabriella thought she was dreaming so she continued to sleep wondering why Alejandro suddenly popped into her head. He snatched the covers when she didn't move and then started to grab a pillow when Gabriella asked What the hell? Her eyes adjusted to Alejandro and her surroundings. Still she didn't get up. Instead she lay on her side facing him and asked What?

Let's go.

Alex it's too early in the morning to be playing. Her cell phone started to ring. Fernando was calling because he hadn't been able to reach Alejandro and needed to talk to him.

Everything okay Fern she asked sitting up in bed.

Yes Mommy, its' just guy stuff. Nothing serious.

She smiled, okay well here's Daddy.

Wassup son Alex asked as Gabriella got up from bed in a sleeveless short pajama dress with her breast and ass all poked out. She stood beside him and stretched. Alejandro put an arm around one of her legs and pulled her center to face him. He rubbed his face between her thighs causing her to bite her lip and smile. He held on to her ass cheeks while he kept at it. Fernando was telling a story. Alejandro would say unh huh or laugh occasionally. Gabriella was hoping they would make the conversation short so Alejandro could handle her. Mr. Pedro got on the phone and the conversation became lengthy. He was no longer into what he was doing. Gabriella starred at him longingly. When she went to kiss his lips he stood up and walked out of the bedroom. She freshened up and found him in the kitchen cooking breakfast.

Where is Satin she asked?

She left a few minutes ago, have a seat. He put a plate of bacon, omelletes and toast in front of her along with a glass of Simply Made Orange Juice. She took a seat, waited for him to fix his plate before they joined hands in prayer.

Why you up and leave like…

Alex please can we not have this conversation. It's barely 8am neither of us have to go to work. The kids aren't here. I'm horny as fuck and the last thing I want to do is argue.

I ain't trying to argue with you G. Just answer the goddamn question. If you so damn horny what the fuck is coming to Phoenix going to solve?

She looked at him and rolled her eyes. I came to help Satin sort through some things and make sure she's alright. I couldn't get sex at home before you left town and obviously I'm not going to get it this morning now that you're here. Use your little friend that you got in the mail. Ain't that what you got it for he asked with a smirk.

Yeah she said as she tossed a napkin onto the table. She decided against having breakfast and opted to go for a run instead, something she hadn't done in a while. When she got back Alejandro was asleep on the couch in the den. She grabbed her rabbit and dildo before making her way into the bathroom. She locked the door and intended to get her rocks off and be done with it. Even the quick orgasm she had wasn't nowhere near satisfying. When she turned off the shower she could hear Alejandro yelling for her to open the door. She wrapped a towel around her body, grabbed her toys and opened the door.

Fuck you locking doors around this muthafucka for?

Alex you should have stayed wherever you were with that attitude she said as she walked over to the bed and took a seat laying her toys beside her.

Did they work Alejandro asked?

Fuck you she told him.

He walked over to her grabbed her legs as she put lotion on and got in between them. He was kissing all over her getting her hot and ready again until the chirp on his cell went off. Deuce was calling to find out where he was. They had both been in PA. Alejandro left in a rush he never thought to tell Deuce.

Yo I'm in Phoenix.

What's in Phoenix?

G done brought her ass down here. Why, what's up?

You coming back this way any time soon?

Nah I gotta deal with G. You straight though right?

Yeah I'm good. Hit me up later.

By now Gabriella's starring Alejandro upside the head. Last night's conversation and the one Alejandro was currently having with Deuce further letting her know Alejandro hadn't been where he said he'd been.

What he asked of the look on her face.

Nothing she said as she pushed him away from her and got up. She grabbed her bra and panties put them on with her back to him. The fact that he watched her and didn't move only made matters worse. Any other time Alejandro would be all over her but lately he hadn't been. There is no way he would still be mad about her going to Georgia when Satin's mom died because Alejandro has never been that inconsiderate. All these things were going through her head as she put on a fitted top and short striped shorts. She slid her feet into a pair of flip flops then went inside the bathroom to pull her hair up into a ponytail. When she came out of the bathroom Alejandro was going through her phone.

Yo G, who is Danny?

Satin's boyfriend.

What he doing calling you?

Satin called from his phone. Get up she said as she straightened the bed. Her cell phone vibrated. Alejandro answered. Yeah what's up? Oh she's busy right now but I will take a message. Oh yeah, she's going to be disappointed but I will let her know. Yeah no problem.

Who was that?

Lawrence, he said the building you wanted in PA sold this morning Alejandro said with a slight smile that didn't go unnoticed by Gabriella.

Inside her head she's thinking What the fuck is going on in PA that he don't want me to find out about? After he couldn't get her to leave he returned to Pennsylvania and went straight to the club upon his arrival. Some dudes started fighting and he ended up getting shot in the leg. When Sherrie found out she rushed to the hospital. The emergency room attendant gave her his status. Upon entry of the room a nurse passed her his personal property because she said she was his girlfriend and completed the financial obligation forms. Alejandro was heavily sedated. When his phone started vibrating Sherrie had no idea what to do. When she realized it was Deuce she tried to answer but he'd already hung up by then. Gabriella was the next person to call.

In a panic Sherrie told Gabriella what happened when the nurses rushed into the room because his heart rate was getting lower and lower. Gabriella told Sherrie to let the doctor know that Alejandro had a heart murmur and the rate of his heart beats are always irregular. Meanwhile she booked a flight to PA after getting the hospital information from Sherrie. She tried calling Deuce but got no answer. His voicemail was full due to his battery having no charge. When Gabriella finally arrived the doctor wanted to speak to Alejandro's girlfriend in regards to his condition. Sherrie stepped up and said I'm his girlfriend but his sister Gabi can give you more information than I can about his medical history.

Gabriella almost lost her balance, not to mention her voice.

Ms. Solera your brother has a heart murmur? Was he born with it?

Yes she sighed as she looked over at him with tears in her eyes.

What's his blood type?

AB negative

Do you have the same blood type?

Yes she said because this was something they realized a while back when he needed blood.

Would you be willing to donate blood?

Yes

You're not pregnant are you?

No she said as she wiped at her tears.

He's going to be okay Dr. Branheart assured her. If you will come with me we can go ahead and get started. He was shot several places in the lower half of his body. Once in the calf of his right leg, twice in both thighs, with a small hand gun. I was able to remove the bullets but he lost quite a bit of blood. We were also able to stabilize his heart rate.

Dr. Branheart had the nurse draw blood from Gabriella. As they were on their way back to Alejandro's room Deuce and some chick came around the corner. When he saw Gabriella he asked Everything okay? Bro still alive right?

Yes she said as she kept walking, For now.

Both Dr. Branheart, Deuce, the chick that was with him and the nurses wondered what that meant.

When Sherrie came out of his room and met them in the hallway waving frantically she said I think he wants you Gabi. When I told him you were here he started mumbling something but I can't understand with the tube in his mouth. He had tears in his eyes and...

Deuce knew what Gabriella meant now, although no one else had a clue. He was trying to figure out how Gabriella knew what happened when the doctor, nurses and Gabi went into his room.

When Alejandro saw Gabriella he could read her facial expression and the tears fell harder and faster. In the hall Deuce asked Sherrie How did Gabi find out what happened?

She called and I told her.

You shouldn't have answered his phone.

What? It's his sister for crying out loud. It's a good thing she came because she was able to give blood and tell the doctor about a heart murmur that I didn't know anything about.

Deuce kept shaking his head as he fell into the closest seat. His cell rang just as Alejandro's cell rang at the same time. Drago was on Deuce's phone and Gordon was on Alejandro's. The owner of the club in which Alejandro had been shot was good friends with Gordon and recognized Alejandro from pictures in the house. He called Gordon when Alejandro was taken to the emergency room by ambulance because no one knew how serious it was. Gordon assured him that Alejandro was in California but started to worry when Alejandro hadn't answered the phone for him or the kids. He didn't want to worry Gabriella so he called Drago. Drago admitted that Alejandro was never in California with them. When Gordon asked Drago what Alejandro was doing in Pennsylvania he couldn't lie to him. Gordon was like a father to him, he couldn't tell him a lie. By the time Gabriella called Gordon to tell him what was going on she was already on a flight to Pennsylvania. When the kids couldn't get a hold to Gabriella or Alejandro they called Adrianna who in turn called Gordon. She knew something had to be wrong because they never ignored phone calls from the kids. They could always get a hold to at least one of the three and that one person could tell you where everyone was. Even when Gordon tried to keep the information to himself to keep everyone from getting all worked up she sensed something was wrong. When she called Deuce he was cussing somebody out about Alejandro's phone. Satin had already told her that Gabriella was on her way to PA because Alex had gotten shot. Adrianna kept asking if Alejandro got shot. Deuce kept denying it. Finally she asked Can I speak to Gabi please? I know she's there and Alex has so fucked up this time.

Gabriella walked out into the hall and asked Sherrie for Alejandro's things. Sherrie gave her a wallet, rolls of money, his cell phone and 2 Desert Eagles in which she had been too afraid to touch. She had them wrapped up in his coat. Neither of them were on safety. Gabriella shook her head in disgust. Deuce couldn't think of anything to say. He knew she was pissed. Adrianna was now yelling in his ear until finally he said Gabi, Adrianna wants you.

Hey what's up Adrianna asked as soon as Gabriella came on the line. Is he alright?

Yes, just lost a lot of blood. They removed the bullet and he will be okay. How are you?

Ooh you just don't know how fucking bad I want to shoot him myself right now she says before walking off with Sherrie and the other chick thinking *Damn,* while Deuce put his head down feeling some of the drama that was already about to pop off. Gabriella didn't go into details about Sherrie. Instead she just said that Alex lied about being in California. Prior to hearing about Alejandro getting shot Adrianna found out he was in PA. She warned him that his lies would catch up with him. She knew by the sound of Gabriella's voice that there was way more to what she was saying and the situation wouldn't go over as lightly as it had with Diana, not that it was taken lightly at the time.

If you need anything sis you call me. I'm about to go to the house with the kids. Don't tell Mom what's going on.

She already knows, she called me. Carmen and Gordon were together when Chaz called so of course she called Mom and…don't tell the kids Alex was shot. I told them we were together out of town. I know I will have to explain in detail later but I don't want it to be right now.

Mrs. Solera, Dr. Branheart said as he walked up. *Can I talk to you for a minute in my office please?*

Sure. Adrianna, I will call you back here in a little bit.

Dr. Branheart said I apologize for what happened here. I didn't know until Alejandro informed me just now that you're not really his sister. Sherrie Seartwz filled out the financial forms and listed herself as the girlfriend so that is why his property was handed to her.

Oh no, I understand Dr. Branheart. Don't worry there won't be any lawsuits filed against the hospital. I mean there is no way you guys would have known had I not shown up. I clearly understand.

We will have him all fixed up. I recommend that he sees his own physician as soon as he gets back to New York. Here are prescriptions for pain and swelling and also to keep his heart rate stabilized. It is very important that he speaks with his physician about the heart murmur. There are treatments available that will work if used correctly. Sherrie has taken care of the medical expenses and if you will just sign these release forms you folks can go ahead and get out of here. He will need to stay off his feet for a good 2-3 weeks. No strenuous activity until he gets released from his doctor.

Gabriella hadn't really heard much of what he said but she had heard it all before. Tago had been shot and so had she. She knew the procedures all too well. She stood up and walked into the hallway. Alejandro was ready in a wheelchair with a look on his face that said he had no idea how things would turn out but he knew he'd fucked up royally.

Sherrie said to Gabi still totally clueless as to what was going on, If you like you can come stay at my place for the night. I have an extra bedroom and I will check flights for tomorrow.

Sherrie she said with a forced smile Thanks but no thanks. You've been a great deal of help but we're leaving tonight. I'm sure Alex will call you when he feels up to it. Deuce, did Alex drive here?

Yeah the car is parked outside. You ready to go?

Yes, please.

Deuce stood up and put his arm around Gabriella's shoulder. She quickly shrugged him off. She followed him, the nurse pushing Alejandro and the chick that came with Deuce out to the parking lot. Deuce pulled the car up to the curb and assisted the nurse with getting Alejandro in the car. Gabriella let him sit in the front seat so he could lounge back while Deuce took the wheel.

Do you want the music on Deuce asked?

Doesn't matter she said as she responded to Antonio's text asking if she was alright.

My heart hurts she replied. He asked, What's going on? Alejandro's okay right? She replied He was shot but he will live. Antonio asked Well okay what's the problem? She replied His girlfriend lives in PA. She was here at the hospital with him. She's the one I spoke to on the phone. She thinks I'm Alex's sister. Obviously that's what he told her because she knows my name. This explains why he doesn't want me to set up CN here. His ass was never in California as I suspected all along. Antonio replied Can you talk? Call me. She replied In the car on our way back home. Will call you when I get settled. He replied Call me no matter what time. She responded Okay.

She didn't want to make any stops, especially if unnecessary so Deuce only stopped for gas once. When they arrived in New York Gabriella had Deuce drive to his house and from there she took over the wheel. She stopped off at a pharmacy to have his prescriptions filled. Uncle Juan picked up the kids and would make sure they got to school okay for the next week or so. When she pulled up Gordon and Alejandro's brother Mateo were there to help him into the house. Alejandro was asleep until they lifted him up.

Hey, hey I can walk. Where's Gabi?

She's in the house getting everything ready Mateo responded.

Everything like what? What is there to do?

Man, just come inside. It's cold out here.

Gordon asked Gabriella Need me to fix you something to eat?

No, I'm about to step out for a minute. Alex has already eaten and I gave him his medicine. He will probably sleep for a while. I will only be gone a couple of hours.

Where are you going?

Somewhere to have a drink or two or four, grab a bite to eat and just think.

You can do all that here. I will fix your drinks and something to eat. We can talk.

Papi I don't want to talk right now.

Gabriella

Papi please.

Alright, alright don't drink too much. 2 drinks is the max and if you need to you call me.

Papi I'm okay, really. Hurt, but okay.

Gordon pulled her into his arms. Hugged her close for a long time. Mateo asked Gabriella can I talk to you for a minute?

Mateo if Alejandro sent you in here to tell me anything you're wasting your time. I just want to…

Mateo not now. I promise you there ain't no conversation that I am in the mood to have.

Alright. Well where are you going?

She bit her lip, took a deep breath, sighed and said Nowhere as she sat her purse on the bar. She fixed a tall glass with Hennessy, no ice, no coke before walking into the kitchen. Gordon made burritos for dinner. She took a plate out to warm two in the microwave. She walked into the bedroom to grab her weed stash.

G, Alejandro called out to her.

What?

Come here for a minute.

Alex what do you want?

Come lay next to me. I want to talk to you.
We don't have anything to talk about.
I got some things I want to say to you.
A bunch of shit I don't want to hear I'm sure. Get some sleep Alex she said walking out of the room.
G come here baby he called out to her. When she didn't come back he attempted to get up but the pain was too much. He fell back down on the bed. Mateo came into the room.
Yo Mat tell my wife I said to come here.
You really know how to fuck shit up don't you?
Alejandro lay his head back on the bed starring up at the ceiling. He lay there a minute in silence.
Yo bro pass me the phone.
Who you calling?
Just give me the phone please.
Mateo passed him the phone and before Alejandro finished dialing the number he wanted to call he told Mateo I'm going to need some privacy. Pull the door close on your way out. When the phone started ringing in his ear he said through tears I fucked up. I need your help.
I'm on my way.
You gone help me fix this?
What is there that you need to fix?
I lied to Gabi about being in California.
That's small time. She will get over that.
Yeah but this chick…
Say it ain't so.
This chick I'm messing around with was up at the hospital when Gabi got there. I told her Gabi was my sister. When Gabi called she told Gabi what was going on and…
Alejandro Solera
I know Ma but I gotta fix this real quick.
Where are the kids?
With Uncle Juan for a couple of weeks.
Whose idea was that?
Gabi's I guess. She called Uncle Juan from the hospital.

Not good.

I know Mom, that's why I need your help. I need you to come do damage control before I lose my family.

Losing your family is the least of your worries. Gabi wouldn't keep the kids away from you.

I'm worried about everything Ma. You know I love Gabriella.

Well why do you keep doing the stupid shit you do?

Ma

Don't Ma me, saying and doing is two different things son. You know that. If you love her so much what logical explanation can you give for the second time around?

It's business Ma.

Alejandro if you really love Gabriella your business would not involve other women that you're sexually active with. And even if it did you would leave her alone until you get to where these other women don't interfere with your relationship with her.

Mom are you coming or what?

Yes son, I'm pulling up out front now.

Thank you.

Alejandro I can't make no promises baby.

Ma just help me do whatever it takes.

Mrs. Lucia rang the doorbell and Gordon answered, the look Gordon gave her let her know there was no damage control that could be done, at least not tonight anyway. Where is she Lucia asked?

In the kitchen, drinking and eating. She doesn't want to talk AT ALL. Mateo's here.

Okay she said as she removed her jacket. Where's Alex?

In his bedroom.

Mrs. Lucia walked to the bedroom to visit Alejandro. She examined the bruise, knew he was in pain for various reasons. She bit her lip and looked at him. She gave him a long hug. Get some rest son.

You staying the night?

Yes, if it's alright with Gabi.

Lucia walked into the kitchen. Gabriella was no longer there but outside on the patio smoking a blunt. When Lucia stepped outside Gabriella was about to put out her blunt.

Lucia told her Go ahead baby, don't pay me no mind. She took a seat beside her on the porch swing, kissed her cheek before wrapping an arm around her. Gabriella laid her head on Lucia's shoulder and cried. Not just little tears but the kind of crying that makes your body shake. The kind that comes from deep within. Lucia hugged her harder and kissed the top of her head. They sat like that for a good 45 minutes. Eventually Gabriella stopped crying but the pain in her heart was still there.

Mind if I stay the night Lucia asked?

Not at all, you're always welcome here. Besides with you and Papi here I'd be less inclined to shoot him.

Lucia didn't comment, she knew what heartache felt like under the same circumstances. She'd stayed with Alejandro's father even after she'd caught him cheating a number of times. At his funeral he had Lucia who was his wife at the time of his death and at least 30 other women he saw on a regular basis. All in which felt like they were entitled to a piece of what her husband had when he died. She knew the pain all too well.

She knew that Gabriella had been thinking about the effect leaving Alejandro would have on the kids the first time around. With their father gone Alejandro had become Daddy. He loved Isabella and Fernando as if they were a part of him just as any father would. They loved him just the same. Gabriella didn't want to mess that up so she worked things out with Alejandro for that reason and the fact that she was still in love with him. Lucia didn't doubt that she was still in love with him now but she also knew that Alejandro had gone too far this time. When they entered the house Gabriella showed Lucia to her room, made sure she was comfortable before going to bed. She walked into the bedroom to find Alejandro still awake waiting to talk.

What are you still doing up she asked as she checked his legs to make sure he wasn't bleeding through the bandages.

I can't sleep. Gabi, we need to talk.

Okay she said as she got up to close the bedroom door. So, talk. While she gathered the items to change his bandages Alejandro watched her. You better start talking now because when I get these bandages done I don't want to hear nothing else. So go ahead, entertain me she said sarcastically.

With those words, the tone of her voice and the look on her face Alejandro had no explanation for what he'd done again. No words he could say would take away her pain. He realized that as she changed his bandages so he remained silent. It took her ten minutes to clean the wound, disinfect it and change the bandages. Once done she placed both of his legs back on to the bed, covered him up before rearranging the pillows so that he'd be comfortable.

Can I get you anything?

A bottle water and some more pain medicine please.

Alright she said as she left the room. She came back a few minutes later with the bottled water and 2 vicodins. She opened the water bottle for him, placed the pills into his hand and stood there as he took the medication. She sat the water bottle down on the nightstand, walked over to her drawers and pulled out her night clothes. When she started out of the room again Alejandro asked where you going? You plan on going to sleep tonight?

Yeah in a little bit. Good night she said as she left the bedroom they shared and went down to the 3rd floor of the house into what used to be Tago's home away from home. It's where he went in order to get away from the world. It held everything a one bedroom apartment would with plenty of space. Gabriella had recently cleaned it out after all those years, put fresh paint on the walls, new furniture, new linen all throughout the space. Nobody understood why. Even she had no clue at the time but upon entering it she knew she'd be spending a lot of time there now.

Gordon was in the kitchen fixing breakfast while Lucia, Mateo and Alejandro sat in the kitchen either reading the morning paper, conversing or starring into outer space.

Alex where did Gabi say she was going Mrs. Lucia asked?

She didn't say. She didn't even come to bed last night he said sadly.

Well she didn't leave in any of the cars because they're all parked in the garage Mateo replied.

Maybe Adrianna picked her up Mrs. Lucia said as she rubbed Alejandro's hand and watched the smile that was usually on his face replaced with a deep frown. Adrianna said she ain't with her. Adrianna's on her way Mateo confirmed.

Alejandro's frown deepened. Gabriella walked into the kitchen. None of the alarms had sounded which means she was already in the house.

Good morning she said while walking over to the refrigerator. She grabbed a carton of orange juice from there and a glass from the cabinet before making her way out of the kitchen.

Gabi baby, you don't want anything to eat Lucia asked?

No, she said as she kept walking.

Gabriella, Gordon called out as he held a plate in his hand, when she turned around he held it out with a look on his face that said Don't argue with me. She walked back over to him took the plate and kissed his cheek. If anybody needs me I'm downstairs. Just call my cellphone.

G, Alejandro said as he looked at her Can we talk?

When I feel like it we will, but it won't be any time soon.

Chapter 20

Adrianna and Gabriella sat inside Bennihana's eating and talking. What are you and the kids doing tonight?

They're having movie night in the home theater. Alejandro had me pick up tons of junk food today. They're supposed to invite some friends over.

BK wants to go out to Kingz tonight. You want to come?

I would, except Gordon's out of town and your Mother is going out on a date.

Yeah I heard. Alex should be okay there with the kids.

Girl I could just hear Isabella now if Alex happens to leak through even a little bit. She will freak out.

He still bleeding, that should have stopped by now.

Alejandro thinks he's He-man or some damn body. He's always up walking around, trying to play football, basketball and everything else. He won't be satisfied until his ass can't move at all.

Y'all still sleeping in separate bedrooms?

Yes

Why?

He better be glad we're still in the same house. Half the time I can't stand the sight of him.

And the other half?

I deal with him because I have to, because of the kids.

You still love him?

Of course I do.

Well why not repair this?

I wish it was that easy Adrianna. I don't want to keep going through the same old shit with him. When he really wants to be with me maybe we can be together but while he's still doing "business" I think it's best that the two of us be apart.

And you've told him this?

No, Alejandro and I haven't talked about what happened. If it wasn't for the kids, your Mom and Gordon we probably wouldn't talk at all.

You know he's not going to be cool with this right? I know not being able to communicate with you is killing him inside.

I'm going to have a talk with him soon, maybe today, maybe tomorrow, maybe next month. Hell who knows?

Adrianna looked at her with sad puppy dog eyes I really hate what Alex did to you and I don't want to lose you.

I'm not going anywhere Adrianna.

What if while the two of you are apart you meet someone else?

And? It's not like I'm going to run off and get married. Issy and Fern aren't going to let that happen. Issy's already upset with me because we don't sleep in the same bed.

Yeah they're still talking about having a brother or sister.

Well that's obviously not going to happen Gabriella said with a sigh just before her text message alert went off. A text from Antonio says Satin's in the hospital. Car accident. Serious. Phoenix Regional ICU

What's going on Adrianna asked?

Gabriella dialed Antonio, What happened?

She and Danny were on the freeway when a diesel driver ran them off the road. He fell asleep at the wheel and Danny lost control of the car.

Okay I'm…I will be there in…

Go home and get the kids settled. I'll book your flight.

Okay.

Satin was in a car accident. She's in ICU. Do you mind…

No, come on let's go. BK and I could use some family time. What better way for he and Alex to bond than to have movie night with the kids.

Thanks girl. I know you wanted to go to Kingz.

I'm cool.

Gabriella explained to the kids what was going on while Alejandro took a shower. When he came out drying himself off he saw Gabi sitting on the bed, he smiled. She starred, he walked over took a seat beside her. He kissed her cheek and asked Why you all frowned up G?

Satin's been in an accident. She's in ICU at Phoenix Regional she said hoping an argument wouldn't follow.

Okay, what time you leaving? What happened?

She and Danny were on the freeway when the driver of an eighteen wheeler fell asleep at the wheel and ran them off the road.

Antonio picked Gabriella up from the airport. He held her in his arms for a minute before they made their way to the hospital. The doctor said that both Satin and Danny would be okay and the baby is fine.

Baby Gabriella asked?

Yes, she's due in exactly 4 months.

Wow Gabriella said as she looked at Antonio. Did you know about this?

Of course not, if you didn't know I didn't know.

The doctor advised that they both would have to spend a few days in the hospital. Antonio and Gabriella alternated between Satin and Danny's rooms. After 3 days the doctor finally convinced them to go home and get some rest. Both Danny and Satin were aware that they had been there the whole time.

Where's the closest hotel?

Hotel, you aren't staying in no hotel.

Antonio

Gabi you know I'm not about to argue with you. I'm tired, all I want to do is get some sleep please he pouted.

Okay, okay but can we get something to eat first? I will even drive.

Antonio passed Gabriella the keys to his Dodge Ram and opened the driver side door for her before going around to the passenger side.

They picked up food to go from Wok & Grill, Pepper steak and combination fried rice, chicken wings and egg rolls. At Antonio's 3 bedroom condo they got comfortable watching Wanda Sykes I'ma Be Me. Gabriella laughed so much that she cried.

You okay Antonio asked as he watched her closely.

No she finally admitted. Without waiting for an explanation Antonio took the seat on the floor beside her, pulled her head onto his shoulder then wrapped his arms around her. She tried to make it as if what was going on between her and Alejandro wasn't really bothering her. Antonio knew it had to be. He held her until the tears stopped. He stood, stretched, removed the containers of food from his living room and took them into the kitchen. From there he went down the hall to the guest room, made sure everything was in order before running her a tub full of bath water. He lit scented candles, dropped some peppermint scented bath bubbles into the water and turned on the music. Conya Doss' Heaven flowed from the speakers. When he walked back out into the living room Gabriella was sitting in the same spot.

He held his hand out to her, she took it. When he pulled her up he said I ran your bath water. Why don't you just go relax.

You coming with me?

He looked at her to see if she was serious. Though the look on her face said she was he assumed it was only because she was emotional. Although he wanted nothing more than to make love to her he had no intention of taking advantage of her vulnerability.

Come on Gabi, quit trippen. You got a lot going on in your head right now he said as he hugged her close and kissed her forehead.

Antonio this has nothing to do with what's going on with Alex.

Yeah okay, well go ahead and take your bath, relax. It might help clear your head.

Gabriella looked at him, rolled her eyes as she walked off but not before grabbing her suitcase and wheeling it into the guest bedroom where she slammed the door behind her.

Hey goddammit Antonio yelled out Don't make me come in there.

She opened and shut the door, slamming it several times to let him know just how annoyed she really was.

What is your problem he asked upon entering the room?

You really want to know?

Yeah, please tell me. Last I checked I was the only one paying bills around this piece so that means I'm the only one allowed to slam doors. Don't do that shit again.

What are you going to do, put me out?

Nah, you know I would never do that. What's the problem?

Never mind she said as she turned her back to him. Sorry for slamming your door, it won't happen again.

It bet not he smiled before leaving the room not bothering to close the door.

She stood there a minute before pulling a Victoria's Secret Pink pajama set from her suitcase, her rabbit, a pink dildo she'd recently purchased when the old ones weren't doing the trick. She really couldn't remember the last time she'd had sex but she knew it had been months. She was beyond horny and her body was dying to be touched and caressed in a sexual way. Antonio thought her tears were for Alejandro. In a way they were because he'd cheated and while he was doing his thing he was too preoccupied with his newest "girlfriend" that he hadn't been attending to Gabriella's needs like he used to. Before he got busted she thought maybe she'd done something wrong, now she knew better. And to think he'd been holding out on her all this time for a ditzy white chick was bullshit. She saw and smelled all that Antonio had created for her in the bathroom and smiled. She decided that she could relax and maybe, just maybe tonight would be the night in which her rabbit and her dildo helped satisfy her sexual appetite. She bathed and tried to bring herself to the point of extreme satisfaction. It just wasn't happening. She was in need of the real thing. Fuck she said aloud before tossing both the rabbit and the dildo out of the bathtub.

You okay in here Antonio asked without looking inside the bathroom. By now she'd been in the bathtub for a little more than 45 minutes. Antonio had trimmed his beard, cut his hair and showered.

Gabriella stood up, grabbed a dry off towel after letting the water out of the bath tub.

Gabi

What?

Talk to me. Keeping everything in is not helping the situation. It's natural to be hurt in a situation like this.

Okay Tony, yes I'm hurt by what Alejandro did. I never denied that.

A whole month later and you bust out crying in the middle of a damn comedy show. What the fuck is up with that? Don't you think that means you haven't addressed something Antonio asked now posted up outside the door with his back on the wall.

Gabriella walked out of the bathroom after applying baby oil gel to her body and putting on her pajamas. Antonio watched her and asked Okay.

Okay what?

What's going on with you?

It's not what you think.

Well what is it he asked as he walked into the bathroom to turn off the music.

I was going to do that Gabriella said as she quickly walked in behind him trying to get to her toys before he saw them.

What the hell is this Antonio asked when he stepped on the rabbit and it started up. He picked it up from the floor. Gabriella quickly snatched it along with the pink dildo and rushed out of the bathroom embarrassed. Antonio bit his bottom

lip. He'd heard her when she said Fuck and wondered what she'd thrown across the floor. Initially he'd assumed it was the shower gel or body wash.
When he walked out of the bathroom Gabriella had her back to him as she unfolded the clothes she planned to wear the following day. Antonio walked into the bedroom and right out of the room. A part of him wanted to do the right thing which was to ignore the feelings he had, the rabbit, the dildo and all things. But the side of him that wanted Gabriella the most wanted to take her into his arms.
Walking out of the bedroom he went into the kitchen, fixed himself a glass of champagne and fixed one for Gabriella. He walked back into the guest bedroom, passed her the flute and took a seat on the bed.
Gabi
What?
It's nothing wrong with having toys Ma.
You got any?
He held up both palms of his hands and smirked. Gabriella smiled as she sat the suitcase on the floor. She plugged her cell phone into the charger and tried calling the house phone and the kids' cell phones but nobody answered. She turned her phone to vibrate then grabbed the remote to flip through the channels until she came across Real Housewives of Atlanta. She posted her back up against the headboard and got comfortable. Antonio dropped his slippers to the floor, got comfortable in the bed then decided to get up to get something to snack on. He came back with fruit; strawberries, pineapples, peaches and whipped cream. He sat the bowl of fruit in the center of the bed, brought more wine into the room. The show was getting started and even Antonio was interested. After the Real Housewives of Atlanta they ended up watching Good Times. They fell asleep in bed together wrapped up in each other's arms.
Gabriella's cell phone was buzzing. Issy was calling.
Mommy
Yes baby she answered groggily.
How's Satin?
She's still in the hospital but she's doing better. How is everything going at home?
Fern has been an angel Mommy. I haven't had to fuss at him yet. Daddy has turned into Dr. Jekyl and Mr. Hyde. Auntie is irritated with him. I'm so glad

Good To Have You Back

Granny's coming over today to stay until you get back and Grandpa is even thinking about cancelling his trip to come home.

If you and Fern are okay and other than your Daddy's mood swings what else is the problem?

Mommy, what's really going on with you and Daddy? You don't even sleep in the same bed together anymore? Ever since he got shot the two of you don't even talk. I know Daddy explained what happened or at least he explained what he wanted us to know but sometimes I wonder.

You wonder what baby?

Like if maybe there is something going on between you and Daddy that you just don't want me and Fern to know about. Like maybe you shot Daddy.

Isabella I didn't shoot your Daddy. Why would you think that?

Because y'all used to be all over each other and now whenever Daddy gets near you, you cringe. And when y'all talk to each other you sound beyond irritated. So really, what's going on Mommy? I'm old enough, you can tell me.

Who you on the phone with this early in the morning Alejandro asked

Mommy. Here Daddy she wants you she lied. She kissed the phone and said Love you Mommy.

Hey baby, how's everything going he asked once he got the phone.

Gabriella snuggled into Antonio's arms and replied Fine. How are you feeling? I'm alright. How's Satin?

She's still in the hospital. They moved her from ICU to a regular room. She should be able to come home in a few days.

Will she be alright?

She will be in a wheelchair for a while and will need a full time assistant.

Man, what about her boyfriend?

Same thing. They're both in the same condition. Satin has a few cuts and bruises on her face, neck and chest that will take some time to heal. Other than that she will be fine. There is even more good news.

What's that? You coming home soon?

Satin's pregnant. She's due in 4 months.

Wow, tell her I said Congratulations. I'm glad somebody is.

Fernando he called out, his attitude and tone had completely changed.

Yes sir Fernando asked.

Good To Have You Back

Here's your Mama he said before passing the phone without another word making Gabriella's blood boil.
Mommy Fern whined I am so missing you.
Oh really?
Yes, I'm craving blueberry waffles and nobody can make them like you.
Gran will be there today, maybe she can make you some.
Yeah maybe. How's Sunshine?
Still shining. Guess what? She's going to have a baby.
Really? Wow, how'd that happen so quick for her and Danny when you and Daddy have been trying for years Fernando asked puzzled.
Gabriella didn't know how to respond to that question. Antonio wrapped his arms around her tighter for support. He could hear most of the conversation.
Isabella asked Fernando why he was all spaced out. His reply was Satin's having a baby. I'm starting to think there is something wrong with Mom and Dad. It wouldn't take a genius to figure that out. Newsflash. They haven't slept in the same bed in over a month. Don't be surprised if...aargh Isabella screamed. All of this is making me sick.
Yeah me too. Here Daddy, telephone. Love you Mommy.
Love you too baby Gabriella replied as she wiped at her tears.
G, I'm just going to tell them the truth. I don't want them to try and put this all on you. I fucked up. I can admit to that. I will explain it to them the best way I know how.
Alex
I know G, look I'm sorry for real.

Antonio held Gabriella in his arms until his cell phone rang. Danny's mother was calling from the hospital to say that both Satin and Danny were awake and had been moved to one big room.
We'll be there in a little bit.
You sure you feel up to this Antonio asked Gabriella for the fifth or sixth time as they walked out of his front door.
Yes Tony, will you stop worrying? If anything goes wrong I got you right here to look after me so I'm good.
He smiled Yeah you're right.

Good To Have You Back

When the two of them walked into the hospital room Danny's family was surrounding both beds.

Well, well, well if it isn't Mr. and Mrs. Smith Danny's sister Danita said with a laugh. She always called the two of them that when they were together. They hugged everybody before they could get conversation time with their friends.

How are you feeling Gabriella asked Satin?

Me, I should be asking you that. You look like you've been crying. What's going on. Whose ass do I need to kick?

I'm going to kick yours Gabriella laughed as she lightly pinched her. How come you never told me you were pregnant?

You know my history with pregnancies.

About as well as I know my own Satin but you still should have told me. I'm so happy for you.

I'm scared.

Don't be, just pray! Everything's going to be alright. You and Danny together are like a breath of fresh air for each other and I believe that this time everything's going to be just fine.

Satin smiled. Thank you for rushing down here to be with me. I know it's not easy for you to leave home right now. How's Alex, how's the kids?

Everybody's good.

Gabi I know you. You're lying. What's going on?

Nothing I can't handle.

Did you at least get some before you left?

No, and I didn't even bother to try.

Where have you been staying since you've been here?

At Tony's she said as she accepted the bottle water and fruit bowl he came back with after taking Danny on a stroll throughout the hall.

You and me need to talk. Now, Satin told her. Me and Gabi are going for a walk. Well a roll, you know what I mean.

Let's meet up outside by the waterfall in say half an hour Danny asked.

Yeah that's cool Satin tells him as Gabriella and Antonio get her safely into her wheelchair.

So what happened Satin asked as soon as they turned the corner in the hallway.

Nothing.

You stayed the night with Tony and nothing happened? Yeah right.

Good To Have You Back

Don't I look sexually frustrated? I pulled out my rabbit and my dildo after he wouldn't give me none. Still couldn't have an orgasm to save my life.

And Tony didn't want to give you none?

I'm sure he did but you know he thinks I'm only doing it because of what Alejandro has done.

Have you not told him that you haven't had sex in months? A woman has needs. No shit Gabriella laughed as she high fived her. No, I didn't tell him. We sat up talking while watching Real Housewives of Atlanta and Good Times before falling asleep in each other's arms. Isabella calls first thing this morning to ask me if I was the one who shot Alex because of the way we are towards each other now. She put Alex on the phone and we start out civil. He asked how you were doing. I told him, mentioned the baby and his whole attitude changed. He told me to tell you Congratulations and commented that at least somebody's having one before calling Fern to the phone. Fern gets on the phone. I know how much he loves his Sunshine and babies so I spread the news. He says "Wow, how is it that Satin and Danny can have a baby so fast when you and Daddy have been trying for years? He and Issy are conversing back and forth and it almost seems as if I'm the problem. Alejandro said he's going to explain everything to the kids because he felt the same way.

Damn, so what happened?

Nobody has called me yet. We came here right after that conversation.

So you're sexually frustrated, slept in bed with a man in which you've been wanting to fuck for years and again I add, you're sexually frustrated but nothing happened. Your daughter thinks you shot her Daddy and both Alex and Fern are mad because you're not pregnant.

So is Isabella and everyone else.

Both Danny and I are laid up in the hospital and you had to come see about us. Oh hursh now, you know I had to come make sure my little sister was okay.

I know but Gabi, you always got so much going on. You're superwoman for real.

Hell, no I'm not. If I was superwoman I'd have gotten super dick by now. I'm about to fucking go crazy.

Satin laughed Shut up before somebody hears you.

Oh please, I'm sure I'm not the only one around suffering from lack of sex.

Okay, what if Tony gives in, then what?

We will fuck and shit…

Yeah my point exactly. You're going to fuck and what? Pretend like it never happened? You will fuck and stop being friends to become fuck buddies? Or will the two of you just try for something more? I mean really, do you still love Alejandro?

Of course I do.

Are you still in love with him?

Yes, if I'm completely honest with myself.

So what would be your reason for being with Antonio? To get even with Alex?

No, simply to awaken the parts of my body that need sexual healing like Marvin Gaye said.

And you're willing to jeopardize everything you have with Alex and the friendship you have with Antonio for just one night?

You act like Alex ain't did the same shit a million and one times. At least my excuse is not "business". I'm doing it solely for satisfaction. Satisfaction I can't get from him right now because I literally can't stand the sight of him. Being around him makes me sick to my stomach. I sure as hell can't have sex with him. Even before I found out about the white chick he wasn't trying to be all up on me like that. So seriously, what is the point?

If Alex finds out you slept with anyone, let alone Tony he's going to flip the fuck out literally.

How is he going to find out? You plan on telling him? You're the only one that knows I'm even considering. Other than the kids you're the only one that knows Antonio is here.

You know I ain't telling him shit Gabi. I'm just saying think this all the way through for all parties involved. Lets' say you and Tony decide to have sex, do you think he will be able to just let you go back to Alex with no drama?

What do you mean, go back to Alex? He and I live in the same house but I sleep on the third floor and have been since all this happened. None of my things are in that bedroom. I live in my own apartment you might as well say and other than not having sex I'm enjoying it.

I wonder what's going through those kids heads.

I told you Isabella thinks I shot Alejandro which is not too far off since I've actually considered it a number of times. Fern is upset because I'm not pregnant.

Shit I bet Tago's turning over in his grave.

Gabriella got quite. Satin realized what she'd said. I'm sorry she said as she took Gabriella's hand as Gabriella slumped onto a bench pulling the wheel chair around to face her.

It's okay, you're right. He probably is for many reasons she said sadly.

Oh Gabi you know you're the greatest at everything you are, mother, daughter, sister, friend. You can't stop people from being people. What I meant is that Tago's probably turning over in his grave because you're still hurting. All he ever wanted was for you to be happy. Every time you get there it's like it's snatched away from you and that is so unfair. Satin still held her hands as 2 butterflies came and landed on Gabriella's shoulder. Satin smiled.

What, Gabriella asked as she turned to look over her shoulder.

Be still, look Satin said as she pulled a mirror from her purse to show Gabriella the butterflies on her right shoulder. Even with two of them talking and moving the butterflies remained. As soon as Antonio and Danny appeared talking animatedly the butterflies flew away. Gabriella's cell phone rang with both Isabella and Fern on the line apologizing for the comments they made and asking when she'd be home.

Satin asked to speak with them, assured them that Gabriella would be on a return flight to New York tonight. She also assured them that she would be alright. Antonio told Gabriella he could handle everything and they would call if they needed her.

Go home Antonio told her. Your family needs you.

Thanks Tony she said as she hugged him.

Any time he tells her as he kisses her forehead before they called last call for boarding of her flight home.

Adrianna picked Gabriella up from the airport. Damn are you really that happy to see me she asked of the kool aid smile Adrianna wore on her face.

Yes, I missed you.

Missed you too. I'm sorry you had to spend all your free time with Oscar the Grouch.

No problem. I enjoyed torturing him with different scenarios about you being with someone else and the kids having a step daddy if he didn't get his shit together.

You didn't.

Yes the hell I did. I was straight up with him. I told him you're a beautiful woman who deserves nothing but the utmost respect and if he can't give it to you there is somebody else that will. I gave him scenario after scenario. That messed him up worse than he already was.

When Gabriella made it home Gordon and Lucia were in the kitchen putting together a meal while the kids and Alejandro were in the family room playing Scrabble.

Mommy the kids squealed jumping up hugging her close for a long time. She was happy to see them. Alejandro smiled at her as he sat on the floor. He attempted to get up but Gabriella stopped him. She took a seat beside him on the floor and kissed his cheek.

How are you feeling she asked smiling at the smile he was giving her.

I'm better now that you're home.

Fernando came over and took a seat in Gabriella's lap. Alejandro argued that he was getting too big to be sitting in her lap. Isabella was so happy that the 4 of them were together and appeared to be happy that she started snapping pictures.

Mrs. Lucia called everybody to the kitchen for dinner. Adrianna had returned with BK. Mateo returned with their other sibling Mariam. Mateo and Mariam had started to come around now that they were of age to venture out on their own. Before their mother did not want them to get to know Alejandro and Adrianna because of her own selfish reasons.

Everyone sat down at the table and enjoyed dinner. Conversation flowed like it used to before everything got out of hand. After dinner they all returned to the family room to play a game of Taboo.

Alejandro watched Gabriella as she changed his bandages. Why are you looking at me like that she asked without looking up at him.

How do you know I'm looking at you?

Feels like you're starring a hole in my back she said as she walked to the bathroom to properly dispose of his bandages.

What, I can't look at you now?

That's not what I'm saying.

Well what are you saying?

I want to know what you're thinking.

How incredibly beautiful you are and how much I miss you. I miss you a lot Gabi. It's too much for me having you not talking to me, not sleeping with you at night. You don't know how it feels to have a woman that you love so much but can't get to.

You're right because I've never had a woman. Never wanted one but I know what it feels like to be ignored and treated like shit by the man you're in love with. I know how it feels to go months without being touched, without being sexed, all because he's so caught up in his "new girlfriend". By the way have you heard from her lately? You should at least call her and thank her for that high ass doctor bill she didn't have to pay.

Alejandro bit his bottom lip as he continued to stare. What can I do to make it up to you he asked after a while.

There's nothing in this world that can make up for that. If you thought there was you're crazier than you look.

Deuce knocked on the bedroom door and asked What up Gabi? Good to have you home.

Hey Deuce, how's the twins?

They're good he said as he hugged her. Y'all need a minute?

No, I'm done. Good night guys.

G Alejandro called out.

What?

You going to bed?

About to take a shower and read for a minute.

Can I come see you later he asked with puppy dog eyes.

Call me.

Deuce asked Where she going?

To her new home.

What? You ain't tell me she moved out. You said she was sleeping in another room.

She sleeps on the third floor. It's like a big ass one bedroom apartment down there. She can shower, cook, do whatever she wants to do. Hell she don't even have to come through here if she don't want to. She can use the elevator to get to the garage. If it wasn't for the kids I wouldn't even see her ass. She would have put me out already.

Damn, how long she been down there?

Good To Have You Back

Ever since this shit happened.

Word? So yo ass ain't getting no love huh? Man, that's fucked up.

Gordon came into the room with a glass of wine for Alejandro and a Grey Goose shot for Deuce.

You going to bed Pop?

Nah, about to play chess with Bella.

Alright

You need anything give me a holla.

Deuce watched the pain on Alejandro's face and asked You want to get out? Go cruise the Ave. for a minute.

Yeah that's cool he said as he raised up slowly. He slid his feet into a pair of slippers, grabbed a hat from the closet. He pulled it down real low over his eyes then grabbed his cane.

You need your cellphone old man Deuce asked?

Nah, it ain't like anybody gone call me.

As they walked out the bedroom down the hallway Gabriella called out from the family room. Deuce you leaving already?

No, I'll be back. We're about to...

Shh Alejandro said as he put his hands to his lips just as Gabriella walked out of the family room.

Alex where do you think you're going?

Come on now G, you know I ain't going to do no dirt. Shit look at me.

Where are you going?

We're just about to go out for a minute to chill.

Chill? You better chill your ass back there in that bed and rest your nerves.

G you trippen, I'm just cruising with Deuce. I'll be back in a couple of hours.

You're not going anywhere she said with her hands on her hips.

Man I'll be back in a little bit Alejandro was telling her when Gordon came out and asked Where you on your way to?

We're about to cruise the Ave. for a minute.

Alright, Derwin don't make me come looking for either one of you.

Papi he shouldn't be going anywhere.

The man has been cooped up in this house for a month and a half now. A little fresh air will do him some good.

Okay, whatever she said as she rolled her eyes and walked back into the family room.

G, I'll be back before 11.

Who cares? Go do what you do she said with attitude.

Alejandro looked at Deuce and then Gordon as they both shrugged their shoulders. Be careful Gordon tells him and stay your ass out of trouble.

It was 10:58, Alejandro hadn't made it home yet. Gabriella was up pacing the floor. Gordon had already gone to bed. Gabriella had called Alejandro's phone at least 6 times before she realized he didn't have it on him, which only aggravated her more. If he wasn't home at exactly 11 she already planned to call Deuce. He walked in at 11 on the nose with Deuce standing behind him. Gabriella flipped on the light in the foyer and asked Why didn't you have your phone?

What, it rang?

Ooh you're so goddamn inconsiderate she said as she walked away from the door headed to the stairs for the 3rd floor.

G, what's up? Why you trippen? It's 11 0'clock. I'm here like I said I would be and I'm alright. Yo Deuce, hit me up tomorrow man. You drive safe.

You go show your girl some love. She obviously wants your attention.

I damn sure want hers. Glad you invited me out. I needed to leave the house, even if only for a minute.

Alejandro made sure the house was locked up, set the alarm and made his way to the bedroom he once shared with Gabriella. He picked up his cell phone, saw the number of times she'd called him and dialed her number. When she wouldn't answer he left the bedroom and took the elevator to the 3rd floor. He knocked on the door.

Yo G, open up. I want to talk to you. When she didn't respond he said I know you hear me. Open the damn door for real before I wake up the whole goddamn house.

She knew he'd do it so she opened the door just enough to peek through and asked What do you want?

I want you to open this damn door he said as he pushed it open and walked inside. If he wasn't hurt she would have pushed back slamming the door on him if necessary. Instead she frowned up at him, tightened the strings on her robe and said Now that you're in here make this quick. What is it that you want?

Good To Have You Back

What you got on up under there?
None of your fucking business she said as she left him in the living area of the 3ʳᵈ floor and walked inside the bathroom located in the bedroom where her shower was waiting.
What you doing in there?
Alejandro you're working my last nerve. Say what you want to say and leave.
I ain't going nowhere he said as he closed the door shutting the 3ʳᵈ floor off from the rest of the house. He locked both locks, removed his clothes and lay them across the back of the sofa. He grabbed two flutes, sat them beside a bucket of ice with champagne chilling inside. He carried it into the bathroom, lit the fireplace, dimmed the lights and dropped a Brian McKnight CD into the CD changer before walking into the bathroom. Through the non-steam shower glass he watched as Gabriella held her head back underneath the spray of the shower head as she bathed her body with Sweet Mango body wash. He starred for a minute before opening the shower door and getting inside. When Gabriella started to protest with her eyes closed and her head still tilted back he kissed her lips before lifting her up in his arms and putting himself deep inside her. Finally he was giving her exactly what she needed without holding back and the two of them experienced multiple orgasms together. After bathing they returned to the bedroom completely naked and lay on the bearskin rug sipping champagne. Gabriella's back was against the lounger in the sitting area while Alejandro's head lay in her lap. Soon he was spreading her legs and using his tongue to bring her more orgasms. When it was all said and done they were wrapped up in each other's arms sleeping peacefully and both extremely satisfied.
It wasn't until Isabella used the intercom to call out Mommy in a voice that woke Gabriella did they both sit up.
Yes baby she asked as she held the intercom button.
Daddy's gone. Grandpa said he was supposed to come home at 11 but I've been calling his cell phone and he's not answering and Mommy his clothes from last night aren't here and Mommy she cried frantically.
Isabella, calm down baby...
But Mommy what if something happened to Daddy?
Nothing happened to Daddy, now calm down before you get everyone worked up.

Good To Have You Back

Mommy nobody knows where Daddy is. Even Grandma and Grandpa are worried.

Tell them not to be. Alex is okay. He's in the house.

No he's not, I've searched all over for him.

Oh really, and did you check the third floor?

No because...Mommy she cried.

Isabella, he's here baby.

Here where?

Here, in the bed with me.

Well why aren't either one of you answering the phone? If Daddy's there let me talk to him.

He's calling you on the house phone now.

Mommy you better not disconnect the intercom she warned. Daddy where are you?

I'm in the bed baby. Quit crying. I'm alright.

Are you really with Mommy?

Yes

You promise? And you're not...say something through the intercom. She needed proof.

When Isabella had her proof she was satisfied, not to mention happy but she had also ruined the moment.

Where are you going Alejandro asked as he watched Gabriella pull on a warm up suit and tennis shoes.

For a run.

It can't wait?

For what?

We were just asleep.

I know and now I'm awake.

Well can we at least cuddle? I mean It's not like this happens all that often here lately,

Gabriella ignored him as she left the bedroom and walked into the living area tightening the case to the I-pod on her arm with Tamia's latest CD playing in her ear. Alejandro was calling out to her. The music was too loud for her to hear. She used the back entrance out of the house and stretched in the alley before starting off on a slow jog. She'd ran a total of 8 full laps when Drago pulled up beside her in his black on black Aston Martin and asked Hey Cutie with the big o'l booty, you need a ride?

Shut up she laughed.

Dang, how long you been out here? You sweating like a....shit like I don't know.

She looked at her watch and said maybe an hour and half now.

Get in.

No she said as she continued to jog in place. I'll see you at the house.

When Drago arrived everybody was fussing about where Gabriella was. Drago told them she was on her way back. He came over to pick the kids up to take them out to Uncle Juan's for the day.

Is Mommy coming too Fernando asked?

I don't know Isabella was saying as Gabriella came in through the front door.

Mommy they screamed. Isabella asked Mommy are you and Daddy coming to Uncle Juan's with us?

Nah Alejandro spoke up. I have a doctor's appointment and we have some business we need to take care of he said as he eyed Gabriella.

What business do we have to take care of Gabriella asked him after everyone left?

Go shower and get dressed. My appointments are all right behind each other.

How many appointments do you have?

3, only 2 are medical. Stop with the questions and come on.

Well damn, rush me because you didn't bother to mention them to me before now.

Gabriella was in the driver's seat of Alejandro's Bentley when she asked Where to first?

Dr. Carver's office.

Inside Dr. Carver's office Alejandro was released from medical care. No more doctor's visits, no more changing of the bandages. Alejandro was back to normal.

Why you all frowned up he asked Gabriella as they were leaving Dr. Carver's office.

Guess this means you will hit the block harder than you were at it the last time she said as she walked ahead of him in the direction of the exit away from all the doctor's offices.

No that's not what it means he said as he caught up to her. G, come on. You're going the wrong way.

The car is…

My other appointment.

What is this other appointment for she asked as he held her hand while walking into Michael Gerbraurd's office. A nurse had him sign in, present his ID and insurance card while Gabriella looked around to try and determine what type of doctor Mr. Gerbraurd was. Before she could find out the doctor invited them back.

Good afternoon Mr. and Mrs. Solera he said before going on to explain his credentials. Mr. Solera please tell me what brought you into my office today.

Well you see Doc, Gabi and I have been without condoms or any form of birth control for a little over 2 years now and we still haven't been able to get pregnant. Gabi has been tested and everything is fine on her end. Her doctor suggested different methods in which are supposed to help but I'm starting to think the problem might be me. I at least want to check to be sure.

Well there's not always a problem. Maybe the timing is just not right. Ever considered that?

We've been together for over 5 years now. I mean if not now then when? Alejandro asked in a frustrated tone.

Mrs. Solera do you have anything you want to add Dr. Gerbraurd asked as he took notes on a notepad.

Are you a fertility doctor or a psychiatrist?

Bae, Alejandro said as he grabbed her hand with a smirk.

No I'm not trying to be funny. I'm serious.

Dr. Gerbraurd laughed too. I could see why you would think that. I'm a fertility specialist referred by Dr. Carver. I typically work with males on anything related to male organs such as impotence, pre-mature ejaculation, etc.

Thank you for the clarification she said just as her cell phone rang. Fernando was calling so she excused herself from the room. She was thankful for the interruption, not at all in the mood to talk about pregnancies or anything related to child birth. Even after the brief conversation with Fernando she stood in the hallway wondering why Alejandro felt the need to be examined now when she'd gone in over a year ago. Why now when their relationship seemed to be one chaotic episode after another.

Alejandro stuck his head out the door and asked Everything okay?
Are you almost through in there?
Why, what's going on he asked in a concerned tone.
Nothing, everything is fine.
Okay well I'm about to have my exam. I'd really like for you to be in here with me. She looked at him a minute before agreeing to join him. The doctor stepped out of the room while Alejandro removed his clothes and put the robe on.
Gabriella watched him strip but turned her head when he looked over at her.
You okay he asked?
I'm good. You okay?
I asked because you haven't said much since we got here. I thought you would be glad that I'm having myself checked out thoroughly as you put it.
I am happy that you're finding out for yourself.
It's not just for me, it's for us.
Gabriella sighed as Dr. Gerbraurd knocked and then entered the room.
Dr. Gerbraurd spent a good 45 minutes along with a nurse running a variety of tests on Alejandro and answering whatever questions they might have.
When it was all over Alejandro confessed to Gabriella that he felt like he was the reason they couldn't get pregnant. He sounded as if he really believed that.
Why do you think that?
I mean, what other explanation is there? We've done everything your doctor said to do a million times over.
Yeah but what Dr. Gerbraurd said is right, maybe it's just not time.
I refuse to believe that. Something is wrong with me.
If there was something wrong Dr. Carver would have mentioned it by now.
I've never asked for extensive testing. Hell even he is starting to worry.
Calm your nerves, besides now is not the time for us to be trying to have a baby anyway.
What do you mean? You want to wait until we're old and gray? G, I ain't trying to be 50 chasing after no kids.
Alejandro you're not even 35 yet. Hell you barely turned 32 and you're worried about turning 50. Hursh now.
Okay, so what makes us not ready? I'm driving.
You…
Dr. Carver said I can carry on as normal.

Yeah that's what I'm afraid of.

Don't be. I promise I won't get out of hand.

Alex do me a favor she said as she passed him the keys.

Anything for you baby.

Don't make me any more promises. The ones that really mattered most to me have already been broken she said as she opened her own door as if he wasn't standing there to open it.

He couldn't say anything against her statement. What she'd said was true. An apology would only annoy her because she'd heard it all before.

What do you want to eat he asked?

Nothing, take me home.

You didn't eat breakfast.

I wasn't hungry then and I'm not hungry now.

As soon as they got home she locked herself in on the 3rd floor and prevented the other floors from accessing the hallway that lead to the 3rd floor. Alejandro started up on the intercom about how important it was for them to discuss their problems. Gabriella muted the volume because the sound of his voice sounded like nails on a chalk board. She even turned off her cell phone after making sure the kids were okay. By the time Gordon arrived Alejandro was clearly heated. Gordon picked up the house phone and dialed the 3rd floor phone. When Gabriella answered he demanded that she get upstairs now. She walked into the kitchen like a teenager afraid of being scolded but knowing it was coming. Yes Papi she asked as she hugged him and kissed his cheek.

He shrugged her off told her to have a seat and called out to Alejandro by name.

Yes sir Alejandro asked?

Have a seat.

Alejandro frowned up at Gabriella and took the seat furthest away from her.

Gordon shook his head sadly and said This shit has got to stop today.

Papi Gabriella said as she looked at him never having heard him curse before.

He glared at them both before saying The two of you are running around here like you're teenagers. This ain't no damn puppy love. This is 5 good years and then some with 2 beautiful kids to show for it. Together you two have raised well mannered, very educated, successful children. You've opened more businesses, created stability for Fernando and Isabella. Heavens knows they need stability. Do you even understand what all this is doing to them? Isabella cries herself to sleep at night. Fernando doesn't believe in love anymore because he never pictured the two of you behaving this way. I'm pissed because I've never seen Bella so happy in all the time I've known her. Alejandro you make her happy but you take away the happiness if you can't fully commit to her. Now, the first time I had your back. Sure enough you messed up, we all make mistakes so I felt like you deserved a pass. She gave you one. You straighten up but then you go fucking up again by getting involved in shit you don't have to and I'm not just talking other chicks. Your excuses are just that, excuses and they don't mean shit.

Gabriella gave Alejandro an I told you so look that didn't go unnoticed by Gordon.

Don't think you're free and clear he said as he looked her dead in the eyes. Fern told me he stated while continuing the stare. She knew he meant he was aware that Antonio was in Phoenix. He went on to say, I assure you that this family doesn't need any more complications.

He fixed himself a glass of Gin, no ice, no juice.

What did Fern tell you Alejandro wanted to know

Gordon wanted to use Antonio as a threat but knew that would only make things worse. Bottom line is that my grandkids are suffering because of your actions. I want you to get it together and get it together quick. There are no other options. Right now you two are the only parents they have. Don't take that away from them. Especially when you know that the two of you really love each other. If you didn't none of this would even be possible. It's alright to have a little fun but you're going about it the wrong way.

Pops, what did Fern tell you?

What did you tell Bella?

About what?

About anything.

I don't know what you're talking about.

Probably because you haven't told her anything. Don't you think it's time the two of you have that talk.

Been trying to talk to her, she don't want to listen.

Well I advise you to try harder if you want things to work out. I mean you are the one that created this problem, and you sure as hell don't want it to get any worse than it already is he said before walking out of the house into the garage.

You got something you want to tell me Alejandro asked Gabriella

Yeah, no point in keeping it a secret. Papi's right, if you don't straighten up things are going to seriously get out of hand. That's not a threat, it's a promise.

Okay, point well taken. What's up?

Antonio...as soon as the name came out of her mouth Alejandro stood up, started pacing the floor a minute before following Gordon into the garage where he got in one of his cars and drove off.

Drago called to say the kids were staying the weekend with him if it was okay with her and Alejandro.

Yes it's fine.

Where's Alex?

He just stepped out.

Where to?

I don't know, he didn't say.

Bella can I say something?

Why not Drago? Everybody has freedom of speech.

Funny, but all bullshit aside.

All bullshit aside.

I don't like what's going on with you and Alejandro.

Nobody does.

Yeah but I'm a grown ass man and normally I'm not bothered by somebody else's problems but sis, you and Alex are like my Mom and Pop. I feel like a teenager watching my parents go through a divorce and the shits ugly yo. I can't even imagine how Fern and Issy feel. When you came back from PA and moved to the 3rd floor I cried. I cried because I don't want it to be over between you two, and you know I don't cry. I know Alex fucked up and that's some shit y'all gone have to work through so I'm not excusing what he did. All I'm saying is that the relationship means a lot to all of us and nobody wants to see the two of you apart. That's all I'm saying.

Chapter 21

*Before night fell Gabriella moved out of the 3rd floor back into her and
Alejandro's bedroom. She thought he didn't come home that night but found him
asleep in the family room the next morning while heading out for a run. By the
time he got up to take a shower he was surprised to see the shower filled with
Gabriella's shower gels and scrubbers. He walked over to the cabinets and saw
all her other personal items. Her huge walk in closet was filled with all of her
belongings and the room was sprinkled with her things. He picked up his phone
and dialed Gabriella's cell phone in which rang on her side of the bed. Glancing
at the time he realized that she was out running. He decided to make breakfast.
An hour passed and Gabriella hadn't made it back. Alejandro was showered and
had planned on asking her to join him in a business meeting. He was standing in
the doorway when she ran up.*

Good morning she said as she kissed his lips and ran past him.

Hey, where you running of to?

I gotta use the bathroom she said as she ran into their bedroom.

*Alejandro followed, as Gabriella flushed the toilet with her back to him and
removed her clothes.*

She turned on the shower and turned around ooh you scared me.

I made breakfast.

Okay, I'll be out in a minute.

Can I join you?

Sure, come on.

*Alejandro washed her body before washing her hair. He kissed all over her neck
moaning all the while. We didn't close the door she warned.*

*Gordon, Mom and Carmen are gone to North Carolina he said as he continued
caressing her body. Soon he was all over her and the two of them were
seriously going at it when Alejandro had a powerful orgasm that left them both
out of breath.*

Shit Gabriella told him, I think you just might have gotten your wish.

What's that he asked as he kissed her lips?

You might have just made a baby.

How do you feel about that?

She smiled as she wrapped her legs around him and guided him inside her. He was hard already and worked her slow and hard. She moaned and said I'm good.

A week later when Dr. Gerbraurd called Alejandro with the results of his tests he informed him that his chances of having a baby were slim to none unless he went through some sort of treatment surgery. Alejandro was so bothered by that information that he stayed out all night drinking. When he got home Gabriella was sitting in the kitchen waiting for him. It was after 4 in the morning.
Sorry he mumbled before kissing her cheek and opening the refrigerator.
You okay she asked him?
Yeah, let's go to bed. You was waiting up on me?
Yes she answered as he walked out of the kitchen towards the bedroom. She turned out the lights and followed. Inside the bedroom she helped him remove his shoes and clothes. She was in the mood for sex.
Nah G, not tonight Ma. I'm fucked up. Let's just cuddle.
Gabriella could smell the alcohol on his breath so she didn't protest. Instead she lay her head on his chest and he wrapped his arms around her.
All week he had an excuse when it came to sex and though he kissed her and showed affection he just wasn't into her sexually like she felt he should be. After trying with no success to get his dick hard she said Okay Alex, who is she this time?
G, what are you talking about?
I've been bugging you for sex, that's crazy she practically screamed.
I just ain't in the mood. You get time off when you're on your period. Can I have my time please he asked in an annoyed tone before getting up out of bed and throwing his robe on. After being out of the room and thinking he came back shutting the door behind him now hard as a rock. He removed his robe and climbed in bed holding Gabriella's legs up in his arms before guiding himself deep inside of her. The sex was intense and when it was over she lay awake on his chest while he snored softly. Whenever she wanted sex after that he'd give it to her to keep confusion down but he wasn't as into it as he used to be. Whenever Gabriella asked him what's wrong he'd say nothing.
Adrianna invited Gabriella out to a block party one of BK's homeboys was having. Alejandro, Drago, Tyren and Deuce all came through. Alejandro noticed

how all the guys that weren't already with their girls and others who didn't give a
damn either way kept trying to get Gabriella's attention. He wasn't into invading
her space but he did do little things to let them know she was taken. When he
and his crew decided to leave he told Gabriella, Yo G, I'm about to bounce.
Alright babe she said as she hugged him close and kissed his lips. I'll see you
back at the house later.
You about to head home right?
No, I'm going to chill a little longer. You're not going home right now are you?
She wiped lipstick from his lips.
What's a little longer?
However long Adrianna decides to stay.
Nah that ain't cool. Adri here with BK. I'ma need you to be at home with me.
Here, I'll leave the car with you.
No need, you know I'm the designated driver. Besides I'm sure I'll be home
before you get there anyway.
You better be.
Yes Daddy.
When Alejandro arrived home at 2 Gabriella wasn't there. When he called, her
phone went straight to voicemail for a good hour before she made it in. He was
pissed.
Where the fuck you been he asked as soon as she pulled into the garage.
At the block party. I didn't expect you to be home so early.
You couldn't answer the goddamn phone?
My battery is dead she said as she stood in front of him. You know your attitude
has been real jacked up lately. One minute you're nice and cool then you just
get nasty. You PMSing?
You calling me a bitch?
Is that what you call me?
Hell nah, quit trippen. I'm just saying, why I got to be PMSing?
It's either that or you…
Or I what?
You got a new girlfriend.
There you go with that shit. There is nobody else Gabriella. Bring your ass in
this house.

Gabriella figured some makeup sex was just what they both needed but Alejandro just wasn't feeling it.

You fucking somebody else? Be straight up with me.

Hell nah, I need to be asking you that. You the one didn't get home until after 3 in the morning and didn't answer when I called. Don't be asking me no shit like that he said as he left the room. When he returned Gabriella was getting up. Where you going he asked?

Somewhere your attitude ain't she said as she grabbed her Gucci travel bag filled with sex toys.

G, bring your ass back here.

Fuck you.

I'ma fuck you up for real he said when he realized she wasn't coming back. He got up and made his way to the third floor. When he twisted the knob it was locked.

Yo G, why you playing? Unlock the goddamn door.

Leave me alone Alex.

I ain't trying to go through this shit with you tonight.

Okay so go back upstairs. You made it clear that you didn't want to be bothered. I made it clear that I'm horny. You do you and I'ma do me she said as she removed her clothes, switched on her real feel Mandingo dildo and lay on the bed with her legs in the air. Alejandro was still talking through the door and she was seriously pleasing herself with her dildo. When she got a quick, yet satisfying fix she got up from the bed with the dildo, walked over to unlock the door. With the dildo in her hand dripping with remnants of her encounter she walked right past Alejandro. Her nakedness turned him on. He was ready to do her, she was clearly not in the mood.

Alex, really what's going on with you? If you're not cheating, what's the problem? You know you can talk to me about anything right?

Gabriella, I'm not cheating on you he said sincerely.

Okay she believed him, let's get some sleep.

A few weeks later the kids are leaving for St. Louis with Lucia. Gabriella gets sick in the airport and thinks it might be from the burrito she had for breakfast. She's feeling ill the next 2 days. Alejandro takes her in to see her doctor. When the doctor tells them Gabriella's pregnant she's all smiles while Alejandro's frowned up.

How many months is she he asked?

Well let's just see.

As the doctor examined her she asked questions. She determined that she was 2 months pregnant. She left the room to set another appointment, write out a prescription for prenatal vitamins and get her set up for Lamaze class. Gabriella said in an annoyed tone, Well damn Alex I thought you of all people would be thrilled. Why did you keep asking if she was sure.

Cause I need to know.

You sat right here and…

Gabriella he said as he looked at her with disgust lose the goddamn attitude he said before the doctor came back in the room with samples and pamphlets concerning this and that. Alejandro's facial expression and attitude had gotten worse as they left the doctor's office. Gabriella continued to ask what's wrong but he would never give an answer. Finally in the garage she yelled out You get on my fucking nerves. Whenever you get what you want you always find a way to ruin it. You're never satisfied.

What the fuck is that supposed to mean?

You wanted me so bad, you get me and you cheat not once but twice. You ask for a baby and we're finally blessed with one and you're giving me attitude like I did something wrong. I can't please you Alex she cried. She walked in the house leaving him alone in the car with thoughts of rage. Throughout the rest of the night his attitude only got worse. It got to the point that they were standing in each other's faces yelling and screaming obscenities. By now Alejandro is drunk.

You all the time asking me who I'm fucking. Wow, does Antonio know he got a baby on the way?

Gabriella stopped hurt by what he'd just said. He wasn't claiming their baby. Yeah, guess you thought I wouldn't find out you fucked him huh? Well guess what? Doc called last week and said the likely hood of me having kids is non-existent. And you already two months pregnant he said as he walked out the front door slamming it so hard behind him that he broke a picture that had been hanging on the wall. After walking for blocks Alejandro was even more upset than he was before so he turned around heading home. When he walked into the house Gabriella had moved to the third floor again. All connections to her were blocked off but she'd left her phone on the charger beside the bed.

Alejandro started going through her call log, her text messages and then her emails before checking her contact list. He found Antonio's number stored up under his name and dialed it. When voicemail picked up he yelled into the phone You piece of shit. I hope you don't think that just because you got her pregnant that she's leaving me. She ain't keeping the baby neither. Her ass is going to the fucking clinic first thing tomorrow morning. You cock sucker he said before hanging up.

Antonio stepped away from the dinner table with his date Lizette and dialed Gabriella back. Gabi he said when her line was picked up.

This Alejandro.

What's up Alex? Everything alright?

Nah, my girl pregnant. What, she ain't called you? I mean considering the circumstances I thought you would know what the problem is.

Alejandro look man, I don't know why you sound so upset. I was under the impression that the two of you were trying to have a baby. If she's pregnant you should be happy.

Would you be happy if your woman of 5 years was pregnant by someone else?

What, Gabi? Nah, quit bullshitten. She wouldn't do no shit like that Antonio said seriously.

You ain't fuck my wife?

No Alejandro, man have you lost your muthafuckin mind? Why would you think some shit like that? Gabriella loves you, even Ray Charles can see that. She wouldn't jeopardize the relationship by messing around.

So you ain't never been with Gabi like that?

Man I put that on my life, hell nah and I hope like hell this is something you thought and kept to yourself.

Nah see, I went and got tested a few weeks ago and when my test results came back Doc said I can't have kids. So you know when we find out she pregnant I'm like shit can't be mine. If she ain't fucking you who else could it be?

Alex listen to yourself man. You don't really believe none of that shit.

Man what the fuck else I'm supposed to believe? She pregnant and I can't have kids.

You get a second opinion?

Nah, what I need a second opinion for?

In cases like this anything can throw the test off. If the doctor said you couldn't have kids what reason did he give? You have to follow up on that kind of shit.
At 8 o'clock the next morning while asleep in the family room the house phone rings. Alejandro reaches over the couch grabs the phone and answers groggily.
Mr. Solera, this is Dr. Gerbraurd. I have some good news and I have some bad news.
Give me the bad news first.
Well, seems there was a mix up in the testing information I gave you. I'm not sure how it happened but your test results ended up in another patient's file and vice versa. I know that's cause for a lawsuit against our practice but please forgive our error. The good news is that you don't have any issues that would prevent you from having children. It's just a matter of time and patience.
By now Alejandro's completely awake. You sure Doc?
I'm positive, even had it tested a second time to be sure. Again I apologize for the error.
You just made me the happiest man alive.
Alejandro had been trying to get Gabriella's attention all day. When she wouldn't come out of the room he had the kids call the 3rd floor phone but even then she wouldn't answer because she'd already spoken with the kids. It wasn't until Gordon came home that he got her to come out of that area. Gordon used the master lock to get through. He pulled Gabriella into his arms as soon as he saw her tear streaked face.
Gabriella I'm sorry Alejandro said to her.
Fuck you she yelled at him as she walked back into the room attempting to close the door behind her. Gordon came inside.
Son, give me some time alone with her, please.
2 hours later they were still on the third floor. Alejandro left out to clear his head and have drinks at a bar. He ended up in jail for driving while intoxicated. He tried calling home to get bailed out. Once Gordon realized he was in jail he posted his bail.
How's my babies? Why didn't she come with you he asked as soon as he was released.
Alejandro she'll be alright but you'd better leave her alone for a while. She honestly doesn't like you right now and if you weren't my son I wouldn't like you either.

Good To Have You Back

Alejandro felt like shit, now sobered up sleeping in bed alone every night until the kids returned home. Gabriella had avoided him as much as she could for two whole months. She moved back into their bedroom with Gordon's help while Alejandro picked the kids up from the airport.

You gone be alright Gordon asked?

If not Papi, I will fake it till I make it.

You called Antonio back right?

No but I will call him today and apologize.

Good because he's worried about you. So is Satin and Danny.

I know. I'll call.

Why don't you go take a shower and get a quick nap in? When the rest of the family arrives we're supposed to have dinner at Houston's. You feel up to it?

Yeah I can use some steak and potatoes.

By the time the kids and Lucia arrived Gabriella was asleep. They all rushed in squealing with delight because Alejandro had told them the good news.

Mommy both Isabella and Fernando screamed out while waking her from her sleep.

Hi babies

Daddy told us the good news. I'm so excited Fernando told her.

Yeah me too she smiled as she caressed Issy's face and kissed Fern's cheek. I missed you guys.

We missed you too Mommy.

Are we going to have a boy or a girl Lucia asked all smiles

We won't know until the week after next Alejandro said as he stood beside her.

Well we better go get freshened up for dinner Lucia advised the kids.

Alejandro asked Gabriella You feeling alright?

Yeah I'm okay.

You need anything?

A glass of water please. My throats a little dry.

Okay he said as he left the room and came back with an ice cold glass of water. Thank you.

He put her sandals on her feet before helping her up from the bed. Gabriella, I'm really sorry.

I know she said as she started to walk away.

He gently pulled her back into his arms and was kissing her passionately when the family stood in the doorway. Gordon had just updated Lucia on what happened so the two of them were glad to see that once again Gabi and Alex had come to their senses. Or so they thought. Alejandro was the one doing all the kissing and just when Gabriella was about to pull away someone appeared in the doorway so she just went along with it. Alejandro stood back, looked her over from head to toe while biting his bottom lip. Damn, I'm one lucky dude he reminded himself.

When they got home from dinner that night Gabriella showered and went to bed. Alejandro was in bed a couple of hours later and snuggled up to her but she got up to use the bathroom so much that he drifted over to his side of the bed but not too far away. He had a smile on his face thinking things would now be okay.

He just so happened to be stepping out of the shower one day when Gabriella came into the house through the garage and removed her clothes in the laundry room. She too was completely naked knowing that the house was empty. Gordon and the kids were in Denver and Alejandro was supposed to be out somewhere with Deuce. They almost ran each other over as she walked into the bedroom and he walked out. He grabbed her to steady her balance.

My bad he said as he looked into her eyes and then down at her body. His body was already tense from lack of sex and his middle always stood at attention whenever Gabriella was around. When she felt his middle poke her leg she had to have him. She started kissing his neck and chest before guiding him to the bed. They were all hot and heavy when Gabriella interrupted asking You got any condoms?

Condoms, fuck I need condoms for?

She frowned as she rolled to the side of him no longer in the mood for sex. Alejandro was confused about the whole condom thing. When she didn't respond he demanded to know why they had to use condoms. Inside his head he was thinking that she and Antonio both had been lying about not being with each other. Never mind the fact that Gabriella already knew of two women that he'd cheated on her with. There was no telling how many others.

She didn't feel like she needed to remind him of this so she moved further away from him and was trying to get up from the bed when he grabbed her arm. Yo G, for real, what the fuck is up with us using condoms all of a sudden? I mean it's not like you can get pregnant cause you're already pregnant. Shit.

Getting pregnant is the least of my worries she said as she snatched her arm from him and walked into the bathroom.

Alejandro was totally clueless, in his head he's thinking everything was back to normal and wanted to forget what happened before and after he got shot.

After Gabriella came out of the bathroom she made her way out of the bedroom with Alejandro calling out to her. She ignored him until he got up and followed her into the kitchen where she grabbed a peach from the refrigerator. He turned her around to face him and asked What's up? All bullshit aside. I want to know what's going on and I want to know now.

When she didn't say anything he asked Gabriella, who you fucking, for real?

I ain't fucking nobody Alex. Don't stand here and act like you have no clue.

I don't. Yo this ain't no muthafuckin game we playing here. Don't play with my emotions. This shit ain't funny.

Play with your emotions? Yeah right, I'm grown. I don't have time to play with anybody. Go ahead with that shit.

So what's up with the condoms for real?

Alejandro she said as she tried to walk around him but he wouldn't allow her to pass so she rested her hip against the counter. You will have to use condoms with me from now on because you have a problem sticking your dick in other women.

He started to interrupt but she cut him off by saying I've decided that I'd be wasting my time and energy being mad at you about the situation and the kids can't handle us being apart any more than anyone else can. I'm not giving you no more free passes. All I ask is that from this point on you wear a condom when you're with me because I'm not trying to catch nothing no other broad passed off to you. Handle your business but don't bring the shit into this house. Don't let your bitches approach me. Don't let them call this house or get out of line in any kind of way. As for you, don't let your side piece take anything away from the kids, that means any and everything. Quality time included. I suggest you start spending more time with them Daddy because right now too much is going on. Although we're not telling them the whole truth we both know they're smart enough to figure things out on their own. I don't want them to resent you and I don't want them to resent me for anything that happens in between us. You know how ugly things can get because you went through enough when your Mom and Dad split. I don't want Issy and Fern or the new baby to have to suffer because of our mistakes. So as far as this house goes all that shit that happened in the past in front of the kids won't be happening again. If you ever decide that you don't want to be here by all means, leave. You're not being held hostage and you're not obligated to Issy and Fern so you're free to go anytime. From now on what we have is an arrangement until one of two things happens, we decide to go our separate ways or get married. In the meantime go out and fuck your bitches. In fact, why don't you go visit Sherrie and properly thank her for that high ass doctor's bill she paid off.

Alejandro looked at her like What the fuck? He knew she was serious but what he didn't understand was why. Why?

Why what?

Why you all of a sudden want to be cool with the shit?

What's the point of not being cool with it? Getting upset ain't getting me nowhere and you haven't changed. So really what's the point?

You don't want to be with me?

If I didn't I wouldn't be standing in your face having this conversation right now, would I she asked him as she finally bit into the peach.

They stood there starring each other down until Alejandro's cell rings and then the house phone. Alejandro doesn't move so Gabriella answered them both.

Deuce is on Alejandro's cell and Satin is on the house phone. Once Gabriella completed her phone call she walked into the bedroom to take a shower.

Alejandro asked You mind if I go to Seattle with Deuce?

Not if you don't mind me going to Florida with Satin.

What y'all going to Florida for he asked as he dried her body.

To finish up the last of her mother's business affairs. What's in Seattle?

Expansion

Cool, how long will you be gone?

A week or two at the most. You?

A week.

When you leaving?

I'll wait until you leave. When are you leaving?

I was thinking Friday, was hoping you and me could spend some quality time together. Go shopping for the baby. We almost 5 months in and we haven't even gotten started on the room yet.

Gabriella and Alejandro spent the next few days shopping for their new baby and bonding much like they used to when she first started coming back to New York after Tago passed away.

Neither of them brought up the subject of sex. Gabriella didn't mention it because she'd said all she had to say and Alejandro wanted things to cool down. He thought Gabriella was just saying things out of anger. She couldn't mean any of it no matter how serious she sounded when she said it.

Chapter 22

They both arrived back home from their trips at the same time.
Hey Alejandro said when he picked her up in his arms inside the garage. I
missed you. He kissed her lips slowly and sensuously. Gabriella bit her bottom
lip when the kiss was over. She was ready to throw caution to the wind and have
sex with him on the hood of her Bentley coupe but then remembered the
conversation she had with him before leaving for Florida and how he reacted to
her asking him to use condoms. She decided not to bring it up. If he was feeling
what she was feeling he'd have condoms or at least go get some. A few
seconds later he had her back against his Maserati while he picked her up in his
arms and pulled her skirt from her waist. In no time his face was in between her
legs and he was seriously going at it. She was moaning and really into it. She
had back to back orgasms before he picked her up and carried her inside to
their bedroom. He was in between her legs with his clothes still on but then
removed first his shirt and then his pants and boxers. His rock hard dick was in
his hands aiming at her center when she asked Alex, did you buy condoms?
He paused, his dick went limp. His face scrunched up before he got out of bed
pulling on his clothes and leaving the house through the garage. Gabriella
thought he was going to get condoms. She was all hot and bothered. An hour
passed, he wasn't back so she dialed his number. What up G he asked?
You busy?
Nah
You okay?
Nah but I ain't in no trouble or nothing like that. I'll be home in a little bit.
Okay, don't forget the condoms.
Fuck the condoms. I'm five years in, can't even remember the last time I had to
use one with you. Why would I start now? You're my woman, about to have my
baby and you talking to me about condoms? Man, that shit is for the birds. If you
want it you gone get it without a condom. I put that on everything I love.
Fine then.
What's that supposed to mean? You take that shit back?
Hell nah, just means I won't be getting none. Oh well, see you when you get
home. Be safe, I love you she said before hanging up without waiting for a
response.

Deuce asked what she say when he noticed the pissed off expression Alejandro wore on his face.

Man, Gabi trippen. She got me fucked up.

What she say?

Nothing, talking all nonchalant like the shit don't bother her either way. I'm gone give it a minute or two to sink in. She will be all over my ass then he smirks. Two months later she's 6 months pregnant. They're having a boy. She hasn't went against her word on the condoms and he's still refusing to use them. He had been suffering from blue balls until he called Sherrie up to apologize for what went on and everything was all good again. He'd make weekend trips out to PA to visit, pretending that he didn't care about sex, just wanted to spend some time with her. After a while she was ready to rape him and he couldn't hold out any longer. He would still rather be making love to Gabriella but with her trippen he would make her suffer, or so he thought. He knew pregnant women stayed horny. She'd give it up soon enough. He had just come back from a trip to Denver with a duffle bag filled with dirty clothes he put in the laundry room and went to the back to take a shower.

Gabriella had ran off to the store to get laundry detergent and immediately got started upon walking through the back door. She was emptying Alejandro's duffle bag and sorting through its contents, checking pockets like she always does. Between him and the kids they were known to leave a number of things in their pockets, cell phones, money, etc. She found a couple hundred dollar bills, hotel key cards that hadn't been turned in, phone numbers, lint, receipts and a number of other things; including an open box of 36 extra large Magnum condoms with only 4 left. She bit her bottom lip, foot tapping on the floor, boiling on the inside as Alejandro walked in from behind her. He noticed the condom box in her hand and quietly walked back out. He waited on the bed wrapped in a towel waiting on her to come into the room yelling and screaming but she didn't. Instead she put the unused condoms, money hotel key cards and everything that wasn't clothing back into the duffel bag. She folded and ironed clothes that had just come out of the dryer before making her way throughout the house to put everything in its designated place. When she walked into the bedroom Alejandro lay with his back posted up on the headboard with his dick hanging out of the towel.

Hey baby, I ain't know you was here he said as he got up to hug and kiss her while rubbing her belly he felt his son kick. How you feeling he asked?
I'm good, how are you she smiled?
Better now that I'm back home with my fam. Where is everybody?
Adventure Landing with Mariam.
Mariam's here?
Yeah she got here yesterday.
How long she staying?
Until the kids go back to school.
Mariam is Alejandro and Adrianna's sister on their father's side. She just turned 19 and was finally able to build a relationship with her older siblings. Her mother didn't want her to get to know them because she felt like Alejandro's father treated them better than he treated Mariam. What Mariam learned is that Mrs. Lucia is the one that always took care of Alex, Adrianna and even Mateo, although he is not her biological son. Their father hadn't done no more for them than he had for her. She loved her big brothers and sister and was happy that Gabriella, Isabella, Fernando and Gordon were all a part of the family.
Why didn't you call me?
I figured you knew she was coming.
If I knew that I'd have been here sooner.
Well you can take that up with Mariam. I assumed you already knew she said as she walked over to the linen closet.
Why you walking away from me?
This basket is heavy.
Why you doing that anyway? Told you to let the maid do it.
The maid does enough as it is. I only keep her around because I know she needs the money. I have no problem cleaning the house.
Yeah, well I have a problem with a whole lot of shit he said as he took the basket from her and told her to go have a seat.
I'm going to cook dinner.
Nah, don't cook. If the kids are going with Mariam you know she's going to feed them. How about you and me step out for the night to say Raven's or Cavallo's to chill?
Sounds like a plan. I need to call Mariam.

I'll call her. You just go get...nah, nah, nah wait. Let's take a bath together. Been a long time since I bathed you. You look like your body could use my touch.

It could she smiled thinking a nice massage would do her just fine. Alejandro's thinking once he gets her in the mood he can go for what he knows. They shared a bath together. He massaged her body, even rubbed his dick across her ass a few times. When the subject about condoms came up again he said Never mind. Let's get dressed.

He finished dressing before she did, said he was going to go clean up the car and gas it up. When he got back she was rocking a strapless Dolce & Gabana fitted pantsuit that she looked damn good in even at 6 months pregnant. Alejandro kept biting his lip. They enjoyed a nice romantic night out on the town, even walked for a minute like they used to before returning home. They stayed up talking with Mariam and the kids before Alejandro said G, come on baby. Let's go to bed.

He had the fireplace lit in the room, music playing softly and Mary B. Morrison's Maneater laying near the bearskin rug waiting to be read. Before they could even get into the book good Alejandro was all over her. He even strapped on a condom and was knee deep inside of her when his dick went limp.

Man, I can't do this shit. It don't even feel right.

Wow, you can't be serious. Your dick was hard as a brick a few seconds ago she pouted.

G, I can't use condoms baby.

Bullshit, a box of 36 only has 4 condoms left in it. Oh yo muthafuckin ass can use condoms obviously.

Oh you all salty about it?

Hell nah, I'm saying your dick goes limp with me cause you don't want to use a condom. That's bogus she said as she got up, pulled on a robe and left his limp dick ass laying in the middle of the floor. She was frustrated for a lot of reasons. As horny as she was Alejandro just knew she'd come back into the room and throw herself on him without the condom. He was still laying on the floor, condom now removed, dick hard once again anticipating her return. She pulled on her panties and pajamas before going to bed.

The next few months were hard for Gabriella as her hormones picked up. She braved the storm and made it through her pregnancy without giving in. When she delivered Alejandro Jr. after 38 hours of labor she was bone tired. Alejandro was excited, a very proud father. All his family and close friends were present. Satin and Danny showed up shortly after the delivery. The kids were also excited. Satin's little girl Sarai was now 3 months old and as cute as can be. You feeling okay Bella, Gordon asked the day after delivery.

Yes, can you get me some ice please. Why hasn't the nurse brought Junior in here yet?

She did, Alex has him. He went for a walk with Deuce and some other dude. Gabriella lay back on the bed too weak to argue about anything. Every time she woke up Junior was always with Alex or in the nursery with the doctor for some screening. She was getting aggravated. Alejandro came strolling in on the 3rd day around 7 pm with Alex Junior on his shoulder.

Can I see my baby she asked in annoyance as he walked in with Tyren and Drago. He gently placed Alex Junior into her arms and watched as Alex's face lit up at the sound of her voice.

What's up sis Drago asked the question Alejandro hadn't. How are you feeling?

I'm alright Bro, thanks for asking. I'm just ready to go home.

You'll be home tomorrow.

Tyren asked You got a brush in here?

Yeah, should be one in my bag, why?

He walked over to her bag for the brush, grabbed it, brushed her hair back into a neat ponytail while Alejandro got comfortable watching a basketball game.

Thanks Ty

No problem sis, any time.

Gabriella had been home from the hospital 2 weeks and finally she'd gotten baby Alex weaned off the bottle his father had gotten him started on even after she told him she was breast feeding. It took a while to get used to the feeling and get Alex Junior to like it but once they both got into it there were no problems.

Alejandro comes into the family room one day with Deuce and two other guys behind him. Originally Gabriella was home alone. The kids were staying over at some friends and Gordon was gone. She was breast feeding baby Alex without a care in the world.

Good To Have You Back

Yo G, goddamn Alejandro said as he quickly covered her chest with a throw.
Why you gotta be sitting all out in the open doing this shit?
She wanted to say cause it's my damn house but instead she said I didn't know
you were having company. She stood up in a shirt that barely covered her ass
after he gave her his pissed off look and walked out of the family room.
Yo D, fix us some drinks. Y'all chill while I go back here and holla at my girl.
The 2 dudes were like Goddamn, mami finer than a muthafucka yo.
No doubt, no wonder he wifed her.
Alejandro walked into his bedroom closing the door behind him. He grabbed his
weed stash, rolled 4 blunts and walked back out of the bedroom. A good 10
minutes later he comes back and asks You done feeding my son yet?
Yeah I'm done feeding hungry butt. I'm about to give him a bath.
Where's Issy? I know Fern had practice.
She's staying over Anita's and Fern's staying all night with Ahmad.
Well damn, what happened to making sure Daddy was okay with it?
They called but you didn't answer so I told them they could go ahead and go.
Y'all gone quit making decisions without me. Hand him here.
I'm about to take him a bath.
You ain't even got the water started yet he said as he took Alex Jr. from her
arms. She stood there watching the two of them for a minute before he walked
out of the room. She had to throw on a robe and go out to the family room to get
him.
Bring him back when you get through. What's for dinner?
I made beef fajitas and rice.
What else?
That's it.
What happened to the beans and corn?
Well it's just me and you so I figured we wouldn't eat much.
Aww G, I see how you do me Deuce joked. I gets no love huh?
Derwin you know that if I'd have known you were coming over I would have
made sure there was enough.
The house phone rang as Alejandro passed the baby off to Gabriella.
What's up sis? Yeah she here. Where else she going? She about to give my son
a bath. I'll have her call you back.

What you waiting on he asked as Gabriella stood there. Get yo ass back there and bathe my son.

Alejandro Jr. was all fresh and clean in his pajamas. Gabriella had brushed his curly hair, cleaned his ears, nose and fingernails. She must have been taking too long because Alejandro came in and asked Damn, you ain't finished yet?
Say yes Daddy, I'm all done she said as she passed him to Alejandro.
To Gabriella he said you need to put some clothes on. Nothing that fits, don't be walking around here trying to show off my shit.
Alejandro's attitude toward Gabriella was starting to piss her off. Originally she thought he was just so caught up on the baby that he wasn't paying her much attention which was to be expected. But the way he treated her was noticeable even to Mariam who just so happened to be over one day while he fussed at Gabriella about the dirty clothes in the laundry room. His argument sounded as if it was about more than just the clothes.
Big brother, give me AJ and go back there with your wife.
For what? I said what I had to say to her.
Yeah but you said it in the wrong way.
What you mean the wrong way? I said she need to clean that shit up. I meant that.
Well damn she is the one that just had a baby.
We just had a baby.
Yeah but you didn't go through the labor, she did.
I was there every step of the way.
You know what I mean.
Nah I don't. Fuck what you talking about. G knows what's up.
Mariam shook her head and walked into the laundry room to start the laundry. She also decided to prepare baked chicken tetrazzini for dinner.
When dinner time came around Alejandro took one look at the food and asked What happened to my gizzards?
You never bought any and I didn't have time to go to the store.
Why not, ain't like you did shit else around this muthafucka.
Alejandro she said through clenched teeth just as the kids came into the kitchen.
I'm going to Jack's, anybody coming he asked?
Ooh me Daddy, the kids squealed as they ran for their coats.

Good To Have You Back

Alejandro there is plenty of food here. I'll cook gizzards tomorrow.
I told you I wanted gizzards today. Learn how to listen. What, having my baby killed your hearing? I mean goddamn. He yelled out Let's go.
Mariam asked, what is his problem?
I have no clue. When you figure it out let me know. Thanks for helping me out.
No problem sis, anytime. Here, have a seat she said as she pulled out a chair. I'll fix your plate and when you're done just go relax.
Mariam agreed to watch Alex Jr. a few hours the next day so Gabriella could get some things done before the kids made it home.
Yo G, Alejandro yelled out from the back door tracking snow all through the house as he walked in.
Shhh Mariam told him. AJ is asleep.
Where G? Why the fireplace ain't going?
Maybe because you never brought the wood she asked you to bring.
My bad, its cold than a muthafucka outside. G sleep too? Fuck she act like she can't hear me.
Gabi's not here.
What you mean she not here? Where she at?
She had to run some errands.
Errands like what? She ain't told me shit.
She went to the grocery store, to get some wood, diapers for AJ. Cleats for Isabella and Fernando's track and soccer registration that you forgot to pay.
Damn, yeah I did forget that shit. She took care of it right?
Yeah, right along with everything else. Alex you really gotta start helping her out.
What you mean? I do what I need to do around here. Don't give me that shit.
You could help out with the simple things like getting wood for the fireplace, washing dishes and clothes and...
Look Mariam you're little sister, I'm big brother. Don't ever forget that. I don't know what Gabi telling you but...
She hasn't told me anything but Alex you need to watch how you treat her.
You trippen, I ain't doing shit wrong. She the one didn't want the maid to come all week, now she have to get all this shit done herself. Shit I hired the maid for a reason. We need a fucking maid.
If you'd help out just a little bit
Yo Mariam, get you some business and get up out of mines alright?

When Gabriella returned after 4pm with Isabella and Fernando they went straight to the family room searching for their little brother.

Yo G, let me holla at you for a minute Alejandro said as he watched her put away groceries.

Holla she told him, I'm listening. I need to get all this put away and get dinner started. Issy's friend and his family are coming over.

What the fuck? I didn't say...

What you said was Issy bring the little nigga over. If I don't like him I'm putting his ass out she repeated word for word in his voice.

He smirked, alright you got that off. Come here, let me holla at you.

Alex how about you put away the groceries while I get started on dinner and we talk in between all this?

Nah, come here now.

Why you gotta be so difficult she laughed?

Do it look like this a fucking joke?

Damn Alejandro what the hell is your problem she asked as Fernando walked into the kitchen and asked Mommy can you help me with my Science project?

Sure baby, you decided what you're going to do yet?

Yes maam, I want to do a 3D solar system. Alejandro stood there impatiently.

And Mommy don't forget we have to finish my Math project tonight and study for my History test.

I didn't forget baby. Isabella has to study too. Why don't you two go ahead and get started and I'll help out in a minute.

Daddy, why are you looking like that?

Like what?

Like you're mad or something. What's wrong?

Nothing. Yo G, come here. I need to holla at you right now. It can't wait.

Once in the room he asked her did you know Geneva was pregnant?

You called me back here with attitude for this shit?

Answer the muthafuckin question.

I haven't heard it and you know I don't fool with Geneva.

He glared at her and asked you ain't see Geneva the other day up at Alley Cats?

Alejandro today is the first time I've been out the house since I had Alex and no I didn't see her today. I haven't been to Alley Cats in forever.

Good To Have You Back

It was a couple of days before Gabriella figured out what that was all about. A local chick by the name of Consuela was claiming to be pregnant by Alejandro. Gabriella found this out through Adrianna when Geneva approached her in the mall one day to spread the word. Adrianna said she asked Alejandro about it and he never denied fucking her but did say she wasn't having his baby and he put that on the kids. Shit had gone from bad to worse in a matter of months and Gabriella felt like Alejandro couldn't handle his issues. As soon as he walked through the door that afternoon laughing and joking with Deuce and the two other dudes that had become regulars Gabriella asked politely after speaking Alex, can I talk to you for a minute?

Come on G, you see I got company.

She gave him the And what look?

His response to that was I'll holla at you in a minute.

She walked up all sexually, grabbed his balls and squeezed them hard. Through clenched teeth she said Fuck that, you gone holla at me now.

He took the hint and left the room without saying a word fearing that the hold she had on his balls would cause him to sound like a bitch. Gabriella bypassed their bedroom altogether and took the elevator to the 3rd floor still holding his balls with a vise grip.

Gabriella, what's up?

I don't know she said as she unlocked the gate to the 3rd floor and raised it with one hand. Why don't you tell me?

You the one walking around with a nigga balls in your hands like they some kind of muthafuckin stress reliever or some shit.

Obviously I ain't holding them tight enough she said angrily as she gripped them even harder causing him to cry out in pain. Now, is there anything you want to tell me?

He thought for a minute. I know Adrianna big mouth ass told you about Consuela.

And?

And that bitch ain't having my baby. I don't know what bum ass nigga she done let knock her up but she ain't putting shit off on me.

Did you fuck her?

I uh, uh. Huh?

Don't insult my intelligence Alejandro. I asked did you fuck her.

Yeah he mumbled so low she barely heard him.

When?

Man, you said…she tried to rip his balls off and he couldn't move.

I didn't ask you what I said. I asked you when?

A couple of months ago.

Did you use a condom?

Hell yeah, fuck you think I am?

If you used a condom what makes her think she can put her baby off on you?

The condom ripped but that was before we even got started. I strapped on 2 after that one for added protection. That's how I know she lying. Can you let go of my shit please?

When she has that baby I want a blood test ASAP.

You gone give me one for AJ?

I most certainly will she said without being insulted or hurt by his comment. And when I get the results I want you to be the first person to see them.

Chapter 23

The results arrived in no time. Alejandro felt a lot of dead weight lifted off his shoulders when the results proved that Alex Jr. was indeed his son. As he and Gabriella sat in the doctor's office Gabriella wanted to cry but she didn't. Of course she'd known all along that AJ was Alejandro's son because she hadn't been with anyone else. As they were walking out of the doctor's office headed towards the elevator Alejandro started apologizing. She tuned him out as she powered on her cell phone and checked her messages. An urgent message from Drago said to call him immediately. She dialed his number in the middle of Alejandro's heartfelt apology.

Sis where are you?

Downtown, Drago what's going on?

I need to talk to you about something important. Come to the house by yourself. Drago.

Sis, this is serious.

She told Alejandro to drop her off at Drago's. For some reason neither Tyren or Drago hung with Alejandro ever since the other two dudes had come into the picture. So when she said she was going to Drago's the only two things he asked was how long you gone be and did you hear anything I said?

Her only response was yes, although she hadn't bothered to listen to anything he said.

Drago answered the door for her, hugged her close and said come on to the back. All the men in the family were present which made the hairs on the back of her neck stand. What's going on she asked?

Bella, have a seat Gordon told her.

I want to know what's going on. Where are my kids?

They're fine, they're with Lucia and Carmen.

What's going on she screamed through tears while still standing. Any time all the males got together something tragic was about to happen or already had. Since everyone was accounted for she figured something was about to happen.

Bella, come on now Drago told her You will want to sit down for this.

Somebody had better tell me what the fuck is going on and make it quick.

Gabriella, baby, calm your nerves a voice from behind her said.

When she turned around she fainted.

Good To Have You Back

Tago pressed a cold towel to her head as he held her in his arms. Gabriella Oh my God Tago. I can't believe you're alive. Where have you been?
I had to get away for a while.
Are you out of your fucking mind she yelled as she got up. Issy and Fern think you're dead. Why would you do that to them?
G-baby, calm down.
Calm down? Oh this is way too much shit for me to deal with in one day. I swear. Somebody take me to get my kids please she screamed. When nobody moved she yelled Now. Gordon, Drago, Tyren and many others were now up and ready.
Gordon tried to calm her by hugging her. She quickly shrugged him off. She asked Uncle Juan to take her to get the kids.
Gabriella, Tago called out as she was leaving. We need to talk.
On the freeway all she could do is cry. Uncle Juan said Bella, I'm going to take you home. I'll call Alex to pick up the kids. You need to pull yourself together before they get there.
Why me she cried? What am I supposed to tell Isabella and Fernando now, after all this time. And Alex is going to flip the fuck out.
I suggest you tell him ASAP.
How?
Just tell him the truth.
Hell I don't even know what that is.
How about we leave the kids with Lucia so you and Alex can talk.
Oh God, can my day get any worse?
There camped out on her doorstep was Consuela and her 2 children, not including the one she's carrying in her stomach. It was below 40 degrees outside and pouring down raining.
Just what I fucking need Gabriella yells.
You need me to get rid of her Uncle Juan asked?
No she said as she dialed Alejandro's number. He answered on the first ring, Yeah baby?
Alex she said barely above a whisper, I need you to come home now.
Okay, I'm on my way. I was grabbing some food.
Make sure you get enough for the kids.

I will. You okay? You sound…

No

Alright, alright I'll be there in like 10-15 minutes.

By the time Alejandro arrived Gabriella helped Consuela get the kids out of their wet clothes and into some dry ones. Consuela was now in one of Gabriella's sweat suits as they sat at the kitchen table with the kids. Consuela's little girl had fallen asleep in Gabriella's arms and cried whenever she tried to put her down. Man what the fuck Alejandro asked in an aggravated tone.

Alejandro can I talk to you for a minute Gabriella asked as he went towards Consuela. Inside their bedroom she rocked Consuela's daughter back to sleep in her arms and said to Alex They need to stay here for a couple of days.

Hell nah, this bitch going around lying on me…

Geneva started that rumor because you told Deuce she was fucking around with Trey.

They can't stay here Gabi.

They have nowhere else to go.

Okay so we will put them up in a hotel.

Why, when we have plenty of room? Look at this baby, both she and that little boy have bruises all over their bodies and Consuela's is even worse.

What the hell happened he asked as he starred at the big bruise on the little girls leg in a rage.

Pen did it when he found out she was pregnant again. It's his baby but he doesn't want any more kids since he's about to marry Z'tasha.

Okay they can stay here for a hot minute then we'll put them into one of the apartments or something. I'm about to go holla at Pen.

No need, Uncle Juan and Tyren are with him now.

Look I'm sorry…

Alejandro it's okay she cried.

Why are you crying Gabi, what's wrong? He took her in his arms when she almost fell out while saying Tago's alive.

Gabi, look at me, what did you say?

I said Tago's alive.

Bullshit, we went to the nigga's funeral. He had an open casket. It was him.

Alex I saw him with my own eyes. He's very much alive.

Alejandro fell onto the bed then quickly hopped up. He ain't taking my kids away from me. I'm not going to let that happen he said through tears.

Look Alex let's get them settled and we'll talk some more.

Where are my kids?

At your Mom's, they're staying the night.

Nah, they coming home. I'll go get them.

I'll have Gordon bring them. Calm your nerves.

Where did you see him at?

At Drago's when you dropped me off.

Alejandro starred at her for a minute looking deep into her eyes. He pulled her into his arms and said don't worry baby. We'll be alright.

Isabella had much attitude towards Consuela having heard Adrianna's conversation with Gabriella about Consuela claiming to be pregnant by Alejandro. She wasn't all that pleased with them staying there even if it was only temporarily. Fernando was cool. He and Consuela's son were the same age. Isabella adored the little girl though and kept mentioning how much she wished they had a little sister. She even sat the little girl down and gave her a head full of pretty ponytails while Consuela got some much needed rest.

Baby, why don't you go take a shower, a bath or something Alejandro asked.

You trying to say I stank she asked as she sat beside him and kissed AJ's forehead while he slept.

Nah, you need to unwind. You all tense and shit.

Daddy, Isabella fussed.

Sorry, go head baby. I got the kids.

Daddy how about you go shower or bath with Mommy and when Auntie Mariam gets here we'll handle the kids Isabella suggested. Mommy already fed AJ so he's going to stay asleep. You and Mommy could use some quality time together. Right?

Yeah we could, come on Big Daddy. Our princess has spoken.

Gabriella you want to tell me what's going on Alejandro asked when they were alone again.

I don't really know. All Tago said was that he had to get away for a while. My head was still trying to come to grips with him standing in front of me. Anything else was too much information.

You need to call and talk to the nigga, see what he's up to.

Tago is not going to talk to me over the phone, at least not about something like this.

Well schedule a meeting with him. Let him know I'm coming too.

He's…

I don't give a fuck what he like. The only way you meeting up with him again is if I'm with you. Understood? Make sure you make that shit clear to him. You're my woman now and I don't want no shit.

Over the next few days Alejandro was the same guy she'd fallen in love with when she came to stay in New York after Tago's funeral.

Sad thing is that he hadn't been that Alejandro in so long that she knew the only reason he was acting this way is because of Tago's presence. Considering everything that happened between the two of them he had every right to be worried. Now he always had to answer her phone when it rang. He went damn near everywhere she went until he was starting to suffocate her. Tago figured Alejandro would be all over her now that he was back in the picture. When Gabriella hadn't bothered to call him all week he called her cell phone. Alejandro answered.

Yo Alex, this Tago. Its time you and I meet.

Yeah, let's do this. The suspense is killing me.

Tago said Let's meet at Barnabee's around 8. No need to bring Gabi. Let's talk man to man.

G, I'm about to step out for a minute he said as he dressed in khaki from head to toe.

Where are you going?

To go handle some business.

Gabriella read a book while AJ rested on her chest with his eyes wide open.

Okay but don't stay out all night. You know the weather is supposed to get bad. You need me to pick up anything while I'm out?

No, we're good. Alex, where are you going?

Out baby, don't start trippen. I'll be right back.

What's right back?

Okay, I'm lying. Nah I won't be right back but I'll be back before midnight he said as he pinched AJ's cheeks. Son, you keep an eye on your mama and hold it down til I get back, aight?

He tongue kissed Gabriella and said when I get back I got to have you.

Bring a box of condoms.

Don't start that shit again Gabi. I'm getting all up in here tonight he said with his hand between her legs massaging her clit. He hadn't touched her in so long that she didn't know how to react to his touch.

Isabella called out Mommy can I get AJ for a little while before he falls asleep.

Yeah Alejandro said Come get him now. He was in the bathroom now coming out of his clothes because Gabriella's wetness just did it for him. There was no way he could leave the house with a hard on like that. Then Deuce started calling him back to back so he ended up putting his clothes back on and leaving.

Alejandro stepped up in Barnabee's and was lead over to a conference room where Tago sat at a round table alone. He stood when Alejandro entered the room, extended his hand. They shook. Tago offered him a drink, a cigar, food, anything to lighten the mood.

So what's been up man, Alejandro asked? Why'd you disappear like that?

I got caught up in some shit and the niggas made threats on my family so I did what I had to do. I made like I was dead and handled my business behind the scenes.

Yeah and you come back looking just as you did when you left here. You didn't bother with a face change, name change, none of that. Ain't you thinking about all the charges you could face by faking your death?

Technically I didn't fake my death.

I went to your funeral, an open casket at that. Yo ass was laying in that casket.

Yeah but the death certificate was my father's information made to look like mines. Even if questions come up there's nothing anywhere that proves I faked my death. My father and I shared the same name, same date of birth. It was just a big mix up.

If you say so. What's your plan now?

If you're worried about me trying to get Gabi...

That's the least of my worries. I know Gabriella ain't going nowhere.

As long as you stay treating her right you ain't got nothing to worry about. She's the most loyal person I know. I'll always love and respect her for that.

You didn't answer my question.

You seem worried about something. Talk to me.

You're back after almost 6 ½-7 years. I've built a relationship with Issy and Fern.

Good To Have You Back

Yeah Tago said as he fired up a cigar and blew out smoke. Heard they call you Daddy. Thank you for treating them as if you're their blood. I appreciate that for real.

Now that you back what do you plan to do as far as the kids go?

I mean I want to see them, spend time with them as often as possible. I'll have to work something out with Gabriella. As much as I would like for them to come live with me I know Gabi ain't gone allow that.

I know I've already put everybody through enough. So if I could just get to know them all over again I'd appreciate it. I know this will be complicated for all of us. So I feel that it might work best if we all work together on this.

You want your house back?

Nah, everything Gabi has is hers, the house, the money, the businesses. I'm good. You tell her you were meeting with me?

Nah, what for?

With all that has been going on with you two secrets is the last thing you'd want to keep.

What do you know about what's going on between me and my wife?

Girlfriend, Tago smirked. Like me you're not smart enough to put a ring on her finger yet. You're too caught up in the business. Trust me, when it's all said and done you'll miss her a whole lot more than you'll miss the business.

You don't know shit about our relationship.

I know more than you think. I made it a point to know all of Gabi's business from the time she left me years ago. I know you cheated on her a number of times but there have only been 2 in which you spent time with, the dead chick and the white chick. I know you didn't think Alejandro Jr. was your son. Tago shook his head. If we as men didn't spend so much time doing dirt we wouldn't be so insecure. Like I said, Gabriella is very loyal. She would leave you before she cheated. You should be thankful that she and the kids love you. Well she could probably get over you if need be. She's a very strong woman, but I'm sure the kids are the reason she's keeping you around. I'm sure you know that too. Man to man, if you know like I know you better play your cards right.

Or else what?

Actions speak louder than words. I'll be calling Gabi to arrange a meeting. You're welcome to join us if you'd like.

I trust Gabriella to do the right thing.

Yeah, and that's why you're always answering her phone now that I'm back Tago laughed.

I trust her, it's you I don't trust.

You don't have to worry about me. Whatever I had with Gabriella is long gone because she's in love with you. All I can tell you is to play your cards right Tago said again as he stood up and downed a shot of Tequila. Have a nice day. I'm out.

After leaving Barnabee's Alejandro needed to clear his head so he hit the strip club with Deuce. After a few lap dances and a whole lot of drinks he made his way home. It was damn near 5 in the morning and Gabriella was up feeding AJ. Wassup he asked without stopping. He headed straight towards the bedroom without waiting for a response. Gabriella didn't return to bed until after she got the kids off to school. She'd stood out front talking with the next door neighbor a good 45 minutes.

Where you been?

Out front talking to Martha. Where's AJ?

Gordon came in here and got him. Get your ass in this bed.

What happened to being home before midnight?

Some shit came up. I had business to take care of.

Yeah I'm sure. Business that has you smelling like another chick's perfume and wearing her lipstick on your collar she smirked.

He looked puzzled trying to figure out how she knew when she hadn't went inside the bathroom where his clothes were at the bottom of the dirty clothes hamper.

I saw the lipstick and smelled the perfume when you strolled through this morning. You really should learn to be discreet. How would you feel if I came in smelling like another nigga's cologne?

Try that shit if you want to. I ain't the one who told you it was cool to sleep with other men.

You didn't have to tell me. You made it perfectly clear when you decided you were going to sleep with other women. Only reason I haven't done so yet is because I was pregnant with AJ.

Yeah what the fuck ever G. Gone on with that bullshit.

Gabriella went into the bathroom, showered and stepped out wrapped in a towel as she walked over to her closet.

What you taking a shower for?

I have plans this morning. I'm not sure what Gordon's going to be doing so AJ is all yours until I get back.

Where the fuck you going?

To get my hair done, nails, toes, a massage and just do me for a day. That alright with you?

Hell nah he says as he gets out of bed butt naked swinging meat every which way as he grabbed his bath robe. Hey Pop, you got anything planned today?

No son, what's up?

Me and G about to go chill. You mind keeping AJ for a few hours?

Nah, grandson's cool with me. We're about to watch Knight Rider

To Gabriella Alejandro said don't leave out that door without me.

I'm still waiting on Adrianna and Mariam to get here anyway.

You didn't tell me they were going with you.

You didn't bother to ask me either.

Gabriella sat in the salon for 3 ½ hours getting the works done to her hair and body. Alejandro sat there falling asleep with her cell phone in his pocket.

Isabella would text ever so often about little boys at school until Alejandro replied You and me gone talk when you get home little girl.

Daddy she replied back.

Yeah and you come straight home from school. Whatever plans you had, cancel them.

Yes sir

Put that damn phone up and pay attention in class.

Yes sir

Chapter 24

G, what Issy doing texting you while she at school?

She always does in between classes, during lunch or whenever she wants to talk.

She go to school to learn. If her cell phones a distraction we taking it away from her.

We ain't taking nothing. She's still a straight A student and all the kids carry cell phones. I've never gotten an email, phone call or letter about her cell phone being a distraction.

What she doing texting you about boys?

Alex, she's 15, what do you think girls her age talk about? Dolls?

She sure as hell don't need to be talking about boys.

I'd rather her talk to me than one of those fass girls at school. You better not make my baby feel like she did anything wrong. I told her she could talk to me about anything. Don't take that away from her.

I still don't think she should be talking about boys.

Alex what were you thinking about at 15 Adrianna asked him.

Pussy, the same thing those no good boys at that school thinking about.

Yeah but you need to trust that Issy's smart enough to know better Mariam cut in. Be thankful she has a mom she can talk to. I didn't have that. Well I had a mom but all she did was tell me what not to do. I was made to feel like her answer to everything was simply don't do it. There was no explanation. If it wasn't for Mama Lucia, Adrianna and Gabi I'd probably be like more than half the girls in my high school, pregnant and dropped out of school.

Oh Isabella ain't dropping out and she sure as hell ain't getting pregnant Alejandro told her.

When Isabella got home from school she found her mom in the kitchen cooking dinner. Hi Mommy, ooh you look so pretty.

Thanks baby, did you enjoy the rest of your day?

No, because I'm in trouble with Daddy now she said with a pout.

No you're not. He's just concerned. Gone on in the family room and talk to him. He's waiting on you.

Hi Daddy Isabella said as she leaned over the sofa to kiss Alejandro's cheek.

Hey babygirl, how was your day? Come around and have a seat.

Good To Have You Back

It was good, can I hold him she asked as she held her hands out for AJ. I already washed my hands.

He passed AJ to her and watched as she made him smile and giggle by telling him all about her day. He asked her a few questions, was satisfied with her answers related to boys and left the subject alone. When Gabriella's cell phone rang he looked at the caller ID and walked into the kitchen. Here he said as he answered and handed it to her.

Hello she answered without being able to check the caller ID because her hands were covered in flour.

Gabi, what's up? I've been trying to call you so we can get together and talk. I've been trying to call you back all day but kept getting your voicemail.

When can we meet? Tonight good? The sooner the better.

Tonight's not good, both Isabella and Fernando have a game. In fact they have games all this week unless you want to meet during the day?

The only way we can meet in the day time is if you come out to PA. That's where I'm living. I still have loose ends to tie up so until I do I won't be spending a whole lot of time at home.

Well I have a business meeting there all this week, maybe we can get together then.

What kind of business?

We'll talk about it later. Issy baby, can you go get my Bluetooth please?

Yes maam. Mommy did you know Grandpa is going to Port Arthur to help that family that lost their house in the fire?

Yes, he told me this morning. Your Daddy is going too.

Who's going to keep AJ while you go back and forth to PA?

Gran's coming over and Carmen will help out around the house.

Ooh Fern's going to be mad if Daddy misses his football game.

They're not leaving until after the game.

Mommy, can I give AJ a bath?

Yes baby, wash his hair too and make sure…

I know, I know, clean his ears, nose and nails.

Man she sounds like a grown woman Tago commented.

And acts like one too, not in the growing up too fast kind of way but she's very smart.

Where's Fernando?

He tutors kids on Tuesdays and Thursdays until 5

Wow, that's great. Man you'll have to fill me in. I know Alejandro's probably starring you upside your head right now.

Gabriella moved to throw something in the trash and bumped into Alejandro who wore a smile on his face like Yeah I'm listening.

I take that as a yes. Well call me when we can meet, the sooner the better.

Okay, I will.

Kiss the kids for me.

What's up Alejandro asked when she hung up.

He wants to get together and talk. When are you free?

Decided I don't have to be there. The two of you probably have a lot to say to each other and I trust that you'll do the right thing. Just keep me posted.

He wants to meet in PA since that's where he's living. Said he's not spending too much time around these parts and we can't meet at night because of all the activities this week.

PA is cool since you're already out that way anyway. Just make sure your ass makes it home before 3 everyday.

Come on now, you know I know that. You sure you're okay with this?

Yeah I'm good. How do you feel about all this?

Better now than never, we need to figure out a way to tell the kids before the rumors start flying.

Make him tell them. He's the one that created the problem.

Yeah but we need to be there for support and be prepared for all the questions. That nigga dug this hole, let him dig hisself out of it.

I wasn't speaking of him. I was talking about the kids. This is going to be so hard on them.

Confusing if anything but they're smart kids. They'll be alright.

Gabriella was dressed in a midnight blue Donatella Versace pant suit that hugged her frame at every angle. Her hair was pulled back in a simple ponytail and she walked with her head held high, a super model stroll that demanded everyone's attention.

Sorry I'm late she said as Tago stood at the table and held a chair out for her. He wanted to wrap her up in his arms and kiss her soft lips.

No problem, I ordered for you. Food should be out shortly. How's your day been?

Productive, the new office is coming along nicely.

What new office?

I decided to expand Computer Networks. We're currently in New Jersey, Pennsylvania, Virginia and soon to be North Carolina.

Well damn G-baby, you really know how to run a business I see. I'm glad to know you're still holding it down. You haven't lost your touch.

Did you expect me to?

No, not at all.

Gabriella's text message went off. Tago asked your boyfriend checking up on you?

No she smirked, it's Isabella.

Why she ain't in school?

She is.

Well what is she doing on the phone?

Telling me about her day. She always does this in between classes or during free time.

Gabriella, I want to say thank you for stepping in and taking care of my kids as if they're your own. You will never know how much I appreciate you. I'm sorry that things had to go down the way they did but things happened the way I needed them to happen. Well, most things anyway.

What exactly were you caught up in that would make you leave your family?

Let's just say it's a lot deeper than you think.

You owe me an explanation.

I know and I have every intention of giving you one. Now is just not the time nor the place.

So what are we here for?

To talk, there's a lot we need to discuss. Shit that we should have talked about long before either one of us disappeared.

I didn't disappear. You always knew where I was.

I made it a point to know. I wanted to make sure you were safe.

You wanted to control me.

That's bullshit. Look, I can't take back what I did. I'm sorry. I told you that and I mean it.

The waitress brought out their food, asked if they needed anything else.

Can I have a to go box Gabriella asked?

A to go box, for what?

The waitress said Yes maam as she walked off.

I didn't come here to eat. You've beat around the bush long enough. What did you bring me here for?

I want to see my kids Gabi and I have to go through you to see them.

You could have said that over the phone.

I don't know what to say to them. Hell I'm not even sure what to say to you. I wish I could turn back...

Yeah but you can't Gabriella said as she accepted the to go box. I'll tell the kids what I know and let you know when a good time to see them would be. After that you're on your own.

Thank you Gabi.

Yeah whatever she said as she closed the lid on her box, dropped a 20 on the table and said I'll call you later.

He watched her walk away. An older gentleman said as he shook his head If I were you son, I'd go after her.

Tago tried to smile.

You love her don't you?

Yes sir.

Well what's the problem?

I messed up too many times to count.

The two of you have kids together?

Yeah, a boy and a girl.

How do the kids feel about the two of you being apart?

They hated it at first.

And now?

I haven't seen my kids in over 7 years.

Why not? She keeping them away from you?

Nah, I kept myself away from them.

You must have had a valid reason. So go get your family back.

She's with someone else now. They have a child together.

She married?

Nah, this guy is just as dumb as I was.

So technically she's still available. What you waiting on son?

Around 7pm Tago dialed Gabriella's number. Gordon answered.
She's back there taking a nap. Hasn't been feeling too good.
What's wrong with her?
She was fine when she left here this morning. What did you do to her?
Come on now Papi you know I would...I didn't do anything to her. She was okay when she left me too. Do you know if she talked with the kids yet?
Isabella's in there now. Fernando is cleaning his room.
Fern, Isabella called out Mommy wants you.

Gabriella didn't know how to tell the kids that Tago was alive without taking away the devastation she herself felt. No matter how she put it, it all still said the same thing. She explained that something happened to where he had to go away for a while. Originally they assumed she meant Alejandro but then she cleared it all up and told them Tago was alive. They both wanted to see him immediately which is what she expected. They had to see him to believe it. The next morning Alejandro and Gordon left for Port Arthur, TX. Alejandro was skeptical about the kids going to see Tago but knew it had to happen eventually. On the way to Tago's house in Pennsylvania Fernando asked Mommy does this mean we will have to go live with...he paused with our Daddy now and does this mean we can't call Daddy, Daddy anymore he asked referring to Alejandro.
You can still call Alejandro Daddy and no, you will not be moving, okay?
Okay.
Issy, you okay baby?
No, Mommy this is so weird. This is straight out of a soap opera. Am I dreaming? I mean I always dreamed that Daddy would come back but I didn't think he really would. I believed he was dead and now I don't know what to think.
Tago paced back and forth as he waited for Gabriella to arrive with the kids. He was nervous and even shed a few tears. Nobody really knew what they planned to say but as soon as Gabi's Bentley pulled into his circular driveway he opened the door and walked out to greet them. The kids were in his arms in no time, almost knocking him over in the process. Gabriella wiped at her own tears.

Come inside. I made Monte Cristos for lunch he said as he ushered them in. He kissed Gabriella's cheek with a smile and said Thank you.

For the next 4 hours Tago sat with the kids, neither of them wanting to leave his side. The kids wanted to stay the night with Tago. Since it was the weekend she tried calling Alejandro before making the decision but he didn't answer. She figured that allowing Tago his time with the kids would keep a lot of confusion down so she left them there but continued calling Alejandro.

When Alejandro called the house phone around 10 o'clock that night Gabriella was half asleep but had explained to him that the kids were at Tago's for the night and possibly the weekend. He hung up in her face. When she kept calling his cell back she would always get his voicemail just as she'd been getting all day. She flipped on the light and checked the caller ID. She was surprised to see Sherrie's name scroll across the screen. When he hadn't bothered to return her phone calls by 5pm the next day she dialed Sherrie's number.

Sherrie answered on the second ring. Hi Sherrie, this is Gabriella. Is Alex in?

Oh hey Gabi, no he stepped out with Deuce somewhere. He should be home in a little bit.

Home as in New York?

No, I mean Port Arthur.

Didn't know you moved to Port Arthur.

Yeah we decided to move closer to my parents so they could be near the baby. So what do you think about having a little niece? You are coming to the baby shower right? Alex said he told you about it.

The phone slipped from Gabriella's hands, she cried the next 2 days. When Tago couldn't get a hold to her he called Gordon. Gordon hadn't made it home yet but had also been trying to call. Tago sent Drago, when he got there he found her in the same spot she'd fallen to after that phone call.

He helped her into the bed. Sis, what's wrong he asked? You okay? Need me to call Alex?

She shook her head no as more tears fell. Her cell started to ring, it was Satin. Satin's calling, you want to talk to her?

Yes

When she passed her the phone he decided to leave the room to fix her something to eat. She told Satin she needed her. She convinced Drago that she was okay, asked that he tell Tago she'd come by later to pick up the kids. She knew Tago wouldn't believe she was okay. He'd keep asking questions until he pulled it out of her.

When Satin arrived she told her all about the phone call to Sherrie. They both concluded that Alejandro didn't even realize he'd called her from Sherrie's number. If he did he'd have called her or come home by now. When Gordon arrived he confirmed what they already suspected, that he thought Alejandro had come home when in reality he'd been in Port Arthur with Sherrie and his baby.

Why the fuck you blowing up my phone like that Alejandro asked Sherrie when he walked in.

Gabi has been trying to call you. She called here. I was telling her about the baby when I heard a loud cry, the phone dropped and I've been trying to call her back but the line is busy. I'm worried about her Sherrie cried.

Gabriella called here? How the fuck did she get this number?

You called her last night.

From my cell phone, that still don't explain why she called here.

You must have grabbed my phone by mistake.

Alejandro checked the caller ID to be sure and saw their house phone number. What exactly did you say to her he asked?

I told her about the baby shower and asked if she was coming.

Alejandro dialed his home number from his cell but nobody answered. He tried Gabriella's cell phone but got voicemail so he tried Isabella's phone. She started crying because she'd been trying to reach Gabriella as well and his phone call made her worry even more. He dialed his Mom's number and asked Ma, where's Gabriella?

She just left here with AJ, said she was on her way to get Issy and Fern from friends. Are you two mad at each other again?

Did she say anything to you?

No, I asked her if she'd been crying because her eyes were all swollen but she told me no. What's going on?

Ma, I'll call you later.

Alejandro she said just before the line went dead. He kept trying Gabriella's cell phone again. She wouldn't answer. Gordon was the one picking up Issy and Fern so Gabriella could avoid Tago. Before leaving the house he'd checked the *caller ID, saw Sherrie's number and called it back looking for Alejandro in order to find out what was going on. Sherrie, thinking Gordon was Alejandro and Gabi's father thought that Gabi must have told Gordon the news. She didn't hesitate to give him the details she didn't get a chance to discuss with Gabriella, including the sex of the baby.*

When Alejandro called Gordon he asked Pop, where's Gabi?

If you weren't in Port Arthur playing house with Sherrie you'd know. I suggest you call someone to come get your shit because if it's not out by tonight its going on the side of the road in the morning.

Pop, come on man. Quit trippen. Can you hear me out, please he asked knowing if he could get through to Gordon Gabriella would be a piece of cake. Gordon sighed, I'm listening.

Shit was ugly with me and Gabi so I was kicking it with Sherrie. One night I slipped without a condom and she ended up pregnant. She refused to get an abortion and you know I just can't put my child out there like that.

So you moved her from Pennsylvania to Port Arthur in hopes that Gabi would never find out huh?

Yeah I mean shit it's not like I wanted the baby. I'm not even trying to be with Sherrie and she knows that he said as she stood in the doorway of the garage listening to him with tears running down her face. That night she tried to kill Alejandro, she shot him once in the chest and again in the leg before turning the gun on herself, killing her and the unborn baby. Deuce had no idea what was going on with Gabi and Alejandro so he called her. She in turn called Lucia and Adrianna before calling Mariam. Lucia and Mariam assumed Gabriella was on her way to Port Arthur but Adrianna knew better. She was at Gabriella's doorstep 30 minutes after receiving the call. When Satin answered the door she knew something was wrong.

Where's Gabi?

On the 3rd floor, she locked herself in and won't come out Satin cried.

Is it because Alejandro got shot?

Adrianna the woman that shot your brother is or was pregnant by him. Alejandro moved her to Port Arthur so Gabriella wouldn't find out. He accidentally called her from the chick's number last night and wouldn't answer his own phone so Gabi called the number back.

Oh God. Gabi Adrianna screamed as she rushed to the elevator only to find that she couldn't access it due to it being locked. She panicked and called Gordon who stood talking to Tago and heard Adrianna's frantic cries concerning Gabriella. Gordon ended up staying with the kids while Tago took a flight to New York.

When Tago walked through the door Adrianna thought she was trippen. She told herself Girl, you're seriously about to lose it, pull yourself together. Gabriella needs you. She bowed her head and prayed for strength. It wasn't until she heard Satin talking that she walked into the hallway.

She heard Tago ask how long has she been down there as he knocked a hole in the wall and put some wires together that activated the elevator. He took it to the 3rd floor and pulled out his keys unlocked first the gate and then the 3rd floor door. Satin and Adrianna both stood with their backs to the wall seeing but not believing the sight before their eyes.

Give me some time alone with her please Tago said in a calm voice. Adrianna call and check on your brother. Satin, fix her something light to eat, get her a drink, preferably something strong. Call Gordon and let him know I made it. Go on, she'll be alright. I promise.

Tago walked inside, closed the door behind him and locked it. Gabriella's soft cries could be heard from the entry area as she lay in a fetal position.

G-baby, Tago called out to her.

Leave me alone she mumbled. I'm having a nightmare. I want to wake up now she cried.

You're not having a nightmare baby he said as he picked her up in his arms and held her close as she cried. He caressed her back, moved her hair from her face wishing he could take all her pain away. For a long time neither of them said anything, only her cries could be heard. He held her as her body started to tremble and her cries got louder.

Tago

Yeah baby

Make love to me

Gabi, I

Please

As much as I would love to Gabi, I just don't think now is a good time. You're emotional and you're not thinking clearly. You and Alex need to clear up some things before I get involved. I know one time won't be enough for me.

Tago you make me sick.

I know, come on let's go get you cleaned up so you can go check on your Boo.

Fuck him. I'm subject to finish him off.

You don't mean that. You're upset.

I'm beyond upset. I feel so stupid.

G baby, come on you trippen for real. You shouldn't feel stupid. It's his loss if he wasn't smart enough to realize what he had in you. It took him forever to get you which means he should have appreciated you even more. That's his bad. Go get cleaned up while I get y'all a flight out. Where's AJ?

Drago came and got him earlier.

You got clothes down here?

Yeah

Why?

Gabriella didn't respond, instead she walked into the bathroom leaving the door open as she removed her clothes and stepped into the shower. Tago bit his bottom lip and said goddamn as he repositioned the huge bulge in his pants and made a phone call on his cell phone. As soon as Gabriella stepped out the shower she called Drago to ask him to remove Alex's things from the house.

Bella, I'm not getting involved right now. You and Alex need to talk first. We both know he ain't going nowhere.

Drago remember the PA chick I found out about the time Alex got shot.

Yeah

He moved her to Port Arthur because she was pregnant with his baby. She just tried to kill him then turned the gun on herself, killing her and the baby.

You bullshitten right?

Hell no, I'm dead serious.

Where's Issy and Fern?

At your brother's.

Does he know?

Yes

And he's still at home?

No, he's here at the house. Gordon's at his place with the kids. I'm on my way to Port Arthur. I want all of Alex's things gone by the time I get back.

Where to?

He still owns the condo he had before he moved here. Take his shit there, that's where he's been pretending to be a bachelor at anyway. I should have listened to Consuela when she tried to tell me.

Next she called Gordon because he'd called about Isabella not being able to sleep.

Mommy she said when she got on the phone.

Yes baby, what's the matter?

I dreamed Daddy had another baby and he was moving away. Is that true?

Yes Issy, Alejandro did have another woman pregnant and he will be leaving for good this time.

Did he get shot too?

Yes

Did he die she cried?

No baby, he's okay as far as I know. I'm getting ready to leave for the hospital now.

In my dream somebody died.

We'll talk more about it when I get back.

Can you tell Daddy to call me please so that I know he's okay?

Yes baby, I will have him call you.

I love you Mommy.

I love you too Isabella. Get some sleep. I'll call you in the morning she said as she kissed the phone.

Good night

Sweet dreams baby.

Did it really happen Fernando asked Isabella after she hung up.

Daddy did get shot but he's not dead. Mommy's on her way to the hospital.

Daddy did have another baby too and Mommy said he's leaving for good this time.

Man, I hate being me Fernando said sadly.

Don't say that, why would you say that?

First our real Daddy dies he says sarcastically and then Alejandro steps in and he's cool. Things start going crazy and he & Mom are acting all weird.

Mom was acting all weird as you put it because Alex was cheating on her. He always was.

Well why did she stay with him then?

She did it for us because she didn't think we could handle them being apart.

Well I would rather not see Mommy hurt and if that means they can't be together then oh well. It's his loss, not ours. At least we still have Mommy and AJ.

Fern you need to let Mommy know that because although she loves Alex she only put up with all that because of us. We have to let her know that we'll be okay and that we'll help out with AJ.

Daddy wouldn't make it hard on her.

Who

Neither one of them.

Mariam ran into Gabriella, Adrianna and Satin in the hallway of Port Arthur Medical Center. I'm so glad you guys made it. Alex keeps asking for you Gabi.

How is he Adrianna asked?

Alive, he'll be alright once he heals. She wanted to hurt him, not kill him. She almost paralyzed him.

Where's Mom Gabriella asked?

In the waiting room, she can't handle it. She just keeps crying.

Gabriella follows Mariam to the waiting room while Satin and Adrianna go to Alex's room.

Mrs. Lucia hugs Gabriella long and hard as she kisses her cheeks. I'm so sorry Gabi.

Don't be, it's not your fault. Come on let's have a seat. You look like you're about to fall over.

She sat talking to Lucia for a good 45 minutes before the doctor came out and called her by name.

Yes she asked?

Mrs. Solera

Ms. Pennington she smiled confidently but yes I am Gabriella.

Okay he said puzzled Mr. Solera was shot in the chest just below the heart and in the leg. Both wounds are pretty deep but I hear you're pretty familiar with gunshot wounds. He stood there and ran down a list of things regarding Alejandro's circumstances as if she would be the one caring for him. She would be under normal circumstances but she'd learned so much about Alejandro's extracurricular activities in the few hours after Sherrie's phone conversation that she wanted no parts of him. She would get him a live in nurse until he could take care of himself. She'd also make sure his medical expenses were paid.

She discussed all this with Lucia and Carmen, gave them all the information they needed to understand her reasoning. Finally after making all the arrangements she went back to see Alejandro.

Gabi he said barely above a whisper with his back turned to her. She was trying to figure out how he knew it was her when he continued to call out her name.

Alex, I'm here.

I need you.

She walked over to him and gently took a seat on the hospital bed. Without words she kissed at his tears and held him while he rested. Hours later he felt her letting go and his heart ached.

Gabriella

Yes

I love you

I love you too Alejandro she said as she kissed his cheek. Take care of yourself. AJ needs you and Issy & Fern are worried sick about you. Call them as soon as you feel up to it.

Even though they hadn't discussed what was going to happen Alejandro knew it was over.

Gabriella powered on her cell phone as she got off the plane in New York. All kinds of alerts started going off, text messages, voice mails, missed phone calls, emails. Most of the messages came from people she'd already spoken to like the kids, Gordon, Drago, Uncle Juan, Tago and others. Antonio had called the most because he was worried about her.

Tony, I'm okay she said when she called him back.

You need me to come take care of you?

I'll come to you she smiled. Give me some time with the kids and I'll call you.

Yeah you do that. Take care of the kids but don't have me waiting too long.

Alejandro never called the kids but called Gabriella to let her know he wanted to talk with the kids face to face. She made arrangements with Lucia to take them to Alejandro's. Tago wanted to spend some time with the kids, even asked about meeting AJ.

Why don't you and Alex work together on the times? I'll be gone for 2 weeks. The kids will be with Lucia, Alex's mother.
Where are you going?
I need a vacation.
Okay so where are you going Tago asked?
Tago for once can you not to be all up in my business she laughed.
He bit his bottom lip and smiled himself before asking you sure you're okay?
Yes, I'm good.

Chapter 25

She never mentioned the vacation to Alejandro so when Tago brought it to his attention he was puzzled for a minute. He asked where did she say she was going?

Tago told him She wouldn't tell me. I kept asking, she told me to mind my business.

Issy, Alejandro called out.

Yes Daddy, she asked before entering the room. Oh hey Daddy she said to Tago. I didn't know you were here.

Hey babygirl he said as he hugged her.

Yo mama go to Phoenix Alejandro asked Isabella.

Isabella looked back and forth between Alejandro and Tago until Alejandro said You don't have to tell me. I already know.

Know what, Tago asked? What's in Phoenix?

Isabella asked Did y'all need anything?

No, but do me a favor.

What's that Daddy?

Text your mama and tell her I said to call me ASAP.

Daddy Isabella said slowly, I'm sorry but your ASAP's don't work with Mommy anymore she shrugged her shoulders sadly.

Alright Issy go get AJ.

Gran's giving him a bath. I'll bring him when she's done.

Thanks

What's in Phoenix Tago asked again

That so called investigator you hired.

Antonio

Yeah

I told him to stop messing around with her when he told me he was catching feelings.

He did, how do you think she ended up with me?

So how'd they hook back up?

He moved to Phoenix a couple of years ago. She ran into him while visiting Satin.

Satin lives in Phoenix?

Yeah, been there about as long as G been here.
What makes you think she's with him?
We ain't had sex since before she had AJ
What?
She started trippen about me using condoms because I fucked off a time or two. I wasn't trying to use condoms because she's the only person I'd been with without one. Plus she's my girl and the shit just didn't feel right. I call myself trying to be strong thinking she'd give in eventually but she wasn't playing about that shit.
So you think she's going to fuck Antonio?
Yeah
Damn they both said at the same time as they whipped out their cell phones and tried calling her. They got voicemail because she was having a 3 way conversation with Isabella and Fernando on separate phones even though they're both in the same house. They were telling her how cool it was to have 2 daddies instead of one and how Alejandro and Tago got along so well.
Unh huh Mommy Isabella confirmed, They're both trying to figure out where you are right now. Daddy has a clue I'm sure and he's going to tell Daddy eventually. Issy you're confusing Fern laughed, you can't call them both Daddy. How will they ever know who we're talking to? How about we call one Papi and one Daddy? They both mean the same thing.
Yeah we can do that.
Alright, well Mom I'm going to finish playing Chess with Daddy's nurse.
Okay baby, I love you.
Isabella asked Mommy, you're not really with Antonio are you?
No baby, Satin and Auntie decide to take me to Venezuela. It's just us girls.
Okay she breathed a sigh of relief as Lucia walked into the living area with AJ.
Gran, Daddy wants AJ. I'll take him back there.
Is your father still here?
Yes maam
It's awfully quiet back there.
Yeah they're trying to get a hold to Mommy. They think she's with Antonio
Antonio?
She's not. She's in Venezuela with Auntie and Satin Isabella winked.
Is that your Mom on the phone?

Yes maam
Let me talk to her
Hey baby, you okay Lucia asked?
Yes Mom, I'm fine. I promise.
What is going through your head young lady?
How I'm about to have them both eating out of the palm of my hands.
You're so bad Lucia smiled.

You call your Mom yet Alejandro asked Isabella as soon as she walked in the room with AJ.
Yes she smiled
Where's the phone? Why'd you hang up?
Gran's talking to her.
Yo Ma
What Alex?
I need to talk to Gabi
You need to get some rest. Hi Tago she said as she hugged him and passed the phone to Alejandro.
Gabi
Yes Alex
Where are you?
Why
Cause I want to know.
I'm not with Antonio.
Alejandro breathed a sigh of relief. I miss you he tells her sincerely.
Not as bad as you're going to.
Gabriella
What, what are you guys doing?
Nothing just talking. Tago's meeting AJ for the first time and he likes him almost as much as he likes me.
I'm sure you don't have a problem with that considering the circumstances.
Nah I'm all good with that.
How are you feeling?
Why don't you come find out?
I'll be gone for another week. I'll stop by when I get back.

Alright, be safe.

I will. You get some rest. Mom says you've been up all day and all night.

Can't sleep, haven't been able to get any sleep since I came home.

You'll have a million and one sleepless nights. I promise you.

What's that supposed to mean?

You will know soon enough. Look, I gotta go. Kiss my baby for me and tell him Mommy loves him.

What about me?

I love you too Alex. Get some rest so your Mom can relax. If you need to, let the kids go home with Tago, even if only for a couple of hours.

Anything else?

No, I think that's about it.

When Gabriella returned home she went to Alejandro's to pick up the kids but Tago had them.

Hey handsome she said as she entered his room and took a seat on the bed.

He bit his lip as he looked her over. Bring your ass here and give me a hug.

She hugged him, then kissed his forehead. You need a haircut.

You'll take me to get one?

Yeah, I guess.

Help me get dressed.

No, you better muster up some strength and do it. I'll be waiting in the living room for you.

G, come on now. I need you to help me shower.

You make me sick.

No I don't. You love me.

I do, come on here she said as she helped him up. He leaned on her without putting too much weight on her trying to be tough shit and almost fell. Alex quit playing, hold on to me. I got you. She had him sit on the toilet while she started the shower. In order to avoid getting wet she had to remove her clothes. After the shower she dried him off. She redid his bandages, put cocoa butter on the rest of his body before putting him on a pair of boxers, a wife beater, white t-shirt, a Crown Holder shirt and a pair of jeans. Instead of tennis shoes she had him step into a comfortable pair of slippers when he argued that he needed to get out of the house. At the barbershop his barber Vic got him right. Told him he'd make house calls if Alex needed him to.

When Gabriella got in the driver's seat Alejandro told her I don't want to go home yet. Let's go somewhere and chill.

Chill where Alex, you're barely standing.

I'm tired of being cooped up in the house Gabi and I just want to be with you.

I gotta go pick up my kids.

Our kids and they're fine. Tago said to take all the time we need.

Yeah and your time with me is up. Unless you need me to feed you.

Licking his lips as he starred at her thighs he said yeah, feed me.

I was talking about food she said with a roll of her eyes. Do you want anything or not?

Mom's usually cooks. Just drop me off at the house.

When they got to his building Alejandro was out the car before she took the key out of the ignition good and limped his way to the elevators.

Alex slow down Gabriella fussed as she hurried to him when he almost fell for the second time.

I don't need your help he said as he snatched his arm away from her and got onto the elevator. He kept his eyes on the doors as they rode up to the 15th floor in silence. At the 11th floor a couple got on, at the 12th a man with a dog and 2 large suitcases. On the 14th floor Alejandro got off because he hates being in cramped spaces.

Here, lean on me.

I don't need your fucking help he said through clenched teeth.

Stop being so goddamn stubborn she said as she snatched his arm and wrapped it around her neck.

I hate you.

Tell me something I don't know. It's gotta be hate with the way you treat me Gabriella said as they stood in front of his door.

I don't really hate you.

You don't really love me either she said sadly as she unlocked his door and let him in.

Gabriella, don't leave. Please.

Alex the more and more I'm around you the less I like you. I think I better just start keeping my distance before my love turns to hate. I don't want that for us and especially not for the kids.

Come on now, you know I didn't really mean that shit back there.

She shook her head Doesn't even matter anymore Alejandro.

What doesn't matter?

I'm leaving. Call me if you need anything.

Gabi, Gabi he yelled out as she closed the door. He limped to the door opened it watched as she waited on the elevator. Come here let's talk.

We don't have anything to talk about.

Yes the fuck we do. You can't just be leaving here all mad and shit.

I'm not mad. I'm hurt, there's a difference.

Look, I'm sorry.

You sound like a broken record Alex. That shit ain't working this time. I can't keep going through this shit with you. I'd rather be by my damn self.

Gabi, can I talk to you please.

Maybe some other time. Go back inside, get some rest.

Come on G, don't do this to me.

You did this to yourself. I have to go pick up the kids she said as the elevator arrived at the 15th floor. I'll call you later.

Gabi he yelled out. She stepped onto the elevator, pressed the button to the parking garage and exited to her car.

Drago called and asked Big Sis, why don't you come have a drink with me?

Where are you?

Wizards

I'll be there in a little bit. She hung up with Drago and called Tago.

G-baby, what's up?

Hey, the kids okay?

Yeah, we're good. They got me playing Twister like I'm still a young buck.

You are, quit playing.

Man, we got some active kids Gabi.

I know, you ain't seen the half of it. Where's AJ?

Watching us bust our butts and laughing every time. Where are you?

About to go have drinks with Bro.

What happened with Alex?

Tago get off my phone. I'll see you in a little bit.
Be safe baby.
I will.

Drago sat in a corner off to himself smoking a Black & Mild dressed in all black. Gabriella stepped up in the spot rocking a Lola Bentley dress and stiletto heels with her hair flowing past her shoulders.
Hey baby brother she said as he stood to hug her. She kissed his cheeks and asked how are you?
I'm good sis, how are you? Long time no see he said as he signaled the waiter to order drinks. They sat talking like old times until Tago called.
Am I gone have to come get you?
No sir, I'm leaving now.
You better be.
She called Alejandro on her way to Tago's. His nurse answered said he wasn't feeling too good, had taken some pain medicine and gone to sleep. The clock on the dash read 11PM and Gabriella was a little tipsy. Tago stood at his front door waiting for her to arrive. He opened it as soon as she pulled up and walked out to open her door.
Why thank you sir.
No problem he said as he watched the sway of her hips in the dress she wore. Where'd you and Drago go to?
The kids still awake she asked as she stepped into the house ignoring his question.
No, they fell asleep about 30 minutes ago and you're not waking them up.
I could have gone home then.
Yeah but you didn't so I suggest you get comfortable.
Still bossy I see. Ain't a damn thang changed.
She found all 3 kids asleep in Tago's spare bedroom. She kissed their cheeks and tucked them in. Surprisingly none of them woke up. What did you do to my babies?
We been playing games all day, just having fun.
Get me some blankets and a pillow please so I can sleep on the couch.
Nah, I'll take the couch. You take the bed.
You sure?

I'm positive Gabi, go ahead. Go shower and get comfortable.

You got a t-shirt I can put on?

Yeah I got you babe.

Gabriella showered in peppermint body wash and washed her hair with the same scents. She stepped out feeling refreshed and energetic. Sleep would not find her anytime soon.

T

Yeah baby?

Can you come light the fireplace in here and turn on this damn projector?

I thought you'd be tired.

I'm not. If it will disturb you it's okay.

No you straight. He flipped on the TV, passed her the remote and started the fireplace.

Need anything else?

A glass of wine if you have it.

Moscota cool?

Yes indeed.

He came back into the room with a glass of wine and a bowl of fruit. Alright Gabi, good night he said as he kissed her cheek.

Good night Tago.

T she said just as he left the room.

Yeah.

Good to have you back.

Good to be here baby.

Gabriella couldn't focus on the TV and she couldn't fall asleep. She kept tossing and turning until Tago came into the bedroom and asked what's the matter?

If I told you, will you solve my problem?

I'll do my best.

I'm horny.

Yeah you ought to be. Alex told me the two of you haven't had sex since before AJ was born. He's almost a year now.

She looked at him like tell me something I don't know.

Get some sleep Gabriella he said before leaving the room again.

She wished she had her dildo in her purse. She kept the rabbit on her but knew that it wouldn't be enough yet she flicked it on anyway and tried unsuccessfully to experience an orgasm. Tago walked into the bedroom closing and locking the door behind him as he removed his clothes while watching Gabriella play with the rabbit.

Need some help he asked as he got on the bed between her legs face first. He used his tongue, along with the champagne and fruit to bring her body to orgasmic bliss. Soon she was returning the favor and Tago who hadn't been with anyone since Gabriella left him couldn't control himself. He was busting off in no time but still remained rock hard.

You sure about this Gabi he asked as she opened a box of condoms.

Hell yeah she told him as she slid the condom on. Soon he had her on her back and was really going at it deep stroking her just the way she liked it. She did so much screaming that she got hoarse. Tago had the biggest and the best she'd ever had. 12 inches of thickness and the brother could put it down. They cuddled until they both fell off to sleep.

Around 5 that morning he tells her Baby, get up and take another shower while I change out the bed sheets before the kids wake up for breakfast.

Tago's dick had Gabriella limping to the bathroom but she wore a bright smile on her face in spite of the pain. She stayed in the shower a good 45 minutes bathing and shampooing her hair. Tago was standing outside the shower when she stepped out holding a dry off towel fresh out the dryer. Tago was irresistible and it wasn't long before the two of them were going at it atop the bathroom counter.

Goddamn I missed you Gabriella.

If I didn't know any better I'd think you hadn't had none in a while or were you just happy to see me?

Both he smiled as he kissed her lips passed her the panties she'd worn last night before she took a shower.

No thanks.

I washed them, they're clean.

I'd rather go without. Can I get some sweats and a t-shirt?

Yeah he said as he picked her up in his arms. He lotioned her body, put on her clothes then brushed her hair back into a ponytail. Get some rest, the kids will be up in a little bit.

I'll fix breakfast.

Nah, I got it.

Well I'll help you.

You sure you don't want to get no sleep?

You trying to get rid of me?

Nah, come on here woman. Let's make our kids some breakfast.

Together they prepared a big breakfast of blueberry waffles, toast, eggs, potatoes, rice, sliced fruit, ham, bacon and sausage with apple and orange juice for the drinks.

Mommy's here Fern yelled as soon as he entered the kitchen hugging her from behind. Gabriella was happy to see the kids. It seemed as if they'd grown in the 2 weeks she was away.

Later Isabella asked Mommy did you stay the night?

Yes she said as she looked at her closely.

Did you and Papi sleep together?

Would it bother you if we did?

No, I was just wondering.

Alejandro called Fernando's cell phone and they passed the phone back and forth between the two of them until Alejandro asked when they planned on coming to see him.

Mommy when are we going to Daddy's Fern asked.

As soon as I get AJ dressed.

Daddy when Mommy puts AJ's clothes on we're on our way.

Isabella whispered is Daddy supposed to know you stayed all night at Papi's?

Gabriella smirked, Issy you are too smart girl. Don't bring it up unless he asks.

Okay. Need something to put on she asked just as Tago came through the door with shopping bags.

Ooh Papi what did you buy me?

Got some stuff for your Mom. We'll go shopping the next time you're here.

Cool she smiled.

Gabriella finished dressing AJ and combing his hair before walking into Tago's bathroom to brush his teeth. He picked out panty and bra sets from Victoria's Secret, shower gels, lingerie, perfume, body wraps and clothes. She was dressed in a velour sweat suit when he walked into his bedroom.

Stilettos and sweat suits she said with a smile.

Nah I got you some shoes to go with the outfits.

I take it that all that I'm not wearing is supposed to stay here?

Yeah cause that means you'll be back.

I will. I'll call you later she said as she kissed his lips.

He hugged and kissed the kids long and hard. Call me when y'all get settled at home.

Okay Papi

Bye Lil Man he said to AJ. Y'all be good.

Alex was in the living room watching Transformers 2 when they arrived. They rushed over to him.

Hey, hey Gabriella fussed. Be careful.

Dada, AJ said as he reached for Alex with a bright smile on his face.

What up son, long time no see he smiled back as Gabriella gently placed him in his arms.

You eat breakfast she asked him but he ignored her question. She warmed his plate, fixed him a glass of orange juice and grabbed a dinner tray.

Issy put AJ in his swing or that bouncer while your Daddy eats his breakfast.

Yes maam.

She sat the tray up in front of Alejandro before going to grab the strawberry jelly and syrup.

Need anything else?

Yeah, have a seat. You making me salute.

She smirked as she took a quick glance at him standing at attention and took a seat beside him. You feeling okay she asked him?

I'm alright.

He barely finished his breakfast before starting back up with the kids. It bothered him that he couldn't interact with them like he used to. He couldn't take them out to play ball or wrestle. He had tears in his eyes when Gabriella noticed and asked what's wrong? You alright?

He tried to get up but stumbled, Where are you going she asked as he rushed past her. When she walked up on his bedroom door he slammed it in her face. Alejandro she called out through the door. He wouldn't answer so finally she said I'm leaving. Call me when you're ready for me to pick up the kids. She kissed them before leaving with no real destination in mind. Tago text her and asked What you got in there? I'm already caught up. She smiled as she headed in his direction.

Chapter 26

Gabriella rang Tago's doorbell an hour later. He'd just stepped out of the shower. Once the door closed they were at it again until the box of 12 extra large condoms were gone.

Gabi, what are we doing?

What do you mean she asked as she lay in his arms.

What is all this?

T, let's not label it. How about we just go with the flow? Right now I'm enjoying myself.

Yeah me too he said as he kissed her lips and pulled the covers over her shoulders.

She picked up her cell phone to check for missed calls, noticed Alejandro hadn't called. She tried calling him. Lucia answered, said he and the kids were watching Everybody Hates Chris.

Is he okay Gabriella asked?

I think everything is starting to set in for him. The more it sets in the grumpier he gets.

Gabriella sighed, I don't know what to do.

Gabi you've done all you could baby. All you can do is continue to be his friend. Lord knows you're more supportive than I would be but I know what love will do to you. It's time you get out and enjoy yourself. Alex and the kids are okay. I'm here, Carmen and Gordon will be here in a minute.

During one of Alejandro and Gabriella's talkative moments they were on the phone watching an HBO special on TV about relationships.

Alex

Yeah bae

You ever wondered about Gordon's relationship with Mom and Carmen?

All the time, shits weird yo.

I think it's cool.

How so?

They all get along really well and I just wonder what it's like. I mean, we're on the outside looking in so everything seems to be all gravy but sometimes I wonder.

What's there to wonder about? Their friendship is like any other.

Alex you've got to be kidding me. Please tell me you don't think it's that cut and dry.

What? They've been the best of friends for years.

They're more than just friends Alex.

What are you saying G?

I'm saying, Gordon's the man. He's got your Mom and Carmen hooked.

Yo, you smoking rocks, sniffing that shit or something? What's up?

Alex, I'm serious.

G quit trippen, the shows back on.

They watched the next episode concerning a threesome relationship. Alejandro said Damn, I wonder what that's like. Could you see yourself with me and another woman?

Seriously, hell no. Maybe just a onetime thing but no relationship.

Man, I wonder what that's like.

You've been with two women before I'm sure.

Yeah but I want to know what it would feel like to be in a relationship where you know there is another person involved and everybody just big kicking it.

You sound as if you really want to know.

Shit, I'm wondering if that's the route I got to go to have you back again he said honestly.

Alejandro

Gabi, I'm serious. I miss you and I can't take this shit no more, straight up.

What's that supposed to mean?

I want to be with you. I want to come back home, be with you and the kids 24/7.

Oh Alex, you so make me sick.

You don't miss me, not even a little bit?

Of course I miss you.

What, since you fucking Tago now you ain't trying to see me at all?

Did I say that?

What, that you ain't trying to see me or you ain't fucking Tago?

Never said I was fucking Tago.

Never denied you was neither. I knew when it happened. Shit woke me up out of my sleep. Why the fuck you think I was so pissed off at you that day?

I thought you were just being consistent, showing the ass that you'd become.

Gabi, come see me.

I'm waiting on Drago to bring the kids home.

Call him and tell him to keep them another night. He's been complaining about not being able to spend time with them anyway.

You better be glad I'm in a good mood. I will see you in a little bit.

She called first Drago and then Tago.

What y'all about to get into Tago asked?

I'm not sure, but Alex was talking about having a threesome earlier.

Tago laughed, Oh yeah, he got it like that?

Yeah, you do too. Why don't you come join us?

Man you must be on cloud nine, that nigga ain't trying to see me.

If he's trying to see me, he's trying to see you and vice versa.

Wow, is that how you doing it now?

I'm feeling freaky and Alex needs some entertainment now that he has healed and tested clean she laughed.

You wild Gabi.

Not as wild as I'm going to get. I'll see you in 45 minutes.

Yo, call that nigga so that I'm not just popping up.

You're good, but I will call to assure you. I'll even have him call you she laughed.

He laughed too thinking this was all a joke until Alex called him up and asked him to keep an open mind. This way they're both winning.

Since neither of them had eaten dinner by the time the three of them got together they decided to have dinner at Turion's. Tago kept looking at Gabriella trying hard to figure out if she was really going to go through with it. He was remembering a time way back when she said she had a fantasy about being with 2 guys at once. He assumed she'd just been talking.

Are we going to do this or what she asked interrupting his thoughts?

Are you serious Alejandro asked?

Hell yeah I'm serious. Weren't you when you brought it up?

Alejandro looked at Tago and asked What we gone do with our woman?

Tago smiled as he and Alejandro both dropped money on the table to cover the bill. Gabriella smirked as she grabbed up both hundred dollar bills, dropped them in her purse and said Our waitress has us covered. She thinks you're both cute. She winked at the waitress on the way out the door.

I booked a honeymoon suite at Intercontinental. I figured since this is as close as I'm going to get I may as well go all out. You only live once she smiled. The honeymoon suite was decked out nicely. Brian McKnight flowed from the surround sound speakers while the fireplace illuminated the room. A bottle of Moscato chilled in a bucket of ice right along with a few other favorites, more drinks, fruit, whipped cream, chocolate syrup and caramel. She had all kinds of toys, creams and gels, along with condoms and other sexual party favors. She popped the cork on the wine and gave them each a glass. She planned to give them just as much as she wanted them to give her so after a few minutes of casual conversation she hit a switch that dropped a pole though a compartment in the ceiling and securely connected to another spot in the floor. She gave them a strip dance better than any stripper either of them had ever seen as they passed a blunt back and forth and sipped shots of Patron. Afterwards Gabriella blind folded and handcuffed them to their chairs by their legs and feet. She took turns feeding them fruit, some dipped in whipped cream, caramel, chocolate or herself. They were facing the table so she lay atop it on her back so they could put their faces right in her place. Pretty soon she'd experienced so many orgasms that they wondered if she'd have to wait for the real thing. She wasn't done with them yet. Still tied up she sucked them both into oblivion before untying them and getting in bed between the two. Alejandro had her upper body while Tago took the lower half. They alternated for a good 30 minutes before Tago watched Alejandro slip himself inside Gabriella and work her slow. She lost track of the number of times she'd experienced an orgasm. They all were feeling the groove as they climaxed together. Afterwards they chill in the Jacuzzi sipping more drinks and smoking more blunts without conversation. Alejandro was in a zone while Tago couldn't get enough of Gabriella. He picked her up in his arms and lowered her onto him. He was really digging in her. Alejandro watched and listened a minute before he decided to join in. By now Gabriella's back is to Tago's chest as she rides him backwards. Alejandro's kissing her lips, sucking her neck and breasts. She wants to feel them both inside of her again, this time with them standing up. Tago was all up in her stomach as her legs wrap around his waist and Alejandro is beating it up from the back. When it's all over they take turns bathing her. She sucks them off again before bathing them, then they all climb into bed with Gabriella snuggled comfortably in between them.

Good night bae Tago says as he kisses her lips.

Good night she whispers to them both before drifting off to sleep.

Alejandro's waking her up the next morning dicking her down while Tago's feeding her his for breakfast.

Damn, am I dreaming she asked aloud before they switched places.

Nah baby Tago responded, you're very much awake. Alert and wet as fuck he said as he filled the condom he wore.

You feel okay Alejandro asked her as he fired up a blunt and passed it to her.

I'm feeling lovely boo.

That's good Tago tells her, Get your ass in there and shower while I cook breakfast. Alex and I need to talk.

Carry on she smirked as she sashayed past leaving them both mesmerized.

I don't know about you Tago told him but I'm trying to get that every night.

Know what I'm saying, you and me both.

You sure you can handle it Tago asked?

Yeah Alejandro said as he licked his lips, hell yeah I'm in.

6 months later Gabriella's tired of driving all the way to PA to visit Tago and Alejandro doesn't like her making the drive all alone. Not to mention that the kids are tired of being all over the place. Gabriella suggests Tago get a place closer.

Alejandro suggests they both move back into the house, Tago agrees.

And what are we supposed to tell the kids Gabriella asked as she got up from the bed naked.

Alejandro smacked her ass and said I don't think they will mind as long as we're all together.

How about we see what they think first?

They get Daddy, Papi and Mommy in one spot. Oh it's all gravy Tago tells her.

Well we have track meets this morning, so let's get moving. We'll talk about it tonight over dinner.

Just like the men said, the kids were all for becoming one big happy family. Gabriella thought, That was easy.

Alejandro said Now we gotta tell Pops, my Mom, your brother and everyone else.

Tago responded And now the drama begins.

Ugh wrong…the hard part was the kids. The rest is a piece of cake.

How you figure both Alejandro and Tago asked at the same time.

Cute she smirked before saying I told you Gordon has the same thing going on with your Mom and Carmen. Uncle Juan and Drago will be cool, Adrianna too I think. Now they all might be a bit skeptical at first and poor Mariam is going to think we're nuts she laughed.

It's all about us and the kids, fuck what everybody else thinks.

Already Tago said as he dapped him up.

<u>Epilogue</u>

Daddy Fernando said as he entered the kitchen. When is Mommy going to be home?

She should be here any minute now. She had a late business meeting. If you had your cell phone you would know that.

He lost it Daddy, thinks it might have fallen out of his pocket at the movies last night Isabella tells him. Where's Papi?

Picking up dinner. You tell your Mom you lost your cell phone?

No because she will think I'm irresponsible.

No she won't. We understand. I think it's time we upgraded anyway. What do y'all say?

Say about what Tago asked as he came in with bags from Macaroni Grill.

Hi Papi, Daddy thinks we need new cell phones.

I agree. Fernando must not be getting his calls or he doesn't know how to answer his Tago commented.

Papi, I lost my phone, not sure where.

You tell your mom?

No but I will when she gets here.

Is AJ asleep Isabella asked?

No, he's with Mariam. She took him out to the park with her boyfriend's son.

Oh, Dominic and Troy.

I guess that's him Alejandro tells her.

Yeah he's cool. He can play football really good Daddy.

How long has he and Mariam been dating?

2 years now Fernando answered.

Unh unh, they've been friends for 2 years but just started dating about 4 months ago. Mommy told her to take her time.

Is he coming over for dinner Fernando asked?

I don't know, why don't you call and ask her?

First we need to make sure it's okay with Mommy.

She's cool. She already met him. She even met his Dad. His Dad was flirting with Mommy right in front of us.

When was this Alejandro and Tago asked at the same time?

A couple of weeks ago when we picked Mariam up from over there. He kept telling Mommy I'm all the man you need. Mommy mumbled under her breath you don't even come close.

They all cracked up laughing as the doorbell rang. Mariam had arrived with AJ and her crew.

Hi Mimi Isabella said as she hugged her before picking AJ up in her arms and swinging him around. Hi little brother, I missed you.

Missed you too, where's Fern?

Here I am Fern said from behind him.

Where's your Mom Mariam asked?

She hasn't made it home yet.

And your father's aren't complaining?

She had a late business meeting.

Tago walked into the foyer shook hands with Dominic after hugging Mariam and playing around with Troy. Y'all come on in and have a seat. Gabi should be here any minute.

She better be Alejandro fussed. She been coming home late all week.

Dominic this is my fussy brother Alejandro.

Nice to meet you Alejandro said as he shook his hand. She had also introduced Tago as her brother. Dominic was puzzled because she said she only had one brother.

Mommy's here AJ squeeled when he heard the sound of the alarm. Lucia, Carmen and Gordon all came in.

Gramps the kids all screamed as they hugged all 3 simultaneously.

Mariam introduced Dominic and Troy to the rest of the family. Everyone sat around talking a while before Gabriella walked in.

Mommy AJ was the first to notice her and rushed her so hard and fast that he almost knocked her over. Tago just so happened to catch her.

You're late he tells her as he kisses her lips.

She bites his and says We ran a little over.

A little Alejandro asks with a frown

And hello to you too she said as she kissed his lips before saying hello to everyone else.

Fernando, where is your cell phone baby? Ahmad has called a million and one times looking for you and the house phone is off the hook somewhere.

I lost my phone Mommy.
When?
At the movies last night, I think.
Why are you just now bringing it up?
Fernando shrugged.
We'll go get new ones tomorrow. Everybody is eligible for an upgrade anyway. Y'all go get washed up so we can eat. I'm starved.
Dominic was even more puzzled after seeing both Tago and Alejandro kiss Gabriella on the lips but concluded that some cultures did that sort of thing. He was next up in the bathroom and was taking Troy to wash his hands when both Alejandro and Tago walked inside the bedroom at the end of the hall. He could hear them both fussing about Gabriella coming home late. After dinner as he and Mariam sat in the family room playing Scrabble he tried to figure it all out.
Why are you looking like that Mariam asked?
Like what?
Confused
Because I am
What, you the extraordinaire she joked?
Nah, I'm talking about your sister, your brothers. What's up with that? I could have sworn you said you only had one brother and why do both of your brothers kiss Gabriella on the lips? Why do the kids refer to Alejandro as Daddy and Tago as Papi? Aren't they the same thing?
It's complicated.
Tell me something I don't know.
Gabriella is both Tago and Alejandro's girl.
Come again.
Isabella and Fernando are Tago's kids. AJ is Alejandro's son. Gabi is their Mom. How did all that happen? I mean I understand the difference in age of the kids but how did they all end up one big happy family? I mean damn, how can I be down?
Things just worked out better this way for everybody. Neither of them were willing to let her go.
Now that's deep. Man so how do they…I mean, you know, sex. What the fuck?
Mariam laughs out loud and says It goes down.
Yo for real? Damn.

Only on the 3rd floor when everyone is asleep though.

What do you do
When The *Love* You Lost Forever
Comes Back Into Your Life?

GOOD TO
Have You
BACK

a Novel

Toriana Jones

Sneak preview of my next novel...

Your Better Judgment Along With My Good Intentions

By Toriana Jones

Chapter 1

Laila was having a hard time breathing. She felt as if someone held their foot on her chest stopping the flow of oxygen to her lungs. Her world was closing in on her. The stress was becoming too much. Her mind was on her daughter Janai who was lying beside her in a hospital bed battling brain cancer. Laila was just informed that Janai was not making any progress and she had roughly 6 months to live.

Dr. Breedlove pulled Laila aside to let her know "Ms. Murray I am doing all that I can to help Janai fight this. I want to be honest with you, she is not responding well to the treatments. I'm afraid that she won't last another 6 months. I'm not saying I give up. I'm not saying you should give up. All I'm saying is that things don't look so good from where I stand. I really wish I had good news Dr. Breedlove said through her own tears. But I don't, 6 months is what I'm praying for. Less is the reality."

Dr. Breedlove held Laila in her arms as they cried and prayed together. Dr. Breedlove has been Janai's pediatrician since she was born 5 years ago today; October 21st, 2006

At the time Janai was said to have been born a healthy baby with no birth defects. It wasn't until she turned 3 that Janai started to complain about things being blurry through her right eye. The eye doctor gave her a prescription for eye glasses, said that it should help improve her vision. Weeks later she started to have seizures, nausea, and vomiting. She would often have trouble moving around, she was always weak. Laila took her in to see Dr. Breedlove, who quickly referred her to the emergency room. This aroused a series of tests to help determine Janai's illness. That wasn't her first trip to the emergency room and as it turns out it wouldn't be her last. Janai had a rough time with her cancer most of the time but there were moments when she seemed so alert and at peace.

Laila tried calling Janai's father Hariam to inform him of Janai's condition. Hariam's a big time drug dealer out in Brooklyn and said that he couldn't take off days at a time to be in Roswell, Georgia to check on his only daughter. Instead he advised his sister Haley to contact Laila to find out how Janai was doing. Like Laila's family, Hariam's family didn't take Janai's illness seriously. It was hard enough watching her daughter go through such a fatal disease but even harder without family and friends to support her. Laila's family couldn't offer support because they were too wrapped up in their own world. Laila's mother Uvonna was living the fabulous life with her new boyfriend Oscar who owned an NBA team that was currently in the playoffs. Laila's sister Nina was strung out on drugs and currently on the Most Wanted List for murder and robbery. Her brother Pharrell was serving a triple life sentence for four counts of aggravated assault, rape and the murder of female police officers in Baltimore. Laila's friend since grade school, Shayla had become an alcoholic and was going through the process of trying to regain custody of her 4 children. Shayla's baby daddies had recently obtained custody of her children when Shayla threw a house party in which all but one of her children consumed large amounts of alcohol and drugs.

As Laila prayed for Janai's suffering to end the sound of the monitor flat lining sounded. Janai had been in the hospital continuously for the past 3 months. Her suffering had only gotten worse. Laila's tears flowed freely and she screamed at the top of her lungs knowing her daughter was now gone forever. The nurses rushed in followed by Dr. Breedlove who tried her best to resuscitate Janai. Janai passed away in her sleep on her 5th birthday. Laila spent hours at the hospital after Dr. Breedlove pronounced her time of death. She just couldn't bring herself to move. Dr. Breedlove and a number of nurses agreed that she shouldn't drive.

One of the nurses who had assisted in caring for Janai and befriended Laila on Janai's initial trip to the emergency room asked if she could drive her home. Sharelle had often sat with Laila and Janai for hours at a time after her shift ended. She and Laila would watch TV shows together, talk about anything that would take their minds off of Janai's condition even if only briefly. Sharelle knew Laila's pain as a mother who lost her son to a fatal illness at the age of 10.

Come on Laila, let me take you home Sharelle said as she wrapped an arm around Laila's shoulders. She gathered both Laila's and Janai's items and guided Laila down the hall to the elevators. Laila was barely holding on, without Sharelle holding her up she probably would have fallen over. Sharelle tried her best to hold her steady as they made their way out of the hospital to her car.

Once at Laila's place Sharelle tried to make Laila as comfortable as possible. Laila no longer felt like someone was standing on her chest. She now had an empty feeling that just wouldn't go away. Sharelle suggests that she make phone calls to her family and friends to let them know Janai had passed. Laila didn't care to inform anyone knowing that no one had bothered to come see about Janai when she was still alive. Sharelle understood her logic but at the same time knew that Laila needed someone by her side at this moment. When she convinced Laila to shower or bath while she prepared dinner she made phone calls from Laila's cell phone. She recalled names mentioned during their previous conversations and called them first.

Uvonna said she was on her way to a playoff game and would call after she left there. Shayla didn't answer. Hariam answered surprisingly and told her that he would get to Georgia as soon as possible. When Sharelle informed Laila that she had spoken with Hariam and that he was checking flights, Laila said Don't be surprised if he doesn't show up. He's been a disappointment since Janai was born. Knowing her condition he didn't get better and I sure as hell wouldn't expect him to have a heart now she said sadly.

I called your mom.

She's at a basketball game, in other words, she's busy. She doesn't have time. What else is new? Shayla didn't answer because she is probably somewhere drunk. Nina never stays in one place too long so don't be surprised if her number has changed. She will call weeks from now to borrow money or to say she's in a rehab and wants to turn herself in. Pharrell, though he's locked up will probably be the only one to come to my aid, IF the prison will allow him to be here for the funeral.

What do you need me to do Sharelle asked?

I don't know Laila cried. I don't know.

Over the next few days Sharelle was able to help Laila make funeral arrangements, contact the prison to get Pharrell released for the funeral and contact a number of life insurance companies. No matter how much Laila thought she had prepared herself for this moment, everyday just seemed to get harder and harder. Everything in the house reminded her of Janai and she cried for days at a time wishing Janai was still alive.

Hariam rushed back to New York after the funeral. His homeboy Allen stayed behind sighting that Laila should not be alone. He argued that Hariam should be there for her, especially now.

Look, I have a business to run, it won't run itself. There is nothing I can do here. Laila got everything under control. The funeral is over with, the insurance is taken care of. What more is there for me to do?

Come on man, there is a lot you can do. You haven't been here for Janai much of her life. The least you could do is try to be here for Laila now. She needs you, she needs somebody here with her.

Why don't you stay? I'll go back home and take care of business. Get at me if something comes up. Cool?

Allen looked at Hariam with disgust. Hariam could be cold in the business world but Allen expected the death of his daughter to soften him a bit. Now he wondered if Hariam even had a heart as he watched him walk away without looking back. Hariam had not shed any tears when he was notified of his daughter's passing, nor did he show any emotion. He showed his face only because Haley and other members of his family argued to no end on it. Allen shook his head as he pulled out a Black & Mild and fired it up.

Sharelle stepped out to smoke a cigarette and asked where did Hariam run off to?

He's headed back to New York Allen said with one hand behind his head.

What?

Don't even ask, I don't have an explanation. I'm here for as long as Laila needs me.

Thank you, other than myself and Dr. Breedlove she hasn't had much help. A few of her brother's friends have come by to bring money and food but that's about all I've seen. I need to get back to work but I didn't want to leave her here alone. I wasn't going to leave.

You can go do what you need to do. I ain't going nowhere.

I will be back once my shift ends. I will call the house to see if she needs anything. I will leave my number by the phone in case you need to call me.

Sharelle, thank you for being here for Laila. I appreciate it.

No problem, that's what friends are for. She would do the same for me.

Chapter 2

After Sharelle left Allen sat around the family room starring at pictures of Laila and Janai from Janai's birth until months before her passing. His heart was heavy with grief. Allen had fallen in love with Laila the first time they met her junior year in high school. Allen was just a freshman at the time and played on the football team as a wide receiver. Laila was over the school newspaper and often ran stories on all the school sports so she knew who Allen was. Hariam was a senior at that time playing basketball and the star athlete for the team. He was very well known and loved by everyone in and out of school. It was during one of Hariam's basketball games that Laila took a seat next to Allen. Nina, Shayla and a few other friends sat beside her. Laila was dressed in a pair of skinny jeans, a Bebe t-shirt and Bebe calf length Chucks. Her hair was up in a ponytail with Chinese bangs, diamond butterfly earrings hung from her ears. Her face was free of makeup, smooth as a baby's bottom and beautiful as ever.

Hey Allen she said with a smile.

What's up Laila? How you been?

I'm good, just ready for the Summer.

You and me both.

Shayla said hey Lai, there go your boy as she pointed to Hariam. Allen watched as Laila smiled big and waved at Hariam. Throughout the game Allen listened as Laila talked on and on about Hariam and how fine she thought he was.

Hariam could have any girl he wanted and was known to have a chick one day and break up with her the next to move on to someone else. Every brother in athletics wanted to date Laila and her friends but they pretty much kept to themselves and focused primarily on school.

After the game all the players planned to meet up at Scooters a local hamburger joint and other students joined them. Laila and her friends were amongst them. Everybody hung out eating, joking around and playing games. Allen sat by watching as Hariam approached Laila. Hariam and his boys later made a bet on how long it would take Allen to get with Laila. Although Laila thought he was cute she wasn't ready to involve herself in a relationship. She wanted to accomplish all her goals, finish school and make something of herself without getting sidetracked. Laila played hard to get throughout the remainder of her time in high school. That only made Hariam want her more. He lost the bet with his friends and decided he would one day get even with Laila. It would take years for the opportunity to present itself.

Hariam and Allen were inside The Burger Shack one afternoon reminiscing about the good old days when in walks Shayla and Nina, still fly as ever.

Hey Laila Allen said as he stood up to greet her. How have you been? Long time no see.

Laila hugged Allen, it had been over 4 years since the last time she'd saw him. Marvelous darling. How about yourself?

Allen smiled, thankful for the hug and the tingly feeling he now felt all over as he responded. Blessed with no complaints.

That's good to know. Hey Hariam she smiled that big Colgate smile. Allen's smile quickly turned into a frown that didn't go unnoticed by Shayla. She figured he was just a hater since he had always been Hariam's flunky.

That day was the start of Hariam and Laila hooking up. He wined and dined her for a good 9 months before he got the goods. Another bet was lost to his friends when he estimated it would take him less than 2 dates to hit. This only added fuel to the fire. It was a known fact that some women pulled scandalous acts while trying to hook men. Hariam's scheme was to get Laila pregnant and drop her thereafter. He switched her birth control pills for other non-prescription drugs that wouldn't do her any real harm. He also poked holes throughout all the condoms he used with her the first and only night they had sex.

Months later when Laila told him she was pregnant he caused a scene in front of his boys just to let them know he still had the upper hand. He fronted her out by saying the baby wasn't his and he knew all about the guy she had been seeing when she was away in college. He implied that the two of them never stopped messing around, that she was nothing but a whore and he wasn't raising another man's baby. He denied Laila's baby up until his mother made him have a blood test once Janai was born. He only accepted her then because of the continued torture he could impose on Laila.

Allen knew Hariam was known to hold grudges but he never thought Hariam would stoop so low. He didn't find out the real deal until they were on their way to Georgia for Janai's funeral. Allen told Hariam that he seemed emotionless. Hariam confessed then that he didn't give a fuck about Laila or Janai. He said he was only showing his face because his side of the family forced him to. He also let out that he had a few insurance policies out on Janai that he would collect on once the death certificate was received.

A few days after staying with Laila she was still grieving yet seemed more stable than she had been the past few years throughout Janai's illness. She stood in the kitchen frying porkchops and sautéing onions to make gravy to smother them in as she read over a letter she received from Gerber Life Insurance concerning a policy Hariam had taken out on Janai. The policy was started around the time she first found out how sick Janai was. The policy was for over eighty thousand, not including medical and burial. She learned that Hariam never produced the required birth certificate and medical records as requested. These records were obtained by Gerber, none of which had his information on them. Hariam never signed the birth certificate when Janai was born and asked that the paternity results be removed from all medical and public records. He paid to have the paternity results become non-existent. In this case with Laila being Janai's only known biological parent all insurance policies he had obtained over the years would be made payable to her. He could argue that he paid all the premiums, that he was the biological father but there was no proof.

She stood in the kitchen laughing from the pit of her soul. Allen who was sitting in the family room catching up on episodes of Tyler Perry's House of Payne smiled after hearing her laughter. He couldn't resist going into the kitchen to find out what was so funny.

Hey Lai, you alright in here? Somebody put a nickel in your tickle box he asked still smiling.

What goes around comes around. God I love Karma.

Who's Karma Sharelle asked as she walked through the back door with dessert from the Cheesecake Factory and a tub of ice cream.

Karma - action, seen as bringing upon oneself inevitable results, good or bad, either in this life or in a reincarnation Laila said as she smiled through her tears.

Okay but what does that mean and for who Sharelle asked?

Laila said nothing as she passed the letter over to Sharelle before asking Allen if he knew how to make potatoes. She had already cooked them, just needed them to be mashed to serve for dinner.

I remember he said, a little butter, milk, I can throw in some ranch seasoning or garlic. Which do you prefer?

Laila paused briefly before saying Yes, that's how you make them. Can you do that for me please?

Sure, you need me to do anything else?

If you want to put the biscuits on I'd appreciate it.

You made homemade biscuits right? You know I've always loved your biscuits. It was one of the things I always tried to make but could never perfect. That, your chicken & dumplings and seafood gumbo. Mines would be good but never as good as yours.

Wow, didn't know you enjoyed my cooking so much. Yes, I made homemade biscuits.

Sharelle said Wow, I love Karma too as she hugged Laila from behind. How many more of these do you have?

I'm not sure, I've been slowly going through the mail today.

How are you feeling?

Laila turned around to face them both, Thank you for being here. You will never know how much this means to me. I don't want to be alone, I don't need to be alone right now. I know you both have lives of your own and I really appreciate you guys taking care of me. I can never repay you.

Being here is payment enough Allen said as he mixed the ingredients of the potatoes.

Sharelle said Woman, this friendship we've come across is the work of God. That is all the payment I need.

That night after dinner Laila and Sharelle discussed the letter from Gerber as well as other insurance companies in which Hariam had taken policies out on. Allen stepped out to go shoot pool.

So all you have to do now is call them with the account information for the deposit, wow Sharelle said as she ate her cheesecake.

Already taken care of.

Hariam is going to be highly upset.

Like a bull seeing red Laila said with a smirk, and I'm glad he will be as disappointed as I've been over the years.

Do you think Allen will tell him?

I seriously doubt it. If he was he would have told him by now and Hariam would be blowing my phone up.

I like Allen, he's a nice down to earth brother with a heart. He seems very sincere.

And mature Laila said as she briefly compared the younger Allen to the new Allen. He didn't seem to be lost in Hariam's shadow anymore. His presence commanded attention of its own.

How long do you think he will stay in town?

I'm not sure but I'm almost positive he has work to do, just like you.

As long as I can get my hours in and get over here after work I'm fine. I enjoy being here with you despite what brought us here. It's refreshing for me to be somewhere other than home for long periods of time.

I know what you mean. I haven't been out in forever. I was always at the hospital or here. We should get out and go somewhere.

Somewhere like where? I hope you aren't talking about a club. I haven't been to the club since Lincoln was in office.

Laila stopped and starred at Sharelle before they both burst out laughing. Let's go to Dudley's in Decatur.

Decatur where it's greater. That's a long drive. Maybe we should get Allen to roll with us. What do you think?

I think that sounds like a plan. Let me call him and see what he's up to.

Laila dialed Allen's number, on his end his cell rang while he was in the middle of a shot. He pulled his phone out and was about to hook it back on his hip when he saw Laila's name.

Yeah Lai, what's up? You alright? Need me to come...

Everything is fine Allen. Sharelle and I decided we want to get out tonight. We were thinking about Dudley's. Do you want to join us?

Dudley's in Decatur, you two don't need to be way in Decatur by yourselves.

Allen, that is why I'm asking you. Now are you going or not?

Yeah, give me like twenty to thirty minutes to get there.

Take your time. You know we have to get dressed. Give us about an hour, hour and a half at the most.

Alright, I got you.

Dudley's atmosphere was on point. Sharelle was up dancing, enjoying herself. Allen watched Laila who sat across from him in a booth sipping on a Hurricane. Though she tried to appear resilient Allen could see right through her. He moved closer to her and asked You okay Laila? If you want to leave we can leave.

But Sharelle is having such a good time she said as she watched Sharelle dip it low and bring it back up with a kool aid smile on her face.

She will understand, I'm sure. Wait here, I will go get her.

I'm okay.

No you're not. Wait here, I will be right back he said as he walked off into the direction in which Sharelle was in. She saw him headed her way and stopped dancing to meet him.

What's going on? Everything okay?

Laila, she…

Okay come on, let's go.

Once back home Laila asked to be alone in her bedroom while she sat in the bathtub in tears. She knew she had to pull herself together. It was easier said than done. She also knew that Allen and Sharelle needed to get back to their own lives. Laila pulled herself together enough to let them both know she could now handle things on her own. Allen would call every day after he left and Sharelle would stop by at least once or twice a week and they talked on the phone every day.

Your Better Judgment Along With My Good Intentions

By Toriana Jones

www.ingramcontent.com/pod-product-compliance
Lightning Source LLC
Chambersburg PA
CBHW070648180626
46817CB00006B/2282